About t...

Like any good Southern belle, Kianna Alex... many hats: doting mama, advice-dispensing sister, and gabbing girlfriend. She's a voracious reader, an amateur seamstress and occasional painter in oils. Life in her world has never been boring, and has come with many twists and turns, but she's taking it all in stride. She's proud to tell stories where Black women are loved, valued, and thriving. A native of the Tar Heel state, Kianna still lives there with her girlfriend, two kids, and a collection of well-loved vintage '80s Barbie dolls.

Meg Maguire has published nearly forty romances and erotic novels with a variety of publishers, sometimes under the pen name Cara McKenna. Her stories have been acclaimed for their smart, modern voice and defiance of convention. She was a 2015 *RITA* Award finalist, a 2014 *RT* Reviewers' Choice Award winner, and a 2010 Golden Heart Award finalist. She lives with her husband and baby son in the Pacific Northwest, though she'll always be a Boston girl at heart.

Elizabeth Bevarly is the award-winning, nationally number one bestselling author of more than seventy novels and novellas. Her books have been translated into two dozen languages and published in three dozen countries. An honours graduate of the University of Louisville, she has called home places as diverse as San Juan, Puerto Rico and Haddonfield, New Jersey, but now resides back in her native Kentucky with her husband, her son, and two neurotic cats (as if there were any other kind).

A Christmas Holiday Romance

KIANNA ALEXANDER

MEG MAGUIRE

ELIZABETH BEVARLY

MILLS & BOON

First Published in Great Britain 2024
by Mills & Boon, an imprint of HarperCollins*Publishers* Ltd,
1 London Bridge Street, London, SE1 9GF

www.harpercollins.co.uk

HarperCollins*Publishers*
Macken House, 39/40 Mayor Street Upper,
Dublin 1, D01 C9W8, Ireland

ISBN: 978-0-263-39664-5

A LOVE LIKE THIS

KIANNA ALEXANDER

In memory of Rev Dr LE Davis. My pastor through childhood, he performed my marriage and became my friend in adulthood. Your smile is lighting up heaven now, Rev.

Chapter 1

Hadley Monroe leaned against the window seat in the living room of rental unit seven, a clipboard in hand. Her eyes swept the room as she took in the flurry of activity going on around her. As office manager and resident jill-of-all-trades at her family's real estate company, Monroe Holdings, she often oversaw the preparation of a vacation property for a client. Today, however, was a bit different.

She glanced over her shoulder briefly, taking in the scenery outside. The bright sunlight streaming through the sheer white curtains gave no clue to the mid-December chill hanging in the air. Less than a half mile from the grassy lawn fronting the two-story town house the frothy waves of the Atlantic lapped at the sandy shore. She smiled as she turned back to the work at hand, reminded once again why she'd chosen to remain in Sapphire Shores after graduation. Her small island hometown just off the coast of North Carolina possessed gorgeous scenery and a close-knit community she doubted she'd find elsewhere.

Stifling a yawn, Hadley shifted her weight and scanned the room for the familiar face of her friend.

Belinda Quick, owner of Quick Transformations, rushed around the room with a clipboard of her own. Dressed in a pair of blue jeans and a red T-shirt emblazoned with her logo, she stood out among the purple T-shirts worn by her employees. It was Belinda's staff that tackled the responsibility of readying MHI's rental properties between clients. Belinda's business handled a bevy of tasks, from general cleaning to decorating, and their efficiency had proven a godsend for Hadley on more than one occasion. Having known Belinda since high school, Hadley placed the utmost trust in her.

Her sneakers squeaking against the recently polished hardwood floor, Belinda sidled up to Hadley. "What do you think? Are we almost there?"

Hadley drew a deep breath as she looked around again, taking in the meticulously placed Christmas decorations put up by Belinda and her staff. The seven-foot Fraser fir occupying the corner by the staircase leading to the second floor was festooned in red and gold ornaments. The color scheme carried through to the tree skirt, the tablecloth and place mats on the dining room table, and the red and gold velvet bows adorning the balsam garland fastened to the fireplace mantel. "It looks fantastic, B. You've done it again, girl."

Belinda winked. "You know QT never slacks on a job. Got a few lights strung outside, too."

Hadley's brow wrinkled. "You remembered to only use white lights, right? Because…"

"I know, I know. Mr. Granger doesn't like colored lights." Belinda rolled her eyes playfully. "It's all good, girl. We only used white lights. On the tree, outside, the whole nine. And no decor on the second floor, just like you asked."

Hadley felt a shiver go down her spine, and it wasn't due to lack of insulation in the rental unit, either. It was the shiver that always moved through her when anyone mentioned Devon Granger's name. *Devon Granger.* Her tongue darted out to moisten her bottom lip as she thought of him. That man had a body so solid and a face so handsome, it was if he'd been hewn from a block of marble. She was sure she wasn't the only woman who found the actor, famous for his performances in action films and Westerns, irresistibly sexy. She was, however, the only woman who'd spent the last four Christmases making sure his every need was met to his satisfaction. Well, his rental property needs, anyhow. Given the chance, though, Hadley knew she'd happily fulfill just about any request he could throw her way…

"Hadley. Hadley!" Belinda snapped her fingers several times. "Are you still with me, girl?"

Blinking a few times until her friend's face came into focus, Hadley smiled sheepishly. "Sorry, B. What did you say?"

"I said, I'm telling my staff to clear out so you and I can make our final walk-through."

"Great. I think we're done here. He likes his decorations to be pretty low-key." Hadley hoped if she steered the conversation right back to the business at hand, her friend wouldn't call her out for daydreaming. *Honestly, it's her fault for bringing up his name.*

No such luck. Belinda's brow hitched upward, as it was apt to do before she commenced grilling someone for information. "You were fantasizing about him again, weren't you." It was a question, yet she posed it as a statement, as if there weren't any doubt in her mind about the answer.

Hadley sucked in a breath. *Oh, the things I could tell her.* She knew there was no point in trying to conceal her plans from Belinda, but that didn't mean she wanted all eight of her friend's employees to know her personal business. "Go clear out the staff, B."

She shrugged. "Fair enough. But once they leave, I want the dirt, Hadley."

Shaking her head, Hadley watched her friend walk away and begin the process of rounding up her employees. She plopped down on the cushion of the window seat, waiting until the last of the staff members had left and watched as Belinda strode back over.

"Let's get this walk-through knocked out." Belinda gestured for Hadley to get up. "And while we do it, you can tell me what you're plotting."

Hadley shook her head as the two of them began walking the property. "You know me too well."

"Yep. So you may as well let the tiger out of the sack."

Hadley sighed. "Well, you know I've had a thing

for Devon ever since he first rented from us several years ago."

Belinda scoffed. "A thing for him? Girl, please. You've been pining after that man like you're a woman in a desert and he's the oasis."

She pursed her lips. "Thanks for that colorful description, B. Anyway, I've stayed away from him because I knew he was grieving, and I respected that. But I think five years is more than reasonable, don't you?" Around town, it was common knowledge that escaping to the vacation house had been part of Devon's way of coping with the loss of his wife. Regardless of her strong feelings for him, Hadley could never bring herself to infringe on his grief.

Belinda nodded as they rounded the corner, passing the tree to head upstairs. "Yes, Hadley. Five years is very respectable. You've been very patient, considering how obsessed you are with him."

On the landing, Hadley gave Belinda a playful punch on the shoulder. "Shut up, B. It's not an obsession. It's not like I have an altar to him or something."

A chuckling Belinda cracked open the door to the master bedroom. "You know I'm just playing with you. But you have to admit, you've got it pretty bad."

Hadley could feel her face relaxing, and she could see her softening expression reflected at her in the bedroom mirror. "Yeah, you're right. And this year, I'm going to do something about it. It's my Christmas gift to myself."

She looked around the space. Belinda's crew had done a great job, and she admired the freshly made four-poster, king-size bed. The bed, along with the matching nightstands and dresser, were all fashioned of polished oak and adorned with an etched ivy-leaf pattern. The soft grey carpet felt like a cloud beneath her feet.

They left the bedroom and continued through the upper floor.

"More power to you. Get your man, girl." Belinda peeked into the bathroom. "Do you have a plan for how you're going to approach him?"

Hadley answered as they finished checking the upstairs room and descended the stairs. "I've got a start. I'm going to meet him at arrival and give him a gift to thank him for renting from us for the past five years. That will get me in, at least." It was something the company did all the time for repeat clients, and making the delivery herself gave her a perfect excuse to spend time in Devon's company.

Back in the living room, Belinda turned to Hadley and tossed her the keys. "That will get you in, true enough. But once you're alone, what are you going to say to him?"

Hadley imagined his face and shook her head. "I don't have the faintest idea. I guess I'm winging it." After all these years of denying herself this particular piece of dark chocolate, she just hoped she'd be coherent enough to get her point across.

The two women left the unit laughing, and Hadley locked the door behind them.

Devon Granger moved around the master bedroom of his Los Angeles home, tossing things into the open suitcase lying on his bed. His flight to North Carolina would depart in a few hours, and he needed to get it together if he expected to make it in time to board the plane. Flying out of LAX was one of his least favorite things to do—the place never seemed to have a time when it wasn't crowded. Still, it was the closest airport to his Silver Lake home. Going a little early meant he wouldn't have to rush.

Devon's work as an actor had left him more than financially secure, but he wasn't the type of guy to spend his money on private jets, yachts and other things he saw as unnecessary. He just flew first or business class, concealed his identity, and kept to himself on flights and in airports. Other than the occasional overzealous fan who'd demand an autograph or selfie, his system had served him well over the years.

He stopped to regard the suitcase, his eyes scanning the contents. He'd packed mainly comfortable clothing for his annual holiday vacation, and he looked forward to lounging around his favorite beach rental overlooking the Atlantic. Force of habit made him also pack slacks, button-downs and a few ties, just in case.

As he leaned over the bed to tuck his socks into an outer compartment, a twinge shot through his lower back. Grimacing, he jerked upright again before uttering a low curse. He was still relatively young, just shy of thirty-five. Despite his youth, his recent injury had made him question whether he should keep performing his own stunts in his action roles.

Before Thanksgiving, he'd shot the final scene for the upcoming *Destruction Derby 3*. When he'd made the daring leap, escaping an explosion that would be added in later via the magic of special effects, he'd landed improperly, resulting in a herniated disk. It wasn't the first time he'd been injured while executing a stunt, but it was his most serious injury to date.

The bed began buzzing, drawing his attention back to the moment at hand. He searched around until he located his phone, tucked between the suitcase and his comforter. Grabbing it, he answered the call on speaker. "Hi, Ma. How are you?"

Eva Sykes Granger's voice filled the room. "I'm fine, but how are you? Is your back okay?"

"It's fine, Ma." It wasn't a lie, per se. Once he took his medication and gave it time to get into his system, he'd be feeling somewhat better.

"Are you sure you're up to that long flight? Don't you think you should sit out the vacation this year?" Her words were laced with motherly concern.

"I wouldn't think of it." He'd come to look forward to this getaway, far from the fast-paced hustle and bustle of LA. He craved the respite of the quiet oceanfront hamlet where he'd been born. "Besides, it's not a nonstop flight. I've got a layover in Dallas, and I'll be sure to stretch."

She sighed. "Well, you're an adult. I don't suppose I can stop you from going."

He shook his head, tucking his last item of clothing into the suitcase and closing it. "Ma, you know why I go home every year. What I don't know is why you and Dad don't come with me. You know I'd cover your tickets."

Another sigh. "Christmas in North Carolina is a bit

much for your father and me. You know we aren't religious, and we're happier keeping things low-key this time of year."

He chuckled. "I know, Ma. You and Dad aren't exactly filled with the Christmas spirit." His parents lived in a palatial home he'd bought them when he had completed his first film, but David and Eva's idea of holiday decoration consisted of battery-operated candles in the front windows and a single strand of white lights, placed in a palm tree by their gardener.

As if reading his mind, she said, "I know what you're thinking, Devon. And I'll have you know Mr. Roper strung lights in *two* of our palm trees this year."

Grateful his mother couldn't see him rolling his eyes, he quipped, "Don't overdo it now, Ma."

She laughed, the familiar sound warming Devon's heart. "Oh, go on with you. Make sure you call us and let us know you got there safely."

"I always do." He zipped the suitcase closed, placing his trusty lock in the loops to secure it.

"Devon…there's one more thing."

Noticing the hesitation in her tone, he sat down on the edge of the bed. "What is it, Ma?"

"Your father and I were talking, and we really want to see you settled down again."

He sighed. He'd been hoping to avoid this conversation this year, but it seemed that wasn't going to happen. "Ma. I don't really want to talk about this."

"I know you don't, son, so just hear me out. It's been five years since Nat left us, and we're ready for you to get off the merry-go-round and find a nice girl to bring home."

"Merry-go-round? Really, Ma?" He'd started dating again about two years ago, and since then he'd gone out with his share of women. He'd even satisfied his urges here and there, but the term his mother had just used seemed to go too far in describing his life as a young widower.

"You've dated plenty of girls but never gotten serious about anyone. I know it must be hard to put your heart on the line after such a loss, but you've got to take the chance, dear."

He felt his brow furrow. *Hard* didn't begin to describe it. His reluctance to enter a serious relationship again had nothing to do with opportunity and everything to do with his feelings. His wife, Natalie, had been only twenty-nine when he'd lost her to an undetected congenital heart defect. It had taken him almost three years to learn to navigate the world without his childhood sweetheart by his side.

"Just think about it, dear. That's all we ask."

He could hear the love and concern in his mother's voice, and it did much to soothe his frustration. "I will, Ma." And he would think about it. But that didn't guarantee he'd come home with a fiancée any time soon, and he hoped she realized that. "I love you."

"I love you, too, son. Travel safe." She disconnected the call.

Devon stood and pocketed his phone, glancing around his room to be sure he hadn't forgotten anything he'd need for his trip. That done, he dropped the wheeled suitcase on the floor, lifted the telescoping handle and pushed it out of the room.

Chapter 2

Hadley pulled her midnight blue sedan up to the curb in front of the rental unit and cut the engine. Unbuckling her seat belt, she dropped the driver-side visor and opened the lighted vanity mirror. She took a moment to make sure her upswept hair and carefully applied makeup were on point, then righted the visor and smiled.

Devon was due to arrive any minute now. She'd always known him to be punctual, and that was just one of the qualities he possessed that made him so attractive. She knew she wouldn't have to wait long for him to appear, so she gathered her wits.

She still didn't know what she would say to him, other than the rote script she always gave to longtime customers when she delivered their appreciation gifts.

She'd thank him for his loyalty, just as her brothers would expect. That would be the easy part. What came after that, she had no idea. There was no point in trying to plan what to say to him now. She fully expected that when she looked into his gorgeous golden eyes, she wouldn't remember her name, let alone any impassioned speech she planned to make.

She looked down at her outfit. She'd chosen a close-fitting sweater, slim jeans and knee-high boots. Her aim was to be appealing to Devon's eyes while still looking professional. She'd also considered the conditions outside. Despite the bright sunshine, the temperature hovered somewhere in the low fifties. She possessed more enticing outfits, but she was looking to make a certain impression. Besides, no one looked sexy while shivering.

The sound of an approaching engine drew her attention, and she checked her rearview. Seeing Devon approaching in a midsize SUV made her lips stretch into a smile. This was another thing she liked about him. Here he was, rich and famous for his acting, yet he eschewed the bodyguards, drivers and entourage many people in his position had. She had no idea how he lived his life in LA, but it was clear that he didn't make himself fodder for the celebrity-gossip bloggers and television shows. And when he was home in Sapphire Shores, he was about as low-key as a person could get. He flew commercial, rented a car and drove himself where he needed to go.

She sighed as she watched him navigate the vehicle into the driveway. *He's so down-to-earth.*

Gathering the large gift basket she'd brought with her from the office onto her lap, she slipped out of the car as gracefully as she could. Once she'd closed her door, she stood by her car, watching and waiting. She tamped down her excitement at seeing him again, not wanting to ambush him before he had a chance to get out of his car.

His driver's side door swung open then, and as he stepped out and stood to his full height, Hadley could feel her heartbeat racing. Dark sunglasses obscured his eyes, but nothing obstructed her view of the rest of his smooth, brown-skinned face. She reveled in the sight of his thick dark brows, his perfectly groomed mustache and beard, and the full, soft-looking lips centering it all. His long, lean body was dressed casually in a pair of khakis, a green sweater and brown loafers. The clothes weren't tight, but they were fitted enough that she could see the hard lines of his muscles flexing beneath the fabric as he moved.

To Hadley's appreciative eyes, he almost seemed to be moving in slow motion. Her lips parted, allowing a pent-up breath to escape into the cool winter air. She tightened her arms around the gift basket, knowing that if she didn't, it might fall to the ground, forgotten, as she stared at her favorite client. *How can he be that damn fine?*

He opened the hatch at the back of the vehicle. Dragging out a wheeled suitcase, he shut the hatch again and turned her way. "Hadley, is that you?"

She shifted the basket, offering a wave before shifting it back into both hands. "It's me," she called. "How are you?" As she spoke, she started walking in his direction.

"I'm good, thanks. How about you?" He remained by the back of the SUV, as if waiting for her.

A few more long steps brought her into his personal space. "Good, good. Can't complain."

He smiled, showing off two rows of shimmering white teeth. "Glad to hear it."

That familiar tingle started at the back of her neck, and she did her best to ignore it. Extending the basket in his direction, she spoke. "This is for you, from all of us at Monroe Holdings. We want to thank you for your loyalty in renting from us for five consecutive years."

"Thank you, Hadley. That's very nice." He extended an arm, taking the basket she'd needed two hands to carry and sweeping it into his grasp as if it weighed nothing. Regarding the selection of fruit, nuts and candy, he looked her way. "Looks like there's some pretty good stuff in here."

She offered a soft smile. "I... I mean, we hope you'll enjoy it." She reached into the hip pocket of her jeans and fished out the key to the unit. "I'll go ahead and let you in so you can put your things down." She started walking toward the front door.

He started to follow, but when he turned, he winced.

The basket slipped from his arms.

Hadley took a wide step and reached out, catching hold of the free end of the shrink-wrap just before the basket could hit the ground. The bottom of it scraped the driveway, but as she raised it to inspect, she found all the contents intact.

He reached up, slipping off his shades and tucking them into the neckline of his sweater.

The moment his intense hazel eyes met hers, Hadley felt a tingle shoot down her spine until it touched the base, then flare out to the rest of her body.

"Wow, Hadley. You've got amazing reflexes." He looked genuinely impressed.

She shrugged, straightening up with the basket in her arms. "I take a kickboxing class." She looked back at him, letting her concern show through. "Are you okay?"

He waved her off. "I'm fine. Just a little twinge in my back that pops up now and again."

She nodded. Even though she suspected there was more to it than he let on, she knew it wasn't her place to press him.

Firmly grasping the handle of his bag, he rolled it to the front door.

As he passed by, she caught a glimpse of his firm backside. It was all she could do to hold onto the basket as she trailed behind him. They walked up the two stone steps to the door. Shifting a bit, she used the key to unlock the place and followed him inside.

He rolled his bag into the nook by the window seat, then glanced around the room. "The decorations are really nice this year. Subtle, but still festive."

She grinned, probably a little wider than she had intended. "That's the look we were going for. I'm glad you like them." She crossed the room to the low mahogany coffee table, setting the gift basket down before any more mishaps could occur.

As she bent, she had the distinct sense that he was

looking at her backside. Acting with intention, she drew out the motion, staying in the position a few seconds longer than necessary as she pretended to fuss with the bow on the basket. When she stood and slowly turned Devon's way, he was sitting on the cushioned window seat.

His hazel eyes were focused squarely on her.

When Devon saw Hadley turn around and look at him, he didn't bother to shift his gaze. He'd misjudged a few things in his day, but there was no mistaking Hadley's flirting. The exaggerated way she'd bent over the table just now had obviously been done for his benefit, and benefit he did. The sight of her round, upturned ass had warmed his blood so much he was tempted to strip off his sweater.

As she caught his eye, her full lips curved into a smile. "Devon. Were you doing what I think you were doing just now?" The teasing in her tone indicated how certain she felt of the answer.

He chuckled. "Only if you were doing what I think you were."

She winked but admitted nothing.

The grin stretching his lips held a mixture of amusement and intrigue. Since when had Hadley been checking for him? He'd always thought of her as attractive. But he'd tried not to dwell on that, since there were two glaring factors that might make her an unsuitable match. She was only twenty-eight, six years younger than him. Not to mention she was the baby sister of his old friend Campbell. He and Campbell had hung out a lot in high school, and Devon had no idea how Campbell would react to his old cutup buddy going after his sister.

She let her gaze drop in a coy manner.

He kept his expression even, hoping not to sway her one way or the other. He was supposed to be resting over the holidays, not entertaining a tender young thing like Hadley Monroe. Still, the man in him couldn't help but be flattered by her theatrics.

Her expression changed then, indicating a return to her usual all-business demeanor. She sat on the sofa, shifting to face his way. "So, tell me all the interesting things happening on the left coast."

He chuckled. "I was about to ask you for an update on what's been going on here over the past year."

"Not much." She shrugged. "We've cleared our last thirty acres of land and are trying to decide what to develop there. A new grocery store opened, along with a few boutiques to appeal to the tourist crowd."

"What about Coastal High? Did they ever finish the new stadium?" When he'd visited last year, ground had been broken for the project, adjacent to the old field.

"Yes. They finished it right after school let out for the summer. By the time the kids got back for the new school year, the football team had already practiced on the new turf."

He nodded, pleased that his alma mater was making improvements. "You know, I haven't been back to Coastal since I graduated." He watched her as she spoke, taking note of her body language. "It's been so long, I don't think I remember how to get there." He had a vague idea of the way to the school and could probably find it on his own. But he wanted to see how she'd respond.

She leaned forward, her face brightening. "If you want to see the new stadium, I'll take you over there."

"Sounds great. Maybe we'll swing by there in a few days." He wondered if he was encouraging her too much, but he did consider her a friend. He saw no reason he couldn't treat her as such. If she were someone else, someone closer to his age and not related to one of his oldest friends, they'd be having a much different conversation right now.

"Really, though. Tell me what's happening in Hollywood. Filming anything? Premieres coming up?" The glint in her eyes gave away her excitement.

He chuckled at her effortless transition from friend to fan. "I wrapped *Destruction Derby 3* about a month ago. Haven't filmed anything since, and no premieres until after the New Year."

She clapped her hands together. "I can't wait for *DD3* to come out. I loved the first two."

His brow hitched. "Really? I never pegged you for the type who'd like the DD series. Explosions, fast cars, fistfights." The films in the series were wildly popular with the young male audience, at least according to the suits at the studio. They were huge moneymakers and kept Devon financially secure, but filming them had been especially hard on his body.

She made a face of mock offense. "That's sexist. Just because I'm a woman, you think I can't get into a good action thriller?"

"You gotta admit, you're not exactly the target audience."

She rolled her eyes, but her smile remained. "Come on, Devon. You know me better than that."

He laughed. "I'm just teasing you. Thanks for the compliment, though."

She leaned in, dropped her voice as if there were someone else in the room. "Listen, just between me and you, is Captain Vicious coming back for the third movie?"

He laughed again at her question. "You're like the fiftieth person to ask me that." The character, a villain in the DD series, was played by veteran actor Rick Rollingsworth. Rick, a contemporary of Samuel L. and Denzel, was about as well loved as a man of color in Hollywood could expect to be. "At least ten people asked me that between the baggage claim and the rental car counter."

"We're friends, though. So, are you gonna tell me?"

He shook his head. "Sorry. The nondisclosure agreement in my contract is in full effect." He knew Captain Vicious would indeed be making a return but couldn't risk his standing with the studio by telling her that. "You'll have to find out with everybody else when the movie drops in May."

She sighed. "Oh, well. I've waited this long, I suppose I can wait till Memorial Day." She stood and he took time to appreciate his view of her. The sweater, jeans and tall boots encased her shapely figure in a way he found very attractive, but not overly revealing. The dark ringlets of her hair were pinned on top of her head, revealing the lines of her face. Her high cheekbones, full lips and sparkling brown eyes were all marks of her beauty, and of the Monroe blood flowing through her veins. Today, Hadley looked much as her mother, Viola, had looked twenty years ago, when they were kids.

A few long, silent moments passed between them before she seemed to notice his scrutiny. Her cheeks filled with a rosy blush, the glittering eyes shifting to the window behind him. Straightening, she began to run through the speech she usually gave him when he checked in to the unit. "The groceries you requested for the first week are already in the kitchen. You have plenty of fresh linen in the closet upstairs, and the housekeeping service will stop by every other day to do laundry and dishes for you…"

He smiled, putting up his hand to stop her rambling. "Thanks, Hadley. I got it."

She shifted her gaze away from his face, running her hand over the red ribbon securing the gift basket. "Is there anything else you'll need?"

He fought the urge to give her one of the many cheeky answers that came to mind. Shaking his head, he said, "No, but if I think of something I'll give the office a call."

She crossed the room toward the front door, passing him as she moved. "Well, I'll stop pestering you and let you get on with your vacation. Just give the office a call if you need anything, or when you're ready to go see the new stadium."

He nodded. "I will. Thanks for everything, Hadley." His words were sincere. She'd seen to his every need for the past four years he'd been coming there, either personally or through the staff. She made it easy for him to leave his work behind for three glorious weeks, and he truly did appreciate everything she did.

"You're welcome." She smiled on the heels of her soft reply, then opened the door and let herself out.

He turned and looked out the window, watching her stroll back to her car.

Something told him this Christmas would be an interesting one.

Chapter 3

Seated behind her desk, Hadley popped a soft peppermint in her mouth and chewed. The desktop was full of paperwork, detailing the long list of repairs waiting to be made at several of Monroe's properties. She sighed as she swallowed the small pieces of candy. She was the office manager, and that entailed a lot of things. What it didn't entail was property management—that was Campbell's job.

Scooting her chair back, she stood and walked around her desk. Leaving her office, she walked down the corridor to Savion's office. The door was open, and a quick peek let her see her brother poring over something on his desk. She tapped on the glass panel next to the door to get his attention.

Glancing up, he waved her in. "What's up, Hadley?"

She entered the office and took a seat in one of his guest chairs. The office, which had been occupied by their father, Carver, before his retirement, still looked much the same as it had ten years ago. Savion had held on to most of their father's books and decor, as well as the navy blue carpet and soft-textured blue wallpaper.

Aware of her eldest brother's obsession with detail, she waited silently for a few moments while he finished reading whatever currently had his attention.

He looked up again, closing his magazine and making eye contact with her. "What do you need, sis?"

Seeing that his body language invited conversation, she sat back in her chair. "I've got a pile of repair request forms on my desk. Again."

"That's Campbell's responsibility, not yours."

She pursed her lips. "I know that, Savion. What I want to know is who keeps dropping the forms on my desk instead of handing them over to Cam."

Savion's exaggerated shrug said all. "Must be somebody on staff. Maybe Belinda? Even though she doesn't work for us, she's in and out of here all the time."

She shook her head. "Belinda knows better."

"I don't know. Maybe it's one of her people. Either way, it's Campbell's job to handle that stuff, so just pass the stack to him." He reached up, stifling a yawn with his hand.

She rolled her eyes. Whoever was leaving her brother's work on her desk would catch pure hell from her if she ever caught them. Pushing that aside for now, she spoke again. "Listen. While I'm in here, what's going on with the shoot for the new TV commercial?"

He opened the cover of the black leather-bound planner he kept with him at all times, dropping it on his desk. His eyes were on the pages as he answered her question. "We're supposed to shoot next Wednesday and into Thursday, if necessary. We hope to get it on the air right after the New Year."

"Does it have a script? Are we doing voice-over? Who's going to be in it?"

He looked up, his brow knitting as if he were confused. "Yes, yes and I'm going to be in it. Why are you asking all these questions about the commercial, anyway?"

She shifted in her seat, pushing away her discomfort with his scrutiny. "I have some ideas for the commercial. You know, to punch it up a bit."

Now he looked annoyed. "What's wrong with the commercials we've been making, Hadley?"

She cleared her throat. "Nothing, per se. I just think it's time to try a new direction."

"I don't know why you'd say that. Monroe Holdings isn't lacking for business, despite competition from Rent-A-Retreat and Homeshare Plus, so the commercials must be working."

"Sure they are. I'm not saying they aren't effective." She did her best to temper her response, knowing how much her brother enjoyed being the face of MHI, and how much he hated being contradicted. She was sure the commercials worked, to a degree, and especially with the female audience. Savion, just like Campbell and their father, was a handsome man, and possessed enough charisma to sell sand at the beach. Still, she thought a change of pace would be nice. "I just think it would be good to film an updated concept, something new to add to the rotation of ads."

He wore his skepticism like a mask. "Hadley, why rock the boat? People know me as the spokesman for MHI. It's comforting, familiar. And isn't that what we're all about? Providing clients with comfort?"

She sighed. *This conversation isn't going anywhere.* Once again, her brother had dismissed her idea before she'd even had a chance to properly express it. "Never mind, Savion." She rose from the seat, vowing not to waste any more of her time on the matter—at least not today. "I'm going to go deliver the forms to their rightful owner."

Savion nodded, then returned his attention to his planner.

On the heels of his nonverbal dismissal, Hadley left the office, seeking out her other brother. Before she could make it to the end of the hall, Campbell dashed out of his office and jogged past her.

Spinning around, she called after him. "Cam. You have to get this stack of repair requests—"

"Not now, Hadley. I've got a meeting." He kept walking, his long strides taking him out of the corridor and into the main lobby.

She followed him, half tempted to shake her fist. "A meeting or a date?"

He glanced back at her long enough to shoot her a crooked grin. "Don't hate, sis."

She rolled her eyes. "Cam. It's the middle of the day. You have to do some actual work around here."

"I'll get to it later," he called back as he slipped out through the glass doors, letting them swing shut behind him.

Standing in the lobby alone, Hadley propped her fists on her hips, feeling her face crunch into a frown. Her work at MHI had begun to seem like a combination of babysitting and playing secretary, neither of which she'd signed up to do. Her brothers had always been expected to remain in Sapphire Shores and continue the Monroe legacy of controlling most of the rental property on the island. As the baby of the family, and the only girl, she hadn't had those expectations placed on her. Still, she loved her hometown, and loved her family more. When she'd turned down an executive position out of state to work for the family business as office manager, she hadn't considered it a sacrifice. But as time went by, and she put in more and more work only to be dismissed and undervalued by her brothers, she wondered if she'd made the right choice.

With a shake of her head, she returned to her office. The small digital clock on the desk told her it was almost noon, and as she plopped down in her chair, she contemplated what she'd do for lunch. Leaving the office sounded fabulous, so she decided she'd walk a few blocks down to the nearby shopping center to grab something. The walk would likely do her good by helping to clear her mind and giving her time to let her irritation with her brothers dissipate.

She eyed the stack of repair requests still sitting on her desk. Eight of their rental units needed some repair or other, and four of those were currently occupied. As was standard, those units with people staying in them would take priority over vacant ones. She thought about Campbell, and with no idea of where he'd gone or when he'd be back, she picked up the phone to call the plumbers and technicians needed for the occupied units.

Erring on the side of caution helped her cope with situations like this, and as she waited for the plumber to answer her call, she vowed to give Campbell a smack upside his head the next time she saw him.

Devon thumbed through the pages of *Reader's Digest* as he sat in the waiting room of Stinger Urgent Care. He'd only been in town for forty-eight hours, and already the pain from his herniated disk had become worrisome enough to bring him here. This was the last place he'd wanted to spend the first Friday of his winter vacation, but there hadn't been any way to avoid it.

Trying to take his focus off the pain in his back, he half read an article in the magazine. While he read, he shifted his hips in the seat, a vain attempt at getting comfortable. But with the searing pain radiating through his low back, achieving comfort was an impossibility.

"Mr. Granger?" A scrubs-clad nurse appeared in the doorway to his left, her gaze cast down at the clipboard in her hand. "Devon Granger?"

He put the magazine down and stood, approaching the nurse.

As he walked up, she looked up from her clipboard. Her eyes immediately grew five sizes larger. "Oh. My. God. You're *that* Devon Granger?"

Despite his discomfort, he managed a smile. He had

a lot of genuine gratitude for his fans—their support had given him a very good life. "Yes. And you are?"

Blushing, she looked away, seeming to struggle to remember her name. "I'm…uh…Marla. It's so nice to meet you, Mr. Granger. I loved you in *Reach for the Sky*… It's my favorite movie of all time."

"Thank you, Marla. And please, call me Devon."

A giggle he'd expect to hear from a teenager erupted from her lips, and she stifled it. "Oh my goodness. Let me stop holding you up. Follow me to your exam room." She started walking down the narrow corridor leading to the rear of the clinic.

He followed her, still a bit amused by the encounter. A few seconds later, she escorted him into a room complete with the typical doctor's office setup: a counter with a sink, a short wheeled stool, a chrome and plastic chair, and a paper-covered bed.

As he took a seat in the chair, she spent a few moments taking his vital signs. That done, she headed for the door.

"Dr. Stinger will be in to see you soon." Still smiling, she departed, closing the door behind her.

The hard seat and backrest of the chair made him nostalgic for the one in the waiting area; at least it had been padded. The stiff material wasn't helping his pain any, so he got up and moved to the bed, which was set in the upright position.

He was scooting his hips onto the paper-covered surface when the door swung open.

Dr. Steven Stinger, dressed in dark slacks and a white medical coat embroidered with his name, entered the room and closed the door behind him. A Black man in his late forties, Dr. Stinger wore a pair of black-framed glasses perched on the end of his nose, as well as the traditional stethoscope draped over his neck. "Mr. Granger. What brings you here today?" He took a seat on the wheeled stool and looked Devon's way.

Settling back against the bed, he released a breath. "My back. I have a herniated disk, and I can't deal with the pain anymore."

Dr. Stinger slid the clipboard holding what Devon assumed to be his medical chart from beneath his arm and jotted something on it. "Which disk?"

He swiveled to his left, gesturing to his tailbone region. "It's in the sacrum area."

"Oh. That's a particularly uncomfortable spot." He scribbled some more. "How long have you had the injury, and how have you been dealing with the pain so far?"

"It's been about a month. I injured myself doing a stunt on my last film…"

Dr. Stinger's expression changed, becoming less serious. "*Destruction Derby 3*, right?"

"Yes." He supposed he shouldn't be surprised that the doctor would ask, given the immense popularity of the series. Still, he wanted to steer the conversation back to the pain that had brought him to the clinic. "Anyway, I've been treating it with hot and cold therapy and some turmeric capsules my trainer gave me."

Still making notes, Dr. Stinger nodded. "Is there a reason you didn't get a prescription from the doctor who diagnosed you? In most cases like this, a prescription is offered."

Straightening, Devon scratched his chin. "My doctor did offer a prescription, but I wanted to try the natural remedies first. I'm not the biggest fan of pharmaceuticals, so I avoid them when I can."

"I can understand that. A lot of my patients feel the same way." Dr. Stinger set his pen and chart aside. "Let me examine you to get a better idea of how I can help you going forward. How long will you be in town?"

"Until just after the New Year."

Dr. Stinger adjusted the bed until it lay flat, and then instructed Devon to lie down on his stomach.

The doctor left the room and returned with a portable X-ray machine and the nurse. Once the examination was complete, and the nurse and equipment were out of the room, Dr. Stinger readjusted the bed so Devon could sit upright again.

"I'm going to recommend a nonsteroidal anti-inflammatory for you. Considering your attitude toward medication, I'll start you at a low dose." The doctor quickly wrote on his prescription pad. "Also, you'll need to remain active—walking will help keep the joints lubricated and lessen your discomfort. Where are you staying while you're here?"

"I'm in a rental town house on Rising Tide Drive."

Dr. Stinger's brow hitched. "Two story?"

He nodded.

"You'll need to stay off the second floor. Walking will help, but climbing stairs several times a day will put undue stress on your injury. Can you make arrangements to do that?"

"I guess so." He knew that would involve calling MHI and probably interacting with Hadley again.

"You may also need some help around the house. Standing in one spot, such as for cooking or washing dishes, is probably not going to be comfortable. You should consider hiring someone for that kind of thing." Tearing the prescription from his pad, he handed it over.

Devon accepted the prescription, tucking it into the hip pocket of his jeans. "I'll look into it." The housekeeping staff already kept the place clean for him, but he'd still need to make some adjustments. Plus, he'd planned to cook for himself, since he didn't want to spend two and a half weeks eating takeout. Now he'd have to see if Hadley could spare a staff member to be at his disposal.

As Devon left the clinic, heading for the pharmacy two doors down, he inhaled, letting the ocean breeze fill his nostrils. The air in Los Angeles was notoriously dirty, and deep inhales there often involved suffering through some unpleasant odors. Here, all he smelled was the salt, the sand and the grass.

Coming here once a year did him a world of good. It wasn't just about escaping the busyness of life in LA—it was about returning home to the place that had shaped his youth. Doing that gave him a sense of peace, and he'd sorely needed that when he lost Natalie.

As he swung open the door to the pharmacy, he contemplated what he would say to Hadley when he called the office to make his requests. She'd said to call if he needed anything, and now he'd have to take her up on that.

Chapter 4

Friday afternoon, Hadley was stretched out on the love seat in her office with her head resting on one of the arms. She held her cell phone to her ear, listening to her mother on the other end of the line.

"Hadley, say something, honey. We need to decide what we're serving so I can send out for the groceries." At fifty-six, Viola Monroe was still as fastidious as ever when it came to her holiday menu. While she loved to cook, she hated to shop and always arranged to have the groceries delivered to the house.

"I know, Mama. I like what you've mentioned so far." Hadley tossed one jeans-clad leg over the other, resting her ankles on the opposite arm of the love seat from where she reclined. "We should definitely do a glazed ham. It's tradition, and I don't think anybody wants to change it. And the turkey breast was a big hit with the guys last year."

"We'll keep those things. But we need to decide on some side dishes to go along with them." Viola paused a moment before launching into a list. "We need at least three vegetables, two starches, desserts…"

While her mother went on and on about the menu for Christmas dinner, Hadley found her mind wandering. That was common whenever Viola started obsessing about the minutiae of the holiday meal. Today, however, Hadley's mind wandered into the most enticing territory. She recalled Devon's arrival in town, and the time she'd spent in the town house with him. Her mind replayed the intense look in his hazel eyes, the way he'd smiled at her. She inhaled and could swear she smelled his woodsy, masculine cologne. She imagined what his arms must look like beneath that sweater, what the hard lines of his chest might feel like beneath her palms…

"Hadley, are you listening to me?"

Snapped back to reality by the harsh tone of her mother's voice, she swung her legs down and sat up. "Sorry, Mama. I'm swamped with work around here, so my mind wandered a bit."

"Mmm-hmm." Viola didn't sound convinced in the least. "I said, we'll have roasted potatoes, stuffing, glazed brussels sprouts, green beans and turnip greens to round out the meal."

"Sounds fantastic."

"Then I asked *you* what we should have for dessert."

Frantically searching her mind for an answer, Hadley nervously drummed her fingers on her thigh. Then she rcmembered a conversation she'd had with Devon the previous year about his favorite desserts. "Why don't we have Dutch apple pie and peach cobbler?"

After a few beats, Viola answered, "I like it. We haven't had those in years, not since your father got on this tiramisu kick."

Hadley breathed a sigh of relief.

"Now that we've settled that, why don't you tell me what you were really thinking about just now when you were ignoring me?"

Her eyes widened as she realized her relief had been premature. "I, uh…well, I found another stack of re-pair request forms on my desk yesterday, and Cam wouldn't—"

Viola scoffed. "Oh, please. You're my daughter. I've only known you since you took your first breath. And I know good and well you weren't thinking about any-thing related to work."

Falling back against the cushioned backrest of her love seat, Hadley sighed. "It's nothing. It's just that Devon checked in Wednesday, and I've been a bit… distracted."

Viola's soft chuckle met that admission. "Honey, I know he's here. He's a celebrity. Everybody knows he's here. What I want to know is when are you going to ask him over for Christmas dinner?"

She bristled. "Mama. I've asked him to join us for dinner for the past four years, and every time he's turned me down." Devon had always pointed to his desire to spend the day in reflective solitude. She wasn't sure that was the full story, but who was she to question his choice?

"Maybe the fifth time will be the charm. I respect his wishes if he says no again, but at least ask him, honey. Nobody should be alone on Christmas, and we have so much to share."

As much as she'd love to bring Devon home for Christmas—if only to corner him under some mistletoe—she still doubted he'd be receptive to her invitation. "I don't know, Mama."

Viola cleared her throat. "Hadley Aria Monroe, you are going to ask Devon to join us for Christmas dinner, do you understand?"

"Yes, ma'am." She could tell from her mother's tone that she didn't have a choice.

"Heavens, girl. The worst he can do is say no. It isn't as if he's going to run you over with his car for inviting him." Viola chuckled again. "Okay, I'll let you go. And tell your brothers they'd better straighten up or I'll send your father over there."

That comment brought a giggle out of her. "Thanks, Mama. 'Bye."

After she ended the call with her mother, she rose from the love seat and returned to her desk. While she usually tried to leave early on Friday afternoons, she had a bit more work she wanted to do before she started her weekend. Easing into the seat, she flipped open her laptop.

Before the computer could awaken from sleep mode, her office line rang. Lifting the receiver from the cradle, she placed it to her ear. "Hello?"

"Hi, Hadley. It's Devon."

Her heart leaped into her throat the moment she heard his voice. He didn't need to identify himself; there was no mistaking the sexy baritone she often heard whispering to her in her dreams at night. It took a few seconds to find her voice, and when she did, her words tumbled out in a rush. "Devon, hi. How are you? Is everything okay with your rental unit?"

He chuckled. "Everything's fine, I just need a little bit of help. I knew you were the right person to call."

She smiled, wrapping the spiral telephone cord around her index finger like a love-struck teenager as she replied, "I sure am. What can I do for you?"

"I went to the doctor to have my back checked out, and it turns out I need to avoid going up and down stairs."

Hadley's mind automatically swung into problem-solving mode. Flipping open the property book on her desk, she leafed through the pages. "We could move you, but I don't think we have any single-story units available until after the New Year."

"That's fine. I love this place, and I don't really want to move out of it, anyway."

Her brow creased into a frown. "So, what would you like to do? I certainly don't want you going against the doctor's orders."

"Oh, I won't. I have no desire for my back to get any worse."

"How can I help, then?"

"Could you possibly spare a staff member to come

over here and rearrange things for me so I don't have to use the second floor?"

It was an unexpected request, but it confirmed her suspicions that he hadn't been telling her the full story about his back. She thought about the layout of the unit for a moment. What he'd asked for seemed doable. Since there was a bedroom and a three-piece bath on the first floor, the arrangement would work fine. "Sure, I'll send someone right over. They will be there within the hour, in fact."

"Great." The tone of his voice indicated he was smiling. "Thanks a lot, Hadley. I really appreciate it."

"You know how much we value your business. Don't worry, I'll make sure you're taken care of."

"Perfect. Thanks again." And he disconnected the call.

Unraveling her fingertips from the cord, Hadley sighed. Then she returned the receiver to the cradle and sat back in her chair, grinning. An opportunity had presented itself, and she wasn't about to miss it. She'd promised to send someone over to help him, and she would. She simply hadn't said whom.

I have the perfect staffer in mind to take care of Devon.

Me.

Devon had just bent to grab a soda from the bottom of the refrigerator when he heard the knock at the door. He shut the fridge, with his ginger ale in hand, and went to answer it. *Hadley wasn't kidding about getting some-*

one over here quickly. It had only been about a half hour since he'd put in the call to the office.

He strolled to the door, looking out the bay window as he passed it. Noting the MHI company car sitting in the driveway, he didn't bother to check the peephole before swinging the door open.

He'd expected to find some guy in the all-blue MHI uniform, ready to do his bidding.

Instead, as the door opened, he came face-to-face with Hadley. She stood on the porch, wearing a long-sleeved blue MHI T-shirt, a pair of dark skinny jeans, high-top sneakers and the most alluring smile he'd ever seen.

He'd been hanging around the town house in a loose tank and athletic shorts and suddenly felt very aware of his attire. Apparently, Hadley shared that awareness, because he saw her eyes rake over his body. Then her gaze lifted to meet his.

"Hi, Devon."

His name on her lips sounded almost musical. "Hi, Hadley. I thought you were sending someone over."

She shrugged, as if she did this sort of thing all the time. "Everyone else was either out on a job or had already gone home by the time you called. Don't worry. I'll take care of you." Her lashes fluttered as she gazed up at him.

He sensed the double meaning in her words. He smiled, folding his arms over his chest. "So, you're sure you'll be able to move everything I need to be re-arranged?"

She laughed, a tinkling sound reminiscent of ice

cubes falling into a glass. Bending her arms at the elbows in a show of strength, she quipped, "Kickboxing, remember? I got it. Now, are you gonna let me come in?"

Shaking his head, he stepped aside to allow her entry. Once she'd crossed the threshold, he closed the door behind her and locked it.

She strode to the center of the living room, near the coffee table, and turned his way. Cracking her knuckles, she asked, "What do you need me to do, Devon?"

The more he watched her move—and considered the way her petite, shapely figure looked even in casual clothing—the more he thought about asking her to do things that would probably be very bad for his back. Shaking those thoughts away, he gestured to the stairs that led to the second floor. "First, I need all my clothes and toiletries moved from the master upstairs into the downstairs bedroom."

"No problem." She crossed the room and jogged up the stairs.

He watched her go, again appreciating the view of her ample backside as she climbed the steps. He took a deep breath, wondering how he would keep his thoughts on the task at hand and off her body. The attraction crackling between them was palpable, and part of him knew it had been there for at least the past three years. It was possible she'd been attracted to him before that, and that he'd simply been too wrapped up in his grief over losing Natalie to notice.

Now, as the passage of time lightened the burden of the loss, he saw Hadley in a new light. But the fact remained: she was Campbell Monroe's baby sister. Not to mention their oldest sibling, Savion. Since Savion had been two years ahead of Devon and Campbell in school, Devon didn't really know him that well. Still, every interaction he'd ever had with Savion painted him a serious, exacting man who'd likely be content with his baby sister staying single forever.

She returned about fifteen minutes later, descending the stairs with his suitcase in one hand and his toiletry bag in the other. "I went through the closet and the dresser, folded all your stuff and put it in here. Then I cleared everything around the bathroom sink and put it in the toiletry bag." She moved toward him, extending the bags in his direction. "Look through it and make sure I got everything. Then I'll help you set it all up downstairs."

He took his bags to the window seat, where he opened them and inspected the contents as she stood nearby, waiting. "There are only two things missing. My sneakers and my slippers—they're under the bed."

"Got it." She dashed up the stairs again, returning with the shoes. "Is that everything?"

He nodded, impressed with her eagerness to help. "Yes, thank you."

She smiled again, the corners of her glossy pink lips upturned. "I was just thinking, you'll need the linens from the closet upstairs, too. Why don't you go ahead and start putting your things in the downstairs bedroom, and I'll move the linens to the downstairs closet?"

"Sounds good." He watched her walk away again, then took his bags into the downstairs bedroom. The room was well appointed, though not as much as the master upstairs. The decor was all done in varying shades of blue, from the dark carpet to the textured medium-blue wallpaper and the softer blues echoed in the bedding. It would meet his needs nicely. The only downfall was the queen-size bed. He preferred the king upstairs, due to his height. But for the sake of his back, he would manage fine with the queen.

He went around the room, putting away his clothes again, the same way he had on the day he'd arrived. Once he'd done that and slid his empty suitcase into the closet, he grabbed his toiletry bag from the bed and headed for the bathroom.

He moved into the bathroom, which was much smaller than the one upstairs, and swung open the mirrored medicine cabinet to put away his stuff. The pedestal sink left him no space to leave toothpaste and whatnot around it, so he tucked away everything he'd need daily and shut the cabinet. He looked to the shower stall, glad the downstairs bathroom had one so he wouldn't have to climb the stairs to bathe. Satisfied, he tucked the empty toiletry bag under his arm and stepped out into the hallway.

Hadley was already there, tucking fresh towels and sheets into the hall closet. Because of the narrow hallway, there wasn't any practical way to go around while she had the closet door open, so he waited.

She shut the door, saw him standing there and jumped. A little squeal escaped her lips.

He chuckled. "Sorry. Didn't mean to scare you, but the hall isn't wide enough for me to have gone around."

She put her hand on her chest, drew a few deep breaths. "No problem. I guess I'm just a bit of a nervous Nellie."

He sensed her tension and instinctively placed a hand on her shoulder. He could feel the stiffness gathered there. "Are you going to be okay?"

She looked up at him, those sparkling brown eyes of hers as wide as the plains in the Midwest. Her mouth fell open in an O shape, but she said nothing.

Something shifted between them as their eyes connected, and he sensed the tension leaving her, the muscles unknotting beneath his hand. "Am I making you uncomfortable?"

She shook her head, eyes still wide. "No."

He gave her shoulder a squeeze before moving his hand away.

Breaking the contact seemed to bring her back to the moment at hand. She blinked a few times, then asked, "Is there anything else you need me to do?"

"My laptop and the binders. I left them in the office. Could you grab them and bring them downstairs?"

She nodded. "Anything else?"

"The writing table up there. I'd like it moved into the downstairs bedroom, if it's not too heavy."

She was already headed toward the stairs. "Nah, I got it. That thing's not as heavy as it looks."

Over the next several minutes, she moved the writing table into the downstairs bedroom. Once she'd set it in the corner near the window, she placed his laptop and the three binders he'd brought with him on the table. He stood in the bedroom doorway, observing her.

She turned his way. "Are you good now?"

"Yes. Thanks for coming over to do this for me."

"You're welcome." Her brow cocked then. "What's going on with your back, anyway?"

He thought about what to say and about how much he wanted her to know. Not wanting her to think of him as helpless, he said, "Let's just say stunt work is hard on the body, and I'm not as young as I once was." *Great. Now I've made myself seem old.*

"Okay, then." She looked as if she wanted to know more, but thankfully, she didn't press. Moving toward him, she spoke again. "I'm headed home."

He moved so she could exit the bedroom, then trailed her to the door. "Thanks again, Hadley."

Opening the door, she turned back toward him with a smile. "Remember, if you need anything else, just call."

"Won't the office be closed over the weekend?"

A sly expression on her face, she reached into the pocket of her jeans and pulled out a business card. She moved into his personal space, adjusting his arm and hand until his palm was up and open, then pressed the card into his palm. "My cell phone number is on the back." Closing his fingers over the card, she slipped through the open door and closed it behind her.

As he flipped the card and read the number scrawled there, he couldn't contain his smile.

Chapter 5

The interior of the Crowned by Curls salon bustled with activity Saturday morning as Hadley entered through the glass doors, with Belinda close behind her. Taking off her sunglasses and tucking them into her purse, Hadley wove her way across the carpeted waiting area to the reception desk.

"Damn, it's jumping in here today. Good thing we made appointments." Belinda ran her hand over her close-cropped hair. "I need my waves redone, like, yesterday."

Hadley chuckled. "Nobody tries to walk in here on a Saturday. At least, nobody who lives here." Only vacationers, operating on the assumption that a Black-owned salon in a small resort town could never be crowded, tried this.

Lisa, the desk clerk, smiled as the two women approached. She wore the hot-pink scrubs and black apron that constituted the salon's uniform. "What's up, Hadley? How you doing, Belinda?"

"We're good, girl." Belinda rested her elbows on the counter. "How the kids doing?"

Lisa rolled her eyes. "Girl, they're as rambunctious as ever."

"Y'all ready for us?"

Lisa winked. "You know how we roll here. You come on time for your appointment and we'll be ready. Go on back—they're waiting for y'all."

Circling around the desk, Hadley and Belinda passed through the beaded curtains to the back area of the salon, where the stylists maintained their stations. The fuchsia-painted walls of the salon were dressed with framed images of famous Black women. There were singers, actresses, educators and other luminaries of the race. The black-and-white tile floor hosted the ten stations for hairstylists, as well as four for nail technicians.

Sandra Jackson, the salon's owner and Hadley's personal stylist, waved her over to her station. Sandra, whose long, thin blond-highlighted dreadlocks were piled atop her head, ran a tight ship. "Hadley, come on over, girl. I'm ready for you."

Hadley waved to Belinda, who'd already slipped into Tammy's chair across the room, and climbed into Sandra's chair. "Hey, Sandra. How you doing?"

"Good, girl. Business is booming, and I can't complain." Picking up a wide-tooth comb, she attempted to sweep it through Hadley's loose curls. "Maybe I can complain. Girl, haven't you been detangling your hair?"

Hadley sucked at her bottom lip. "I have, but I didn't do it last night. And I fell asleep without my silk bonnet."

Sandra shook her head. "Tsk, tsk. I told you if you don't want to take care of your hair between visits, we can always shave your head." She gave Hadley's shoulder a gentle jab with the end of the comb.

Feeling properly chastised, Hadley shook her head. "No, no. I'll do better. I just want my usual wash and set. And I probably need a trim."

Sandra ran her fingers through her hair. "Yes, you do. Your ends are looking a little raggedy, girl. Let's get you to the shampoo bowl."

Once Hadley's tresses had been washed, trimmed and set on rollers, she sat underneath the hooded dryer. No sooner than she opened a magazine to pass the time, Belinda was ushered over and put beneath the dryer next to her.

The moment she was seated, Belinda spoke. "So, tell me. What's going on with that fine Devon Granger?"

Thanks to Sandra's investment in ultraquiet hair dryers, Hadley couldn't pretend not to have heard Belinda. Odds were most of the people in the back of the salon heard her, as well. "Pertaining to what, exactly?"

Belinda rolled her eyes. "Come on, girl. Did you ask him about Captain Vicious coming back for *DD3*?"

Hadley glanced around and noticed more than a few sets of eyes on her. Apparently, she and Belinda weren't the only ones curious about what to expect from the next film in the trilogy and the villain everyone loved to hate. "I did, but he's under a contract that says he can't tell anyone."

"So much for getting the scoop on that." Belinda leaned to her left a bit, as if trying to get closer to her friend. "Did you get any juicy Hollywood news out of him?"

She shook her head. "No filming and no premieres until after the New Year."

"Sheesh." Belinda popped her lips. "Well, let's get down to the real deal, then. Have you made your move on him yet?"

"Nice segue, B."

Belinda shrugged. "I do what I can. Now give me the dirt."

Hadley cocked her head to one side, hoping to redirect the hot air to a spot where her head felt more damp. "There's no dirt. At least, not yet."

"What are you waiting on? You had better make your move on him before some other woman does." Belinda tossed one leg over the other. "Remember, Sapphire Shores is a resort town. That means your competition is bigger than just the local girls. It's all the women traveling here as tourists, too."

Hadley sighed. She had history with Devon, and not just the past five Christmases spent seeing to his needs at the town house. They'd known each other since childhood, and while they'd never been more than friends in the past, she liked to think their long association counted for something. "True enough, but Devon and I have history."

"History, indeed. Your history is as the pip-squeak little sister, and his is as the hot friend of your older brother." Belinda chuckled. "Yeah. Y'all go way back."

Hadley stuck out her tongue at her friend. She loved Belinda like a sister, but sometimes she could do without her plainspoken honesty. "Thanks for the vote of confidence, B. If you feel that way about it, then why are you pushing me to go after him?"

"It's like I said. If you don't, someone else is going to move in on him."

Hadley fixed her with a glare and waited.

Belinda sighed. "Fine. Look, I've known you how long now? Approximately forever, right?"

"That's about right." They'd been the tag team of terror for more than a decade.

"In all that time, I've never known you to be into anyone the way you're into Devon. The way I see it, y'all are soul mates. I get that he's all famous now, and that makes it harder to approach him. But you're in a unique situation that gives you total access to him."

With her chin resting on her fist, Hadley nodded. "I suppose that's true. I even have a key to the town house...but I would never infringe on his privacy by using it without his permission."

"I'm not suggesting you do that. But I think it would be pretty stupid of you to let the opportunity to make your feelings known pass you by." Belinda's expression changed, becoming more serious. "I just want you to be happy, Hadley. You work so hard at MHI, picking up the slack for everyone else. You deserve to be happy, girl."

Despite her earlier annoyance, Hadley felt the smile

tipping her lips. "That's really sweet, B. Thanks for caring so much."

"Hey, somebody's got to look after you." Belinda playfully punched Hadley on the arm, an accompaniment to her teasing. "You're too busy looking out for everyone else."

Mulling her friend's words over, Hadley turned her attention back to the magazine still lying open across her lap. She continued to flip the pages and read some of the text, but her mind insisted on playing out possible ways she might approach Devon. She didn't want to come off as desperate or pushy or do anything else that would lead her efforts to crash and burn before they even got off the ground.

Her interactions with Devon so far made her aware of how much he valued his solitude and privacy. As much as she wanted to get his attention, she knew he wouldn't go for being openly pursued. No, it was best to bide her time and wait for the right moment to let him know exactly how she felt.

Somehow, she knew that moment was coming.

With his tablet in hand, Devon slid open the glass doors leading to the back patio. The stone courtyard, with its resin-and-glass dining set, gas grill and comfortable resin love seat, was one of his favorite features of the town house. The location of the property, near the southern tip of the island, meant he could enjoy ocean views from both the front and back of the house. He eased onto the cushioned love seat and settled in. Just beyond the five-foot powder-coated iron fence surrounding the patio lay a wide band of sand that gave way to the blue waves of the Atlantic.

He turned his attention to the tablet, adjusting the screen brightness for easier viewing in the sunlight. The day was temperate, in the midfifties, and he'd donned a pair of gray sweatpants and a long-sleeved black T-shirt. Usually at this time on a Saturday afternoon, he'd be working out, but his injury prevented him from doing much in the way of exercise other than walking. The prescription he'd gotten from Dr. Stinger did a lot to ease the pain, but he didn't want to risk making matters worse by hitting the gym.

He took a deep breath, inhaling the fresh air. As he exhaled, he made sure to force the air out from his diaphragm. Despite his inability to do his usual number of sit-ups, he was determined to maintain his core strength. He was no doctor, but he knew that abdominal strength and stability would only help his back.

He tapped the screen, intent on opening the web browser, but an incoming video call interrupted his effort. Seeing the face of his old friend and mentor on the screen made him smile. Swiping across, he answered the call. "Rick! How the hell are you?"

"Great, great. How are you doing, young buck?" Rick Rollingsworth, a consummate actor who was considered Hollywood royalty, smiled from across the miles. The man was in great physical shape, and the only hint of his nearly sixty years of living was the small streak of gray hair running across his hairline. "Enjoying your vacation?"

"Yes. It's beautiful down here. And far more quiet

than LA could ever be." Devon raised the tablet, turning it so Rick could see the water. "Look at that ocean. And barely a soul out here to disturb my peace."

Rick chuckled. "I'm jealous. I'm still on set for the Teddy Pendergrass biopic." He panned his camera around, showing Devon the bustling activity going on in the studio. An outdoor backdrop, depicting a city street, hung behind Rick. People rushed back and forth through the cavernous space, carrying props, chatting noisily and pushing carts. "They're moving equipment between soundstages right now, then they'll set up the next take."

Devon shook his head. He admired Rick's work ethic, and he knew a large part of Rick's success as an African American actor in a less-than-hospitable film industry could be traced back to it. "Jeez. It's little more than a week before Christmas. When are they gonna wrap this thing up?"

"Hell if I know." Rick shrugged. "Filming is going to continue in the New Year, probably. But I expect they'll let us go for a holiday break in the next couple of days. Even if they don't, I'm out by the twentieth. My wife isn't going to have me staying any longer than that."

"How is Odetta, anyway? I haven't seen her in a while." Devon was particularly fond of Rick's wife, who loved to bake and often sent cookies, pies and other homemade sweets to the film sets they worked on together.

"She's great. She's out shopping right now, no doubt. Between her and Richelle, I gotta take most of the roles that come my way." He laughed as he spoke of his twentysomething daughter, his and Odetta's only child. "They're both spoiled as hell, but I wouldn't have it any other way."

Devon chuckled. "We both know that. So, what's up? There's got to be a reason you're calling me from on set."

Rick snapped his fingers, as if remembering something. "Yes, there is. I've been called to consult on a new film project. The screenwriter wants to put together a whole new team of up-and-coming talent. You know, a new director, producer, actors at the beginning of their careers, the whole nine."

Devon's ears perked up. "Really? So, what's the project about?"

"It's a romantic thriller, exploring the Black Panther Party in the '60s. I've seen the script, and it's pretty impressive writing. The man's got a gift, and if he can pull the right team together, he's got a hit on his hands."

Scratching his chin, Devon thought about what he'd just heard. The film's premise was intriguing, and he always sought out roles that allowed him to tell stories he thought were important. "How are the Panthers portrayed?"

"Pretty objectively, from what I can tell. You won't find any of that manufactured lore about them being a criminal organization, but they aren't painted as saints, either."

The more Devon heard, the more he liked the project. "So, I guess this means you're ready to deal me in, then?"

Rick nodded. "Yeah. I thought you might like to step

in as one of the Panthers' enforcers. The role is available, and you've definitely got the body type."

Devon sucked in a breath. "Okay, Rick. I'm interested in participating, but not as an actor."

Rick's thick brow rose a few inches. "Then what, pray tell, would you be doing?"

"Directing." He kept his expression even, hoping to convey his seriousness.

It was to no avail, because Rick immediately burst out laughing.

Devon sat there, watching the screen and waiting for Rick to recover.

When he finally stopped laughing, he said, "Okay, Devon. I'll let the screenwriter know that everyone's favorite action hero wants to direct."

Devon frowned. "Come on, Rick. I'm serious."

That only started the laughter again. "I hear you, man." Rick inserted his words between guffaws. "Look, I'll let you go. I'll get back to you on your directorial debut. 'Bye, Devon." His image faded from the screen as he ended the video call.

Setting the tablet on the cushion next to him, Devon folded his arms over his chest. He'd put himself out there, made his aspirations known, only to be laughed at by the man he looked up to.

He shook his head ruefully. This was precisely why he hadn't told anyone of his aspirations. Moving behind the camera wasn't some fly-by-night idea he'd come up with on the plane ride. He'd been thinking about it for the past two years, at least. He loved acting and loved his fans even more. But the stunt work side of things only became harder and more physically taxing as the years went by. He wasn't foolish enough to think he'd stay young and able-bodied forever. Even though he kept himself in excellent physical shape, his efforts hadn't prevented his recent injury.

All he could do now was wait and hope Rick put in a good word for him. With no information on the project other than the general premise, he'd be hard-pressed to find out any more about it on his own.

His face tight with tension and worry, Devon closed his eyes and set his focus on the sound of the rolling waves.

Chapter 6

Standing in line at Della's Delicatessen, Hadley tapped her foot to the rhythm of an '80s pop song playing on the jukebox. There were still three people ahead of her, as well as five or six behind her. She'd been waiting about ten minutes so far, but this wasn't anything new for the Monday lunch rush. There were no other delis in town, so if you wanted a great sandwich that you didn't have to make yourself, you stood in line at Della's with everybody else.

Once the person ahead of her was served, she moved forward in time with the rest of the line. Her phone buzzed in the hip pocket of her slacks, and she reached to check it.

It was a text message from Belinda.

Lunch today?

She typed a quick reply.

Can't. Grabbing lunch for the office. TTYL.

Sending the message off, she tucked her phone away just as the line moved again. Observing the faces of the people around her, she saw many that were familiar. Della's was an out-of-the-way spot, tucked in a nondescript one-story building on the southwestern side of the island. Only the intrepid tourist in search of a quick lunch or light dinner found the place, which was a hit among the locals. There were several chain restaurants that were more centrally located, and Hadley had driven right past them on her way to Della's.

When Hadley got to the counter, the woman herself greeted her. Della Hall, her gray hair covered in her signature white hairnet, leaned over the counter as she approached. "Hey, Hadley. How are you? How are your parents and those crazy brothers of yours?"

Smiling, Hadley set her purse on the counter. "Everybody's good, Della. You ready for the holidays?"

"Yes, if you mean ready to take myself a vacation. We close up on the twenty-third and don't open back up until the second of January."

"Here's the order, Miss Della." A young man in one of Della's famous green-checked aprons passed her two plastic bags brimming with food.

"Thank you." Della placed the bags on the counter in

front of Hadley. "Okay, love. Got your order right here. Let's run through it and make sure everything's there."

Hadley ran down the office lunch order, which included seven different sandwiches, a salad and all the side items. The fridge in the break room was usually stocked with drinks, so she'd left those off when she had called in the order earlier. As Hadley went down the list, Della produced each item from one of the bags. "Looks like we're all set." She passed Della the company credit card.

After Della swiped the card, she handed it back to Hadley with her receipt. "There you go. Y'all enjoy."

"Thanks, Della." Hoisting the two bags down from the counter, Hadley turned and started to leave.

"Wait a minute. Let me ask you something."

She turned back to face Della. "Sure. What is it?"

"Any word on what y'all are going to do with that last plot of land you just cleared?" Della tapped the end of a short pencil on the counter as she waited for a response.

Hadley shook her head. "Not yet, but there's a meeting about that after lunch. Whatever I find out, I'll pass on to you."

"I'd appreciate it. If it's possible, I'd love to build a bigger deli, and that's about the only place left on the island where I can do it."

Hadley nodded. "I'll look into it and let you know." With that, she took the food and exited the deli. Outside, she set the bags on the passenger floorboard of the company car, climbed in and drove away.

Back at the office, she hoisted the bags out of the car. At first, she thought she'd be hauling them in, but one of the two young male interns from Campbell's department helped her bring everything in and set it down in the break room. Campbell had only had his interns for about three weeks, and Hadley wondered when he'd start putting them to full use. Maybe then he'd stop leaving his work on her desk. After thanking the young man, she claimed her salad box and took it to her office to eat at her desk.

After lunch, she filed into the conference room with her brothers and the five other staff members who normally attended these meetings. Savion, as chief executive, sat at the head of the table, with Campbell to his right and Hadley to his left. The receptionist, marketing officer, operations officer and the two interns rounded out the group.

Once everyone had settled into their seats, Savion stood and grabbed a long tube of paper that had been leaning against the wall behind his chair. "Good afternoon, everyone. I called this meeting to share with you an interesting proposal that has come in for the remaining land MHI plans to develop." He unfastened the band around the paper and opened it, rolling it out on the table.

Campbell, poring over the paper with the others, asked, "What is it?"

"This is a concept drawing for Sapphire Landing. It would be a place designed specifically for the convenience of the tourists who visit Sapphire Shores."

Staring at the oversize paper to view the drawing, Hadley could feel her brow furrowing. "It looks like a mall. All I see is a bunch of chain stores and restaurants clustered together."

Savion shook his head. "No. It's not a mall. While there is shopping available from familiar brands, there are also condominiums. We could rent them out at a premium price because of their proximity to restaurants, shopping and the beach."

Hadley frowned. From what she could see, the whole thing looked and sounded gaudy and overly commercial. Savion seemed to have dollar signs where his pupils should be, and she was afraid that he couldn't hear what she was saying over the sound of the imaginary cash register ringing in his head. "What happened to donating some of the land to the municipality for public green space? Or offering plots to local businesses that want to relocate and expand?" She thought about Della and her desire to grow her business. In a prime location, Della would do very well.

Martin, the marketing officer, piped up then. "There's still the possibility of that. We all know that donating land would only benefit our public image."

Hadley sighed. Martin was the only one who'd offered any defense of the green space idea, and it had been solely based on building up the company's reputation, not on building up the community for the island's residents. She turned to her older brother. "Savion. This development is all wrong for our island. It just doesn't fit the way we live here."

"And what brings you to that conclusion, Hadley?" The condescension had already begun to creep into his tone.

Struggling to keep her frustration with him in check, she answered, "We're a close-knit community, and I think bringing in all these chains and fancy condominiums will diminish the special charm of Sapphire Shores."

Savion shook his head. "You're so young and idealistic, Hadley. It isn't just about the money we'll make on this deal. Think of all the new jobs this would bring to the island. Construction jobs at first, then jobs within the establishments once they're open."

At the opposite end of the table, the receptionist, who'd been busy taking notes, glanced up on the heels of his words. As if sensing the rising tension, she immediately turned her attention back to her laptop.

Hadley pursed her lips. Her brother had just dismissed her, again, and everyone in the room could sense it. Leaning back in her chair, she vowed to keep quiet the rest of the meeting. Arguing with Savion was about as effective as arguing with a telephone pole. As the rest of the staff talked excitedly about what it would be like to have a place like Sapphire Landing in town, she tuned them out. Her focus was better spent on coming up with a way to stop this development and formulating an alternate plan for the land.

She loved Sapphire Shores. She stayed because she loved this place.

And she wouldn't sit idly by and watch some developer ruin everything that made it unique.

Tuesday afternoon, Devon was sitting sideways on the couch with his feet propped up on the backrest. The television was on, but he wasn't really watching it. He'd spent the better part of the day calling around to see if any agency could send over a housekeeper or personal chef to handle his meals.

His search had been largely fruitless, since Quick Transformations was the only agency on the island that handled such requests. He supposed he understood that, as there was probably very little call for personal chefs in Sapphire Shores. Since Quick Transformations already provided housekeeping for MHI, he'd thought he might be able to request some extra service.

"We'd love to help you, Mr. Granger," the receptionist had told him. "But I'm afraid our staff is already greatly reduced this time of year. We'll be closing in a few days and won't reopen until after the New Year."

With a sigh, he readjusted his position as he tried to come up with a way around this little problem. He'd already tried to cook for himself, against Dr. Stinger's advice. That had been a colossal mistake that had led to him having to take an extra dose of the painkiller he'd been prescribed. Standing in one spot for more than a few minutes was simply not going to happen again, at least not without pain.

He'd been in town a little less than a week now and had already grown tired of takeout food. What he wanted was a home-cooked meal, as many of them as he could get. Obviously, he wasn't going to be the one doing the cooking, and therein lay his dilemma.

He looked at his phone lying on the coffee table in front of him. Hadley popped into his mind. She had said to call her if he needed anything. Cooking for him seemed to be well outside her job description, but then again, so had rearranging things in the town house. She'd come over and done that without any complaints.

Contemplating his options, he realized he didn't really have anyone else to call. He'd have to walk a fine line between asking her for help and burdening her. He knew Hadley was already busy with things at MHI, and he didn't want her to think he was taking advantage simply because she'd made herself available to him.

In the end, logic won out, and he gave Hadley a call.

"Hello?"

"Hi, Hadley. It's Devon."

With a smile in her voice, she asked, "Do you need something?"

He took a deep breath. "Yes. I have kind of an unorthodox request."

"More unorthodox than rearranging the town house?"

He chuckled. "I'm afraid so."

"I'm listening."

"I'm not supposed to be standing on my feet for long periods of time. That's fine, since I'm on vacation, but it does leave me with a problem."

"What's that?"

"I can't cook. I've got a refrigerator full of groceries here, and no way to indulge my love of cooking."

"I'd hate for it all to go bad."

"So would I, since I paid for it." A nervous laugh left his throat, and he decided to just come out with his request. "I know you're busy at the office, but I'm tired of eating takeout. Is there any way you could cook for me? It doesn't have to be every day, and you don't have to come here and do it. Since I'm asking you for a favor, I'll let you decide the parameters."

The line was silent for a few moments.

Was she thinking it over? Or had they been disconnected? "Are you still there?"

She laughed. "Yes. I'm just trying to decide what I'll cook first."

He felt the smile stretching his lips. "So, you'll do it?"

"Sure. It's not a problem if I can cook what I'm already making for myself. I'll just double my recipes, and voilà, your problem is solved."

"When could you start?"

"How about tonight? I was going to make Chinese, and I don't mind coming over there."

He felt his nervousness dissipate, replaced by the anticipation of her presence. "I have just about everything here. Whoever did the shopping was very thorough."

"Sounds good. I'll just bring over some spices, and we should be good to go." She paused. "You realize you're going to have to tell me the entire truth about what's going on with your back, right?"

"Yes. If you're willing to do all this for me, I owe you that much." He reclined against the backrest of the sofa. "I'll tell you the whole story tonight over dinner. How's that?"

She sounded pleased. "Then I'll see you tonight around seven. 'Bye, Devon."

"'Bye." He disconnected the call and set his phone aside. His eyes focused on the view through the patio doors, he wondered what tonight would hold. He'd be out of his mind to deny the attraction sparking between them. Would it all come to a head tonight?

He didn't know, but he planned to let things progress naturally. Wherever that led, he'd be ready.

Chapter 7

Hadley knocked on the door of the town house at a few minutes past seven. With a paper grocery bag balanced on her hip, she waited, marching in place to stay warm. The temperature had dropped after the sun went down and the chilly day faded into a cold December night.

Devon swung open the door, greeting her with a smile. "Hi, Hadley."

His lips continued to move, as if he were saying something more. But everything he said after his initial greeting went unheard as her eyes raked over him. She hadn't intended on staring at him, but she couldn't help it. He wore a closely fitted long-sleeved black T-shirt that displayed the outline of the ripped upper body beneath. Charcoal-gray slacks encased his powerful thighs and legs. A thick gold rope chain hanging around his neck suspended the head of a roaring lion in the center of his chest.

How can he be this fine? Every time she saw him, her brain shut down. When it came to concentrating in Devon's presence, the struggle was quite real.

"Hadley, did you hear me?" He touched her arm. "Come on inside out of the cold."

His velvet voice brought her back to reality, and her awareness of the frigid air swirling around her returned. She offered a crooked smile to her amused host. "Thanks."

He stepped aside to allow her in. Once she was inside the town house, she carried the paper bag to the kitchen while he locked up. Setting the bag on the counter, she removed the supplies she'd brought over to supplement Devon's grocery stockpile.

He entered the kitchen, and she felt his presence the moment he did. Her nose twitched as she detected the familiar woodsy fragrance of his cologne. "You look nice tonight, Hadley."

"Thank you." She'd donned a green turtleneck sweater dress, black leggings and tall black boots to work this morning, and had come straight to the town house from the office. She arranged the sesame oil, sesame seeds, soy sauce and rice wine vinegar she'd brought on the counter, trying not to get too excited about his compliment.

A tremor shot through her as he moved closer. He entered her space, standing directly behind her as he placed his fingertips on her shoulder. "Thank you again for doing this. I really do appreciate it."

Her conversation with Belinda in the salon came to mind, and she remembered her decision to seize the opportunity with Devon when the moment was right. Standing there, with his warm breath on the back of her neck, she knew what she needed to do. Drawing a deep breath, she turned around to face him. "Before I start cooking, can we talk for a minute?"

He nodded, backing up a bit. Leaning his hips against the opposite counter, he looked her way. "Sure. What's on your mind?"

This was the moment she'd been waiting for. For the last four years, she'd been waiting to tell him how she felt, never planning a speech. She just wanted to speak from her heart. "I don't want you to think I'm just being friendly and helpful by doing this."

His thick brow cocked upward. "Oh, really?"

She nodded. Maintaining eye contact with him was something of a struggle, but she refused to look away until she'd said what was on her heart. "I...have feelings for you. Strong feelings that tell me I want to be more than just your friend."

His expression remained unchanged, revealing nothing about his reaction. "And how long have you been feeling this way?"

She hesitated. *Maybe I should have come up with a speech.* "At least three years. Maybe longer. But I know you're a widower, and I wanted to be respectful of your grief."

He straightened then, taking a few steps, which brought him back into her personal space. "That's very considerate." He reached out then, his fingertips grazing down the sleeve of her dress until he clasped her hand in his own.

Her heart jumped into her throat as she realized he was receptive. Drawing her bottom lip into her mouth, she lowered her gaze. She didn't know what else to say. Thankfully, it appeared she wouldn't need to say anything else.

He squeezed her hand. "I'm honored that you feel this way about me, Hadley." He raised her hand, lifting it to his lips. Brushing a kiss over her knuckles, he set his golden eyes on her face. "You're an attractive, intelligent and caring woman, and I'm very open to seeing what we could have."

Her breath escaped in a rush, then a wide grin broke over her face.

His smile melted her heart. "Are you still cooking?"

Laughing, she nodded. "Yes. We still have to eat, right?"

"I suppose." He released her hand, gesturing to the stove. "I'll leave you to it."

She took a few deep breaths to settle herself before her hormones got the better of her. Then she went back to the sink to wash her hands.

He strolled to the dining room table and took a seat. The open layout of the town house meant there was no wall separating the kitchen from the other common rooms on the first floor. "I think I'll stay here and keep you company while you cook, if you don't mind."

"I don't mind at all." Concentration be damned, she loved having him nearby. With him sitting at the table only a few feet from her, she started to cook.

Within the hour, the kitchen was filled with the savory aromas of the dishes she'd begun to prepare. One skillet held the cornstarch-battered chicken, frying in a shallow bath of vegetable oil. The other held baby peas, diced carrots and chopped onions, sizzling in oil along with cooked brown rice.

"Smells fantastic in here. What are we having?" Devon leaned forward, resting his elbows on the surface of the table.

"Sesame chicken, fried rice and egg rolls." She looked at the digital display to check the oven temperature. Satisfied that it had heated up enough, she slid in the waiting sheet pan.

"I'm impressed. I've never had homemade sesame chicken."

"You'll love it." She tucked the cutting boards she'd used to dice the chicken and onions into the dishwasher. After washing her hands again, she grabbed a paper towel from the standing dispenser to dry her hands before chucking it into the trash. "Or at least I hope so. It's hard work making this stuff from scratch, though I did use precooked brown rice."

He chuckled. "Nothing wrong with a shortcut now and then." He stood then, slowly making his way back into the kitchen.

She watched him, feeling her heartbeat hasten as he approached. "Shouldn't you be resting your back, Devon?"

"I promised to tell you the problem, and I'm telling you now. I have a herniated disk near my tailbone.

That's why I need to take it easy and stay off the second floor."

Concern swept over her, and she resisted the urge to chastise him or try to force him to sit back down. "Are you sure you should be on your feet right now?"

A wicked smile lit his face as he came abreast of her. "I'm fine. Now, like I was saying. A shortcut is okay now and again, but not when it comes to us."

She noticed his quick change of subject but chose not to address it. "What do you mean?" She trembled as his nearness threatened to overwhelm her.

He placed his palms on her arms. Though she was encased in the dress, his touch seemed to penetrate the fabric.

"There won't be any shortcuts with me and you. I want to get to know you, and I want to take my time doing it." He leaned low, his face mere inches from hers. "No shortcuts."

"Mmm." It was the only sound she could manage. She looked into his hazel eyes and felt her insides melt.

Hooking his finger beneath her chin, he whispered, "Can I?"

She didn't need an illustration to know what he was asking. "Please do."

She saw him smile as he tilted her face to an angle more to his liking. Seconds later, his lips touched hers, and her eyes closed as the sweetness spread through her like wildfire. His lips were soft, and she relished the feeling of them. None of her fantasies matched this fiery reality. He kissed her solidly yet gently, lingering for a few long moments before easing away.

Only the sizzling of the food on the stove broke the silent aftermath as she stared into his eyes.

He is one hell of a man.

Tuesday afternoon, Devon sat on a padded stool at the bar inside the Salty Siren. He'd been coming there every year since he started vacationing in Sapphire Shores for the holidays, and he loved the food, the top-shelf drinks and the laid-back atmosphere. There was always a game on the television, plus all the giant chicken wings you could eat and a great selection of beers on tap. Holiday decorations consisted of several wreaths fashioned from beer can tabs and a single four-foot Christmas tree occupying the corner behind the hostess stand.

He'd decided to break the cabin fever that had begun to set in by meeting his old friend Campbell for a quick chat. Even as he stared absently at the highlight reel on the television in front of him, he couldn't shake his memories of the previous night.

When Hadley had revealed her feelings to him, he hadn't been surprised. He'd mostly been pleased, flattered and happy that she'd decided to make a move. He still held on to some nervousness about dating his friend's younger sister. But the kisses they'd shared last night made it clear that he had no choice but to give in to the attraction between them. Like the pots of food on the stove last night when they'd shared that initial kiss, the feelings had been simmering for a long time and had finally reached their boiling point.

Campbell, who'd been sitting on the stool next to him

for the past fifteen minutes or so, perused the laminated menu. "I get the same thing every time I come here."

Brought back to reality, Devon shrugged. "If it ain't broke…"

Chuckling, Campbell laid the menu on the bar. "You're right. I'm just gonna order the wings."

By then, the bartender in the fitted T-shirt bearing the namesake Salty Siren sidled up. The blue-eyed brunette had been openly flirting with Devon ever since he and Campbell had entered. She leaned over the bar in front of him, the V-neck of her shirt revealing her ample bust. "What can I get ya, Mr. Granger?"

Giving her the practiced smile he gave all his overzealous fans, he replied, "Call me Devon."

She sighed. "I'd just as soon call you handsome. Did I mention how much I loved *Reach for the Sky*?"

Campbell rolled his eyes. "Yes, twice. You do see me sitting here, right, Maddie?"

She cut her eyes in his direction. "Yeah, I see you. And I know you want teriyaki wings and a Blue Moon. You order the same thing every time you come in here."

Devon hid his amusement as he watched the exchange.

"You're coming off a little salty today, Maddie." Campbell folded his arms over his chest. "You can't be acting up just because we went to school together. Expect that to be reflected in your tip."

Did we go to school together? Devon searched his memory bank for a Maddie in his graduating class but came up empty of one that fit her description.

She giggled and stuck out her tongue at him. "Whatever." Smoothly switching her focus back to Devon, she continued, "It isn't every day we get a bona fide celebrity in here."

Devon waved his hand in a show of modesty. "You're too kind. But I'll have the chicken nachos and a Sprite, please."

"Coming right up." Maddie winked at him as she walked away.

"No beer today?" Campbell asked.

"Nah. Mixes with my pain meds, and I gotta drive myself back to the town house."

Maddie placed a tall glass of iced soda in front of him, then set a frosty bottle of beer in front of Campbell. Tossing another grin in Devon's direction, she moved away.

"I feel ya." Campbell relaxed his arms, resting his elbows on the bar. "Meanwhile, looks like Maddie's trying to get with you, man."

Devon shook his head. "Not interested."

Campbell's eyebrow cocked. "What? You're not down with the swirl? I'm shocked, with you coming from Hollyweird and all."

Devon gave his buddy a punch on the shoulder. "Shut up, Cam. It's not that. There's somebody else."

"Oh, really? Who?"

Hesitating for a beat, he replied, "Your sister."

Shock registered on Campbell's face, and he shifted positions on the stool so he faced Devon. "What? When did this happen?"

"Last night."

Face scrunched into a frown, Campbell shook his head. "Bro."

Realizing his error, Devon chuckled. "No, no. It's not like that."

"It better not be."

"I should rephrase." He'd wanted to be honest with his friend, but it hadn't come across the way he'd intended. "Last night, Hadley told me that she's been attracted to me for a while, and honestly, I've been interested in her, too."

Campbell asked, "And what does that mean?"

"It means we're going to take our time getting to know each other better."

That seemed to satisfy him, at least to a degree. His shoulders dropped, and he turned back toward the bar. "Okay then. That sounds a lot better."

Devon watched his friend, gauging his reaction. "So, does that mean you're okay with this?"

Campbell looked him in the eye. "Your playboy days are over, right?"

"Those ended years ago, before I married Natalie."

He shrugged. "Then it's cool with me."

"Really?"

"Hadley's grown. It's not really my place to interfere."

He nodded, taking in the response. It was lukewarm, neither for or against. The more he thought about it, the more he realized it was just typical Campbell, one of the most laid-back dudes he'd ever known.

"My only request is this—don't hurt my sister. If you do, we fighting."

"Understood." Devon expected nothing less, because if he hurt her, he deserved a swift kick.

"I'm not the one you should be worried about, though. Savion's the one who's always trying to tell Hadley what to do." Campbell chuckled. "She usually does what she wants anyway, but that's never stopped him from trying."

Devon let out a chuckle of his own, one fueled by his nerves. He hadn't given much thought to Savion, the oldest Monroe sibling. Odds were Savion wouldn't take too kindly to Devon dating his baby sister. "He's probably not going to like it. But I don't intend on letting Savion tell me what to do, either."

Maddie returned with their food then, sliding the plates in front of them.

Digging into his wings, Campbell smiled. "I'm actually looking forward to Savion's reaction to all this. Should be pretty entertaining."

Devon couldn't help laughing at that. "Hopefully we won't have to square up." He picked up his soda and took a long drink.

"And if it came to that?" Campbell's eyes widened as he awaited an answer.

Setting the glass down, Devon looked his friend right in the eye. "Then it's on. She's worth it." He meant every word. He'd had his share of liaisons with women, and he could see Hadley's worth. It was all over her, glowing as brightly as a neon sign on a moonless night.

Campbell nodded, his expression showing his approval. "My man." He offered his fist.

Bumping fists with Campbell, Devon settled in to his seat and dug in to his meal.

Chapter 8

Wednesday afternoon, Hadley arrived at Oceanview Grill at a few minutes past noon. The OG, as the locals called it, was known all over the island for its top-quality seafood prepared on a wood-fired grill. She inhaled the delicious woodsy aroma as she strolled up to the hostess stand and gave her name. Hadley had arrived first, so she followed the hostess to a booth near the rear of the restaurant, situated beneath a large window.

Settling into the soft brown leather cushion, Hadley picked up one of the two menus the hostess had left on the lacquered wood table. It took her only a few moments to select the day's special: mesquite salmon with braised brussels sprouts and mushroom risotto. Laying the menu back down, she directed her attention to the view outside the window. The temperature had risen into the sixties today, but the hazy gray sky heralded a coming rainstorm. The restaurant's perch on a hill overlooking the sand dunes and the Atlantic on the southeastern tip of the island gave it a beautiful view. She stared out to where the water seemed to rise to meet the sky, sighing contentedly.

I don't know which is better here—the food or the atmosphere.

Voices and footsteps near the entrance drew her attention to a view almost as breathtaking as the one outside the window. When she turned her head, she saw Devon approaching the table. He wore a white button-down shirt, dark denim jeans and black moccasins. The top two buttons of the shirt were undone, giving her a view of the powerful, muscled lines of his neck and upper chest. A pair of dark sunglasses were tucked in his shirt pocket. His hazel eyes swept the restaurant's interior until they landed on her. Then his soft, full lips turned up in a smile that threatened to be her undoing.

He walked up to the table. "Hello, Hadley. You look beautiful."

She felt the warmth filling her cheeks. "Hi, Devon. And, thank you."

He slipped into the booth, sliding over until he was in the center of the bench. "Have you been waiting long?"

She shook her head. "Just a few minutes. The waiter hasn't even been by yet."

He picked up his menu, opening the laminated pages.

She watched the way his large hands grasped the menu, her mind drifting toward other things he might grip with both hands. How would his hands feel holding her hips that way? And just like that, the familiar tingle rose again. It started at the base of her spine and snaked its way up until the hairs on the back of her neck stood on end. What was it about Devon that put her in this state? He made her feel like an enamored teenager.

"What will you be having today, Miss Monroe?" The waiter's question drew Hadley back to the present moment.

Clearing her throat, she passed him the menu. "I'll have the daily special, please. And an iced tea." Looking down at the table, she saw the two glasses of ice water and a basket of rolls that had materialized while she'd been lost in her own thoughts.

Devon handed over his menu, as well. "I'd like the same, with root beer, please."

After the waiter left them alone, she turned her attention back to Devon. Thinking of him that way made her smile. "So, how's your back today?"

"It's feeling pretty good. I've done my stretches, and I'm taking my meds and staying off the second floor as instructed." He rested his elbows on the table and laced his long fingers together. "I see you're still looking out for me."

"Now more than ever." She winked.

"I think it's really sweet." Separating his fingers, he reached out and captured her hands in his. "Now, tell me what's on your mind." His golden eyes locked with hers.

Should I tell him I'm thinking of what it would be like to have him touch me? Her mind wandered back to that night two years ago, when they'd almost kissed. Belinda had stealthily hung a sprig of mistletoe by the front door of the town house, and Hadley had come over to drop off a batch of Christmas cookies from her mom. He'd said something about tradition, and leaned in, but before she could even pucker, the damn sprig fell off the doorframe and landed on the floor. Her cheeks had been so hot, she must have been twelve shades of red as she'd made her hasty retreat.

Thinking of that now made her feel awkward, so she decided against bringing it up.

She blinked a few times as she became aware of his scrutiny. "I...uh..." Yes, they were dating now, but she felt their relationship was a little too new for her to unleash her intense physical desire on him. No, it would be better to tell him about the other thing weighing on her mind. "There's another developer vying to purchase the land we just cleared. It's the last tract of Monroe family land on the island. We have our own plans, but now things are up in the air."

His brow creased. "What developer? And what do they want the land for?"

She sighed. "The company is called Neville South, and they want to build a tacky, oversize mall filled with nothing but chain stores."

"No room for local businesses to rent shops there, I'm guessing?"

"None. You seem familiar with this type of thing."

He shrugged. "I see it in LA all the time. Company swoops in, buys land, pushes folks out and slaps up some pretentious commercial center."

She snapped her fingers. "Yes. Exactly that. The only

difference is no one lives there, so it seems like an easy, mess-free land grab for Neville South."

He shook his head. "Wow. How do your brothers feel about the offer?"

She rolled her eyes. "Campbell isn't going to say anything one way or the other—that's just how he is. But Savion is basically ready to sign the land over."

"Why would he do that?" His face showed genuine confusion.

"Because as part of the deal, Neville South will build some upscale condominiums. They would take on all the building costs, but let MHI collect the rental fees and handle the maintenance." She could imagine how excited her brother had been to hear that part of the deal. The idea of collecting fees on a property MHI didn't pay to build probably made Savion want to break-dance. The company did far more business in real estate, partly because of the overhead involved in property development.

"It's obvious you're not down with this offer."

"That's an understatement." She frowned. "I hate everything about it." She stopped, realizing how negative she sounded. "I don't want to drag you down with this stuff, Devon."

"You're not." He gave her hands a squeeze. "This is bothering you, and I want to hear about it."

She smiled, despite the bad feelings that had been brought up by talking about Neville South. Gazing into his beautiful eyes, she could see his concern, and that made her comfortable enough to go on. "I've lived here most of my life, and I stayed after college even though I had offers to go elsewhere. I love this island, and I know this development will ruin everything that makes it special. Denying the chance for expansion to our local businesses…increasing traffic from the mainland as people flock to these chain stores…more trash… There are so many reasons I oppose it."

"You're pretty fired up about this. Now the question is, what are you going to do about it?" He watched her, awaiting her response.

Shrugging, she replied, "I don't know if there's anything I can do."

He gave her a crooked grin. "Come on now. MHI is your family's company. If you really want to stop this development from happening, I'm sure there's something you can do."

"But what?" She genuinely didn't know how she could impact the outcome. "Talking to Savion is like talking to a brick wall, and Campbell's too busy avoiding work to care."

"You say you can't talk to Savion." He fixed her with a direct, telling look. "Try going over his head." He released her hands to make room on the table for the plates the waiter brought.

She mulled over his words. *I wonder what Mom and Dad would have to say about this deal?*

As they each took their respective plates, Devon stole glances at Hadley. She looked beautiful in the black turtleneck and long denim skirt she wore. Her hair was swept up into a ponytail.

They shared most of the meal in companionable

quiet. By the time dessert came, he found that he couldn't tear his eyes away from her.

He watched her lift a forkful of strawberry short-cake to her lips. She opened her mouth, tucked the cake inside and chewed gracefully. Her eyes closed, and a soft groan escaped her throat. The look of pleasure that came over her face affected him more than he would ever have expected.

She'd only expressed her feelings the night before, and already, he was prepared to act on them. The truth was, she wasn't the only one with feelings. If he were honest, her admission had given him permission to act on his own attraction to her. It hadn't always been there, because he'd loved Natalie with all his heart. But as time had passed, putting more and more distance between the loss of his wife and the present, his pain had also less-ened, making room for him to notice Hadley's appeal.

He started eating but continued to watch Hadley be-tween bites. She continued to wear that blissful ex-pression, giving away her enjoyment of the meal. He wanted to put that look on her face and give her all the pleasure she deserved. But he knew better than to say something like that aloud at this stage in a relationship, most of all in public.

So he grabbed his glass and took a long swig, will-ing the icy root beer to cool his hormones as well as his throat. Needing to make conversation to break the ten-sion, he asked, "Did talking about your concerns make you feel a little better?"

She nodded, taking a sip of her tea. "It did. Thanks."

"No problem." He felt good about helping her on their first official date.

Laying her fork across her nearly empty plate, she sat back on the bench. "You know, I'm just thinking. Even though we're just starting out on this relationship journey, I feel really comfortable with you."

He nodded. "I agree. I think it's because we started out being friends. You've always been chatty and sweet to me whenever I came into town." Unable to resist the urge to tease her, he winked. "Last night I found out why."

She laughed, shaking her head. "Oh, hush, Devon. You know we've always had good chemistry." She hesitated a moment before her next statement. "I feel like I can trust you."

He smiled. "You can."

"Do you feel that way about me?"

"Yes. Everything about you tells me you can be trusted." He pushed aside his own clean plate, settling his focus on her.

"Good. So now that we've settled that, what's on your mind? Maybe I can help you out the way you helped me." She leaned forward again, indicating her interest in whatever he said next.

He thought about his aspirations to direct. No one knew about them except Rick Rollingsworth, and Devon wasn't entirely sure Rick had taken him seriously. And even though he sensed Hadley wasn't the type to make fun of his dreams, he still wasn't quite ready to tell her about that, at least not in detail. "I've been thinking about making a change in my career."

She looked thoughtful for a moment. "Oh, you mean not doing your own stunts anymore? You did say it's hard on the body."

I did say that. Since he didn't want to go into the complexities of his plans, he went along with what she'd mentioned. "Yes. I'm not really into stunt work the way I once was. It's time for me to move on."

"I totally understand, and I agree. I mean, look at all those other big-name actors who don't do their own stunts but still make a killing doing action films." She folded her arms over her chest. "There's no reason you should sacrifice your physical well-being for your work."

"You're right. I've already spoken to Rick Rollingsworth about a possible project, one that could take my career in a whole new direction."

A bright smile spread across her face, her eyes sparkling with excitement. "I love that you get to just call up *Rick Rollingsworth* and talk to him like a regular person."

Her exuberance made him chuckle. "Rick *is* a regular person." He paused. "Well, that's not entirely true. He is strangely obsessed with doing internet searches on himself."

"I can't help but be amazed, though. Weird quirks aside, the man has an impressive body of work, and probably enough Oscars and Golden Globes to fill an entire trophy cabinet."

"That's why I called on him for help with this. Rick's

a good friend, and something of a mentor to me in the business." He drained the last of his root beer.

"If anyone can help you, I'm pretty sure he's got the connections you need." She turned her head to gaze out the window. "Promise me you'll go after what you want, Devon."

"I will." He watched her, taking in the regal beauty of her profile. She seemed to be admiring the scenery outside, and the enjoyment of that played over her features. She wore her emotions all over her face, and he knew from that moment that he'd do just about anything to make sure she was always happy.

Without taking her eyes off the window, she said, "I know you usually like to spend Christmas in quiet reflection and all, but…"

His brow cocked up. "But what?"

"My mother asked me to invite you to our house for Christmas dinner."

He hesitated.

She turned his way, her gaze dropping to the table. "Sorry. I just realized how that must have sounded." Her dark eyes lifted, and she looked right at him. "I would love it if you'd join us for Christmas dinner."

"Thank you for the invite." He had every intention of accepting, but he wanted to tease her a bit more.

"I have to warn you, the Monroes are big on Christmas. You can expect a huge tree, gaudy decorations, colored lights, gift exchanges…the whole nine yards." She smiled nervously. "I know you're not really into all that, but I'd appreciate it if you came."

"Will there be mistletoe?" He fixed her with a sly look, as if it weren't obvious why he'd posed the question.

She blushed. "Yes. Typically, no one makes use of it except Mom and Dad…"

"We'll just have to remedy that, won't we?" He winked.

The blush coloring her cheeks deepened in response, and she looked away.

"Don't get shy on me now, Hadley. We're in this thing, for real."

The waiter appeared then. As if he sensed he might be intruding, he quietly placed the bill on the table and slipped away.

Devon picked up the black leather folio, tucking a fifty-dollar bill inside. The amount covered both their meals, as well as a generous tip for their server. Then he stood, rounding the table, and offered his hand to help Hadley up from her seat. "Are you ready, baby?"

He'd thought her cheeks couldn't get any redder. But somehow they did as she accepted his hand. "Sure." Once she was on her feet, she slung her purse strap over her shoulder.

With a gentle tug, he pulled her into his embrace. "You seem a little nervous about the whole mistletoe thing. So, let's practice."

And before she could utter another word, he pressed his lips to hers. She was a little stiff at first, as if the kiss caught her off guard. Within seconds, she relaxed, draping her graceful arms around his shoulders.

He kissed her long and deep, ignoring the few other

people in the restaurant. And when he released her, breaking the seal of their lips, she sighed softly.

Pleased that he could get her to make that sound, he smiled and escorted her out of the restaurant.

Chapter 9

Hadley entered the family room at her parents' house quietly that evening. She'd come straight there after leaving the office, hoping to act on Devon's advice about going over her brothers' heads. In any other instance, she might have waited awhile and taken a shot at reasoning with Savion, but with so much at stake, she didn't want to risk wasting valuable time.

Monroe Manor, as the family referred to the house, was a two-story brick-and-stone structure occupying a five-acre lot on the northeastern side of the island. Her childhood home was roomy, over three thousand square feet, with six bedrooms and three and a half baths. The verdant green lawn behind the house went on for several hundred yards before it gave way to a broad strip of sand, then to the cerulean waters of the

Atlantic. It wasn't the largest home on the island, but it was in the top five.

She'd used her key to get inside and shut the door behind her. There was no telling what her parents would be up to this time of the day, but she knew they were home. She'd passed through the three-car garage and entered through the kitchen, and noticed both cars and both motorcycles were parked inside.

The family room was Hadley's favorite room in the house. The crisp white walls, along with the soft shades of blue, green and tan her mother had chosen for the furniture and decor, were a perfect reflection of the coastline outside. The picture window behind the beige sofa allowed plenty of light to shine in. Making herself comfortable on the couch among her mother's bevy of throw pillows, Hadley looked outside at the grassy expanse that led to the road. She loved looking out the window at the pristine scenery of the other homes and landscaped lawns nearby, so she thought she'd watch before she combed the house in search of her parents.

She didn't have to go looking, because her mother strolled into the family room, carrying a magazine and a cup of hot tea. At fifty-six, Viola Monroe still possessed the appearance of someone fifteen years her junior. She wore a pair of white palazzo pants and a white T-shirt and had her gray-streaked curls, as well as her reading glasses, piled on top of her head. She looked up from the magazine as she sensed her daughter's presence. "Hello, sweetheart. What are you doing here in the middle of the week?"

"Hi, Mom." Climbing up from the couch, Hadley

went over to give her mother a kiss on the cheek. "I was hoping to talk to you and Daddy."

Viola's brow furrowed as she set her teacup and magazine on the side table. "It must be important for you to come over out of the blue. Your father's in his study, flipping through that stamp book again."

Hadley sighed. Tugging her father's attention away from his prized stamp collection would be a challenge. "I'm going back there."

Settling into her favorite armchair, Viola cracked, "Good luck, dear."

Hadley walked through the foyer, past the staircase and into the rear hallway. There, she knocked on the solid oak door of her father's study. "Dad? Can I come in?"

A few seconds later he answered, "Sure, Hadley."

She pressed down on the gold handle and opened the door. Peering into the room, with its pine wainscoting, flooring and bookcases, she saw her dad in the center of it all.

Carver sat behind his big pine desk, leaning forward. She could see the light from his desk lamp reflecting off the top of his head, which was sparsely covered by his thinning, close-trimmed gray hair. He clutched a magnifying glass in his hand as he pored over the open pages of the stock book holding his stamps. Without looking up, he said, "Hi, honey. What are you doing here in the middle of the week?"

She chuckled, releasing some of her nervous energy. "Mom just asked me the same thing. I was hoping to talk to you and Mom about something."

"Okay." He flipped the page, closely studying the contents.

She watched him for a few minutes. When she realized he'd fallen back down the stamp rabbit hole, she spoke again. "Daddy, could you come in the family room with us, please? It will just take a few minutes, then you can get back to what you're doing."

"Sounds reasonable." He set his magnifying glass aside and closed the book, following her to the front of the house.

Once they were all comfortably seated in the family room, Hadley and Carver on the sofa and Viola ensconced in the overstuffed armchair across from them, Hadley squared her shoulders.

Taking a deep breath, she started talking. "I'm here because I think Savion is about to make a bad business decision, and I'd like to prevent that, if possible."

Carver's brow cocked. "What bad business decision?"

"Do you know about the Neville South offer on our land?"

He nodded. "Of course I do. But what does that have to do with anything?"

Hadley frowned. "Everything. Daddy, Neville South doesn't care about the people in Sapphire Shores or creating jobs or any of that. They're just out to make a buck, while pushing out the people who already own businesses here on the island."

He chuckled. "There's that youthful idealism of yours."

She wasn't amused, especially since his tone and

his expression were basically the equivalent of patting her on the head. "It's more than that, Daddy. Bringing all those chain stores to the island is going to ruin the unique charm we have here. And why can't they make room for local businesses, anyway? Della already told me she wants to expand, and I—"

Carver sighed, placing a hand on his daughter's shoulder. "Hadley, calm down. No one has signed anything yet. But I'm going to be honest with you. I agree with your brother. It's a good offer, and it could bring a lot of good things to the island, too."

Resisting the urge to roll her eyes, she turned away. "You sound just like him. I'm sure you're thinking of the money right now, aren't you?"

"I'd be lying if I said I wasn't." Carver shrugged, his arms moving beneath the fabric of his pajama top. "Did you know that they're offering two and half times what the land is worth? I don't see accepting that as a bad business decision."

"Daddy, you're not listening."

He patted her shoulder. "I've heard everything you said, honey. I just disagree."

She swiveled toward Viola. "Mom. Please jump in here and tell Dad…"

"Oh, no, you don't." Viola waved a hand from behind the pages of her magazine. "I'm not about to step into that minefield."

"Mom, I just think…"

"This is precisely why I retired. After almost forty years taking care of this family, plus helping to run the business, I'm tired."

Hadley stared at her mother, amazed. "Come on, Mom. You must have an opinion on this. I know you do."

"I sure do. And I'm keeping it right to myself." She raised the magazine a little higher, turning the page as she lapsed back into silence.

Letting her head drop back against the cushions of the sofa, Hadley sighed. She wasn't going to get anywhere with her parents on this issue. If she was going to stop the Neville South deal, she'd have to do it herself.

Devon strolled out onto the patio Thursday afternoon with his tablet in hand. He wanted to do a little online shopping with the local grocery store, Shoreside Foods. The locally owned market had embraced the rise of technology and leveraged it for the convenience of their customers. Because of that, they now had a delivery service, so customers could shop online and have their items delivered to their door. The service had been implemented since Devon's last visit, and now that he'd discovered it, he was quite pleased. He needed to replenish a few things he'd used up since his arrival—milk, eggs and the like. He also planned to order some fresh flowers and a few surprises for Hadley.

Seated on the resin love seat, he started perusing Shoreside Foods' website. The day was partly cloudy, with mild temperatures and a cool breeze blowing from the Atlantic. In his gray sweats and sneakers, he was comfortable and warm despite the crisp air. The quietness, broken only by the soothing sound of the waves, helped to still his mind. This was why he chose to spend his holiday vacation here, in his hometown. No other place on Earth had ever seemed so peaceful and so antithetical to the pace and tone of life in Los Angeles.

A notification on an incoming video call filled the screen, blocking his view of the store's website. Seeing the name on the display, Devon smiled as he swiped the screen. "What up, Rick?"

"Hey, youngster." Rick's grinning face appeared on the screen. He gestured behind him, indicating that he was on foot and walking outdoors. "Look at this. Finally got away from the set and out to the ranch."

"I bet the wife and daughter are happy about that. Where are they?"

"Up at the house. I'm just out for some fresh air." He huffed a few breaths, as if taking on hilly terrain. "Whew. Anyway, I've got some news on the Panther project."

Devon's face brightened. "Great. Let me hear it."

"Well, first off, the movie's got a title now. *Love in the Revolution.*"

"Nice." He was eager to hear what else Rick might have for him, so he encouraged him. "Go on."

"The other news is that I was able to pull some strings for you and snag you a role." The moving scenery stopped as Rick dropped down onto a bench somewhere on his property.

Devon's chest tightened as his excitement rose, but he kept it low-key. "Great, sounds great. So, when will I meet the screenwriter? Get a look at the script and all that?"

Rick's face crunched into a frown. "When we start

prepping for filming in February. Your agent will get all the details ironed out. Since when have you wanted to do all that before a role?"

Hell, now I'm confused. Frowning, Devon asked, "Okay, let's back up here. What role are you talking about?"

"They offered you the role of Stokely Carmichael, which I think is pretty damn good considering this isn't an action flick. Stokely played a big part in the party back then. It's an honor, really. I'm playing Bobby Seale."

He felt his frown deepen. "Rick, I thought I was clear when I said I was looking for a directing job, not an on-screen role."

Scoffing, Rick said, "You were clear. And I thought you were clearly joking."

He met that remark with silence, letting his expression speak for him.

Rick's face changed then, to a display of disbelief. "You mean you were serious?"

"Yes, I was."

Shaking his head, Rick replied, "So are you turning down the role? Because they already have a director."

Blowing out a breath, Devon nodded. "Yes, I'm turning down the role. I think it's a great concept, but I'm not looking for any more on-screen roles right now."

Rick shrugged. "All right, I'll let them know. But let me give you a little advice. You know, as a friend."

Devon braced for a real gem. "Sure. What is it?"

"Nobody here is going to take you seriously about this directing thing, Devon. You've been in the game almost ten years now, and you've never done anything but action and stunt work. That isn't gonna translate to you sitting in the director's chair."

He sighed. "That may be so, but it doesn't change what I want. I plan to find the right project and start my new career in directing."

Rick shook his head again, as if pitying Devon. "Do you, man, but don't expect any help from me. Later." And just like that, he disconnected the call.

Devon stood, tossing the tablet on the cushion. Frustration coursed through him like hot lava. Stripping off his sweatshirt, he stepped away from the love seat. If he were able to do so, he'd get in his car and head for the gym to take out his feelings on the heavy bag.

Yet his body had betrayed him, all because of the work he'd done—the work he was trying to leave behind. He looked back on his efforts over the years. After seventeen films, millions made at the box office, tons of fan mail and a beautiful home in one of the swankiest neighborhoods in Los Angeles, he wondered if it had all been worth it. Acting had taken him so many places and provided him with so many relationships and experiences. Still, how much did any of those things matter if he didn't have his health?

And as for those relationships he'd developed with his colleagues in the film industry, he wondered what they amounted to, as well. He'd considered Rick Rollingsworth, the Oscar- and Golden Globe–winning actor, to be one of his close friends. When he'd first come to Hollywood, he'd looked up to Rick. They'd worked together on half a dozen films, gone to countless red carpets and after-parties together. Devon had even spent time with Rick's wife and daughter. Yet none of that had meant a damn when it came time for Rick to help Devon achieve his innermost dream. Nothing in their past had stopped Rick from laughing in Devon's face when he'd shared his career hopes.

Pushing those thoughts away, he widened his stance. With his bare feet planted hip-width apart on the cool stone of the patio, he stretched, careful not to put too much stress on the muscles around his damaged disk. With his bare arms stretched up toward the sky, he took a series of deep breaths, focusing on the waves until he felt centered again.

With his peace restored, he grabbed his tablet and headed inside. Leaving the device on the coffee table, he retrieved clean linen from the closet in the hallway.

Later, under the hot spray of water flowing from the waterfall showerhead, he let his mind drift to more pleasant things—namely, Hadley. He hadn't called her today because he knew she was busy with end-of-the-year duties at work. That didn't preclude him from thinking of her, though. As he soaped his body, he recalled the way her lips felt pressed against his, the way she'd moaned when he'd darted his tongue over them.

His line of thinking soon began to affect his anatomy, so he tucked his fantasies away for later.

He would see her soon, and then perhaps his fantasies of her would become reality.

Chapter 10

Hadley was both pleased and anxious to go over to Devon's place Friday for dinner. He hadn't given any indication that he'd tired of her cooking yet, and the thought made her smile. Now as she stood on the front porch of his town house, she smoothed her hands over the fabric of her cream-colored A-line skirt. She'd paired the skirt with a V-neck crimson top and understated gold jewelry and left her shoulder-length curls to hang down around her face.

She'd been standing there for a few moments but hadn't knocked yet. First, she needed to get her mind right. While her attraction to Devon was a long-standing part of her life, their relationship was still new. Logic told her she should take things slow and easy with him, but her body wanted the fast track. He'd mentioned not wanting to take the shortcut route with their relationship, and she'd agreed. Now she wondered if taking it slow would mean quelling the powerful physical desire that hung between them.

Drawing a deep breath, she knocked on the door.

He opened it, greeting her with a bone-melting smile. He wore a pair of well-fitting black jeans and a vintage Free Huey T-shirt. "Hadley. Come on in." He stepped aside to allow her entry.

She stepped out of the cool air and into the warmth of the town house, and he shut the door behind her. Before she could reach the sofa, he walked up behind her. His presence in her personal space threatened to overwhelm her.

He leaned into the crook of her neck and inhaled. "You smell wonderful."

With the fragrance of his cologne invading her senses and his muscular arms snaking around her waist, she barely managed a reply. "Thanks. So do you."

He placed a soft kiss against her throat before releasing her. "Let's sit down for a minute and talk." He moved to the window seat and patted the cushion next to him.

She eased onto the seat, close enough that their thighs touched.

He draped his arm around her lower back. "What would you like to make tonight?"

She shrugged. "I thought I'd make a nice pasta Bolognese. How does that sound?"

"Sounds great. Do I have all the things you need?"

She nodded. "Yes. I checked the refrigerator when I was here last time, so we're good."

He gave her a squeeze. "A man could get used to this, you know."

"Get used to what?" Being this close to him made it difficult to think critically. She'd come over to cook for him, and at this point it would be a miracle if she could remember the recipe. All she wanted to do was fall into his arms and have him carry her to the bed. The direction of her thoughts, coupled with the touch of her handsome companion, made her blush. *I have got to get it together.*

"Having a beautiful woman who's intelligent and loves to cook…" He paused, his gaze settling on her lips. "And kisses oh-so well."

A small sigh escaped her throat.

Seconds later, he pressed his lips to hers.

His kiss was gentle, yet held a fiery passion. His tongue darted along her lower lip, teasing and coaxing her to open her mouth. She did and was treated to the best, most intense kiss of her life. Their tongues mated, and she sank into his embrace as if she was made to be in his arms; that was how she felt.

A few breathless moments later, she eased away from him, a difficult but necessary action. Once she got her breath, she said, "If you want dinner, we're going to have to postpone the kissing until *after* I cook."

He chuckled as he put some distance between them. "I think you're right. If we keep this up…" He didn't finish his statement, but his eyes implied the rest.

She scooted off the window seat and scurried into

the kitchen. There she assembled everything she'd need for her Bolognese sauce on the countertop. To keep the sauce hearty while cutting cholesterol, she was using ground turkey instead of beef or pork. She'd also set out a large can of crushed plum tomatoes, white wine, chicken stock, minced garlic and various seasonings. Once she got the sauce simmering and the pasta boiling, she went to the sink to rinse her hands. As she dried them, she hazarded a glance his way.

His eyes were waiting.

To break the tension, she asked, "Has anything new happened with your career change?"

It worked, because his expression changed immediately. "Yes, but nothing good. Turns out Rick thought I was joking about the favor I asked of him. Basically, he dismissed me."

She frowned, sympathetic to the betrayal she sensed he felt. "I'm sorry that happened."

He shrugged. "It's no big deal. I'm going to put out some feelers elsewhere, see what I can come up with. Thankfully he's not the only person I know in Hollywood."

She returned to the stove, using a wooden spoon to stir the sauce. "You've got a good attitude about it. I'm sure things are going to work out eventually."

"What about you?" He shifted a bit, raising his legs up to rest his feet on the window seat's cushion. "How are things going with the developer's deal?"

The relative quiet of the space allowed her to hear him clearly. "We haven't made any official moves at the office yet." She lowered the burner temperature to keep the sauce from scorching. "But I did try talking to my parents the other night."

"And?"

She shook her head. "No luck there. Dad took Savion's side, per usual. And my mom is just too through with this kind of thing. She's vowed to keep her opinion on the matter to herself."

"Looks like we both struck out, huh?" He chuckled.

She shrugged. "Well, at least we live to fight another day. I don't intend to give up on my goals. Do you?"

His expression conveying his determination, he shook his head. "No way."

"Good." The pasta water bubbled up then, the foam threatening to spill over the rim of the pot. Slipping her hand into the oven mitt, she turned off the burner. Waiting a few seconds for the water to still, she then hauled the pot to the colander waiting in the sink and drained the contents.

As she worked on putting the pasta dish together, she could feel his eyes on her. Holding her awareness of him at bay for a moment, she scooped some of the sauce into a small bowl. Taking a spoon from the silverware drawer, she made her way to the window seat. There, she dipped the spoon into the sauce. "Want a taste?"

His brow hitched, as if he read the double meaning in her statement. "Yes. I definitely do."

She brought the spoonful of chunky red sauce to his lips.

He opened his mouth and tasted the sauce.

As she drew the spoon away, she asked, "How is it?"

"Delicious." His gaze met hers. "Almost as appealing as the chef."

Heat rushed into her cheeks. "Devon."

He grazed his knuckle over her cheek. "I meant exactly what I said." Then he snaked his right arm around her waist, drawing her close until she stood between his parted legs.

That damn tingling returned, buzzing through her body as the pace of her heartbeat increased. "I... I thought you didn't want to take shortcuts?" It seemed like the right thing to say, to remind him of what he'd said before.

"This isn't a shortcut. It's a natural progression." He nuzzled her neck.

She sighed, losing her grip on the spoon. It fell to the floor, and she couldn't muster an iota of concern.

He placed humid kisses against her throat, her collarbone and the shell of her ear. "If you want me to stop, Hadley, just say so."

She shivered. "Don't stop."

He lifted his head, looked into her eyes. "You're sure this is what you want?"

She nodded. "Yes."

"Then you'd better make sure the stove is turned off."

Once she'd done that, she returned to the window seat and climbed up.

Devon swept Hadley onto his lap as she scooted up on the window seat with him. Between them, his hardness pressed against her hip, making his longing for her clear. She settled in, a brief flicker of surprise passing over her face. Yet she gave no indication of being put off by his involuntary physical reaction to her.

Cradling her in his arms, he pushed a wayward curl out of the way with his fingertips. She trembled, and he wondered if she felt nervous now that the desire that had been bubbling between them had finally boiled over.

"Are you nervous?" He watched her face to gauge her reaction to the question.

She shook her head. "No. I feel safe with you."

Hearing that, he smiled. "Good. Because I would never hurt you." He slid his hands up to her shoulders, beginning to knead the tight muscles gently. He could feel the tension melting away beneath his touch as her back slumped against his chest.

She sighed. "That feels so good."

"Trust me. It gets better." He placed a soft kiss against the graceful line of her collarbone.

She hummed low in her throat.

He lifted his eyes to hers.

She swiveled to the side, her hands coming up to cup his jaw.

Moments later, his lips crushed against hers. Their bodies became a tangled mass as they embraced each other, his arms around her waist and her arms thrown around his neck. She opened to him right away, and his tongue explored the sweet, warm cavern of her mouth. She continued making the low humming sound, an indication of her enjoyment, against his lips.

When the kiss finally ended, their gazes met in the dim light. Only the light over the stove remained on, as full darkness had fallen outside. Yet even in the soft glow coming from the other room, he felt sure he read the wanting in her sparkling eyes.

What he saw didn't matter, not until she said yes. So, putting aside his own needs, he sought to draw out her true feelings.

He stroked her jaw, feeling the satin texture of her skin beneath his fingertips. "I didn't plan for this to happen so soon, Hadley."

She dropped her gaze. "Neither did I."

With crooked fingers, he tilted her chin so he could look into her beautiful eyes again. "I would never pressure you. But if you'll let me, I want to make love to you tonight."

She ran her index finger down the center of his chest. "Yes, Devon. Yes."

Needing no further encouragement, he stood. Once he was on his feet, he reached for her hand and tugged her up. Leading her by the hand, he walked through the living room, down the short hallway and into his bedroom.

Standing by the foot of the bed, he drew her into his arms. He didn't know how much experience she had with this, and in a way, it didn't matter. It was their first time together, and he fully intended to take things slow and give her all the pleasure she could stand.

Raking his hands through her loose curls, he kissed her lips again. Then he moved to her neck and the upper part of her chest, revealed by the V of her red top. She smelled of citrus and flowers, and he found the fragrance as soft and intoxicating as the woman wearing it.

He stepped back for a moment to peel off his T-shirt

and toss it aside. As he drew her back into his arms, she stroked her hands over his bare chest, fueling the fire already burning inside.

He kissed her again then, and the next few moments blurred into one another as he kissed and caressed her out of her top and the camisole she'd worn underneath.

With his arms still around her, he eased them both back toward the bed. Sitting down, he positioned her between his parted legs. He moved his hands to the side zipper on the waist of her long skirt. "Can I?"

With a wicked smile, she nodded.

He eased the zipper down, and she stepped out of the skirt. In nothing but a black lace bra and panties, she looked like an absolute goddess. The sight fired his blood even more.

He leaned forward, kissed the tops of her breasts where they rose above the bra. Her sighs were like music to his ears as he began to slip her out of the undergarments. As he undressed her, he kissed each new inch of bared skin. Her soft moans rose in the silence, and by the time she kicked her panties aside, her legs were shaking.

"Lie down," he instructed her quietly.

She did as he asked, and he stood to strip away his jeans and boxers.

Her gaze swept over his body, lingering on the hard evidence of his need. When she looked there, her lips tilted into a sensual smile. "Aren't you going to join me?"

"Soon." While he appreciated the invitation, his first mission was her ecstasy. With that in mind, he dropped to his knees at the end of the bed. His hands guided her hips to the edge of the mattress, and he nudged her thighs apart with his chin. She gasped as he placed a kiss on the inside of each thigh.

He lingered over her most intimate place then, bestowing her with the joy she deserved. Soft kisses gave way to lingering licks and impassioned sucks. With each gesture, her body arched, and her cries filled the bedroom. And as he gave her one slow, thorough lick, she shouted his name.

While she lay trembling on the bed, he stood. He gently readjusted her, moving her up toward the center of the bed. When she was properly positioned, he eased away to retrieve a condom. Sheathing himself with protection, he returned and moved on top of her, aligning his body with hers.

Before he could do anything else, she snaked her arms around his waist and pulled. Her action effectively brought their bodies together, and she purred as his hardness slipped inside her.

He had little time to settle into her insane tightness before instinct took over. He rocked his hips, stroking her with abandon. She met each stroke with one of her own, her hips rising off the bed.

They moved together as if their bodies had been made for oneness. He shifted, sliding his open palms down her sides and then beneath her. Filling his hands with her ample backside, he lifted her, angling her more to his liking. She squeaked out his name between fast, panting breaths. Then she lifted her legs and locked them around his waist. The new position allowed him to achieve deeper penetration, and he groaned with delight.

He watched her eyes close, then pop open again as the building sensations got the better of her. He struggled to keep a hold on his own pleasure, but as he watched her head drop back, he knew what was coming. She screamed, her body overtaken by waves of trembling as an orgasm carried her off.

And as he watched her climb to the highest heights, he followed her, growling as his own release propelled him heavenward.

Chapter 11

Hadley opened her eyes to darkness and to the distinct feeling of not being in her own bed. As she blinked, letting her bleary eyes adjust to the low light, her mind began to awaken. She became aware of the strong arm tossed over her waist and the hard, naked body pressed against her back.

It didn't take long for realization to hit. The erotic memories of Devon's loving flooded her mind, bringing a smile to her face and a tingling warmth to the place between her thighs.

She shifted slowly, trying not to wake him. He groaned in his sleep, tightening his arm around her waist. The action caused her body to press closer to his, something she hadn't thought possible a few moments ago.

She felt his manhood awakening and stretching against her hip, and wondered why she'd wanted to get up in the first place.

She felt the movement as he tilted his head, then she felt his warm, soft lips lacing kisses along the side of her neck.

"Were you going somewhere?" His deep voice, thick with sleep and unmasked desire, reverberated in the silence.

"No." Why would she, when getting up now would mean denying herself another taste of his delectable lovemaking? She wanted this, wanted to let her body's cravings guide her actions instead of following the rule of logic.

So, as his kisses lingered, traveling lower, she gave herself over to the bliss. When he rolled her over a few moments later, she fed on his kiss greedily, wanting everything he had to give.

Their tangled limbs were wrapped in the bedsheets, but she adjusted accordingly until she was atop him. Straddling his strong hips, she made sure there was nothing between them.

Desire pushed her on, urging her to sink and take him in, but his hand on her belly stayed her. "The condom." His whispered reminder made her stop and move aside so he could retrieve the protection. When he returned to the bed with it, she took it from his hand. Encouraging him to lie on his back again, she knelt next to him and rolled the condom on.

The moment he was covered, she climbed into the saddle again. And this time, she didn't waste a moment lowering herself onto him. As she settled in, her inner thighs flush with his pelvis, she remained still for a moment. She savored the feel of him stretching her, filling her so gloriously. Then she began to move her hips, enslaved by the enticing sensations.

She leaned forward, bringing her upper body over his. He growled, his hands reaching up to cup her breasts. When he began to thumb her nipples, she answered with a purr of her own.

He continued to caress her fevered skin as she quickened her pace. She moved as fast as her desire demanded, until the rising ecstasy became too much. The glow of completion started where their bodies connected, radiating out through her belly and into all her limbs until it touched the very tips of her fingers and toes. And when she exploded, shouting her orgasmic joy into the steady strength of his muscled shoulder, he followed her a short time later.

Breathless and trembling, she lay against his chest in the aftermath. A sheen of sweat was the only thing between them, and that was just the way she liked it.

He slipped his arms around her, nuzzling her neck. "You're amazing."

She smiled, even though she knew he couldn't see her face. "You're not so bad yourself."

A snort of laughter met that remark. "Oh, so I guess you're gonna act like you weren't just screaming my name."

She blushed. "No, I'm not. Ain't no denying that." She'd never had a lover like him, someone who seemed almost obsessed with her pleasure. No man had ever

made it so clear to her that he valued her sexual fulfill-
ment over his own. The feeling she got from that was
unlike anything she'd ever felt before.

Maybe things would change between them one day.
Maybe he'd become as selfish as the other guys she'd
been involved with. Whatever the case, she'd never forget the care he'd shown for her tonight, or the way he'd
pushed her to the absolute limits of passion.

Emotions were running high—she could feel it.
Lying against him like this felt so good and so right,
it almost frightened her. What did it mean to be so
wrapped up in a man, especially one who had an entire
life waiting for him three thousand miles away? One
night with him had already changed her world, altering
her in a way she didn't think could be undone. What if
he decided she wasn't enough, that she wasn't a suitable replacement for the glitz and glamour of life in
Los Angeles? What if he chose his thousands of ador-
ing fans over her?

She wanted to ask him these things, but she couldn't
work up the nerve. Besides, parts of her were afraid of
what his answer might be.

So she set the questions aside for now, choosing instead to focus on the happiness she felt in the moment.
She'd finally made love to Devon after years of barely
contained attraction, and that warranted celebration.
Best of all, his loving had been better than any fantasy
she'd ever conjured up, and well worth the wait.

She wanted to say something, to tell him how wonderful a lover he'd been. But before she could get the words out, she heard his snores ruffling the silence.

With a sigh, she closed her eyes and let sleep claim her, as well.

Devon could have lain in bed forever with Hadley asleep in his arms. But morning eventually came, as it always did. And when the sun rose into the steel-blue sky, his eyes opened to the new day—and the new reality of the rapid progression of their relationship.

They'd shifted positions during the wee hours, and she now lay next to him, with her side resting atop his outstretched arm. Her wild curls lay spread across his pillow, highlighted by the golden rays of sunlight streaming through between the slats of the bedroom's vertical blinds.

He could feel the smile tilting his lips. There she lay, asleep and unadorned, and she was likely the most beautiful thing he'd ever laid eyes on. Fueled by his rising admiration, he leaned over and placed a gentle kiss against the warmth of her cheek.

She smiled first, then slowly opened her eyes. "Good morning."

"Morning." He pushed a few curls away from her face. "Sleep well?"

"The sleep I got was good, yes." She looked at him pointedly.

"I'm not sorry for keeping you up."

"And you shouldn't be. I'm not sorry about it." She lifted her face, puckering her lips.

Seeing no reason to deny her request, he kissed her,

slow and sweet. When he broke the seal of their lips, he said, "I'm guessing it's pasta Bolognese for breakfast?"

She laughed, nodded. "Yes. I'm not about to cook again, or let my made-from-scratch Italian feast go to waste."

He crawled out of bed then, extending his hand to her once he was on his feet. "Fair enough. But first, a shower." He didn't bother to hide the wicked glint in his eyes. She went along despite it…or maybe because of it.

He told himself they would simply shower and get out, because he didn't want to hold her captive all day. But as he stood beneath the stream of hot water, her lush, soapy nakedness so close to him, the idea of simply showering went out the window like a bird escaping its cage.

He pulled her body close to his, and she leaned forward, bracing herself with her palms against the shower wall. The sight of her positioned that way in the steamy stall threatened to make him spill then and there. That reminded him of the lack of protection and helped him quell his desire long enough for them to finish showering, get dressed and return to the kitchen.

At the dining room table, they enjoyed the meal that was supposed to have been their dinner the night before. The pasta was tender and the sauce flavorful with just a hint of spice. The similarities between the meal and its beautiful chef could not be denied.

As morning waned into afternoon, he stood by the door, giving Hadley a lingering kiss. She smiled up at him when they separated. "I have to go. I have something important I want to take care of today. But I'll call you, okay?"

He nodded, despite his selfish reluctance to let her go. No matter how much he wanted to hide her away and keep her all to himself, she had a life outside him, and he respected her enough to let her go about it. "Have a good day, baby."

With a blush reddening her cheeks, she wiggled her crimson-tipped fingers at him and left. He watched her climb into her car and drive away. Then he slipped back inside the town house and shut the door against the cool air.

Alone again, he settled down on the window seat with his phone and tablet. Turning sideways on the cushion, he stretched his legs out in front of him. The first doctor he'd seen after his injury had instructed him to put his feet up whenever he could, to take some of the stress off his lower back. He knew he could rest his feet on the coffee table, especially considering the rates he paid to rent this place. But when he was growing up, his mother had always forbidden him from putting his feet on her wooden furniture. Even though he was well into adulthood now, old habits died hard. The window seat was the perfect width to allow him to put his feet up while resting his back against its inner wall.

He opened the blinds, allowing the bright sunlight to provide light and warmth to his comfortable sitting spot. Picking up his phone, he put in a few calls to some of his friends and acquaintances on the left coast.

First, he called Corey Drake, his agent. Corey, who, at forty-three, had been in the game for more than a decade, was barely able to suppress his laughter as Devon spoke of his desire to try his hand at directing.

"Corey, remember, this is a partnership. So I'm going to need you to contain your amusement and put out some feelers for me, okay?"

"I get it, Dev." Corey sounded as if he were someplace crowded and shouted a bit to be heard over the noise around him. "I'll look into it."

"Good. Because the last thing I need is an agent who doesn't take me seriously." He hung up the phone then, before he was tempted to use a few choice words to tell Corey about himself.

The next call was to Glenn O'Hara, a set designer he'd met while filming the original *Destruction Derby* movie. Glenn was a little more respectful of Devon's request, though he seemed somewhat unsure of how he could help.

"What do you need me to do, Mr. Granger?"

Devon chuckled. "First, call me Devon. I'm asking you to keep your ear to the ground. I'm serious about moving out of acting and into directing, and you've got relationships with plenty of producers and screenwriters."

"That's true." Glenn seemed to be turning the request over in his mind. "I'll see what I can do, Mister... I mean Devon. Sorry about that. Most actors at your level don't go for being called by their first names."

"You and a whole lot of other folks are about to find out just how different I am from *other* actors. Thanks for your help, Glenn."

"No problem." And he ended the call.

Devon set the phone aside for a moment. He didn't know what or how much Glenn would be able to do for him. But the man had been receptive, so Devon placed the call firmly in the win column.

He didn't expect anyone to give him special treatment or to go out of their way to lay rose petals at his feet. All he asked was that people not lay traps and obstacles along the new path he was trying to take. His college coursework had yielded him a dual degree in drama and film; he'd done a short film on systemic racism for his senior project. He knew he had the skill to sit in the director's chair, and he intended to put it to use. That was why he was still angry with Rick Rollingsworth. Rick's callous dismissal of Devon's aspirations had been a hard blow. But at least Rick had shown his true colors, so Devon would know not to expect much from him in the future. He did, however, vow to rub his directorial success in Rick's face the very moment he made it.

After a quick break to grab a glass of iced tea and a bowl of popcorn, Devon returned to the window seat and to his task. He used the tablet to fire off a few emails to people he was acquainted with but unable to reach by phone. He kept his messages short and succinct, mindful of the abject busyness that plagued most folks in the industry, and of his own annoyance at getting long-winded emails. Once he'd finished that, he set the tablet down on the window seat and relaxed against the wall behind him.

As the sweet tea rushed in a cool torrent down his throat, he thought back on the previous night. He imagined that from now on, whenever he didn't have something pressing on his mind, his thoughts would always return to Hadley. In the few days since she'd been his girlfriend, she'd already left an unmistakable imprint on his world. And now that they'd made love, the connection between them had only deepened.

He looked out the window at the overcast day. Even though he knew he needed his rest, he craved some fresh air. So, donning his sneakers, he tucked his phone into the hip pocket of his track pants, slipped on a jacket and left the house to take a short walk.

As he locked the door, a thought made him smile.

If I'm going to have a woman like Hadley in my life, I'd better keep my blood pumping.

Chapter 12

After she swung by her house for a change of clothes, Hadley went out with a single mission in mind: proving to her brothers that the offer from Neville South wasn't good for Sapphire Shores. In her mind, the best way to do that was to ask the citizens. After all, the island was their home, and they deserved to have a say in the matter.

Anticipating that she'd spend most of the afternoon on her feet, she'd dressed casually in a pair of white jeans, a dark blue sweater and blue-and-white sneakers. Tucking her hair up into a haphazard bun, she grabbed her supplies. Filling a canvas beach bag with two clipboards holding printed copies of her petition, and about thirty ballpoint pens, she left the house and headed for downtown.

Before she left work Friday, she'd spent time at her desk, working out her plan. She'd made a list of business owners in town she wanted to approach, as well as places frequented by everyday citizens of the island. Then, she'd written up a simple petition with spaces to collect signatures. Her main goal wasn't necessarily to convince people to sign the petition, though that would further her cause. She really just wanted to hear from the people of Sapphire Shores. Unlike her brothers, she cared about their opinion. And if the overwhelming majority of them wanted to let the developer go ahead with construction, Hadley would be willing to lay down her weapons. She wasn't one to fight a needless battle.

When she parked in the main lot near the intersection of Fable Drive and Story Road, she got out with the bag slung over her shoulder. Her first stop was an easy and familiar one. Wearing a smile, she pushed open the doors to Crowned by Curls and went inside.

The salon was just as crowded as it was on most Saturday afternoons. The interior bustled with activity and conversation, from the filled chairs in the waiting area to the reception desk and the styling floor behind the beaded curtains. Seeing Sandra standing at the desk talking to Lisa, Hadley made her way over.

"Hey, Sandra. Hey, Lisa." She touched Sandra's arm. "Can I talk to you for a minute?"

"Sure, girl." Sandra gestured for Hadley to follow her, then passed through the beaded curtain and across the styling floor, leading Hadley into her office in the back of the building. She sat at her desk and gestured for Hadley to sit across from her.

"This won't take long, because I know y'all are busy today."

Sandra shrugged. "It's cool. I don't have another client for an hour or so. What's up?"

Settling into her seat, Hadley spent a few minutes explaining the Neville South offer. When she finished, she asked, "What's your opinion on this?"

Sandra's brow furrowed. "So, you're telling me this developer is dead set against having local businesses in the new shopping area they want to open?"

She nodded. "Yes. They plan to fill most of the storefronts with chains and franchises, and the few that are left may be open, but only to new small businesses. Existing small businesses won't be eligible to lease space there, at least not at the rates they'll be charging." Even as Hadley explained the proposal, she shook her head. For the life of her, she couldn't understand the developer's seemingly malicious intent to squash the island's economy.

Sandra rolled her eyes. "Do they think that if they keep us out of their saditty development, we'll be forced out of business? Because Crowned by Curls is making good money, and we aren't going anywhere."

"I know. And I can't help being worried about the other businesses that are established here but aren't as quite as successful as you are." She didn't mention them aloud, but she thought of Della's, the Shoreside Foods and all the small boutiques selling handmade jewelry, stationery and things that represented hours of creative labor.

Sandra snorted. "You're right. Maybe they think they

can force us out and take control of the island's whole economy."

Hadley's eyes widened. "That's it, Sandra. All this time, Savion has been ignoring me when I said the developer was motivated by greed. But I've had this horrible feeling about Neville South, and you just articulated why." She leaned back, tenting her fingers. "I can't imagine he'll keep ignoring my warnings when I point this out to him."

"I hope you're right." Sandra sighed, her expression still communicating her anger at what she'd heard. "Listen, is there anything I can do to help you stop this from happening?"

With a smile, Hadley took a clipboard and pen out of her bag. "There sure is. Sign this petition."

Sandra scribbled her signature in the first open space. "And I think once we talk to our clients, they'll all want to sign it, too. At least the locals. I'm not sure how concerned the tourists will be." She passed the clipboard and pen back.

Hadley accepted the items and stood. "That's fine. I'm really looking to show my brothers the will of the island's full-time citizens, anyway. So it's all right if the tourists don't want to sign."

"Cool. Come on up front and I'll let you use the PA system."

Sandra went around the styling floor, asking all the stylists to turn off the all the dryers, both handheld and hooded, so everyone could hear Hadley's announcement. Using the handset of the desk phone, Hadley gave an honest account of the developer's offer to the patrons in the salon. She kept it brief but detailed and ended by asking that anyone interested in signing the petition against the new development report to the desk.

By the time she set both clipboards and her stash of pens on the counter, a line had already started to form. Apparently, the women of Sapphire Shores didn't appreciate the blatant profiteering Neville South sought to engage in at their expense. Hadley watched woman after woman—most of them draped in styling capes and sporting curlers, conditioning caps or coloring foils—sign the petition. It gratified her to know that so many of her fellow citizens were of a similar mind as her.

When she left with her clipboards, she'd collected twenty-six signatures from the patrons and staff of the salon. Outside, she started down the sidewalk. A few doors down from the salon, she stopped by the bakery and spoke with the proprietor there. It wasn't as crowded as the salon, but she collected seven more signatures, which accounted for all but one of the people inside the establishment.

She traveled on foot as far as she could, visiting four more businesses to collect signatures. Then she climbed back into her car, having collected fifty-seven signatures total during her time downtown. Starting the engine, she set off for Della's.

The deli was much quieter than during the weekday lunch rush, but was still mostly full. Hadley spent time talking to Ralph, Della's husband, who worked on Saturdays so his wife could have some time at home. Their conversation led to Ralph's signature on the petition, and Hadley left with a sandwich and thirteen additional signatures on her petition sheets.

As the afternoon faded into evening, Hadley visited several more businesses, and then drove home. Inside the house, she laid her petition sheets out on the table and counted the signatures she'd collected. Altogether, she'd managed to get 217 people to sign. Since Sapphire Shores had a year-round population of fewer than seventy-five hundred people, she considered that an impressive number, especially since she'd collected them all in a single day. Tucking the signed pages into a folder, she left it on the table.

She thought of all the people she'd spoken to today, and those she hadn't. Whether she talked to them, and regardless of if they had agreed with her or not, many of them would be adversely affected if the developer's proposal was accepted.

She looked at the bright red folder holding the petition and smiled.

When the time came to defend her hometown and theirs, she'd be ready.

Devon strolled along the beach Saturday evening, enjoying the feel of his bare feet sinking into the cool sand. What he enjoyed more was having Hadley walking next to him, her small hand in his. The darkened sky above sparkled with stars and the faint light of a crescent moon. The tableau was beautiful but came in close second to his companion.

She'd changed after she left that morning and now wore a pair of jeans and a sweater. When he'd invited her to walk on the beach, he hadn't been sure she'd go for it. But she'd accepted right away, though she'd refused to take off her shoes, preferring to keep her feet out of the sand due to the coolness hanging in the air.

"So, what did you do today? If you don't mind my asking."

"Remember how I didn't have any luck with my parents about this Neville South thing?"

"Yes, I remember."

"Well, today I went into town and collected signatures on a petition against the developer's proposal."

He nodded, impressed with both her efforts and her determination to take on one of the largest developers in the Southeast. "Wow, Hadley. That's a brilliant idea. How many signatures did you get?"

"Over two hundred." She smiled, looking proud of her accomplishment. "It's more than enough to keep Savion from ignoring my concerns this time."

"I agree." He knew the island wasn't big enough to support a very large year-round population, so the signatures she'd gotten represented a good cross section of them. "I'm really impressed that you came up with this and that you were able to execute it so quickly."

She asked, "What about you? Any progress on your career move?"

He could only shrug. "I'm not sure yet. I did put in some calls and send emails to a few contacts. I'm hoping at least one of them will come through for me."

"That's good. At least you're still trying." She squeezed his hand.

"Yep. And I fully intend to keep at it until I make

this move." He looked up at the sky, observing the rising darkness. "It's time."

"You know I'm behind you. Whatever it is you're after, I'm sure you can do it." She moved a little closer to him as they kept walking.

He released her hand so he could drape his arm around her shoulder. Having her close to him made him feel as if he could accomplish anything, even his so-called crazy dream of becoming a director.

She stopped suddenly, moving closer to the water and casting her gaze up to the sky. "Look at that. Isn't it gorgeous?"

"Yes, it is." His response was as much about her as the sky. He looked to the heavens, taking in the deep richness of the night sky, punctuated by gleaming silver stars. She stood on her tiptoes, raising her face toward his.

He leaned down and kissed her on the lips. His arms circled her shapely body, pulling her flush against him. Her lips were pliant and soft, and when he swept his tongue over the petal of her lower lip, she opened to him without hesitation.

He could go on kissing her for hours, but after several long, torrid moments, he released her.

She looked up at him, silently regarding him.

He watched her as well, lost in the shimmering beauty of her dark brown eyes.

Without thinking, he murmured the words that seemed to fit this moment, the words that his heart had kept locked away for so long.

"I love you, Hadley."

Chapter 13

Hadley blinked a few times as her mind worked through what Devon had said. *Did he just say what I think he said?* After a few moments of confusion, she finally put her mouth in gear. "What did you say?"

His beautiful golden eyes locked on her face. "I said, I love you, Hadley."

Her heart fluttered in her chest, and tears sprang to her eyes. "Oh, my."

He met her exclamation with a soft chuckle. "That wasn't the response I expected."

She could only nod to convey her understanding. This relationship was still so new. But after all the time she'd spent fantasizing that he would say those words to her, it seemed like she'd been waiting an eternity to hear them.

"You don't have to say it back." His deep voice cut through her thoughts.

She looked up at him, searching his face. Was he angry? Hurt? Embarrassed? She didn't see any of those things. His expression exuded nothing but affection for her.

"I... I..." she stammered, searching for a way to express what she felt.

He smiled. "It's cool. I know you have feelings for me, or else you wouldn't have approached me."

She inhaled, filling her lungs slowly.

He placed gentle hands on her shaking shoulders. "Remember what I said. No shortcuts. No pressure."

A wave of emotion came over her, the force of it surpassing the ocean crashing against the shore. She leaned into him, craving him.

He caught her in his embrace and wordlessly turned, walking them toward the back patio of the town house.

He stooped to pick up the moccasins he'd kicked off by the back door, then left the patio door open after he escorted her inside.

He stopped at the dining room table. When he sat down at the head of it, she assumed he would pull her onto his lap.

Instead, he brought her to stand next to him. Then he ran his palms over the flat of her stomach before circling her hips. "You seem tense. Let me relax you, baby."

Trembling, she watched his hands move around to the front of her waist, where his fingers lingered at the button of her jeans.

"Can I?" He looked up for her answer.

"Yes…" Her answer came on the heels of a sigh. Swirling heat began to gather between her thighs as her body anticipated the things he would do to her.

So he undid her jeans, first the button, then the zipper. As he tugged them down her legs, she helped him along by wriggling out of them and then kicking them aside. Next, he helped her out of her sweater, leaving her in only her camisole, bra and panties.

He patted the table in front of him. "Have a seat."

She did as he asked, rising to rest her hips on the tabletop. He eased her thighs apart, then shifted until he pulled his chair up between them.

A shiver ran through her as his fingertips grazed over her skin, tracing a pattern from her ankles to the insides of her upper thighs.

"So sweet…" His murmured words accompanied his motions as he stroked his knuckle over her core, with only the thin satin of her panties between his hand and her sensitive flesh.

The touch hit her like a thunderbolt, as if there were no barrier between them. She fell back then, resting on her elbows to support her upper body.

He smoothly pushed the fabric aside, easing his hand into her panties. His touch was gentle, purposeful and skilled as he swept two fingers over her damp warmth.

Another wave of trembles took over her body as the bliss began to build. What was he doing to her? He seemed to have mystical power over her body, something that gave him the ability to send her beyond the limits of self-control.

Her head dropped back as he continued his ministrations, and when he tugged her panties away, she offered no protest. Then, with her legs spread and her very center bared to him atop his dining room table, he leaned in and kissed the place he'd been so skillfully stroking.

A strangled cry left her lips when she felt his first lick, and more cries and moans followed as he continued. Reality fell away; time became meaningless. All she cared about was Devon, his hands gripping her hips and his wicked mouth driving her out of her mind.

He kept up his attention, never wavering from his mission until she screamed into the silence of the room. Orgasm tossed her toward the stars, and as she came down, shaking and sighing, she knew no other man would ever compare to him.

When she got her bearings enough to move, she sat upright again. Seeing the wicked smile on his face, she said breathlessly, "You are too much."

He shook his head. "Nope. I'm exactly what you need."

She smiled. *He's certainly not lacking in charm.* "What I need right now is help off this table before you get any more ideas."

"I was just about to help you." He stuck out his hands.

She grabbed hold of them, only to be tugged down onto his lap.

"Does this suit you better, baby?" He held her close, watching for her response.

She shook her head, knowing she had little to no resistance when it came to him. "I think I can work with it."

* * *

Late Sunday morning, Devon awakened in his bed alone. Hadley had gone home after their interlude in the dining room. She'd said exhaustion had taken hold, and they both knew if she stayed, no one would've gotten any sleep.

Climbing out of bed, he went about his usual morning routine. Refreshed from a shower, he sat down to a simple breakfast of cereal, toast and a banana.

As he walked across the room to the couch, intent on spending some time reading, he heard his phone ringing. Grabbing it from its spot on the coffee table, he answered it. "Hello?"

"Good morning, Mister... I mean, Devon."

Recognizing the voice on the other end, Devon smiled. "What's up, Glenn? I didn't expect to hear back from you so soon."

"I've spoken to several writers already, as well as a studio head I know." Glenn paused. "I already had a meeting scheduled at the studio, so I figured I'd go ahead and ask around."

"And what did you find out?"

Glenn's tone changed, becoming less upbeat. "It's not looking good. The studio head says you're crazy. Most of the writers laughed. I can't say I made much headway for you."

Devon sighed. When he'd realized Glenn was calling him back on a Sunday, he'd thought the news was good. "Tomorrow is Christmas Eve. This is a hell of a present."

"There is one positive, though. One of the writers—
the one who didn't laugh—had a suggestion for you."

Devon rolled his eyes. This ought to be good. "And
what was that?"

"Open a production company." Glenn paused, and
took a deep breath. "Think about it. You have the industry experience to get it done, and if it's your company, no one will be able to stop you from directing, or
doing anything else you want."

Flopping down on the couch, Devon touched his temple. "I don't know, Glenn. Going indie is a lot of work,
and I'm not sure I'd be able to handle everything that
entails."

"It's just a suggestion. I respect you, and I believe
you can do well as a director." Glenn sighed. "If there's
anything else I can do to help you, please reach out. But
I think you've probably hit a dead end out here."

He sighed, knowing Glenn was probably right. Now
that he'd reached out to so many people about this directing thing, the word was out. Odds were there were
a bunch of studio types laughing at him all over Los
Angeles. "All right. Thanks anyway, Glenn."

After he disconnected the call, Devon sat back
against the sofa cushions. As he turned Glenn's secondhand suggestion over in his mind, he wondered if
starting his own company was really his only solution.
Running a business wasn't something he'd ever aspired
to. All he really wanted to do was the creative, artistic work of bringing a writer's vision to life on screen.
Now he was moving into territory he wasn't sure he
wanted to explore.

Tossing the phone aside, he scratched his chin. He didn't want to think too hard about it now; after all, this was supposed to be his vacation. He turned his mind to Hadley and to the Monroe family Christmas dinner. He'd asked repeatedly if he could bring something and had been turned down each time. Hadley had warned him that the Monroes were big on Christmas, and that he could expect to find the atmosphere "overwhelmingly festive." He'd chuckled when she'd described it that way, but parts of him wondered if he could sit through it. He was honored to be invited, but he didn't have much interest in holiday movies, gift exchanges or dramatic readings of "A Visit from St. Nicholas."

In the end, he decided not to worry about it. All that really mattered was getting to spend the day with Hadley. And if that meant participating in her family's holiday jamboree, so be it.

If he was lucky, he'd be able to hold on to some of that holiday cheer to get him through the following day. December 26 would be the fifth anniversary of Natalie's death. Though time seemed to soften his pain, that day still usually felt dark and somber.

Setting aside his worries, he turned on the television. He flipped through the channels until he found some trashy reality show. Then he settled in to watch the train wreck, letting it take his mind off his troubles.

Chapter 14

Christmas day was here, and as Hadley buzzed around the house that day helping her mother set up for dinner, she kept thoughts of Devon in the back of her mind.

Viola, dressed in her traditional Christmas outfit of a red sweater and emerald green skirt, tied an apron over her clothes. "Hadley, set the table for me. I'm going to start pulling out the things that need to be warmed up."

"Yes, ma'am." Hadley knew that was the only acceptable response to her mother's shouted instructions. Viola had never been particularly stern with her children, but when it came to her holiday dinners, Viola Monroe meant business.

As Hadley rolled the silver cart with the holiday china and table service on it into the dining room, she wondered what Devon was doing. It was midafternoon, and he was due to arrive within an hour or so. Thinking of him made heat rise into her cheeks as she recalled the naughty way he'd calmed her nerves a few days ago. It certainly wasn't something she should be thinking of while setting her mother's table, but she couldn't help it. The man was a champion lover, and keeping her mind on the straight and narrow when it came to him was very difficult.

She laid out the snow-white tablecloth, then set the table with dishes, stemware and silver, following the pattern her mother had taught her as a child. Being the only girl in the Monroe family had meant spending hours with her mother learning how to do traditional women's work: setting tables, cleaning, cooking and taking care of her appearance. Her father had balanced it out by taking her fishing and golfing. Hadley supposed all those things made her a well-rounded individual. Given the choice, though, she'd probably never go golfing again. The game had bored her so much she'd often nodded off sitting in her father's golf cart.

Once she'd finished setting the table, she pushed the silver cart back into the pantry and turned to her mother for more instructions.

Before Viola could open her mouth, the doorbell rang.

Hadley couldn't hold back her smile as she jogged past her mother, through the kitchen, into the foyer and to the front door to open it.

On the porch she found a smiling Devon. He looked delectable in a pair of black slacks, a tan sweater and tan-and-black dress shoes. A silver chain hung around his neck, and he had a velvet wine-bottle bag tucked under his arm. With a blinding smile, he greeted her. "Merry Christmas. You look beautiful, baby." He leaned in and pecked her on the cheek.

She knew he was prone to kissing her way more intensely than that but figured he was being respectful of her parents' house. "Thank you. And merry Christmas." She'd dressed as her mother's dinners demanded—a little black dress that barely grazed her knees, black pumps and a string of pearls. Eyeing the wine, she said, "You brought something."

He passed her the bag. "Yes. I know you said not to, but I appreciate the invite."

"I'll give it to Mom. Come on in." She stepped aside so he could enter, then retraced her steps toward the kitchen. She could feel Devon following close behind.

At the kitchen door, Viola greeted them. She'd taken off her apron and now held her arms up for their guest. "Devon. It's so good to see you."

Sharing an embrace with her, Devon smiled. "Good to see you, too, Mrs. Monroe."

"Oh, none of that. Call me Vi." Seeing the bag Hadley held, she took it. "Did you bring this? You know you didn't have to bring anything."

He chuckled. "I know. Hadley told me. But I thought you'd enjoy it. Merry Christmas."

"Aren't you sweet? Merry Christmas to you, too." Viola undid the strings, lifting the bottle from its bag. Her eyes widened as she looked at the label. "My word. Ten-year-old cabernet! Thank you, dear."

"You're welcome." He draped his arm around Hadley's shoulders. "Thank you for raising such a classy, wonderful daughter."

Hadley looked to her mother for a reaction. She hadn't really spoken to Viola about what was happening between her and Devon. Viola's grin told all, communicating her approval even better than words could have. "Well, look at you two. Come on in the family room and see the boys."

Hadley groaned inwardly. Ever since she could remember, her mother had referred to the men of the household collectively that way. She braced herself for whatever crazy reactions her father and brothers might have to her new boyfriend.

Carver, seated on the couch, looked up from the open book on his lap as they entered, and he smiled. "Devon Granger. Merry Christmas. Long time no see. How are you, son?"

"Merry Christmas. I'm good, Mr. Monroe. How about you?"

"Can't complain." The older man nodded, then his eyes moved lower, settling on Devon's hand, which was wrapped around Hadley's. His expression changed then, becoming less open and more questioning.

Hadley held her breath. She knew better than to read too much into her father's use of the endearment *son*—Carver frequently used the term when speaking to younger men. Truthfully, she had no idea what he would say next.

Carver started to speak. "Well, I—"

Before he could get his sentence off the ground,

Campbell entered the room, arms laden with wrapped gifts. "Merry Christmas, y'all."

As everyone in the room responded in kind, he set the gifts under the seven-foot Fraser fir occupying a corner of the room. "Savion is on his way in with the rest."

Hadley took the opportunity to sit down next to her father. His body language seemed a bit stiff, but he said nothing.

Devon sat down in one of the two armchairs.

Savion entered then, toting several gift bags, which he also placed beneath the tree. "Ho, ho, ho, folks."

Viola took the empty armchair, and Savion leaned against the back. Campbell took a seat on the carpet near the tree.

A few moments passed in silence before Carver asked, "Devon, what's going on between you and my little girl?"

Hadley fought the urge to roll her eyes. She was damn near thirty years old, and had long since grown tired of her parents referring to her that way.

Devon, on the other hand, appeared completely relaxed. "As of last week, we're dating. And you should know that I plan to treat her like the queen she is."

Warmth rushed to her cheeks in response to Devon's words.

Carver looked less impressed but said nothing more.

Savion inclined his head. "You'd better. We Monroe men are very protective of Mom and Hadley. I'd hate to have to kick your ass."

"Duly noted," Devon answered with a smile. If he

was at all intimidated by the Monroe men, he didn't let on. He remained just as cool while they continued to pepper him with questions, both about his intentions with Hadley and the latest happenings in his career.

Hadley felt some of the tension leave her body, and the room. Devon's ability to remain calm impressed her and added to his list of positive qualities.

When Viola called them to dinner, they sat around the table, and after Carver blessed the meal, they all dined on a sumptuous feast. Glazed ham, garlic mashed potatoes, roasted root vegetables, homemade rolls and more all made their rounds of the table. Conversation flowed easily, even as Savion and Carver attempted to intimidate Devon. He let their barbs roll of his back, answering with a smile.

After the plates were cleared away, Hadley grabbed Devon by the arms and secreted him away to the rear of the house. Just outside the back door, she draped her arms around his neck. "Look up."

His gaze lifted to the strategically placed sprig of mistletoe. "You put that there, didn't you?"

She winked. "You know the deal, Devon."

"Yes indeed." And he pulled her closer in his arms and kissed her until her knees went weak.

Devon pulled his rental car into the small parking lot of Mt. Ephraim Baptist Church and cut the engine. The day after Christmas had dawned cloudy and overcast, and those conditions continued to linger. Stepping out of the car, he closed his lightweight trench against the chill hanging in the air and hurried to the main doors of the church.

The redbrick church he'd attended with his parents as a child hadn't changed much since last year. But he did notice new brass door handles as he stepped up onto the cement pad in front of the entrance. For the past four years, he'd come here on December 26. He didn't consider himself especially religious and knew he certainly wasn't as pious as his mother would like. Still, coming here each year, on this day, helped him deal with his reality as a widower in a healthy way.

He gripped one of the shiny new door handles but didn't pull. He knew why he was hesitating. This was his tradition, his routine on the day of Natalie's death. Deep down, he knew this year was different. Up until now, there had been no other woman in his life since his late wife. Now that things had gotten serious with Hadley, he sensed there had been a cosmic shift in his perspective.

Taking a deep breath, he tugged the door on the exhale. It opened, and he stepped into the warmth of the vestibule, letting the door swing shut behind him. As he crossed over the soft burgundy carpet toward the sanctuary, he heard footsteps from the west hall.

Camille, the church secretary, approached with a smile on her face and a stack of papers in hand. The moment she saw him, she made a beeline for him and folded him in a hug. "Devon! How are you, son?"

He looked down at her, matching her smile. She was only about five feet tall, and well into her sixties. She had been church secretary from his earliest memories. "I'm good, Ms. Camille. How about you?"

She shrugged. "You know, I can't complain. The Lord is keeping me, my grandchildren are thriving and I still have my Sam. You know Celia lost Frank in the spring."

He nodded. "I heard about it. I sent flowers." Celia was Camille's twin sister and a gifted musician who served as the church's organist.

Camille stepped back then. "Well, I know why you're here, so I won't keep you. Stop in and see Reverend Keene before you leave, okay? He's been asking after you."

"I will, Ms. Camille." He leaned down to give her a peck on the cheek.

Still grinning, she left, passing him and disappearing down the east hall.

Turning back to the sanctuary doors, he pushed them open and entered. The space was as devoid of people as he'd expected. It was Wednesday, and all the happenings at the church that day were scheduled for the evening. He looked around, taking in the familiarity of the place. The lacquered oak pews with their red velvet–upholstered cushions still held a few scattered hymnals and programs from the Christmas Eve service. The scant sunlight filtered through the stained glass windows, casting a rainbow of colors on the hardwood floors.

Walking over the red carpet that spanned the center aisle, he quietly went to the first pew on the right, the one nearest to the altar. Sitting down, he looked up at the raised pulpit, his eyes finding the wall behind the choir stand. The painting there depicted a blue sky filled with puffy white clouds. The center-most cloud, the focal point of the image, held up two golden gates. A golden cross topped the gates, and a brilliant white light emanated from them.

He smiled, despite the melancholy that had brought him here. The painting was an artist's vision of heaven, and he liked to think Natalie was there, resting comfortably. Her last days had been trying, and his grief at losing her had been tempered with a sense of relief that she no longer suffered.

Alone on the pew, he let his memories of her wash over him. There were parts of his heart that would always hold her dear, but he knew his mother was right. The time had come to get off the "merry-go-round" and settle down again. Since he'd lost Natalie, being in a serious relationship had been the farthest thing from his mind. He'd taken a few women out for drinks, dancing or coffee. That had only led to zealous paparazzi snapping and publishing pictures to make him seem like a playboy. The reality was that no woman had really enamored him or captured his attention beyond the surface level since his late wife.

No woman until Hadley.

Now, in the silence, he grappled with this new reality. Hadley had worked her way into his heart, and he knew he couldn't stop it from happening. What really stood out about the situation was that he didn't *want* to stop himself from falling in love. Not this time. Hadley had effectively changed the way he looked at his life.

She'd touched his soul, reminding him that beneath his grief and his efforts to keep women at a distance, there was something else: loneliness. Somehow, she'd dug down into his very core and revealed his vulnerability. Yet for some reason, he trusted her not to take advantage of him.

Letting a sigh escape, he closed his eyes and dropped his head into his hands. He'd never thought this day would come, and now the stress of it had begun to get to him.

A voice echoed in the silence. "It's time, son."

Opening his eyes, he looked up toward the sound.

Reverend Keene stood to the left of the pulpit. Clad in the casual jeans and sweatshirt he often wore on weekdays, he rested his hand on the organ. The older man's deep brown face, punctuated by white whiskers, held concern and empathy. "I don't mean to interrupt, but I know why you're here."

Devon nodded. "It's not an interruption. Actually, I could use some counsel."

The minister walked over, taking a seat next to him on the pew. "You've done right by Nat, Devon. We all loved her, too. I know you've closed yourself off out of respect to her."

He shrugged. "I guess I have." Natalie had moved to Sapphire Shores with her family during Devon's seventh grade year, and remained until graduating high school, so she'd been well-known around the church, too.

Reverend Keene narrowed his eyes, observing Devon's face. "But this year, something's different. You met someone?"

Devon nodded. "I'm surprised you haven't heard about it, since the island's so small and close-knit."

"There's been some chatter around the fellowship hall, but you know I don't condone gossip." He winked. "Whatever the case, if you're closing your heart off to someone because of the specter of Natalie's memory, it's time to stop."

He looked at the man, who'd played a role in his upbringing, and felt the rightness of his words. "My mother said the same thing to me before I left LA."

"Eva's right. Remember what Ecclesiastes teaches us. 'To everything there is a season, and a time to every purpose under heaven.'" Reverend Keene patted Devon's shoulder as he stood again. "If the Lord has sent someone to touch your heart, then you know what it means. Okay, son?"

"Yes, sir." He watched as the minister walked down the aisle and through the sanctuary doors.

As he faced the pulpit again, his eyes settling on the image of heaven, Devon clasped his hands and let the guilt leave his body like a rising vapor. He tossed aside any concern for time, allowing himself to work through it all. He would never forget Natalie. Fortunately, moving on with his life didn't require him to do so.

Letting that settle into his spirit gave him the sense of peace he'd been seeking for the past five years. And when the lightness came over him, heralding his freedom from the negative feelings, he quietly left the church.

Chapter 15

Hadley, dressed in an old pair of sweats and a T-shirt, curled up on her couch with her feet tucked beneath her. After busting her hump at work all last week, she'd finally started her winter vacation. With yesterday's holiday meal now out of the way, she was looking forward to spending her Wednesday night vegged out in front of the television. She had a glass of wine and big bowl of fresh popcorn next to her.

She grasped the remote, pointing it and flipping through the channels. Coming across a marathon of *Say Yes to the Dress*, she set the remote down and settled in. She loved this show. It amused her to watch women cry, scream and get all bent out of shape over a wedding dress. For the life of her, she couldn't fathom the level of emotion the women put into a piece of clothing, or how much money they were willing to drop on something they'd wear only once. When her day came, she planned to wear a simple white pantsuit and call it a day.

During the commercial break, she let her mind wander. She hadn't heard from Devon today, and she hadn't expected to. She could sense he'd been overwhelmed by her family during dinner. The barrage of questions from her dad and brothers, plus the all-out gusto with which the Monroes celebrated Christmas, had taken it out of him. While he'd been perfectly calm all afternoon, by the time he'd gone home for the night, he'd told her himself that he'd need a couple of days to himself to recuperate and recharge. She respected that. She'd never been one to cling to a man, and she didn't plan to start now.

Admittedly, she did miss him. She wondered what he was doing and how he was handling his meals all by himself. At any rate, she planned to leave him alone until he was ready.

The show was back on, and a bride was going on and on about how much she hated lace when Hadley heard a knock on the door of her apartment. Her brow furrowed, because she hadn't been expecting anyone to stop by. Clambering up from her comfortable position, she padded to the door and checked the peephole.

Savion stood on the concrete balcony, tapping his foot impatiently.

Opening the door, she asked, "What are you doing here? You couldn't call first?"

He leaned against the door frame, looking over her

head into the apartment. "Why? You're not doing anything except bingeing on TV and snacks."

"Whatever." Rolling her eyes, she stepped aside to let him in.

He flopped down on the couch, gesturing to her popcorn. "May I?"

"Yeah, go ahead." She joined him, tucking her body against the right armrest while he sat on the left-most cushion, munching on her snack.

"Is this that wedding dress–shopping show?" he asked around a mouthful of popcorn.

She folded her arms over her chest. "Savion."

He shrugged. "What?"

She gave him a playful punch on the arm. "I know you didn't come here to watch TV with me, so what do you want?"

"I want to know what's going on between you and Devon." He looked pointedly at her as he chewed, waiting for her answer.

"I don't see how that's any of your business." She was already annoyed by his showing up without calling, eating her snack and interrupting her show.

"You're my baby sister, and it's my business now and any other time I think you might be in danger—"

"Danger? From Devon?" That seemed a bit far-fetched. They hadn't been at this dating thing long, but he'd always treated her well. Devon was, as the classic Ralph Tresvant song proclaimed, a stone-cold gentleman.

He rolled his eyes and set the popcorn bowl aside. "I

don't mean physical danger—unless you come across one of his overzealous groupies."

She side-eyed him. "Really, Savion?"

"Don't you know what you're dealing with here?" Savion shook his head, his expression reading as if he knew something she didn't. "Devon is a big action star. He probably gets panties thrown at him everywhere he goes."

"That's really crude." She tried to push away the imagery of her brother's rather blunt statement. She had no desire to contemplate the number or the types of propositions Devon received from random women on the street. She would then question whether she could compete with those women, which in turn led down the rabbit hole of doubt.

"Still, you have to admit women are probably sweating him all the time." He sat back against the sofa cushions. "Plus, if you read the blogs, you'd know he has a bit of a, shall we say, reputation. Campbell knows about it, too."

"Oh, please." She was shocked her serious, staid brother would even admit to reading trashy online gossip. "If you and Cam spent more time working and less time on the internet, my life would be a whole hell of a lot easier."

Savion's face folded into a frown. "Baby sis, I'm sure you're not implying that Cam and I are lazy." He fixed her with a searching look.

She pursed her lips. "You're right, I'm not trying to imply that. I'm saying it straight-out. Y'all are lazy."

He cut his eyes at her, as if she would rescind her statement if he eyeballed her hard enough.

Undeterred, she stared at him. "Lazy. L-a-z-y. You're not lacking in skill, you just leave entirely too much of the work around the office to me."

He sighed. "Cam does, I'll admit that."

"How charitable." She was quickly growing tired of her brother's foolishness.

"I give you more because I'm so busy. Every time I turn around, there's some executive decision to be made, a call to take or something to sign off on. You're more than capable, though."

"Savion, don't patronize me or else—"

"I'm sorry, Hadley. I'm not trying to insult you." He gave her a crooked smile. "I never thought much about it until now, but you do a lot."

"You're damn straight. And despite everything I do, you and Cam still treat me like a little girl. You ignore my suggestions, talk over me and in general make my workday difficult." She watched his face, seeing the guilt playing over it, and felt a modicum of vindication.

"But I didn't—"

She wasn't hearing any of it. "And now you have the gall to come here, to my home, and tell me what to do in my personal life."

His eyes widened. "Hadley, I didn't realize—"

She pinched her fingers together in midair. "Clam up, Savion. I'm tired, and all I want to do is watch TV in peace. You're welcome to think about everything I've said…on your way out." She pointed at the door, beyond ready for her brother's departure.

He stood, strode to the door. Opening it, he started to go out, then stopped and turned back. "Hadley, I know Cam and I can drive you crazy—Dad, too, probably. But remember, it's just because we love you so much."

"I love you, too." She winked, then shooed him out. "Now go love me from a distance."

Chuckling, he stepped outside and shut the door behind him.

Shaking her head, Hadley grabbed her popcorn and went back to watching her show.

These Monroe men are such a handful.

When Devon got up, he quickly got himself together then headed to the kitchen for some cereal. With his bowl and mug of coffee, he sat down to enjoy his breakfast and the morning silence.

While he ate, he used his tablet to check emails. He perked up when he saw that all the contacts he'd emailed about helping him find a lead for a directing gig had replied. The feeling was short-lived, though, because none of the three respondents could help—or were willing to. Two of them went into the reasons why they didn't have anything for him, citing his reputation as an action star and nothing more. The third hadn't even bothered to write out a sentence, and instead had responded with a single phrase: LOL. Closing his email program, Devon slid the tablet away and returned his attention to his breakfast.

He thought back on the conversation he'd had with Glenn about branching out on his own. Glenn had been right—if Devon owned his own production company, no one could stop him from directing. So far, every contact he'd reached out to had either refused him help or made jokes about his dreams. At this point, he only hoped no one had mounted a campaign to actively block him from being part of the industry.

What would I need to open a production company? Where would I even start? He knew he'd need a building with space for offices, soundstages and more. He'd have to decide where this company would be headquartered. Then there would be staff to hire, projects to vet and more. Draining the last of his coffee, he decided to put a pin in it. This was a big undertaking, and it was just too damn early in the morning to be thinking this hard about anything.

As he set his empty bowl in the sink, a knock at the front door broke the silence. He went to answer it and was surprised to find Campbell standing on his doorstep. He opened the door, letting in a blast of cold air. "Hey, Cam. What's up?"

"What's up, Dev. Can I come in for a minute?" He stood with a stooped, closed posture, as if hiding from the wind. "It's cold as hell out here."

He stepped back. "Yeah, come on. I'm not gonna just stand here letting all that icy wind in the house." Once Campbell was inside, Devon shut the door and gestured to the couch. "Have a seat, man."

"Thanks." Cam shrugged off his black parka and sat down.

"What brings you over?" He couldn't help but wonder why Campbell was there so early on a weekday.

He knew MHI's office was closed until the second of January, but he hadn't expected Campbell to stop by.

"I just wanted to talk to you really quick. Shouldn't take too long."

Curiosity furrowed his brow. "Is it about the property?"

Campbell shook his head. "Nah."

"Okay." Realizing he should be hospitable, Devon added, "You want something to drink? Coffee, maybe?"

He shook his head again.

By now Devon was plenty interested in knowing what had brought his friend to the town house. "So, say what you gotta say, man."

Scratching his chin, Campbell looked at him. "It's about you and Hadley."

Ah, hell. Brow furrowed, Devon waited. He should have expected this. After he'd spent most of Christmas dinner with the other two Monroe men interrogating him, now it seemed Cam wanted a shot.

"I'm not trying to tell you what to do. You're grown." He paused, took a breath. "But things between Hadley and Pops are not great. And I know she's also not too pleased with Savion."

He folded his arms over his chest. "But you're on good terms with her, I assume?"

Campbell nodded. "I had sense enough not to say anything to her. Plus, I already told you, I don't have a problem with you two seeing each other."

"I see."

"Anyway, I'm sure you remember how they acted on

Christmas. And then Savion took it upon himself to go over to her house yesterday and lecture her."

A snorting laugh escaped Devon's lips. "Why in the hell would he do that?"

With a shrug, Cam surmised, "Because he's a glutton for punishment? I don't know. Everybody who knows my sister knows she's her own woman."

Devon chuckled as he imagined what had gone down at Hadley's place when Savion had shown up, trying to tell her what to do. "How hard did she hit him?"

This time Campbell laughed. "Lucky for him, she didn't. But she did kick him out."

While this whole thing was amusing, he still didn't see the connection. "Okay, I hear what you're saying. But what does that have to do with you being here?"

"With all that's going on, I have to ask you. How serious are you about my sister?"

"Very." Devon could see his entire future in Hadley's eyes. "More serious than I've ever been about anyone."

Campbell sighed. "I guess that means you're not going to back off, then."

He shook his head. "Nope. But why would you ask me to? You've told me more than once that you don't have a problem with us dating."

"Personally, I don't. Still, I hate to see all this drama going on between my family members." Campbell ran his hand through his beard. "You know me. I'm not one for drama."

Devon nodded. Even back in high school, Campbell had avoided conflict whenever he could and had been known for stepping in to break up arguments and scuffles.

"I'm not backing down. I love your sister, and I've already told her as much. I'm in this thing, all the way."

Campbell's expression was one of resignation. "Just thought I'd ask. If you love her, she'll be worth the fight, right?"

"She already is." He locked eyes with his friend so he could convey his seriousness. "She's everything I want, everything I need."

"Wow. Never heard anyone speak about Hadley that way before." He clapped his hands together and stood. "I'm not going to take sides if the crap hits the fan, you know."

"I know." He didn't expect Cam to do something that went against the core of who he was.

"I'm still cool with this relationship. Not that y'all need my permission." He stretched, then reached for his parka. "I suggest you gird your loins to do battle with Savion and Pops. But you'll have no trouble out of me."

Standing, Devon extended his closed fist toward Campbell. "Thanks, man."

Bumping fists with him, Campbell headed for the door. "No problem. I'll let myself out."

Devon waved as Campbell opened the door and walked out, shutting it behind him.

Chapter 16

Friday morning, Hadley sat in her usual seat at the conference room table, tapping a pen on the lacquered surface. She knew her face was scrunched into a frown, but she didn't care. It was a few days after Christmas, and she should still be home enjoying her vacation. Instead, because the reps from Neville South couldn't wait to make their pitch, she and her brothers were at the office.

Savion, seated at the head of the table on Hadley's right, was busy flipping through the full-color proposal the developer had sent over. He'd been engrossed in the booklet for the last fifteen minutes.

She cut her eyes extra hard in Savion's direction. He was the one who'd caved to the developer's offer to hold the meeting today, taking away a full day of her vacation.

Campbell sat across from her, scrolling through something on his phone. He hadn't been particularly happy about coming in today, either. Now he seemed to be making a show of his disinterest by refusing to look up from his phone.

Hadley, on the other hand, intended to redeem the time, as her grandmother used to say. If she had to sacrifice her hard-earned vacation time, she wasn't going to waste the opportunity to be heard. She looked at the folder she'd brought with her, lying on the table next to where she'd been tapping her pen. Her brothers had no idea of the contents of the folder, and she planned to keep it that way until the right moment.

Campbell's phone buzzed, loud in the quiet of the room. After a few taps on his screen, he said, "The people from Neville South are here."

Savion smiled and stood. "I'll go let them in." He disappeared from the room.

Arms folded over her chest, Hadley waited for the developer's salespeople to appear. She expected they'd come in grinning, all ready to win her over with their carefully crafted pitch.

Nope. I'm not having any of it. She'd already heard everything she needed to know she was against the proposal. Since Savion had set up the meeting, she supposed the polite thing to do would be to let them talk for a while before she made her play.

Savion entered the room again then, followed by two men in dark suits. One was fair-haired, with blue eyes. The other had skin the color of milk chocolate and brown eyes that seemed to be assessing everyone in the room—Hadley noticed the way his gaze lingered on her.

Hadley and Campbell each stood. Gesturing to the two newcomers, Savion introduced them. "This is Alvin Clark—" he motioned to the Black man "—and this is Gordon Young."

Handshakes were exchanged, and Hadley almost had to pry her hand from Alvin's grasp. She kept her expression even, but her eyes let him know, plainly, that she wasn't playing games.

Once everyone was seated at the table, with Gordon sitting next to Hadley and Alvin next to Campbell, the presentation began in earnest. Gordon laid out maps and concept drawings on the table, droning on about landscaping and parking.

Campbell seemed to be paying attention, offering a nod or a short comment here and there. Savion appeared enraptured by all the concept drawings, even though he'd already seen them. Hadley closed her eyes momentarily, thinking of all the effort that had gone into the materials, yet unable to muster much interest.

Then Alvin took over, presenting his charts and graphs of expected revenue from the new development. "As you can see, both Neville South and Monroe Holdings stand to turn a tidy profit. We think this development will be immensely beneficial for both our companies."

Savion's eyes lit up at the phrase *tidy profit*.

Hadley sighed. Her brother wasn't a greedy person, but he was fastidious in his efforts to increase revenue and decrease expenses for Monroe Holdings. This part of the presentation seemed to tap into his greatest desire: to make MHI as profitable as it had been under their father's leadership.

As if to put a finer point on the potential financial gain, Alvin continued, "We think this development will be immensely beneficial for both our companies. The location is perfect for a venture like this, and with Gordon and his team handling the aesthetics, people will be drawn to it in droves."

Their concerns seem to rest solely on profit, and therein lay the problem. Hadley felt the frown creeping over her face. The time had come for her to make a stand before her brother signed over the land. "Excuse me, Mr. Clark—"

He stopped her with his raised hand. "Please, call me Alvin."

"Fine, Alvin. I've heard a lot about how much money our two companies can make from this development. What I haven't heard is how it will help the island's citizens. Can you elaborate on that?" She sat back in her chair, awaiting his answer.

Savion shot her a dirty look.

Hadley didn't care.

Alvin cleared his throat. "Well, Ms. Monroe, that's a great question. Of course, the development will bring jobs to the island. People will be needed in the shops and restaurants, as well as to maintain the condominiums. We estimate two hundred positions will be created by the—"

"Yes, I heard that before. Two hundred jobs, most of them paying at or below minimum wage. What do you have to say about what seems like a concerted effort to keep local businesses from becoming tenants in the shopping center?"

Blinking rapidly, Alvin stammered. "I...well, we plan to allow new businesses to come and—"

"And what about existing businesses? We have plenty of skilled entrepreneurs already here, and I think shutting them out of the development is misguided and downright wrong." She rested her elbows on the table and tented her fingers. "What do you have to say about that?"

Alvin's eyes registered panic. He looked to Gordon, who only shrugged.

Savion raised his hand. "Okay, Hadley. I realize you're passionate about this, but let's not attack our guests."

She glanced at her brothers, then at the developer's mouthpieces. "I'm not attacking anyone. I'm simply asking pertinent questions. I don't know why these two gentlemen would come here unprepared to answer them."

Alvin remarked, "I wouldn't say we're unprepared."

She smiled the smirk of a woman about to make a point. "Fine. Let's just say you're uninformed." She opened the folder and took out the copies of her petition. "This is a petition signed by almost three hundred of the island's citizens. All of them are opposed to the construction of Neville South's development. A few have even lodged complaints with the town council." She riffled through her papers. "I have copies of the complaints as well, if you'd like to see them."

The four sets of male eyes around the table widened.

Hadley sat back, waiting.

Campbell chuckled. "That's our girl. Kicking ass and taking names."

Savion frowned. "Why didn't you tell me about this, Hadley? And when did you even have time to start a petition?"

"I tried to tell you. You just weren't interested in hearing anything that didn't line up with your vision." She turned back to Alvin and Gordon. "Would you like to see the town council complaints, gentlemen?"

Gordon shook his head. "That won't be necessary."

Alvin, already on his feet, gathered up his charts. "Considering what we've just learned, I think we'd better postpone any major moves on this project, Mr. Monroe."

Savion nodded. "I agree. We'll reconvene after the New Year."

Gordon took a moment to roll up his images, and after that, he and his partner left in a hurry.

After they were gone, Savion turned to her. "Hadley, you are something else. You're determined to stop this development, aren't you?"

She winked. "I thought I'd made that clear, Savion." Satisfied that her point was made, she gathered her copies back into the folder. "Now I'd like to continue my vacation, if you don't mind."

"Go ahead." Savion waved her out.

The still-amused Campbell remarked, "You're a real pistol, sis."

Smiling as she carried her purse and folder to the conference room door, she tossed back, "Damn straight." Then she strode out.

Devon had just parked in the MHI lot when he saw Hadley marching out of the double glass doors. Gathering the dozen blush-pink roses he'd brought with him from the passenger seat, he climbed out of the car, careful not to damage the blooms.

He took a moment to enjoy the view of the beautiful woman he called his own. She had the sexiest walk of any woman he'd ever seen. He could almost hear "Love's Theme," the classic instrumental by Barry White's Love Unlimited Orchestra, playing in his head as he watched her. She was dressed in a white blouse and a pair of fitted gray trousers that hugged her bottom nicely. Her black pumps clicked on the pavement in time with her steps. Her soft curls were tucked up into a high bun, giving him a full view of the graceful lines of her face—which was scrunched into a perturbed frown. He couldn't help but be concerned.

What's going on with her? He adjusted the flowers, the plastic overwrap crinkling as he tucked them into the crook of his arm. He quickened his steps, aiming to meet her on the sidewalk.

She looked his way then, and her expression softened considerably and surprise lit her eyes. Slowing her steps, she stopped and waited for him until he stepped up on the curb. Leaning up, she gave him a peck on the lips. "Devon, what are you doing here?"

He handed her the flowers, which were miraculously still standing up despite the unusually high humidity. "When you texted me that you had to come in on vacation, you seemed upset. So I thought I'd try to lift your mood."

"You're so sweet." She smiled, but only for a moment before the frown returned.

He asked, "What, you don't like pink?"

She shook her head. "It's not that. The roses are beautiful. It's just that you just reminded me that I forgot my phone."

"Inside the office?"

She nodded.

"That's an easy fix. Just go back in and grab it."

She pursed her lips. "I've had enough of Savion for the day. Let me borrow your phone. I'll call Cam and ask him to bring it out."

He shrugged, dragging his phone from his pocket and passing it to her. "Sure thing."

While he waited, she called her brother and asked him to bring out her phone. Then she passed the phone back to him. "Thanks."

He tucked the phone away again. "So, how did the meeting go?"

She smiled then, making his heart sing. "I think it went pretty great. Remember the petition against the development I spent last Saturday gathering signatures for?"

"You spent most of the day on it."

"Yep. I knew most of the places downtown would

have a good amount of business on a Saturday afternoon."

"Very astute. I see why you were so insistent on leaving."

She nodded. "It was my last chance at gathering that many signatures before we went on holiday vacation. I didn't expect to have to put the petition to use until after the New Year, but Neville South insisted on this early meeting."

"I see." He remembered how she'd left that morning, after they'd made love all night and well into the wee hours. The memories of her lush nudity rose again then, and he licked his lower lip. *She's a hell of a woman.*

Her lips kept moving, indicating she was saying something.

Most of what she'd said went underwater, as he struggled to focus. Visions of her beneath him, moaning as he stroked her, were making it difficult for him to keep his attention on the present. "I'm sorry, baby. What did you say?"

She laughed and gave him a playful punch on the shoulder. "Stop daydreaming and listen this time."

He placed his hand over his heart. "I promise I will."

"Anyway, I had said that I hadn't told anybody in the office...until today, when I slapped it down on the table during the presentation. You should have seen the looks on those guys' faces." She seemed pleased with herself. "Then they packed up their stuff and got out of here quick. It was pretty epic."

Chuckling, he gave her shoulder a squeeze. "I'm

proud of you. You saw a problem and tried to fix it. And when the first try didn't work, you didn't give up."

Her smile grew broader. "Thanks, Devon. You know, I owe this to you. You pushed me to keep at it, even when it looked pretty grim."

He looked at her, amazed at her determination. "I never would have thought of the petition, but I'm glad you did it. What a way to get your point across."

"So I have you to blame for this?" A male voice cut into their conversation.

Both Devon and Hadley swiveled toward the voice.

Savion stood on the sidewalk a couple of feet away, brow furrowed. He stuck out his hand toward his sister. "Here's your phone."

Rolling her eyes, she took the device and dropped it into her purse. "I thought Cam was bringing it."

"I was on my way out," Savion said before swinging his eyes back to Devon. "So you're the one who's been encouraging her in this crusade against progress?"

Devon turned toward him. "Not really. She was just following her convictions, and I'm behind her one hundred percent."

"You'd deny the islanders this shot at hundreds of new jobs, more housing and more tourism revenue? Just to get brownie points with my sister?" He folded his arms over his chest.

"This isn't about brownie points."

"Oh, yeah? Then why do you care either way?" Savion walked a few steps closer. "You haven't lived here full-time in over a decade. Why are you suddenly so concerned about what happens to the island?"

Devon rubbed his hands together. "That was a low blow, Savion."

Savion shrugged. "Truth hurts."

Hadley snapped, "Savion, enough of this."

Shaking his head, Devon touched her shoulder. "Don't worry, baby. I've got this." He turned back toward Savion. "Look, I grew up here, too. Where I live now has nothing to do with the fact that I care about Sapphire Shores and the people who do live here year-round."

"Yeah, right." Savion tapped his foot, as if growing impatient. "I've been over the numbers and statistics more than once, and I'm telling you, this development is just what the island needs."

Rolling his eyes, Devon remarked, "There are two sides to every argument. Just because you feel a certain way, that doesn't mean it's right."

"I could say the same thing to you." Savion gave him a hard stare.

They stood there in silence for a few long moments, observing each other. Hadley looked somewhat uncomfortable, but she didn't interfere.

Devon sensed Savion was waiting for him to back down, but it wasn't going to happen. Placing his hand on the small of Hadley's back, he stood his ground. "We can agree to disagree on this. But if you expect me to change sides or run away because you're eyeballing me, you're sadly mistaken."

"That's how it is, Devon?"

He cocked his head to one side. "That's exactly how it is." With that, he turned away from Savion, done with the conversation. He stooped to kiss Hadley on the cheek. "I'll see you later, baby." Then he turned and strode back to his car.

He could feel Savion's eyes on his back, but he didn't turn around.

Chapter 17

That night, Hadley knocked on the door of Devon's town house. When he opened the door and stepped out onto the porch, she greeted him with a smile. "You look handsome, Devon." She made no effort to hide the fact that she was ogling him. Dressed in brown slacks, a tan button-down shirt and tan-and-brown loafers, he had a brown sport coat tossed over his shoulder.

He leaned down, placing a soft kiss on her lips. "You look gorgeous, as always." Holding her hand, he stepped down off the porch. "Here, do a little turn for me, baby."

Blushing, she executed a full 360-degree turn, showing off the long-sleeved shimmering gold sweater dress she wore. "I'm glad you like it."

As they walked toward her car, he remarked, "You

know, you didn't have to do this. I don't expect you to apologize for Savion."

She nodded, tapping the button on her keys to unlock the car doors. "I know. But I still feel bad about the way he sniped at you today."

He shrugged. "I get it. That's how a classy woman rolls. And I'll gladly accompany your fine ass to dinner, whatever the reason." He winked, going to the driver's side and opening the door for her.

She climbed in and buckled up while he closed the door and went around to his side. Once they were both in the car and strapped in, she backed out of the driveway and headed down the road.

Hadley kept her eyes ahead as the car moved through the darkened streets. Devon's large hand rested on her thigh as she drove, sending tingles of anticipation dancing over her skin. Soft R & B music poured from the stereo system, the lyrics reminding her of what she'd like most for dessert. Oceanview Grill boasted an extensive selection of desserts, but only Devon's loving could satisfy her sweet tooth. A smile tilted her lips as she thought of all the ways she wanted to savor him.

Once they reached the restaurant, she parked and he escorted her inside. The heavenly aromas of the wood-burning grill and the fresh herbs used to season the food greeted her the moment they entered. She'd anticipated the Friday night crowd, and had made a reservation to ensure they'd get a table without a long wait. The place was just as packed as she'd expected it to be, and the din of various conversations and silverware clanging against dishes echoed through the interior.

The hostess escorted them to a booth along the back wall, where the windows looked out on the sand dunes and the beach.

Seated in the booth, Hadley picked up her menu. "Maybe I'll try something new this time. Have you ever had red snapper?"

"Yeah. There's a place in LA that makes a fantastic broiled red snapper." His gaze rested on his own menu as he spoke. "I'm in the mood for something else, though. Maybe surf and turf."

When the waiter came by with their glasses of water and the basket of rolls, she looked up from the menu. "We're still deciding. Can you swing back in a few minutes?"

"Of course." The waiter left to take care of his other tables.

"I think I'm gonna just do the surf and turf." Devon sat his menu aside. "Listen, can I talk to you about something?"

Reading the seriousness on his face, she put her own menu down. "Sure, what is it?"

He drew a breath. "I spent some time over at Mt. Ephraim on Wednesday."

She nodded. "I know. You go there every year on December 26."

One of his thick brows hitched up. "How do you know that?"

She shrugged. "Small island. Plus, my parents still go to that church."

"If you know about my trips, then you probably know why I go. Natalie passed on December 26, and going there every year has been my way of dealing with my grief. I'm not all that religious, but it really has helped to go there, pray and reflect."

"I understand." She felt honored that he would share something so personal with her.

"This year was a little different," he continued. "It's the first time I've gone when I've been seriously involved with someone, and—"

She reached across the table, grabbed his hands. "I don't mean to cut you off, but I love you, Devon, and it's high time I told you."

A broad smile spread over his face. "I'm glad to hear that, because…"

Hadley's eyes drifted from Devon's face as a familiar yet disturbing feeling came over her. The feeling of being watched. Sure enough, when she looked around, she saw a man sitting across from them, alone in a booth. The man was attempting to be discreet, but it was obvious he was watching them over his menu. "Devon, I think you've got a fan in here."

He chuckled. "Maybe so. We'll wait and see if they come over and ask for an autograph."

She swung her gaze back to her handsome companion, pushing away the creepy feeling she got from the menu watcher.

"What were you saying, Devon?"

"I was saying that I had a talk with Reverend Keene, and I think it's time I moved on and—"

Shouting broke out at the hostess stand, and both Hadley and Devon turned in that direction.

A tall dark-haired man, wearing a camera on a strap

around his neck, was arguing with the hostess. As the man's hands flailed around, he seemed to be gesturing toward Devon's table.

Devon frowned. "That guy looks familiar."

"Someone you've worked with?"

Shaking his head, Devon's frown deepened. "He's a paparazzo. But what the hell is he doing here?"

Tension crept into Hadley's shoulders. Something told her that things were about to go sideways, in a big way.

A flash went off to her right, by the window.

Swiveling her head, Hadley's eyes grew wide when she saw two photographers crouched outside the restaurant window. "Shit."

Devon was already on his feet. "You can say that again. Let's get the hell out of here."

Grabbing her purse, she took his hand and the two of them darted across the restaurant. Hadley's heel caught on a tablecloth, dragging the dishes set up on the unoccupied table to the floor. She heard the crash and cringed but didn't stop.

They flew past the hostess stand, with both the menu watcher and the hostess harasser on their tail. More flashes went off around them, illuminating the blurred scenery as they ducked into Hadley's car.

The menu watcher shouted, "Miss Monroe! Why would you tip us off it you didn't want to be photographed?"

"I don't know what you're talking about!" She called back just as loudly.

While they buckled up, some of the photographers

circled close to the car. More shouted questions were thrown at them.

"Is it true you two are an item?"

"Devon, will you be returning to LA?"

Hadley turned the engine over and looked directly ahead. Her eyes communicated that she was leaving, but just in case, she tapped the gas pedal to rev the engine.

The photographers backed away, and Hadley peeled out of the lot.

For the first few minutes of their escape from the photographers, Devon looked out the window, watching the scenery roll by. He'd thrown on his sport jacket while they'd been rushing out of Oceanview Grill, to stave off the wintry chill in the air. Now, trapped in the car with the heat flowing from the vents and the tension snapping between the two of them, he wished he could take it off again. In his mind, he wondered how he'd ended up in a situation like this. He'd been coming back home for years now and had never been harassed by photographers before. The whole reason he chose his hometown for his vacation was peace and quiet, but that concept had certainly been shattered tonight.

He waited, thinking that if he gave Hadley time, she'd apologize for calling in those media goons. As he tried to settle his racing pulse, he retreated into his own thoughts. He had so many unanswered questions about what had just happened, and all of them centered on Hadley. His familiarity with the photos-for-profit crowd was surface level, but he knew enough. Candid shots were worth far more than posed ones. The photographers knew that and would do anything to get their next high-paying shot. Paying someone who had intel on where celebrities would be wasn't outside their comfort zone.

So, was that why had Hadley summoned them here? *How much are they paying her?*

What did she have to gain by alerting them to my whereabouts?

Several blocks away from the restaurant, Devon looked at Hadley. "What just happened?"

"I don't know." She seemed bit out of breath. "I never expected anything like this."

His face creased into a frown. Was her expectation a subtle admission of her guilt in all this? "Even though you called them?"

Stopped at a red light, she turned to stare at him. "Devon, I didn't call anyone."

"One of the reporters said you tipped them off." How would the guy even know her name if she wasn't the one who'd dimed him out?

The light changed, and she went through the intersection. "He's lying. I never contacted anyone. Why would I do that?"

"I don't know, Hadley."

"Besides, I'm not the only one who knows you're in town."

"Yeah, okay." He didn't bother to hide the impatience in his tone.

Her brow furrowed. "Come on, Devon. Plenty of people have seen you this year, and most folks on the island know you come every year around this time."

If he weren't so irritated, he would have laughed. "That's true. But the fact remains that in all the years I've been coming here, no one has bothered me up until now."

"That's true, but—"

He cut her off. "And today, when this crap happened, the only name mentioned was yours." His face was now tight with anger. It seemed she was determined to deny her involvement in this whole mess, but he was going to see to it that she took responsibility for her actions.

Her expression was a mixture of sadness and confusion. "Devon, I don't know what's going on, but I swear I didn't—"

He held up his hand. It had become clear that she wasn't going to admit to anything, and that meant there was no point in continuing this fruitless conversation. "Don't say anything else, please. Just drop me off at the town house."

Her jaw tightened, but she did as he asked, lapsing into silence.

He kept his eyes on the horizon, not even wanting to look at her. After everything they'd shared, how could she do this to him? He'd opened his heart to her in a way he hadn't with any woman since Natalie. And now she betrayed him this way? Calling in the same overzealous photographers who chased him around Los Angeles so they could infringe on his privacy there? He depended on his three-week vacation on the island to restore his peace of mind after the other forty-nine weeks spent on the left coast depleted it. Now, not only had he lost the woman he'd come to love, but he'd lost the one place he'd considered sacred. And it had all gone down in one night. He sighed, mourning everything that had been taken from him.

When she pulled up to the curb in front of the town house, he climbed out. "I'm leaving on the next available flight. My assistant will make sure the bill is handled."

Tears began to fill her eyes. "Devon, please."

He said nothing more. Though her tears moved him, activating the part of his heart that belonged to her and longed to comfort her, he quashed the urge. She couldn't be trusted, and he wouldn't be in a relationship with someone he couldn't trust.

He turned his back to her and started walking. Every step increased the physical distance between them, and he felt the emotional distance growing along with it.

He heard her crying behind him. But he didn't turn around. He wouldn't.

By the time he reached the front porch of the town house and inserted the key in the lock, he heard her switch the car into gear.

Only when he heard her drive away did he look back at the spot where she'd been parked.

Clenching his fist, he pushed open the door and went inside, shutting the door behind him. Shrugging out of his sport coat, he tossed it over the back of the couch and cracked his knuckles. The first order of business was to adjust his travel arrangements. He'd planned to stay on the island until after the New Year, but not anymore.

Settled in on the couch, he took out his phone and dialed Mimi, his assistant. Young, driven and something of a workaholic, she rarely took vacations and always answered his calls. He tried not to take advantage of her ambition, but this particular request couldn't wait.

He held the phone against his ear, waiting through two rings before she answered.

"Hello? What do you need, Mr. Granger?"

"Hi, Mimi. Can you please change my flight for me?"

She chuckled. "Sure thing. You wanna stay longer and enjoy some more relaxation?" The keys on her computer clicked as she began typing.

He frowned. "Afraid not. I need you to book me on the next available flight. And make sure my bill for the rental property is settled."

She paused, and when she spoke again, she sounded surprised. "Okay, I'll handle it. But as far as the flight goes, on this short notice, tickets will be hard to come by if you go commercial."

"That's fine. You know I don't do private jets." He considered the small aircraft, outfitted with wet bars and televisions, to be a wasteful extravagance. He made enough money to own a jet, but practicality ruled his spending, and he just couldn't muster the desire for one.

"You may even have to fly coach," she continued. "Is that okay?"

"That's fine." He wasn't the kind of guy who thought himself too good to fly coach. He'd be just fine alongside the regular Joes and Janes, traveling for work and play. "Do what you have to do to get me on a flight. Email me the details when you're done." He ended the call and went to pack his things.

The faster he got out of Sapphire Shores, the better.

Chapter 18

The last Saturday night of the year found Hadley on her couch in a camisole and fuzzy pajama pants. All over the island, folks were celebrating, if the fireworks she heard in the distance were any indication. Usually she'd be out with Belinda and her girls. They'd all be enjoying a glass of wine on the beach, reveling in one another's company.

Her blowup with Devon last night had left her feeling anything but celebratory. She'd spent most of the morning calling and texting him, hoping he'd answer. She had to get him to listen, to hear her out. Apparently, he didn't want to talk, because her efforts had been ignored.

Now, curled up with the remote and her misery, she brushed away the tears yet again. She'd managed to screw things up with Devon, and she didn't even know how she'd done it.

Her front door swung open then, startling her. She yelped in surprise, but relaxed when she saw Belinda walk in. Her best friend had a key to her apartment, which explained her ability to get in, but not her sudden appearance.

Hadley sat up, using the tail of her top to dry her cheeks. "What are you doing here, B?"

"Girl, please. You think I couldn't tell something was wrong when I called you this morning?" She moved farther into the apartment, shifting the grocery bags she was carrying. "The better question is, what's wrong with you?"

She sighed. "Plenty. Close the door and I'll tell you all about it."

Belinda shook her head. "I can't close it yet. Somebody else is coming up."

Hadley's eyes shifted to the door as her ears picked up the sound of another pair of feet climbing the stairs outside. "Who else is coming? I'm in no mood for a party."

Belinda rolled her eyes. "Hush, Hadley. I wasn't sure how big the problem was, so like any good friend, I called in reinforcements."

And as Belinda finished her statement, Viola entered through the open door. Her eyes went straight to Hadley's. "Oh, Lord. What's wrong? Who's made my baby cry?"

For once, Hadley appreciated her mother's tendency toward babying her; she could certainly use the comfort right now. Standing, she went to her mother and let herself be enfolded in her soothing hug. She managed to hold back her tears until Belinda dropped her bags and joined them. That set her off again, and the tears flowed anew.

They separated and went to sit down. Hadley sat between her mother and her best friend, who occupied opposite ends of the couch. Once she was composed enough to speak, she took a deep breath. "Let's just say things have crashed and burned between me and Devon."

Belinda's lips curved downward. "Oh, no."

"Oh, yes." Hadley sniffled. "It happened last night, and he's been ignoring my calls and texts all day."

Viola, who sat shaking her head, asked, "What could have happened? Y'all looked so sweet together when he was over to the house for Christmas dinner."

She remembered well; it had only been a few days ago. *How did things go so wrong between us in such a short span of time?* "I don't really know myself. But he's probably back on the West Coast by now, because when he got out of the car, he told me he was leaving right away."

Belinda groaned. "That's why my housekeeping crew got a call today. He must have checked out of the town house."

Hadley had known he was leaving, but for some reason, hearing Belinda confirm it only made her sadder. "Damn."

Viola tilted her head to the side. "Hadley, just tell us what happened and we'll try to help you figure things out."

Inhaling deeply, Hadley gave them a rundown of her date with Devon, including the sneak attack mounted by the photographers. "One of them claimed the tip about Devon's location came from me. That's outrageous, because I never contacted anyone."

Belinda looked genuinely confused. "So how did these people get your name?"

She shrugged. "I don't have a clue. I've been asking myself that ever since I dropped Devon off. But I swear, I didn't contact them. I know he comes here for peace and quiet. I would never do that to him, even if we weren't dating." Saying that aloud reminded her that they were no longer a couple; he'd made that clear with his cold manner last night, and solidified it by ignoring her attempts to reach him.

Touching her shoulder, Belinda gave her a sad smile. "I'm sorry, Hadley. This is a tough one."

"You're telling me." She sank back against the overstuffed cushions, trying to fight off the rising sadness. "After all this time pining after Devon, I finally get the courage to tell him how I feel. And after a week and a half of absolute bliss, this happens. Just when it seems we're making a real connection."

Viola patted her thigh. "At least your conscience is clean. If you say you didn't contact those people, I believe you. I raised you better than to lie."

Hadley blew out a breath, struggling against the emotions roiling around inside her. "In the short time we were together, he did so much for me. I mean, I never would have thought to petition against the Neville South development if he hadn't encouraged me not to give up."

"Wow." The usually stoic Belinda seemed impressed.

"Yeah. He pushed me to stand up for my convictions,

even when it became hard to do so. Aside from that, he was such a gentleman. He treated me like a queen. Opened doors, pulled out chairs, the whole deal." She shook her head ruefully. "What am I going to do now that he's gone?"

Viola stood then. "I'll tell you what I'm going to do. I'm going to stop sitting on the sidelines about this Neville South development."

Hadley looked up at her mother. "Mom, I love you so much. But if you're going to side with Daddy and Savion, you're welcomed to keep sitting this one out." She couldn't take any more bad news right now.

Viola pursed her lips. "Oh, hush, child. I'm on your side. Truth is, this development is too big for a place as small as Sapphire Shores. I've lived here for forty years, and I can see this deal for what it is. The benefits aren't worth the traffic headaches, litter and increase in property taxes it will also bring."

That triggered a small smile for Hadley. "So, if the Monroe men stand their ground on this…"

Viola clapped her hands together. "Then you and I go into battle together, honey. Your father needs to be contradicted now and then, and he's about due."

Refreshed by her mother's declaration, Hadley nodded. "I appreciate that, Mom. I really do." This was the first time she could remember her mother standing firm on something that was in direct opposition to her father. Knowing Carver Monroe, and how stubborn he could be, Hadley assumed it wasn't easy for her mother to do this. "But what am I going to do about Devon?"

Belinda piped up. "Now, this is my wheelhouse. As

your best friend, I'm gonna advise you to do not one damn thing."

Confusion knitting her brow, Hadley said, "Say what?"

Folding her arms over her chest, Belinda doubled down. "You heard me. You didn't dime him out, so he's in the wrong here. So you need to stop calling and texting him, and go on about your business. When he realizes how stupid he's been, he'll be back."

"I don't know about that, B. He was pretty angry."

"Yep. And he'll be just as contrite when he comes to his damn senses." Belinda gave her a curt nod. "Trust me, girl."

"Despite your lack of a man?" Hadley knew her skepticism showed in her expression.

Belinda rolled her eyes. "Yes, because my lack of a man is by choice. It certainly isn't from a lack of offers." She flipped her ponytail and winked.

Snickering despite her mood, Hadley shook her head at her friend's shenanigans. "Girl, you're crazy."

"That may be so, but I'm right, too." She rested her back against the armrest, as if indicating that her job was done.

Viola headed for the kitchen. "Okay, enough of this depressing talk. I say we watch a movie, and I'll make the popcorn."

"Great idea." Belinda was already shrugging out of her jacket. "Don't you have *Beyond the Lights* on DVD?"

"Yeah." Knowing that neither of her houseguests

was leaving any time soon, Hadley got up and went to her entertainment center.

Her mother and her best friend were real pieces of work, and she felt fortunate to have them in her life.

Devon stood in his mother's kitchen Sunday morning, filling his plate with her famous breakfast. Though she'd lived in Los Angeles for more than a decade now, Eva Sykes Granger hadn't lost her touch for Southern cooking. As he loaded up with cheese-laden eggs, country sausage, seasoned grits and fluffy biscuits running with butter, he smiled for the first time in a few days.

As he carried his bounty to the table to join his parents, he took in the familiar room, the heart of his parents' home. He'd purchased the twenty-five-hundred-square-foot Echo Park home for them after the success of *Reach for the Sky*, his first Western film. And while his mother had initially complained about his "extravagant" gift, declaring the house "too large for folks our age," she'd soon forgotten her protests and started decorating. The kitchen was painted a dark blue and white, displaying a blueberry motif in honor of Eva's favorite fruit.

Sitting down, he grabbed the little ceramic bunch of blueberries that held the black pepper and sprinkled a bit onto his eggs.

Eva was already eating, her eyes on the pages of *Better Homes & Gardens*. Her white hair was up in curlers, and she wore a blue T-shirt and a pair of bedazzled blue windbreaker pants. In her hand was her favorite mug, emblazoned with the words *49 and Hold-*

ing. The cup held her favorite blend of herbal tea, since she didn't like coffee.

Across from her, David Granger flipped through that day's edition of the *LA Times*. He was bald, having long ago given up the ghost regarding his receding hairline. His thick eyebrows and trimmed mustache were the color of fresh-fallen snow, standing out in contrast to his deep skin tone. As he read, he absently nibbled on a biscuit, the crumbs falling onto his Marine Corps sweatshirt.

With a contented sigh, Devon dug into his breakfast. This was why he'd come here from the airport instead of going home. It would be several more weeks before he could stand in one spot long enough to cook, so his mother's cuisine had drawn him. But beyond that, he felt a certain peace in the presence of his parents. They were about as laid-back as parents could be.

Devon was chewing a forkful of eggs when he heard his father clear his throat.

"Now, Eva?" David asked the question without looking up from the local section of his newspaper.

She glanced up from her magazine, looking right at her son. "Yes, David. Now is good."

A confused Devon looked back and forth between his parents while tucking a piece of sausage between the split halves of his biscuit. "What's up?"

This time David closed his paper and folded it up. Resting his arms on the tabletop, he tented his fingers.

Uh-oh. Devon's eyes widened. Nothing good ever came of his father's finger tenting, at least not where he was concerned. He felt like a wayward teen, staring down the business end of an epic lecture.

David cleared his throat again. "What's going on with you, son?"

He blinked a few times. "Um, nothing."

David scoffed. "Something brought you here. And you may as well tell us what it is."

"You know we love having you, baby," Eva added. "And you're welcome to come and stay with us anytime. But we're entitled to know what's going on with you."

Feeling out of sorts, he shrugged. "I'm not supposed to be cooking, remember? And where else am I gonna get real Southern food cooked with this much love?" He hoped flattery would distract his mother from this rare quest to find out about his personal life.

It didn't. "Nice try, Devon. But I brought you into this world, and I know something's on your mind." Eva sipped her tea. "So, spill it."

Taken aback, Devon dropped his fork and put his hands up. "Now, wait a minute. What makes y'all so sure there's something wrong?"

David fielded that question. "You've been moping around this house ever since you got back from the island. Don't think we haven't noticed."

"Not only that, but you're been eating everything I cook, as fast as I can make it," Eva quipped as she flipped the page in her magazine.

"Sure enough." David reached out and patted his son's belly. "Much more of your mama's cooking and you gonna pop, son." He winked. "Why don't you go on and tell us what the problem is."

It had become clear he couldn't squirrel his way out of this conversation, so Devon acquiesced. "Can I at least finish my breakfast first?"

"Go ahead." Eva nodded in his direction. "We'll wait."

Shaking his head, Devon scooped up the last of his grits and eggs, then tucked the last piece of biscuit in his mouth. As he ate, he wondered how to best phrase his "problem," though he considered it more of a revelation. Washing down the food with a long swig of orange juice, he set the glass down. "My holiday vacation was a little more eventful than I'd hoped."

"That's pretty obvious, from the way you've been acting." David took a draw from his mug of black coffee. "Can you be a little more specific?"

He sighed. "Y'all remember Hadley Monroe, right?"

Eva's face brightened at the mention of her name. "I sure do remember little Hadley. Those rambunctious brothers of hers kept her running all the time when you all were younger. How is she doing?"

Devon slanted his eyes in his mother's direction. "First, she's not so little anymore. She's twenty-eight. And…she and I started dating while I was in Sapphire Shores."

David grinned, slapping his open palm on the table. "Well, hot damn. Never would have thought of you two as a match."

"She's a real sweet girl, so you've got my approval." Eva closed her magazine. "But I know that's not why you're sitting around my house looking like a little lost puppy."

He gave his mother a wry smile. "Actually, it is. Hadley and I already broke up."

David's brow crinkled. "Well, that was short-lived, then."

"Yeah, it was." *And it's a damn shame.* "For a while there, I thought she was the one."

Eva exchanged a look with her husband. "And what changed that?"

"She showed me who she really is." Draining the last of his orange juice, Devon stood and took his dishes to the sink. "She can't be trusted."

Quiet settled over the room for a moment, making the sound of the china dishes landing in the stainless-steel sink seem much louder. Walking back to the table, he sat down.

Both of his parents eyed him expectantly—waiting for him to elaborate, he assumed. So he told them about the night at Oceanview Grill when the paparazzi had shown up, seemingly out of nowhere. "In all the years I've been vacationing back home, this has never happened before."

Eva frowned. "How does that make it Hadley's fault?"

"I wouldn't even have considered that angle, Mama, until one of the photographers looked right at Hadley and called her by name. Asked her why she'd tipped them off if she didn't want to be photographed." He scoffed. "I guess he was surprised that we went out of our way to avoid him and his ilk."

David shook his head. "Did you ever ask her if she contacted them, Devon?"

He thought about it for a moment. As he recalled, he hadn't so much asked her as he had accused her. "I asked her why she did it."

Rolling his eyes, David got up from the table. "Eva, you take this one. This boy is obviously out of his mind." Tucking his folded newspaper under his arm, he shuffled out of the room.

Eva fixed her son with a hard glare. "I know you're not going to sit here at my table and tell me you accused that girl of betraying you without even giving her a chance to tell her side."

Singed by his mother's fiery gaze, he looked away. "Mama, all she had to say was that she didn't do it. She never even admitted—"

"Hush up." She sat her mug down. "Son, you ought to be ashamed of yourself. I've never known Hadley to be dishonest, have you?"

Unable to think of such an occasion, he shook his head.

"I can't believe you. You were probably so busy yelling at her that you missed the whole point of what she was telling you." Folding her arms over her chest, she continued. "Have you even considered that she's telling the truth? That she wasn't the one who called those people?"

Inhaling deeply, he realized his mother was right, as usual. He hadn't stopped to think about how vehemently Hadley had denied having a part in this debacle. "How did they get her name, then?"

Eva shrugged. "I don't know. That's for you to investigate if you want. But I tell you what." She stood, gathering her dishes and her husband's. "You're not going to sit in my house with your face all screwed up. You messed up, now do something about it." With a huff, she walked away with the armload of china and silverware.

Devon sat at the table alone for a few minutes, thinking over what had just happened. If his parents had noticed his foul mood and been concerned enough to bring it up—in direct contrast to how they usually operated—that meant something. It was quite a wake-up call.

He'd been missing Hadley fiercely—her smile, her touch, the sound of her voice. Even his anger did little to temper his longing for her. Taking his phone out, he dialed Mimi. He had arrangements to make.

Mama's right. It's time to fix this.

Chapter 19

As Hadley looked through the papers she'd brought, she realized how unusually quiet the interior of Della's was. It was Monday, just after two. The morning New Year's Eve service crowd had already hit the deli, seeking to fill their grumbling stomachs after sitting through the sermon. She surmised that some of the other folks who usually stopped in had kicked off their New Year's celebrations early.

She sipped her iced tea, observing the gray day outside before returning her attention to her papers. One sheet among the stack was much larger than the others and occupied most of the square table, which was meant to seat four people. She'd taken it over when she came in, since no one had been sitting there, and she needed the space.

Della appeared behind the counter then. The older woman saw Hadley, waved and took a moment to slip her checked apron up over her head. Hanging the apron on a wall hook, she used a few pumps of hand sanitizer and made her way over to the table.

"Hi, Della. You ready?"

Sitting down, she grinned and clapped her hands together. "I sure am. I'm so excited about this."

Hadley returned the smile, looked around a bit. "Is Ralph going to sit in on this?"

Della shook her head. "You know how he is. He told me to look things over and decide, since this is my place."

"Okay, then." She spread out the large sheet. "I'm not an artist, but I brought over this diagram of MHI's last land plot. As you can see, I drew out the basic shape and location right here." She gestured to the rectangular object she'd added to the diagram with the tip of her pencil. "I think it's the perfect spot for the new Della's."

Eyes wide, Della looked over the image. "Are these dimensions in square feet?"

Hadley nodded.

"Wow. This is really a big building you're talking about." Della inhaled. "A big undertaking, too."

"I know. But you do good business here. Everybody agrees you're the best deli in town, way better than those two chain places." She tapped the rectangle for emphasis. "Having a space like this means you'll be able to accommodate everybody who wants to get into your place during the lunch rush."

Della sat back in her chair, as if thinking it over. "I

can see the benefit of that. Let me see what else you brought."

"Glad you asked." Opening a manila folder, Hadley pulled out the cost estimates and timelines. "I've got a friend who's an architect and another who's a contractor. Benefits of working in real estate. Here are the numbers they mocked up for you." She slid the small stack of papers across the table.

"There's a lot of information here."

"I know. Take your time going over it." Hadley got up and crossed the dining area with her frosted glass in hand. She stopped by the dispenser to refill her iced tea, then started back toward the table.

The bell over the entrance rang as the door swung open.

Hadley turned toward the sound and saw Savion standing there. She was still a little annoyed at the way he'd acted with Devon, but she supposed it didn't matter much now. "Hey, Savion."

"Hey, sis." He walked farther into the deli as she passed him, returning to the table with Della. Watching them, he asked, "Can a brother get some service?"

Della chuckled, "Boy, if you don't go on to the counter and order. Don't you see Marcelle standing there?" She gestured to the counter, where the young woman at the sandwich station waved.

"Okay, but I'll be back after I order." He went to the counter.

Della turned to Hadley. "That brother of yours is something else."

She rolled her eyes. "Trust me, I know."

"Handsome as all get-out, though." Della looked his way as she made the remark. "When the right woman comes along to tame him, he'll make a fine husband."

"Well, let's both pray for the day when that woman comes and takes him off my hands." Hadley giggled at the thought of her staid older brother strung out over this nameless, faceless woman. It was almost too much to hope for, but she had to admit she'd love to meet the lady who could capture his heart.

They chatted until Savion interrupted them, taking a seat at the next table with his sandwich and chips.

Sipping his drink, he asked, "What are you two doing?"

Hadley answered the question. "Well, Della is considering ways to expand her business. As for me, I'm taking the sage advice of my best friend by getting on with my life." She didn't want to think about Devon, so she pushed the thoughts away.

"You miss him, don't you?" Savion's eyes held hers, and he looked almost sympathetic.

"I thought you'd be happy about it." The words came out a bit snippier than she'd intended, but she couldn't take them back once she'd said them.

Savion didn't respond to that. Instead, he ate some of his food. He was quiet for so long, Hadley thought he was done talking. She returned her attention to the contracting estimates she'd had drawn up for Della.

Finally, he spoke again. "Hadley, I have something to tell you."

"What is it?" She glanced up from the estimates.

A deep sigh preceded his words. "I'm the one…who reached out to those photographers about Devon."

Hadley's eyes widened, her jaw tightening in anger. When she thought of what she'd lost because of her brother's actions… "Savion. How could you?"

He wore a mask of regret, and it looked genuine. "I'm sorry, Hadley. I used your work email to contact them—you had left your computer on."

She stood up, fists clenched at her sides. "I should pop you right upside your square head! I can't believe you."

"I know. It was childish and petty, and I really do regret it. I never expected things to blow up the way they did, but that doesn't matter." He pushed aside his half-eaten food. "I'd decided I didn't like Devon, that he wasn't good enough for you. I let the overprotective brother in me take over and did something against my better judgment."

"You're damn straight." She sat down again, flexing her fingers before the stiffness set in.

"Seeing you unhappy is driving me crazy. I had to confess, and I hope you'll forgive me. I promise I'll never pull a stunt like this again."

Della shook her head. "Honestly, Savion. I expect better of you."

He sighed. "I know. And from now on, better is what you'll get."

Hadley took several deep breaths. While she was angry with her brother, she also felt vindicated. This revelation solved the mystery of who'd ratted Devon out. Now that she knew, she felt better. But Devon…

"Savion, I'll forgive you under one condition."

"Anything. Just name it." He seemed contrite, and eager to get back in her good graces.

"Reach out to Devon and tell him what you just told me." She folded her arms over her chest. "This idea that I called in those photographers is what ruined things for us, so he needs to hear from the real culprit."

Savion nodded. "That's reasonable. I'll get in touch with him right away." He paused, as if he'd just thought of something. "But I can't guarantee this will fix things between you two."

"I'm not asking you to do that." She wasn't naive enough to think her brother had that ability. "Just tell him the truth. What he decides to do next is on him."

"Then I'm on it." He stood, tossing away his trash. "Is it too much to ask for a hug? Just so I know we're cool and you're not going to draw on my face while I'm asleep?"

She stood and hugged her brother, laughing at his reference to a prank she'd pulled on him when they were kids. "We're cool, if you do what I've asked. Screw this up, though, and you'll wake up looking like a Picasso."

The siblings separated, and Savion left.

After he was gone, Della asked, "What do you think is going to happen next?"

Hadley shrugged. "Who knows? I'm just going to wait and see."

"And keep living in the meantime."

Hadley smiled. "Yes, ma'am."

* * *

Devon rolled his bag across the polished floor of the concourse, moving at an easy pace. Spotting an empty seat in the terminal his connection would depart from, he strolled over and sat down. Jogging through airports was probably one of his least favorite ways to spend his time. But if the cause was worth it, he'd travel wherever it required.

He still had a good hour or so before his connecting flight, so he pulled out his tablet. He started putting together a virtual jigsaw puzzle to pass the time, but quickly lost interest in that. Turning off the tablet, he tucked it back into the outer pocket of his carry-on.

Absently watching the teeming crowd of people moving through the terminal, he couldn't keep his thoughts off Hadley. Did she miss him? Was she even thinking about him? He'd been so harsh with her the night he'd left the island. In his mind's eye, he could see her beautiful face, lined with worry as she tried to get through to him; he could see the tears coursing down her satin cheeks.

He'd hurt her, and he was having a hard time forgiving himself for that. She was about as sweet a woman as he'd ever encountered. Beneath the confidence she exuded lay sensitivity, and she'd made herself vulnerable by telling him how she felt about him. He'd repaid her bravery in revealing her innermost thoughts by basically calling her a liar and dismissing her attempts to explain herself.

He cursed under his breath, mentally kicking himself for being such an ass. Unfortunately, there was no way to go back and undo it now. All he could do was return to the island, and to her, and beg her forgiveness. He'd do whatever was necessary to prove that he loved her, tell her that he was sorry and that his life would be empty without her. He'd have to humble himself, let her inside to see the core of his being. He'd give her what he sensed she craved most: he'd trust her fully, the way she trusted him.

He'd been sitting there strategizing for about twenty minutes when his cell phone rang. Fishing it out of the hip pocket of his slacks, he answered it. "Hello?"

"Devon? It's Savion Monroe."

Surprise made him lean forward in his seat. "Hi, Savion."

"You sound surprised to hear from me."

"I am. I can't think of any reason you'd be calling me." And he couldn't. Despite the caffeine buzz from the two cups of coffee he'd had before leaving LAX, he couldn't think of a single motivation Savion would have for wanting to talk to him.

"I'll get right to it, then. I have something to tell you, related to my sister."

He rolled his eyes. "If this is about us seeing each other, I don't want to hear it."

Savion cleared his throat. "No, no. Nothing like that. I just want to clear up something about this whole paparazzi thing."

He shifted, seeking comfort on the chair's hard seat. *This ought to be interesting.* "And what's that?"

"I'm the one who tipped them off."

Devon frowned but said nothing. If Savion was feeling guilty enough to confess, he wanted to hear the whole story.

"Hadley has this bad habit of leaving her computer on at work, logged in to everything. So I used her email address to reach out to them."

He groaned. "You wanna tell me when you did this?"

"Christmas Eve. Took them a few days to get their crew together and make it to town, though. Then it was just a matter of figuring out where you would be." Savion paused. "I'm sorry, man. I really didn't expect things to turn out like this."

He was pretty sure Savion hadn't spent much time at all thinking about how things might turn out. It seemed the brother had mostly been concerned with driving a wedge between his sister and her new man. "I gotta say, man, this was a pretty childish stunt to pull. What are you, fourteen?"

Savion released a sigh. "I deserve that. I thought I was protecting my sister. The truth is, what I did was wrong. I shouldn't have interfered with her relationship, and it won't happen again."

"Did you tell Hadley what you did?"

"Yes. And she insisted I let you know, though I intended to do that anyway." Savion paused again, as if choosing his next words carefully.

Devon thought that wise.

"Look, she misses you. She's probably not going to call you, but if you do reach out to her, I know she'd be receptive."

Devon chuckled. "Oh, so you like me now?"

"In a word, yes. You make my sister happy, and that's all I ever really wanted for her."

He took a moment to let that settle in. Hearing Savion say those words made Devon feel good, maybe even a bit smug and self-righteous. But he was mature enough not to say any of that aloud.

"Would you consider giving her a call, Devon?"

He snorted a laugh. "I'll do you one better. I'm coming back for her."

Savion's tone brightened. "Really? When?"

Looking around the terminal, he smiled. "Actually, I'm at Chicago O'Hare right now. Should be there before nightfall, if all goes well."

"Awesome." Savion sounded genuinely pleased. "Listen, Devon, again, I'm sorry about all this."

"It's water under the bridge. As long as she's willing to take me back, I don't have any beef with you, Savion."

"Thanks, man. I appreciate it."

"Yeah. I respect your ability to admit to me that you acted like an idiot." He laughed. "Just don't do it again, and we're cool."

Savion laughed in response to that. "Trust me, my days of butting in on Hadley's life are over. Listen, when you get in town and have some time, call me. I'll take you out for a beer."

"Bet. Later, Savion." He disconnected the call, tucking his phone away. Sitting there in the terminal, he thought back on his mother's stern lecture. She'd been right about everything—Hadley had been telling the truth, but he'd been too blinded by his anger to see that.

It had been a long time since he'd been this wrong, and he was almost certain he'd have some tall apologizing to do when he arrived—if she would even talk to him.

It didn't matter, though. Being without her had taught him how much he needed her in his life. He needed her softness, her sweetness and, yes, even her sass. If she took him back, she could give him lip every day for the rest of his life if she wanted to, and he'd gladly accept it. She was the key to his future happiness, the only woman who'd managed to work her way into his heart since he'd become a widower.

Yes, Hadley Monroe was meant to be Mrs. Granger.

Now he just needed to get back to Sapphire Shores and prove it to her.

Chapter 20

As day turned into night, Hadley settled in on her couch for a marathon of Eddie Murphy movies. Belinda had pestered her most of the day about going out to participate in the revelry of the night and bring in the New Year with some drinks and shenanigans. Hadley had turned her down, choosing a quiet night at home instead. The *Beverly Hills Cop* movies, *Coming to America* and *48 Hrs.* were on tap and sure to lift her mood. Besides, the New Year would come anyway, so she'd decided to spend the night in the comfort of her home rather than being pushed around some smoky club.

She started *Coming to America*, humming along with the iconic chant in the opening sequence as she fetched her popcorn and wine from the kitchen. Sitting down on the sofa, she placed the bowl in her lap.

During the scene where Prince Akeem and Semmi were deciding where to look for a suitable bride, a knock sounded at her door. She shook her head as she set her popcorn aside and climbed to her feet. *It's probably Belinda, trying to convince me to go out.* Her friend was about to be out of luck, because she'd removed her bra already and donned a rather matronly nightgown. Hadley wasn't going anywhere and no amount of convincing would change her mind.

Since it was dark outside, she stood on the tips of her toes to check the peephole as a precaution. Her brothers often lectured her about that.

When she saw Devon standing on the doorstep, her heart stopped. She dropped back down, wondering if she were seeing things. There was only one way to find out.

Opening the door, she saw that he really was standing there. Not only that, but he had another armful of roses—this time they were sterling. "Hi, baby."

Standing there in wide-eyed amazement, she managed to mutter a greeting. She let her hungry eyes devour his tall, handsome frame, draped in a pair of charcoal-gray slacks and a crisp white button-down shirt.

"These are for you." He handed her the flowers. "Mind if I come in?"

She took the roses, cradling them against her chest. Looking down at her nightgown, she sighed. "Here you are, looking like a million dollars, and I'm dressed like this."

He smiled. "You look beautiful to me."

She stepped back. "Come on in out of the cold."

Once he was inside and she shut and locked the door, he leaned against it. "Thank you for letting me in. After the way I treated you, I'm not sure I deserve your courtesy."

She blinked a few times. "I can't believe you're really here."

He reached out, dragging his fingertip over her jawline. "I'm here, baby. For real."

The tingle that went through her confirmed his words. Thinking of the flowers she still clutched, she took them to the kitchen. "Let me put these in water."

Once she'd taken care of the roses, she returned to the living room, where Devon remained in the same place, leaning against the door. He seemed to be waiting for her to say something. "Come over to the sofa and sit down."

Seated next to him, with the popcorn between them, she watched him, waiting.

He took a deep breath. "I'm sorry, Hadley. So very, very sorry."

She wanted to make him work for this, she really did. But the reality was that she'd missed him terribly. Hearing him apologize made happy tears spring to her eyes.

"Your brother called me today and admitted what he did. But even if he hadn't called, I was still wrong for the way I treated you, for not believing you."

Their gazes met.

"How did you get here so fast?"

He smiled. "Easy. I was already on my way—I was sitting in the terminal at O'Hare when he called."

She sniffled then as the tears continued to spill. Confusion mixed with her joy at seeing him again. "You were?"

"Yes." He moved the popcorn bowl, setting it on the coffee table. Before he moved, he asked, "Do you mind?"

She shook her head to let him know it was all right.

He scooted next to her, and his first move when he entered her personal space was to brush away her tears with the gentle touch of his fingertips. "I was on my way back already because I missed you. I realized how much I need you in my life, Hadley."

"I missed you, too." She could hear the emotion in her own voice, so she assumed he could hear it, as well.

He laid his hand against her cheek. "Again, I'm sorry, baby. Please forgive me. Regardless of what happened, I should have believed you. I should have trusted you."

She sobbed then, overwhelmed by the rising emotions of the moment.

"Please, don't cry. You've shown me what it means to truly trust someone." He tilted her face up, looked into her eyes. "And I trust you now. Completely and without reservation."

He kissed her then, and she welcomed it. Her lips parted immediately, allowing his tongue to search the depths of her mouth as she explored his. By the time she broke the kiss to catch her breath, she was panting as if she'd just run a fifty-yard dash.

He reached into his hip pocket and pulled out a small black velvet box.

She recognized the size and shape of it right away, and her hand flew to her mouth.

"I know this may seem sudden," he began as he rocked the lid open on its hinge. Inside was a cushion-cut sparkler on a rose-gold band. "But since you waited so long to tell me how you felt, I don't want to waste any more time. Hadley Aria Monroe, will you be my wife?"

"Yes!" She nodded, sticking her hand out for the ring. He slipped it on to her finger, and she admired its immense beauty. "This is gorgeous, Devon. How did you know that I like rose gold, and that my middle name is Aria?"

He shrugged. "Your brothers gave me all the information I needed."

She sighed happily, holding her hand up and turning it from side to side. She just loved the way it sparkled. "Seems those two knuckleheads are good for something. Guess I'll keep 'em."

He pulled her into his arms then, letting his desire show through in his gaze. "Fancy a little celebration, baby?"

She smiled a wicked smile. "Oh, hell yes. What better way to bring in the New Year than making love with my husband-to-be?"

He whistled. "See, that's why I love you. Beautiful, intelligent and freaky."

"Only when it comes to you." She leaned up for his kiss.

The kiss deepened, escalating into more, as passion rose between them. She straddled his lap, splaying her fingers across the back of his head as he brushed his lips over the tops of her breasts where the gown revealed them. She popped the buttons off his shirt in her eagerness to get him out of it, but neither of them cared.

Shirtless and breathing heavily, he stood, holding her close to him. She locked her legs around his waist, peppering his face and neck with kisses and licks. He felt a twinge in his back, but it was slight. It might mean taking an extra dose of his meds tomorrow. He moved across the room to the bare wall in the hallway, his big hands cupping her ass to support her body weight. In the hall, he pressed her back against the wall. He used one hand to rip open the snaps running down the front of her gown, and moments later, he drew her nipple into his warm mouth.

She sank her nails into his shoulders, her head coming to rest against the wall as the ecstasy built. They'd made love before, but nothing compared to this primal, passion-fueled encounter.

When he lifted his head from her breasts, he asked huskily, "Can I…"

She knew what he was asking, and she wanted it just as badly as he did. "Yes, Devon. Yes…" To further encourage him, she reached between them to undo the button and zipper on his trousers. Working them down around his powerful thighs, she groaned when he rubbed his hardness against her.

A few quick movements later, he'd freed his erection from his silk boxers. His searching fingers slid her panties aside, finding her center. She was hot with desire, and as he teased her a bit with his fingertips, her passion only grew.

"Now." She ground the word out through clenched teeth, pressing her pelvis against his.

He obliged her, pressing his length between her thighs and entering her in one swift, smooth motion.

A high-pitched cry left her throat as she experienced the sheer joy of him filling her.

And there, with the moonlight streaming in between the slats of the shutters, he made love to her until she screamed his name in the darkness.

Devon looked up at the cloudless blue sky, thankful for the warmth and beauty of the day. He stood on the beach, flanked by Campbell and Savion. They each wore crisp white shirts and black slacks, though Devon was the only one with a sterling rose pinned to his shirt pocket.

Belinda stood close by as well, wearing a lavender robe. She'd recently gotten ordained on the internet, at Hadley's request. Belinda wasn't especially religious, but if her outfit was any indication, she was taking her role as minister seriously—at least for the day.

From where they stood, they had a full view of the back of Monroe Manor and its grassy lawn, which was miraculously green despite the lingering winter.

That wasn't the view that concerned him, though. He was watching the back door, waiting for Hadley to make her appearance. He supposed he should be more patient, because it was a bride's prerogative to take her time getting ready on her special day. It seemed their relationship had spoiled him, because he'd gotten used to things flowing quickly but naturally between them.

It was early February, barely a month since he'd proposed, and they were already about to take their vows.

The old saying said, "You can't hurry love." As far as Devon was concerned, there wasn't any need. It moved fast enough without any interference from him.

Finally, she walked out on her father's arm. The white runner than had been spread out from the back door to the spot on the beach where everyone had gathered served as her path as she walked slowly toward him. He couldn't hold back his grin as he took in the sight of his radiant bride. She wore a white halter-top pantsuit encrusted with crystals and pearls. A sheer white coat covered her bare arms, and her feet were bare, save for the jewelry around her ankles. As he'd asked, she left her hair down, accenting her flowing curls with a large white flower tucked behind her ear.

By the time Carver placed his daughter's hand in her fiancé's, Devon could barely contain his excitement. He couldn't believe how incredibly fortunate he was. The fact that she'd agreed to be his wife seemed like a miracle to him.

They turned to Belinda, who performed the ceremony with a broad smile on her face the entire time. Devon was aware of the watchful gazes of their parents, her brothers and the few friends he'd invited, but he had eyes only for his bride. He spoke his vows loud and clear, to let her know that he had no doubts about their future. She spoke hers in kind, and the softness in her eyes as she pledged her love to him touched his heart.

When Belinda pronounced them man and wife, Hadley threw her hands in the air and gave a little cheer.

He cut her impromptu celebration short by pulling her into his arms for a lingering kiss.

The party went on late into the evening, underneath a tent the Monroes had set up in their backyard. Sitting in the throne-like chair he'd been assigned, Devon cradled his wife's hand in his own.

She stood suddenly, then leaned down to kiss him on the forehead. "I've gotta go to the little brides' room. I'll be right back."

After she walked away, Savion strolled up, a glass of champagne in his hand. He reached out to shake his brother-in-law's hand. "Welcome to the family, man."

"Thanks."

"Got a little something for you. Call it a wedding gift."

Devon leaned forward in his chair. "Aw, Savion. You didn't have to…"

"Listen up, Devon. Remember what you said a couple of weeks ago about opening a production studio here on the island?"

He nodded. "Of course. I've been looking into what I need to do, and I'm ready to make some moves as soon as I find a location."

Savion winked. "You're in luck. Neville South withdrew their proposal, so…it looks like that last piece of Monroe family property is yours now." He reached into his shirt pocket, pulled out a folded sheet of paper and passed it to him.

Opening it, Devon's eyes widened. "It's the deed to the land plot."

"Congrats, man." Savion turned and started to walk away.

"Hold up, Savion. This is too much. I mean, I can buy the land…"

Carver strode up then, smiling. "Nonsense. It's my wedding gift to you, and in our family, we don't turn down generous gifts such as this." He patted him on the shoulder. "Just say thank you, son."

An amazed Devon parroted his new father-in-law. "Thank you, son."

Chuckling, Savion and Carver walked away.

When Hadley returned, she climbed into his lap instead of returning to her own throne. "What's up? Your expression tells me I missed something."

He passed her the deed. "Looks like we have land for my studio."

She covered her mouth, tears springing to her eyes. "Wow."

"Come on, don't cry." He used his thumb to dash away her tears.

She looked into his eyes then. "Stay with me forever, and I won't have any reason to."

He touched her cheek. "It's a deal."

And to seal the arrangement, he pressed his lips to hers.

* * * * *

PLAYING GAMES

MEG MAGUIRE

For my husband – copilot for all my best road trips, bedmate in sketchy, spiderful honeymoon suites.

1

CARRIE LEANED TO one side, stealing a glance at the line's progression—or lack thereof. Seemed as if it hadn't moved in ten minutes or more.

One of the clerks behind the rental car counter boomed, "Again, any customers with reservations, please move to the right-hand line. Everyone else, please stay to the left, and we'll do our best to accommodate you."

Carrie willed her heart to slow, but it was looking grim. Her Sacramento–Portland flight wasn't the only one to get canceled. The unusual ice-and-wind storm that had hit western Oregon was laughable by Midwest standards, but it was more than enough to grind the under-prepared region to a halt. Everyone in this line had the same idea—screw waiting for the next available flight north. That could take a day or more. Instead, rent a car and drive an all-nighter, whatever it took to get home for Christmas morning.

There were businessmen in the queue, ones who probably had kids looking forward to their arrival as much as they did any gift from Santa. There were families, too, like the young mom a couple spots ahead of Carrie, with a toddler flopped unconscious on her chest, chubby cheek on her shoulder. There was Carrie, who didn't have kids to see, but whose younger brother, Shawn, was due to pull into the Grafton Amtrak station the following lunchtime. She wasn't going to miss greeting him for the world, waving from the platform beside their mom and dad. She hadn't seen Shawn in over two years. Not since she'd hugged him goodbye before he'd shipped out for his second tour in Afghanistan. Normally, sure, she'd defer to the people with kids to get home to. But she needed this car as badly as any of them.

One person who *didn't* need a car so badly, she imagined, was the guy in front of her. She hadn't seen his face, but he was probably her age—thirtyish—and he was single or at least childless. She knew because she'd listened to his phone call when she'd gotten in line half an hour earlier. He'd greeted his mother, explained that his flight had been nixed and that he'd call when he had an update. That was that. No, "Tell the kids I'll get there as soon as I can." No follow-up call to the wife. If anything, he'd sounded tired and cranky, his entire aura transmitting that his trip was one-hundred-percent obligatory.

You, Carrie thought, glaring at his neck above his smoky-smelling black hoodie, *should spend the night in the airport if they run out of cars. Let the people who want to get home be on their merry way.*

She studied his short dark hair, trying to find fault with it. No luck. Or with the olive duffel bag slung over his shoulder, but that reminded her of her brother, so no criticism there. With his butt in those jeans... Damn, no issues with that, either.

Finally, the line progressed a space. The mother and co-matose toddler stepped up to the counter, which put Carrie within striking distance right after the grump. Thank *God.* She couldn't stand keeping still. It was a wonder she hadn't been labeled ADHD in grade school. Instead, her mom had diagnosed her with a severe case of ants-in-the-pants and signed her up for peewee athletics. She'd gone to the state championships for track and field her junior and senior years, and had gotten a scholarship for it, too. So, hey, good as medication. What she'd give for a jog bra right now... Though, God knew what the TSA would do with random women caught running laps through the terminal to save their sanity.

"Next," called the clerk, and the grump stepped to the counter.

"Whatever you've got," the man said.

"What we've got is exactly one car," the clerk replied, typing.

Carrie's heart stopped.

"Hope you like subcompacts," the clerk added with a smile, and Carrie surged forward on a wave of desperation.

"Wait! Hi, sorry," she said, half to the clerk and half to the grump. "There's only one car left?"

Murmurs rose behind her from the dozen or more people still trapped in line.

Seeming to steel herself, the clerk told the crowd firmly, "That's correct. There is only one car left. I suggest you all try the Avis counter. They may still have vehicles."

"When is the next car due to be returned?" someone called.

"The Avis counter," repeated the clerk gruffly. "I'm sorry. The cancellations have created a volume we're not equipped to deal with."

This invited more grumbling, but also the scuffing of shoes as many hurried away to try their luck in the other rental car queue. Carrie didn't bother. She had line fatigue. She was punchy. She was righteous, and this guy did *not* deserve the last car.

"Can you check again?" she asked, standing right beside him as if they were a couple. She didn't look at his face, but she could guess he was miffed. "Please," she said. "I *have* to get home by tomorrow morning."

"Don't we all," muttered the clerk, and she swiveled the computer monitor, tapping a little box in the upper corner that read, *Vehicles in reserve: 0.* "I'm sorry, ma'am, but we're all out."

Carrie turned to the grump and was met by hazel eyes—brownish gold—and black stubble. She was zapped by a weird recognition, one she couldn't place. He was freaky handsome, though. Was she bickering with someone famous? Right now, she couldn't manage to care.

"I'll give you a hundred dollars," she told him. "Please. A hundred bucks for that car."

"Ma'am," began the clerk, probably about to point out some bribery law Carrie was trying to violate. But whatever the woman said next went unheard, as the grump's brows drew together and he said, "Carrie?"

"Excuse me?"

"Carrie Baxter."

She blinked. "Yes. Do I know you?"

Something went dark in his eyes at that, and he probably would have frowned if his expression wasn't already thoroughly sour. She studied him, and there was that spark of familiarity again. She definitely hadn't slept with him. She'd remember sleeping with someone this handsome. With those cheekbones and black brows, and intense eyes. Oh, shit. Wait. Those eyes.

A surprised "Daniel" fell from her lips.

Daniel Barber. Oh Lord, her high school boyfriend's best friend. Her line-up mate for much of school until Andrea Batagglia had moved to town their sophomore year and wedged herself between them alphabetically. Jesus, he looked as broody and annoyed as he had as a teenager. And as unapologetic as the day he'd destroyed her relationship.

"Are you going home?" he asked. "To Grafton?"

"Yeah." Oh, hey… "Are you?"

"Yep."

Oh—*hey!* Oh, no. Eight hours in a car with Daniel Barber, probably longer if the roads were icy.

"Two hundred dollars?" she ventured.

"Let's just…carpool." He said it stiffly, his tone suggesting that had there been extra cars, there was no way in hell he'd have made the offer.

And did she have a choice, really? Hours in a car with the grown-up version of the ill-tempered boy who'd intimidated her in high school, scowling every time she interrupted him and her ex when they'd been talking about dude crap. Who'd smiled at her maybe twice in their entire twelve years of overlapping, small-town education. Who'd smoked beneath the bleachers during her track practices, those hazel eyes finding her through the steps and beaming the coldest mix of judgment and ambivalence. He'd played bass in her ex's awful band, too, shooting her dirty looks when she sat in on their practices. Figured. The attitudinally challenged burn-out and the overachieving jock girl—different species back then. Back when he'd dismantled her relationship, ostensibly for the sport of it.

But now, more than a dozen years later, they were just strangers. Two thirtysomethings headed in the same direction, both wanting only to get home for Christmas.

"Fine," she said. "That'd be good. We can take turns driving." And sleeping. That way, they'd never have to talk.

Daniel turned back to the clerk and continued the trans-action, and Carrie offered her driver's license so she could be covered by the insurance. Just like that, she was bound to the man who'd made her teenage years especially awkward.

Daniel Barber, with the king-size chip on his shoulder. Daniel Barber, who'd never once cast her a glance that wasn't adversarial or at least annoyed.

Daniel Barber, who'd driven a wedge between her and her first love, inspiring Matt to break her heart two days before their senior prom.

He was the scourge of her youth and now the harbinger of awkward road trips.

Though, goddamn, she thought, stealing a final glance at that stern face. The bad boy had blossomed into one stun-ning grown-ass man.

2

"SERIOUSLY?" DANIEL ASKED, standing before their rental in the near-empty lot.

The car was tiny. And girly. An eggnog-colored Fiat 500. Under any other circumstances, Carrie would have been delighted, but there was a reason it was the last vehicle to get rented. Taking this little gumdrop of a car into an ice storm wasn't the smartest move.

But *smart* was a luxury that neither of them could afford at the moment.

"It's cute," she said in its defense.

"Let's enter the Iditarod with a team of weenie dogs while we're at it."

"Shut up before you hurt its confidence." She grabbed the key from his hand and unlocked the trunk to stow their bags. "I'll drive first. I want to get this thing figured out before the roads turn sketchy."

Daniel seemed fine with this, obediently heading for the passenger side. He moved his seat back and settled in while Carrie familiarized herself with the controls.

"Buckle up," she said, and then the road trip was on. "Here." She handed him her phone. "Open the map thinger and see if you can program Grafton in."

"No." He set it in the cup holder between them.

"Yes," she said, and shot him a look as she pulled the car out of the lot. "I'm not getting lost in the middle of a freak storm because you think you know the way."

"And I'm not spending the next five hundred-plus miles listening to some robot tell us to stay on I-5 North."

"Tell me how to *find* I-5, then, genius."

He pointed to a sign that very conveniently, very annoyingly appeared as the road curved.

She frowned. "Fine. But I get to pick the radio station." And once they'd merged onto the freeway, she scanned for the perkiest, pop-iest one she could find, just to punish him.

"You're way bossier than I remember," Daniel said.

She considered it. Yes, she was acting a touch pushy. Preemptively, because she was poised for him to do the same. To be all brusque and tactless. To be Daniel Barber, basically.

"People change a lot in thirteen years," she told him. And in more ways than simply becoming devastatingly handsome. Not that she even cared.

"Did you go to our ten-year reunion?" he asked.

"I did." And though it had been more than a decade since she'd last seen Daniel, she'd mingled and danced with her heart throbbing in her throat the entire evening, wondering if he'd show. And if she'd still be livid with him. Was she livid with him now? No, not really. It wasn't as if she and Matt had been destined for wedding bells. All they'd probably been destined for was a half-assed attempt at a long-distance romance when college started, then a breakup that would've ruined both of their Christmas breaks. A mercy, in the end, although *so* not Daniel's place to instigate.

"Did Matt go?" he asked.

"Yeah."

"You guys rekindle your little high school romance?" he asked, a snide edge to the question.

Oh, you mean the two-and-a-half-year, most formative relationship of my life? That you ruined, by telling Matt God knows what horrible lie about me? That old thing?

"We did not," she said coolly. "We danced a few times, but he's married now with a toddler. Do you guys not talk anymore?"

"Facebook's not really my thing."

"Are telephones your thing?" she countered. "Because Matt's vocal cords were working just fine."

She heard him hiss a little sigh through his nose. That sound brought back memories. If the man ever released a fragrance, she knew precisely what to name it: Derision by Daniel Barber.

"He seems really happy," she said. "I met his wife and she's very nice. They only live ten miles from his parents."

"She cute?"

"His wife? Yeah, she's pretty."

"Was that weird for you?"

Ugh. Why did he have to be so exactly like himself even after thirteen years? So mean, always angling to make people uncomfortable?

"No, it wasn't. There's nothing weird about a guy I dated marrying somebody else ages after we broke up. No matter how attractive she is."

"Even though he's the one who dumped you?"

She gritted her teeth. "Why do you ask? Are you making notes for yourself on how human emotions work?" God knew he could use them. She glanced to the side to find him smiling to himself in the faint glow of the dash display. Oh, he had emotions all right. All the jerky ones like smugness and scorn and self-satisfaction.

"Are you still angry about whatever it was you found so repugnant about me back then?" she asked. "Whatever it was that inspired you to convince Matt to dump me?"

Could loyalty actually be on his short list of acceptable feelings?

"Just making conversation." Christ, he didn't even bother denying being the catalyst.

She turned up the radio.

AFTER TWO HOURS of uneventful travel, Carrie pulled off the freeway near Red Bluff. "I'll do another hundred miles, but I need a pit stop."

"Suit yourself."

She pulled the car into a gas station. Daniel topped off the tank while Carrie got a coffee and stretched her legs. She watched him through the store's front window, that familiar person standing beside the little car, his attention on the pump's meter. In all the ways that counted, he hadn't seemed to change. Same attitude issues, same callous sense of so-called humor. But the packaging was new. A little taller, a good deal broader. She could make out the planes of his chest beneath the jacket, and he'd filled out in the legs and hips. And butt. He was a man now, but still dragging around the same teenage boy's baggage.

Same eyes, too. She squeezed her own shut, feeling a headache brewing.

And the saddest part was there'd been a time when he'd kept her up nights. When her body had positively hummed with curiosity over his, back when she'd still been with Matt. She'd considered breaking things off over it, thinking herself a monster for being attracted to her sweetheart's best friend. What kind of girl *did* that?

She'd had it all wrong, she knew now. All that attraction had indicated was that she'd been a horny teenager. Carrie hadn't understood the difference between romantic longing and plain old sexual infatuation then. Lust—that's what she'd felt for Daniel. And she'd read too much into it, let it gnaw at her until it had soured into guilt and nearly driven her to break up with Matt, before he'd ultimately beaten her to it.

When she climbed back behind the wheel, she resolved to pinpoint something redeeming about Daniel. She refused to believe she could have lusted so intensely for this guy if she hadn't sensed *something* intrinsically worthy in him.

Once she'd gotten them back on I-5, she turned down the radio and hazarded more small talk.

"Well, I guess neither of us lives in Sacramento, otherwise we'd be making this trip in our own cars. Where's home for you these days?"

"Coalinga."

"Is that near Fresno?"

"More or less. You still in San Francisco?"

How about that? He'd actually returned her conversational serve.

"I am," she said. "Sunset."

Funny, he'd remembered where she'd moved for school. Then again, the number of things she remembered about him was embarrassing. *Like the way his old jacket smelled.* She'd found that gray hoodie tossed over a chair in the kitchen of Matt's parents' house. He and Daniel and the rest of the band had been practicing in the basement. She'd given in to the urge and had brought the jacket's collar to her nose and breathed him in. She'd caught a hint of cigarettes but other things, too. The curious scent of young manhood, kind of like Matt's, but different.

It had made her wonder if he'd taste different than Matt if she kissed him. It had made her wonder a lot of things that had left her feeling guilty. That curiosity had put her on the road to realizing that, counter to what the fairy tales and romantic movies suggested, loving one person didn't stop you from craving another.

Of course she'd wondered what her attraction to Daniel had meant. Had it meant she didn't love Matt? Or had the fact that Matt hadn't been able to hold her attention been proof that something about her love had been faulty or selfish? He'd been so much *nicer* than Daniel, after all. So much more lovable.

"What kind of degree did you end up earning?" Daniel asked after a couple minutes of silence.

"Business."

"You put it to much use?" he asked. She couldn't tell if he was being snarky again, though no doubt he held business-people in contempt. He was probably a clerk at the country's last surviving record store. Or a professional heckler, something that played to his primary talent—douchiness.

"I manage a climbing gym," Carrie told him.

"Come again?"

"You know, those places where you can do indoor rock climbing. Best in the Bay Area," she chirped, mimicking the TV ads. "With a sixty-five-foot roof and over seventy routes for all skill levels!"

"Weird."

"Yeah, a bit. But it pays pretty well and they let me try new things. It's a good chance to make contacts, too, since I'd like to start my own business someday. Plus, now I've got really good arms, and there's always lots of shirtless men hanging around. As it were."

He didn't even sniff that bait.

The chatter was flagging, so she asked, "Do you still play bass?"

"Nah."

"That's a shame. You were the only half-decent one in the band."

"*Half-decent* hardly equals an artistic calling. I only ever really did that as an excuse to hang out at Matt's, anyway."

She pondered that. She'd always suspected his home life had been less than idyllic. Those suspicions had become starker as she'd grown up, met new friends with dysfunctional families and had come to realize exactly how awful some childhoods could be. Toward the end of high school Daniel had lived with his grandma, which had seemed like a red flag. Maybe she'd find the nerve to pry in the next however many hours of driving.

The conversation lagged for a long time. Carrie caught

herself squinting, her contacts growing sticky and her eyes strained. "I hate night-driving."

"I'll take over."

"That might be smart." The closer they drew to the Oregon border, the gustier it got. "I'll keep going till we're near Shasta."

They made the switch a half hour later, and just in time. Carrie's headache was intensifying, the caffeine leaving her dried out and dim-witted. She sighed as Daniel merged them back onto the freeway, the end nowhere in sight. "We should both be in Grafton by now. And I should be on my second glass of wine with my mom, staring at the Christmas tree."

Daniel didn't volunteer his own plans, and she tried to guess what they might be. She'd never been inside his parents' place—a dumpy little house on the outskirts of town with a steadily rusting hot rod parked on the side lawn. The kind of place where people stocked twenty-four packs of beer and argued a lot. *Merry Christmas from the Barbers.*

"Did your dad ever fix that car that was always sitting in your yard?"

"No. He never finishes anything."

"Do they still live in that same house, by the pond?" she asked.

"Yeah."

"Is that where you're staying?"

A light drizzle had begun to fall, and Daniel switched on the wipers. "No, at my grandma's house. My mom was supposed to pick me up from Portland and drop me there. I'm sure she's happy the storm's saved her trip."

"Grandma's house… Now I'm picturing you sipping tea and eating homemade cookies."

"My grandma's not that wholesome, though she does bake good cookies."

"Frosted with sprinkles?"

He shook his head. "Gingerbread."

"Hot toddies?"

After a pause. "I don't drink."

"Oh." Interesting.

"Not for a few years now, anyway."

"Do you have issues with it or…?"

Another curt, "Yeah."

"Like addiction?"

He laughed softly. "No. More like it turns me into an even bigger asshole than I usually am."

"Ah." A corner of Carrie's heart softened to hear him admit he was a jerk. "Well, that's a good reason to abstain. I like what a glass of wine does to me. Gives my brain permission to quit overthinking stuff for a couple hours."

He smiled faintly, eyes on the road. "You were funny drunk."

"Oh, God. I don't drink like that—like I did at those parties."

Amateur hour, for sure. Who knew how dumb she'd looked to sober outsiders. To Daniel. She remembered a party at one of the popular kids' houses, drinking a couple too many tumblers of Sprite and vodka, and Daniel showing up late in the festivities, grudgingly at Matt's insistence. He'd been sober. She'd been drunk. She remembered sitting on the floor, giggling at something or other. Some people had been playing a video game and Daniel had crouched beside her. She couldn't recall what she'd said to him, but more than a decade later she knew his response word for word.

You're super wasted, aren't you? He'd said it with a little smile, a glimmer that she'd taken for true fondness amid the teasing. Not that her judgment could have been trusted. He'd probably been mocking her.

She told him now, "I've graduated to beer and wine—and moderation—since then. You still smoke," she added.

Daniel shook his head.

She laughed. "You think I can't smell you?"

"I quit when I was twenty-two."

"High time you washed your— Shit, look out!" A large delivery truck was fishtailing in the slow lane.

Daniel scanned left and merged, giving the truck room to right itself. "Jesus." He sounded rattled.

"Black ice must be forming already." She put a hand to her pounding heart, checking the side mirror and finding the truck stable again. "Nice maneuvering there, Barber."

After a minute, he asked, "What were you saying about me needing to wash something?"

"Your jacket. You kinda reek."

"It's from my job." His tone had changed, tinged with a little defensiveness. Would wonders never cease?

"Jeez, what do you do? Bouncer?" It was the only job she could think of that involved standing around soaking up people's secondhand smoke.

"I'm on a wildfire crew."

She blinked. "Oh."

"This jacket was stuffed in the same bag as the last shirt I worked in," he said, sniffing his sleeve. "Forgot about it until it was time to head out the door for the airport."

"Wildfire crew," she murmured. "That's very…manly." And very admirable, which didn't quite square.

"It's a job," Daniel said. "Interesting one."

Interesting and *dangerous*. Ah. Putting her finger on it, Carrie had to laugh. "You always did have a death wish. Just like my brother—and he's coming back from Afghanistan tomorrow."

"Shawn's in the service? Damn." Then, after a moment's thought, "I could see that, actually. He was bound for that or pro football."

She smiled, surprised he even remembered her brother's name. "Yeah, whatever gave him permission to put on a uniform and go tearing toward enemy lines. Trust me, I wish he'd made pro. I'd take the concussion risk over the dangers he faces over there any day."

"Sure."

"How do your folks feel about the fire-crew stuff?"

He shrugged. "We don't talk much. They seem fine with it. They're probably impressed I have a job at all."

"What about a girlfriend?" Carrie asked, a lump lodging in her throat. "I don't know how I'd sleep if my boyfriend was out in the middle of that stuff. The news footage is terrifying enough without worrying about someone you know."

"A woman who cares enough to worry about me isn't a problem I'd know much about," Daniel said.

She stared at the swatting wipers, her emotions humming static, caught between two frequencies—sadness and relief. The sadness was novel. Daniel had always been too prickly to inspire sympathy, at least when she'd been younger. The relief was simply alarming. Why on earth should she care if this man was single?

She'd been over him for years—both the lust and the bitterness. And the latter should have ruined the former for good. *Should* have.

He was *still* a prickly jerk.

They lived two hundred miles apart.

She shoved that stuff aside. "How did you get into firefighting?" It seemed like such a cooperative job. So not the Daniel Barber she'd known.

"I did some logging out of high school. Then wound up in the park service for a while, but I didn't really have the people skills for that."

"You don't say!"

He shot her a funny look and Carrie laughed. "Sorry. Too easy."

"Anyhow, I dunno quite how it happened. Saw a crew opening listed someplace or other, and it sounded exciting. Pays good."

"And is it exciting?"

He nodded. "I'll do it till I'm dead."

The way he said that gave her a shiver. That was where his recklessness and her brother's adrenaline addiction varied. Daniel really did have a death wish, she thought. Or, at the very least, a lack of concern for his own safety. He'd always been the kid who'd climb forty feet up a tree and turn a sixth-grade field trip into a scene. Always diving off the trestle or driving too fast or picking fights with grown men for the sport of it.

"From chopping trees into timber to trying to keep them from burning up," she mused.

"That's me."

Was it? They'd known each other since kindergarten. How come Carrie didn't feel as if she understood this man at all?

"You're a weird guy, Daniel."

"Don't remember asking your opinion."

"Don't remember you ever caring what anybody thought of you." Least of all Carrie. His best friend's annoying girlfriend, that was all she'd ever been to him. Some grade-grubbing jock girl loitering in the basement during their band practices, probably wrecking the bro vibe.

"You don't get into as many fights as I did if you don't give a shit what people think," Daniel said absently.

She frowned, mulling that over. "That's probably true. I guess maybe I always figured you just *liked* fighting."

"Surprised you thought about me at all."

She spoke carefully. "You were Matt's best friend. And it wasn't exactly lost on me that I never had your endorsement."

"You got that part wrong," Daniel said. "You and Matt were perfect for each other."

She sensed something mean coming, some jab that proclaimed both her and Matt equally boring or upstanding or overachieving.

"Go on," she said. "Go ahead and qualify that statement."

"Qualify it? It's true. You guys deserved each other."

"And…?" She twirled her hand. "Because I know for a fact Matt dumped me because you told him to."

"And nothing," he said, shrugging. "He was a good guy. You were a nice girl. And I never told him to dump you."

"Well, you told him something. He said so. He said you guys had a long talk and he realized he had to end things. So forgive me if I assumed you were going to say something mean just now."

"Give me long enough, I probably will."

She sighed, headache reasserting itself. "Four hundred miles to go."

3

DANIEL EYED THE intensifying rain with worry. Rain for now, but the farther north they went, the colder it'd get. This water would be ice and snow before long, and he didn't have a ton of faith in their little wind-up rental.

The highway was quiet, and small wonder. Only the desperate and dumb were out driving in this. The smart people were comfortable indoors sipping eggnog with their loved ones, or whatever it was nice people did for the holidays. Like he'd know. He hadn't celebrated Christmas in six years, probably.

If it was only him along for this ride, he'd have downed a few Red Bulls and powered through the trip, getting there as quickly as possible. But sliding sideways off the road and trapping Carrie with him all night.... The drive was punishment enough for her, surely.

He didn't even want to be making this trip. He wouldn't be if his grandma hadn't called him directly and demanded he come.

This is probably my last Christmas, she'd told him. She was eighty-two and she wasn't a dramatic woman. If she thought this was her final winter, he believed her. *And there's only one thing I'm asking for—everybody to get along for one lousy day. Put aside whatever hurt feelings there are for twelve hours. Suck it up and give me a nice Christmas to remember you all by, wherever I'm headed next.*

He hadn't needed to think twice about it. If that was what she wanted, that was what he'd do. He'd hug the parents he couldn't care less about, swallow his resentment, ignore whatever bait came his way once his dad got toasted, stay away from alcohol himself and keep his cool. For his grandma. He owed her. And he loved her, which he couldn't say about anyone else in the world. Who knew what would've become of him if she hadn't taken him in for his last two years of high school. Probably would've flipped his shit and wound up in juvie or jail if he'd been forced to stay at home.

So, yeah. Whatever Grandma wanted, Grandma would get.

He eyed Carrie, wondering how many people *she* loved. Probably a hundred. And probably they all loved her right back. He didn't even envy whatever happy, homey Christmas she had waiting for her in Grafton. Like he'd even know how to enjoy all that niceness and love and crap. He was allergic to sincerity.

He remembered watching a documentary about the real-life Horse Whisperer and getting that suffocating feeling in his chest. Whatever that emotion was, he didn't even know. He hated feeling touched by things; always felt as if he was choking on something. He avoided interacting with puppies and ducklings and babies. Adorable things made him feel vulnerable, like if he held a baby, it would sense the rottenness in him and start crying, and probably need therapy for the rest of its life. Any time a coworker forwarded an email about a firefighter rescuing an animal, Daniel immediately deleted it. Couldn't risk the sensation. Like a sucker punch to the heart.

The last time he'd cried had been four years ago when one of his colleagues had died in a wildfire outside Yosemite. The reaction had freaked him out so much that he'd had a panic attack and had been rushed to the hospital for shock.

Never again.

Though, God help him when his grandma really did pass away.

In the passenger seat, Carrie was leaning against the window, using a folded sweater as a pillow. He wondered if she was asleep.

He wondered if she still snored.

He wondered if she still used the same shampoo she had in high school, the one that had made her hair smell like strawberries.

Daniel jumped when she spoke, breaking over an hour of perfect peace. "It's after midnight."

"Yeah."

"Merry Christmas, Daniel."

"Oh, right. You, too."

"You can change the station if you want."

He'd forgotten it was even on. The ads and pop music had faded into the droning swish of the wipers. He switched it off.

"It's really coming down." Carrie sat up straight, balling her sweater in her lap. She was right. The drops had turned to slushy flakes. This wouldn't end well. Western Oregon was useless with snow and ice, unequipped to handle either. Three or four inches of snow could shut down a whole county for days.

"If it gets too shady to risk, we'll find a motel," he offered. Hopefully there'd be vacancies, with most people already at their destinations.

"Or a manger," Carrie joked. "In case my virgin birth kicks off early." She rubbed the sweater bulge in her lap.

Daniel smirked at that, then stifled a stupid little pang of jealousy. He knew beyond the shadow of a doubt that she wasn't a virgin. He'd gone camping with her, Matt and another friend once, and had suffered through noises evidencing that fact. He didn't *care* if she was a virgin, her or any other woman. Didn't care what intimate things his best friend had been privy to about Carrie Baxter, not the feel of her body, the smell or taste of her excitement, or the words she'd whispered in the dark tent. Totally. Did not. Care. At all.

Christ, you're such a creep.

IN TIME, THE late hour began to assert itself. Daniel would have berated himself for not napping while Carrie had been driving, but there was no chance he would have succeeded, anyhow. Too shell-shocked, finding himself in this situation— closed in this tiny car with the girl it had taken him so long to get over. It had been three years after graduation before he'd quit thinking about her. Quit dreaming about her. Quit conjuring up her face in less polite moments—which had taken a concerted, cold-turkey effort. Three years, even though he'd never even kissed her, never even held her hand. So, yeah, sleep wouldn't be coming tonight.

"Oregon welcomes you," Carrie murmured as they crossed the border. They'd been climbing steadily for a while when the sign appeared on the right, the wind peaking as they neared the summit of Siskiyou.

"Check your fancy phone." Daniel nodded to where it still sat in the cup holder. "See what the weather's doing in the Rogue Valley." Not that knowing would change a thing. There was pretty much one civilized route to take.

"Yikes," she said. "Only one bar."

He stole glances at Carrie's face, lit up by her phone as she typed. She still had amazing skin. Her hair was shorter, with layers and stuff, but she hadn't gone California blonde or anything. She wore it long enough to put in a ponytail; running still shaped her aesthetic, he'd bet.

He'd smoked under the bleachers and watched her at practice, and he'd thought she looked like somebody who'd run right out of their stupid hometown, ponytail swinging as she'd book it to someplace better. He'd always liked that about her, how she'd been pretty enough to be one of the popular girls, only she always wrecked it—no makeup ever, no qualms about being seen all flushed and sweaty in her track clothes, brown hair frizzy from practice and curling at her temples.

"It's thirty-two in Ashland," she said. "Freezing rain but not crazy heavy."

"What about Grants Pass?"

She tapped and waited. "Thirty-four. Heavy rain."

That could get nasty if the temperature dropped much more. And this car was about as surefooted as a hockey puck.

"If it gets worse we really might want to stop until the morning. Until it's light out and the road crews have a chance to do their inadequate best."

Carrie looked alarmed.

"What?" Daniel asked.

She sank back in her seat. "Nothing. You're right. We can't be stupid about it. I just really, *really* didn't want to miss meeting Shawn at the train station."

"Oh, right."

Man, what did it feel like, missing someone? Daniel loved his grandmother, but he wasn't sure if he missed her. She was so woven into the mess of his childhood and adolescence that it was hard to crave a reunion. Plus, a reunion meant going back to Grafton, a place that held very few nice memories and a ton of bad ones. Why didn't he miss Matt? His best friend, whose house Daniel had escaped to who knew how many times, with whom he'd shared a band, as crappy as they'd been. He didn't really *like* the sensation of being known, though. Anyone who'd ever known Daniel well— Matt, his grandma, that one nice guidance counselor—knew he had feelings, and knew what had made him put up walls and push people away. Anyone who knew you also knew how to hurt you.

Daniel hadn't missed Carrie, either. For those few years after graduation, before he'd managed to forget about her, he'd *craved* her, badly. But that was different.

Beside him, she fidgeted, shifting her legs around.

"You okay?"

"Just achy. This always happens during long car trips."

"You never could sit still."

She smiled, he thought. He sensed it in his periphery as he might feel a warm breeze.

"You—" He gasped, control of the car gone in a breath.

Carrie yelped, gripping her seat as they slid at thirty miles an hour straight across the shoulder and along the guardrail. The front passenger side was screaming, metal-on-metal, sparks flashing. With a hammering heart, Daniel pumped the brakes until the car finally came to a stop.

"Oh, God," Carrie said. Beyond the sturdy rail was the black of a drop-off. A deep ditch, not a cliff, but the way Daniel's body was pulsing, it could have been the Grand Canyon.

He gulped a massive breath. "Holy shit."

They'd lost a headlight and the side mirror, but the car was still running, and the dash wasn't blowing up with any truly fatal warnings. Tires, brakes, axels—all apparently were intact.

After a minute filled with nothing but the pulse of adrenaline, Carrie said, "Thank goodness we got insurance."

He was too freaked to laugh, and instead let himself collapse against the steering wheel, overcome with horror and relief and guilt. Christ, he could have gotten her killed.

He sat up straight. "Screw this shit. We're stopping someplace." No more bumper bowling with the guardrails. No more driving for a minute longer than they had to.

He aimed them toward Ashland. Even at a crawl the car slipped often, but not as badly as the first time. It was snowing, but as they neared civilization the temperature rose to just above freezing. The road was suddenly glazed in black ice, the little car losing its traction every few hundred yards and stopping Daniel's heart all over again. Carrie probably couldn't tell, since her hands weren't on the wheel as his were. She also couldn't feel how tired he was, how sluggish his reflexes were in the wake of the adrenaline rush and at the end of a long-ass week. Though winter was typically kinder as wildfires went, they still happened. Daniel had helped battle a nasty one in southwest Nevada three days earlier, and he never slept well the week after an intense job. With the hour now approaching 1:00 a.m., he was starting to feel impaired.

He exited at the next ramp. "We'll get up early," he promised. "Once it's light and the roads have some sand on them. Better to be trapped in motel rooms than in a tiny car on the side of the road in the middle of nowhere."

"Fair enough."

"Want to see what your phone says there is for motels around here?"

"Sure."

"Oh, wait. I see one." The familiar logo glowed through the drizzle and fog like a beacon.

"That was easy."

Only it wasn't. No Vacancy, read the neon sign. Daniel pulled into the lot anyway. He parked under the awning, grateful that at least they wouldn't break their necks slipping on the icy asphalt.

"Down one eye and one ear," Carrie said sadly, surveying the car's light and mirror and patting its hood. "Poor thing."

"Better it than us." He headed for the door and the front desk.

"Sorry, we're full up," the woman on duty said with an overdone, patronizing frown. "Lots of travelers got stranded on their way north."

"Are there any other places nearby?" Carrie asked.

"Yeah, two—but the La Quinta's full. We called before sending some other folks over there. Last I knew, there were still a few rooms at the Evergreen. That's about three miles east on this same road."

"Thanks," Carrie said. "We'll try there."

Even after just a five-minute stop, the roads had become worse. They were practically laminated in ice, and no sand trucks were to be seen.

"Jesus," Daniel muttered. "Only thing that could make this road slicker is a Zamboni. This place better have rooms."

"Fingers cross—"

The car slipped dramatically on a diagonal, front tires

seeking the shoulder. Daniel wrestled back control and slowed them to ten miles an hour.

After a seeming eternity, the cheap sign for the Evergreen Motor Inn finally appeared down the road. If there weren't any rooms, driving anyplace else wasn't an option. They might just have to beg to rest in the lobby for a few hours until the road crews could do their thing.

"Vacancy sign's lit," Carrie said hopefully. Once they parked she took her suitcase out of the trunk. Daniel followed suit. He nearly wiped out on the ice as he slammed the trunk, and Carrie almost fell trying to catch him. Somehow or other, they both stayed vertical, then skate-shuffled their way to the motel office.

"Merry Christmas," Carrie called when the clerk looked up from her computer.

"And a Merry Christmas to you both. You two sure are intrepid."

"Please tell me you've got rooms," Carrie said, setting her bag before the desk.

"You're in luck! Exactly one left."

Daniel's eyebrows rose to perfectly mirror Carrie's.

"Okay," Carrie said. "Now please tell me it's got double beds."

A shifty smile. "You two not together?"

They both shook their heads emphatically.

"Sorry, just the one bed. It's a big bed, though," said the clerk. "Honeymoon suite."

Daniel shot Carrie a dry look. Christ almighty, now there was a cosmic joke.

"We'll take it," she said. Only choice they had. Daniel gave the clerk his credit card.

"Honeymoon suite comes with a complimentary bottle of wine," the woman announced.

"I don't drink," Daniel said stiffly, but Carrie grinned.

"More for me."

They were handed a key card and a chilled bottle of white.

"Ooh, Willamette Valley," Carrie read off the label.

"Oh, and this," the clerk said and passed Daniel a coupon for ten dollars off a couple's massage at a spa down the road. He forced a smile for the clerk's sake.

"I can't figure out if this is awkward or hilarious," Carrie said as they made their way gingerly across the slick walkway to the one-story motel's farthest room.

"It's lucky," Daniel said, caught by a rare moment of gratitude. "We get to sleep someplace, which is more than the next person to pull in can say."

"True."

Carrie unlocked their door and they finally left the ice rink behind.

"Jeez, it smells like your jacket in here." She set down her bag. "Clearly people don't take the no-smoking rule seriously."

"Probably distracted by all the consummation. Yikes." Daniel looked around. Pretty big room and, cigarette-stink or not, it was heated and looked passably clean. The bed was gigantic, done up in a tacky peach satin comforter with a couple of heart-shaped pillows to round out the farce. He tossed his duffel bag by the door and pulled the curtains shut. Yellow light from the parking lot slipped through the gaps.

"Oh, my God," Carrie said, the final word gobbled up by laughter. "Come here." She was in the far corner, standing before a large pink hot tub.

"Oh, Jesus. Is it heart-shaped?"

She clapped. "It *is!* And that's not all."

He came to stand by her side, ignoring the little rush he felt as their arms brushed. Perfectly centered in the bottom of the tub was a dead black spider, big as a dime.

"Our marriage isn't going to survive this, is it?" he asked.

Carrie punched his shoulder. That chiding little smack affected him the way a tender kiss might.

He was his teenage self again in a flash. She touched me. On purpose.

"Who puts a hot tub in a carpeted room?" he asked.

"The Evergreen Motor Inn, that's who."

He spent a minute leaning over the edge of the tub and blowing on the spider to make sure it really was dead, and Carrie wandered away.

"If we wake up to find it mysteriously missing," he said, straightening, "this honeymoon will be an official success."

She didn't reply. He turned to find her sitting on the edge of the king-size bed, her phone at her ear.

"Mom? Hi. Sorry to call so late. Bad news—we had to stop for the night. The roads are insane down here…. Near Ashland. We're going to wait until they've put some sand down in the morning….I know, but I'm still frustrated. I really wanted to be there to meet Shawn…. Uh-huh…."

Feeling misplaced, as he always did in the presence of familial affection, Daniel headed to the bathroom and shut the door. He stared at himself in the light of the too-bright bulbs above the mirror. How on earth was this happening? How, after thirteen years, was he suddenly spending the night with Carrie Baxter? And *so* not under any circumstances he might have fantasized about when he'd been sixteen, eighteen, twenty.

Is she single? He hadn't had the balls to ask, even after she'd posed a similar question to him. His stubborn, defensive self wasn't programmed to admit that he gave a shit—not about anything. *Especially* not about Carrie's personal life, something that he'd never be a part of.

He wet a washcloth with cold water and scrubbed his face. The lighting made him look about eighty. Not that he cared how he looked.

Goddamn it, he did care, though. Cared more than he had since this woman had last been a part of his daily life, whether she'd realized it or not. Now he had to share a bed with her.

It didn't matter that they'd likely keep on all their clothes. It would still haunt him deeper and longer than any sex he'd ever had. No doubt about that.

Daniel was broken when it came to sex. He'd never once felt close to any of the women he'd taken to bed. He'd felt grateful maybe, and excited of course. But he'd never felt anything that had made him understand why people seemed to think it was a special, joyous thing to do with another human being. He was okay at the actual mechanics of it, he suspected, but he always felt unbearably awkward the second the sweat cooled, leaving two strangers lying on a rumpled bed surrounded by that sex smell. It was only by the insanity of biology that he got laid, really. If it had been up to his brain, he'd deem it more uncomfortable than it was worth.

And what a wonder you're single.

He left the bathroom, and found Carrie filling a plastic cup with wine.

"Sure you don't want any?" she asked.

"Very." He sat on the rim of the hot tub.

"Your loss. It's screw cap." She took a sip. "Oh, it's nice, actually."

"That coupon the desk lady gave me was for a couple's massage," he said.

"Erotic massage, I trust."

Daniel looked dryly around the room, from the satin pillows to the smoke-scented carpet, to the outmoded tube TV, to the pink fiberglass beneath his thighs. "I think this is erotic enough for me already. Best not to chance a heart attack if it gets any hotter."

She smiled at that and drained her cup.

"Slow down there, champ."

"It's been a long day. You're sure you don't—"

"Yes."

Her eyes narrowed. "If you're an alcoholic, you can just tell me. I won't judge you. In fact, I'll dump the rest of this, if—"

"I'm not."

Like he'd told her, alcohol simply turned him into an ass. Of course, he'd really only drunk on his own or in dive bars, and neither setting had been especially cheerful to begin with. In truth, alcohol probably only had done to Daniel what it did to everyone—saturated his emotional armor until it softened enough to let him feel stuff. He didn't like feeling stuff was all. Made him punchy, like strangers were poking at him. Strangers named vulnerability and sadness. And worst of all, loneliness. He remembered Carrie's little slug on his shoulder, and, without meaning to, palmed the spot.

She poured herself another cup, took a sip and then set it on the nightstand. She flopped back on the massive bed, legs dangling over the edge. He studied the shape of her breasts before he caught himself. *No doubt she doesn't want to be here with you.* Especially not if she knew precisely what he'd said to Matt, to cause their breakup. *At least spare her the perving.*

"I'm gonna shower," he said, and stood to shrug out of his jacket. He cast the spider a backward glance, making sure it hadn't moved. "Keep an eye on our mascot."

"Hang on. I need to get these contacts out." She got up and jogged to her bag, then the bathroom, which she vacated a minute later wearing glasses. She flopped back across the covers as Daniel rummaged for his deodorant and toothpaste.

"Toss me the remote," she said.

He did and then shut himself in the bathroom once more. He stripped his clothes, then the paper wrapper from the bar of soap. A small box caught his eye. Sitting beside the lotion and shampoo bottles was a three-pack of complimentary condoms.

"Rub it in, why don't you?"

Carrie's shout came through the thin door. "What was that?"

"Nothing!"

"There better not be spiders in the shower."

"Nope," he called, tugging the curtain wide. "No spiders. Just some asshole you went to high school with."

Her distant laugh made his body warm.

An "Oooh," came from the room. "Hurry. *Gremlins* is on!"

"Get some sleep, you drunkard." He turned on the tap, drowning out whatever retort would have answered him. He kept the water cold and let it scare away the unnerving, giddy feelings that bantering with Carrie had pitching around in his chest. Stupid crush. Couldn't just stay dead like a hot-tub spider.

They could wind up spending eighteen hours together, yet he'd be stuck waiting to forget about her again for another three years, probably.

Goddamn woman.

Goddamn feelings.

Goddamn Christmas and family and guilt and weather.

And goddamn his heart for aching. Figures it'd pick a freak ice storm to finally thaw again, as broken as it was.

4

DURING A COMMERCIAL, Carrie took advantage of Daniel's absence and changed into yoga pants and a long tee. She tried hard to concentrate on the movie, and not imagine what he might look like in the steaming shower, naked.

It was weird, being around him—the subject of her guilty infatuation at age seventeen, eighteen. She would have expected time to neuter the attraction, the way it had her crushes on the celebrities of the day. But Daniel had matured right along with her taste. Subtle changes to his face marked him as a thirty-one-year-old man, not a teenaged boy. Probably had chest hair, too. And rough hands. Maybe some scars from his work—not burns, hopefully, but interesting scrapes, with interesting stories to match. She sipped her wine, blaming her warming body on the alcohol.

The bathroom fan flared as the door opened, and Daniel emerged wearing the same clothes minus his stinky jacket. He looked way too good in jeans. And his arms looked way too nice in that gray T-shirt. And his hair, wet? Forget it.

"Please tell me that's making you tired," he said, nodding to the cup in her hand. "The point of this sleepover is so we're ready to drive again when it gets light out."

"I thought the point of this sleepover was so we wouldn't die on the icy roads."

He frowned. "That, too."

"It's Christmas. Lighten up." Carrie was lounging on what she'd come to think of as her side of the bed, three pillows piled under her head. Daniel eyed her, then went to his duffel and rooted around before disappearing back inside the bathroom. When he came out he'd swapped his jeans for flannel bottoms.

"Oh," she teased, sitting up. "Now it is *officially* a slumber party."

He rolled his eyes at her before tossing his jeans onto his bag and heading for the other side of the bed. She'd stolen most of the pillows, so he sat up against the awful wicker headboard.

"What sleepover games shall we play?" she asked, and sipped her wine. "Truth or Dare?"

"Sure. I dare you to shut up and get some sleep."

"I dare *you* to be nice to me for twenty minutes."

"I lose."

She smiled sadly at that. "What's your problem, anyway?"

He stared at her.

"I never had the guts to ask you that in high school," she said. "But seriously—why were you such a jerk to everyone?"

He shrugged. "I dunno. Maybe some people are just naturally unpleasant."

"Maybe if you had some of this," she said, and leaned over to grab the wine off the nightstand, "you'd discover you have feelings aside from pissed off and judgmental." She refilled her glass.

He reached over and took the bottle, surprising her. He held it in both hands, resting it between his spread legs. Carrie gave herself a hot second to admire those hands before meeting his eyes.

"Want me to dare you?" she offered.

He rolled his eyes, but wonder of wonders, he tilted the bottle to his lips and took a drink.

"Wow, you're surprisingly susceptible to peer pressure."

He made a face as he swallowed, and tried to hand the wine back, but Carrie wouldn't have it. "Hang on to that. Might help you fall asleep."

"So would shutting off the TV and lights."

A tipsy, mischievous corner of Carrie's brain could think of some other things that might put him to sleep. *Bad girl. Worst.*

"Have you played Never Have I Ever?" she asked.

"No."

"Do you know how to play?"

"No. And I don't want—"

"It's easy. Whoever's turn it is makes a statement, like, 'Never have I ever sky-dived.' And if I said that, I wouldn't have to drink, since I've never sky-dived. But if you have, you *do* have to drink. Basically, you try to say something you *haven't* done that you think the other person has, if you want them to get drunk." Before he could protest, she said, "Never have I ever battled a wildfire."

His eyes rolled ceiling-ward.

"Go on. I know you have."

"You realize we're thirty, right?"

"Thirty-one. But we're also trapped together in this weird-ass thirteen-year high school reunion for the night. Let's be eighteen again."

"Thirteen years," Daniel said through a sigh. "Like cicadas."

"Exactly. Every thirteen years I'll sweep into your life like a plague," she threatened grandly. "And I know you've fought a fire, so drink."

"Only to make this game be over quicker." He took a sip.

"Now you," she prompted. "You say something to make me drink."

"You don't seem to need much motivation."

"I was hoping those jeans were your grumpy pants, but clearly your pajamas have the same issue. Just be fun for ten minutes and do the stupid game."

"Fine. I've never—"

"Never have you ever," she corrected.

"I'm meeting you halfway, okay? I've never come first in a track and field meet."

"Only in one event." She took a drink. "Some of the point

of this game is to find out stuff about each other. So we can't just say stuff we already know the other person's done."

He waved a hand to tell her to get on with it already.

"Never have I ever…" Man, what did she want to know about him? "Been in love." And she drank.

Daniel didn't, only held her stare for a long moment. She was about to tell him it was his turn when he slowly brought the bottle to his lips.

Carrie sat up straight. "Oh, ho! Who was she? Who managed to melt that frosty heart of your—"

"I'm playing the game, okay? Can't that be enough?"

She sank back against the pillows. "Fine. Your turn."

He thought. "I've never lived with anyone. As a couple."

She drank. "It lasted, like, six weeks. Okay…never have I ever saved anyone's life."

His gaze ran away at that, darting around the room. The bottle stayed between his legs and his expression went dark.

"Is that a no?"

"Even if it wasn't, that's not something you acknowledge within the context of a drinking game."

Whoa. Daniel Barber had a serious side. Who knew? Then her heart dropped. What if he'd had the opportunity to save someone's life, but had fallen short of the task? Shit. The gravity of his job hadn't fully registered.

"Okay. Sorry. That was too heavy. Let me think of another one.… Oh, I know. Never have I ever had sex outdoors."

The sternness left his expression, nostrils flaring with a silent laugh—a fond remembrance of an extramural fling? She couldn't feel jealous about that. The humanity inherent in it was too exciting. He drank.

"Your turn," she said.

"Drink," he said, nodding to her glass.

"I haven't had sex outside."

"You and Matt when we went camping in the North Santiam with—what's his name?—Pete Pollard. Junior year spring break."

"What? Matt told you guys?"

"Like he needed to. You two probably scared all the bears away."

She smacked his arm and he laughed, a sound she liked way too much. A sound she wondered if she'd ever heard before.

"Well, that doesn't count anyway," she said. "We were in a tent."

"Drink," he proclaimed, leaning over to top off her dwindling cup.

"Technicality," she grumbled, and took a half sip.

"Shit, I'm already kinda drunk," Daniel said, and then stifled a laugh, if she wasn't mistaken.

"Wow. Cheap date."

"It's been years. I probably have my high school alcohol tolerance back."

"It's adorable. You should drink more often."

He began his turn, probably to change the subject. His cheeks were pink, his eyes bright. "Never have I ever…shit. Um, never have I ever…"

"Just ask a sex question. That's the real point of the game."

"Man, girls are perverted. Uh, never have I ever…done anything with another guy. Or a woman, in your case."

Carrie took a sip, and Daniel's eyes widened. "Long story. Tequila shots. Gay bar. It was just frenching."

"How was it?"

Carrie smiled, making her expression wistful. "She had a crew cut and amazing arms, and a tattoo of a dancing skeleton. And she could kiss, I must admit. Okay, never have I ever…said the wrong name during sex." And she drank.

Daniel stared at her and then began laughing, half-doubled over the bottle.

"Shush. It was really embarrassing."

"With who? And whose name did you say?"

"This guy I dated in college. And I said our RA's name, by mista—"

Daniel just about lost his shit.

She gave him a limp shove. "Shut up. I pled drunkenness."

"Classy. I'm detecting a theme."

"Whatever. You've never done that? Little slip, wrong name pops out?"

He smirked. "Never have I ever been much of a talker in bed."

"Oh, Lord." She took a big slug for that one. "Which apparently you already knew about me."

His smile seemed to soften, and he nodded at her cup. "Your turn."

"Never have I ever met a person I thought I might like to marry. Yet."

Daniel didn't drink. "Never have I ever imagined being a parent."

Carrie took a sip.

"Even though you've never wanted to marry anyone?"

She nodded. "Sure. I'm not saying I want to do it alone, but I'd like to have a kid someday. I can imagine motherhood without picturing the father's face. Or, I can now that I'm over thirty, anyhow. Treacherous ovaries," she grumbled, glaring down at her middle.

"I don't think I could ever imagine that without imagining the marriage, first."

She smiled. "I'm slightly shocked you even believe in marriage."

"Didn't say I did. Hell, I dunno. The wine's working." He took an unsanctioned drink.

"Whose turn is it?" she asked.

"Yours."

She tapped her lips with the rim of the cup. "Never have I ever made a sex tape. That I know about."

Daniel didn't drink. "Never have I ever…had sex with a woman I love."

She frowned, feeling clouded. Feeling confused by that statement, disappointed, sad and strangely relieved. "You said you've been in love, though."

He nodded.

"Oh. Was it unrequited then?"

He drank, seemingly in the affirmative.

She cocked her head. "Was it recent?"

The bottle stayed where it was.

"While ago… Ooh, was it high school?"

He brought the bottle to his lips.

"Oh, wow!"

"Jesus, calm down."

"No way. Okay, let's see… Was it someone in our class?"

Another drink, and the wine was nearly gone.

She dredged her memory for likely girls. Cool, tough ones that fit Daniel. "Was it Michelle Sobiari?"

Nothing.

"Was it one of the burnout girls? Like Amanda Duffy, or that one with the dreadlocks and the ear stretchers?"

More nothing.

"Was it one of the popular girls?"

He hesitated, but didn't drink.

"So not totally *un*popular. Right, who's the exact opposite of you? Oh. Nicole Pelletier? Or the girl who won all the debate things, Jamie something. Or—"

"Jesus Christ, Carrie. Shut *up* already."

She started, taken aback. He'd gone from nearly fun to mean again in a breath, eyes cold. Apparently drinking really did crank his jerk dial to eleven. She shivered.

"Fine. Sorry." Annoyed, she drained her cup and left the bed to toss it in the little trash can next to the bureau. She crouched by the door to unzip her suitcase and dug for her toothbrush and paste.

A word she didn't think she'd ever heard Daniel say drifted softly through the room behind her. "Sorry."

"It's not like you didn't warn me." She shut off the TV on her way to the bathroom. "I'm setting my alarm for six."

"Carrie."

She took a deep breath and then turned to meet his stare. What on earth had she expected? That they'd bond or something? "It's fine. Sorry I upset you. I thought we were having fun…and you're really hard to read."

"I know."

"Let's just get some sleep. You want some water, so you don't wake up totally hung over?"

A pause. "Sure. Please."

She went into the bathroom and peeled the plastic off one of the cups by the taps. She filled it and padded back into the main room, finding Daniel sitting at the end of the bed, hands clasped between his knees. He accepted the cup. "Thanks."

"Sure. My fault if you wake up feeling gross, really."

She was about to step away when his warm, rough fingers circled her wrist. Her heart stopped. Limply, she tried to tug her hand away. "What?"

"I'm not sure if I'm drunk or not," he said, holding her stare. "But I'm going to say I am and blame this on the wine."

"Blame what on—"

"It was you. I was in love with you. In high school."

A deep numbness consumed her body from soles to crown, chased by a hum of rushing chemicals—hormones or adrenaline, she couldn't say which. "You what?"

He let go of her wrist. "You heard me."

"I don't care. Say it again."

"I was in love with you."

"But you hated me. Didn't you?"

"I hated everything *but* you. And Matt," he allowed, breaking their eye contact.

"Whoa."

"Like I said, I'm probably drunk."

"That's...okay. I need to.... Excuse me." She turned, marched to the bathroom and shut herself inside.

5

"IDIOT. IDIOT, IDIOT, IDIOT." Daniel thumped his forehead with the butts of his fists. Rubbed his temples. Stared at his bare feet on the mangy carpet. Christ, if only he could leave. Except stranding Carrie in the middle of the Rogue Valley in an ice storm was definitely more of a jerk move than making her uncomfortable with the world's most awkward love proclamation.

Past tense. He'd told her he'd loved her in high school. And that was true, right? He didn't love her now. Drinking games aside, he didn't know her now. So, how could he—

He froze, watching the bathroom door open and the light inside go dark. He stayed where he sat at the end of the bed, unable to move. She didn't look at him, just walked to her side and tossed one of the hoarded pillows back to his.

"Sorry," he offered, speaking mainly to the hot tub, perhaps the spider. He wasn't brave enough to meet her eyes.

She said nothing at first, stoically folding her glasses and setting them on the nightstand. "That was ages ago… Though, tell me this. Was that why Matt left me? Did you tell him something awful to get him to dump me, thinking I'd run to you instead?"

He huffed a soft laugh. "Yeah. Like you would've ever left him for me."

"What did you say to him, Daniel?"

He swallowed, throat aching. "I told him I thought I was in love with you."

A pause. "And what did he say?"

"I don't want to tell you."

Her smile was dry. "Well, consider it the fine you owe me for making everything awkward."

"At first…we fought. Almost physically. And I told him I knew you'd never want to be with me over him. That I'd only told him because it was eating away at my insides. I felt like, how could I feel all this for my best friend's girlfriend? I'm such a shit. Maybe I wanted him to take a swing at me. I thought, maybe, that'd make going our separate ways after high school easier—him to college, me to whatever. If we ended it on a fight, I could tell myself I didn't care."

"So, why'd he dump me?"

His heart twisted, throat dry and sore, and he spoke to his hands. "He was going to dump you anyway after graduation. That's what he told me after it happened, when I asked if I'd fucked it all up for you guys."

"Oh."

"We had that big blowup, and I guess maybe he felt shitty after, for dragging it out with you. Or maybe guilty, because what I felt for you… It had faded, for him. I don't know. But it sure as hell wasn't to free you up to date me. Neither of us believed for a second you'd ever want that."

She was silent, and he found the nerve to turn and make eye contact. He couldn't read her face, for once. Normally, it was easy. Whatever she felt was written right there. Happy, sad, angry, embarrassed. But the chalkboard was blank.

Whatever she's feeling, it can't be great.

He stood and skirted the bed, and stretched out on his side on top of the covers.

"You'll be cold like that."

He shrugged, shoulders swishing over cheap satin.

Carrie switched off the lamp, and they laid for ten minutes or more in a pathetic charade of sleep. He could hear her breathing as surely as she could hear him. Neither was anywhere close to relaxed. Didn't help that he was all punchy from the sugar, head spinning slightly from the alcohol. Coherent thoughts were about as easy to catch a hold of as gnats.

In barely a whisper, she asked, "Are you awake?"

"Of course I am."

"What are you feeling?"

"I dunno. I never know what I'm feeling. Stupid, maybe. Or creepy. What are you feeling? Pissed?"

"It was thirteen years ago. I don't know that I feel much of anything except surprised. And relieved."

"Oh?"

"I always imagined you must have told him some nasty lie about me or something."

"Never. There's nothing nasty to be said about someone like you."

"That's one man's opinion. But, in all honesty, I think it's kind of sweet."

Daniel sighed. So the last thing he wanted to hear. That his only experience loving a woman was quaint and adorable. Plus it *hadn't* been sweet. Who lusted and ached after their best friend's girlfriend? It had been ugly, made him feel shitty and jealous and wound up and crazy. And, at times, euphoric. The nice-feelings equivalent of the rush he got standing in the path of a wildfire. "Great."

"I had feelings for someone in high school, too."

"Duh."

"Not Matt," she said evenly. "Someone else. While I was with Matt."

"Oh. Wish I'd known that then. Might've wrecked my crush on you."

"It ate me alive, too. I kept waiting for it to go away, but it never did. I felt so guilty about it, that Matt was so great, yet he didn't seem right. Or like, enough. I almost broke up with him, too. You could say he beat me to it."

"Oh?"

"No one had ever told me you could love one guy and still be turned on by other ones."

He turned that around in his head. "Guys get told that sort

of crap, too. About which kinds of girls are just for sex, versus the one magical woman you marry, and who's too good for you to want to do nasty things with."

"Ugh. Why do we feed ourselves that bullshit?"

"I never bought into it. I always thought, why wouldn't I want to marry the woman who makes me feel that the most? Why wouldn't I want to do those nasty things with my wife more than anybody else?"

Carrie laughed softly in the dark. "I'm with you there. I'd be really pissed if I married some guy and found out he used up all the really hot sex with all these skanks who came before me. Maybe *I* want to be his one, most special skank. A skank for keeps."

Daniel snorted. "Yeah. I always thought that was a crock."

"I wish I'd known the whole having-feelings-for-two-people-at-once-is-unforgivable thing was bull back then. I'd have beaten myself up about it a lot less."

"And gotten to be with that guy you liked more than Matt."

"I don't know if I liked him more.... Just differently. He made me feel such different things than Matt did." She laughed. "Matt was the marrying kind."

"Who was your skank, then?"

"Someone I never could have been with."

"Was he dating someone, too?"

"No. He was just off-limits."

"Oh," he said. "Not like...not like a teacher or something?"

"What? Ew."

"Just asking."

"Anyway, I couldn't have been with the other guy. End of story. I was tempted to break up with Matt just so I wouldn't have to feel guilty about it anymore."

"Wish I could have turned off how guilty I felt all the time," Daniel murmured. "From how I felt about you."

"That's so strange."

He frowned, unseen. "I don't think it's strange. Then again,

I couldn't imagine why everyone *wasn't* in love with you. I thought you were amazing." And it was just as amazing that he was even saying these things. Amazing and oddly calming. Freeing.

"I never, *ever* would have guessed," she said. "I was positive you hated me."

"You remember those stupid parties at Jenny Holmes's house, every year when her parents went to the Bahamas?"

"Stupid? I think you mean the awesomest parties of all time."

"Those ones. Where the cool people always wound up in that basement rec room, playing Spin the Bottle."

"And you were always too cool for the so-called cool people," she said. "I don't think I ever once saw you play."

"Like any of the girls would've wanted to kiss me."

"That's not true. Girls can't resist a bad boy."

He smirked. "I didn't wear a leather jacket and have a tattoo, Carrie. I was just an asshole."

"Trust me. You would've been well received."

"I think I was afraid of how you'd react if I played and you got stuck kissing me. Or if your friends would've teased you. Maybe that's why I acted like I thought it was all too stupid to bother with."

"You acted like *everything* was stupid."

He chewed on that. "Yeah, I did. I've never been good at admitting I care about stuff."

"How come?"

"Because if you do, then you have to admit it hurts if you can't have it. Or if it goes away." Goddamn, stupid wine, letting his feelings leak out. He felt a sting in his sinuses and immediately fought to get ahold of himself.

They were silent for a long time, Daniel staring at the stripe of sallow parking lot light painted across the far wall.

Carrie broke the silence. "I wouldn't have given a shit what the other girls thought if I'd kissed you. And if you'd been good at it, I'd have told them so."

He smiled at that. "I always liked that about you. That you could've been one of the popular girls so easily, but even at sixteen, or whatever, you already knew it was bullshit."

"You're giving me way too much credit."

"You could have been the queen of our school. Easy."

"I don't know about that. But if there was any reason I didn't become one of the popular crowd, it wasn't because I thought it was dumb. It probably was because it looked like too much work. You had to look good all the time—makeup and hair, and cute shoes or whatever. Running isn't compatible with any of those things, and I liked running more than I ever wanted people to like me."

"You know, I only smoked for an excuse to stand around under the bleachers and watch you at track practice."

No reply. Shit. Shit, shit, shit. *How much of a stalker could you sound like?*

"Sorry," he added. "That probably came out creepy."

"Nah. Just…surprising."

"You'd have thought it was creepy back then, though. If you'd known."

"You don't know that."

He laughed sadly. "I'm pretty sure you'd have sided with Matt on that. And I'm pretty damn sure he'd have disapproved."

She didn't answer.

"Guess that's enough truth for one night," he said. "We should probably get to sleep."

And he thought he *could* sleep, now. He still felt foolish but also relieved. And it wasn't as if he'd expected this little confession to be received with enthusiasm or for Carrie to echo his feelings. There was no disappointment to suffer. If anything would change, it'd be that this woman wouldn't have to go forward assuming he'd disliked her back then. Not that she'd likely think of him at all in a few weeks...

Ouch.

"'Night, Baxter," he said, and rolled over.

"Good night, Barber."

6

CARRIE DIDN'T THINK she'd ever felt quite what she was feeling now—no longing even half this deep. So deep it hurt. She wanted to turn over, to reach out, to wrap herself around Daniel and feel his body against hers. To kiss him and taste her own desire mirrored in him. To slide her hand low and find him excited—hard from wanting her. Flushed and thrumming, exactly how she felt between her thighs.

Fear held her back. Fear that if she made the leap and bridged the gap, he'd clam up, his muscles being the only part of him growing hard as he locked her out, shut himself down. But she didn't know if fear could hold her back much longer. Fear froze, but desire burned. And everyone knew which would win in a fight between ice and fire.

She'd willed him to press her for the identity of the boy she'd liked as much as Matt, but he hadn't. She didn't know how to make such an announcement now that the conversation had petered out. She only knew what her body wanted to say to him. And she'd always trusted her body above her brain—it was her physical self that kept her mental one in check, after all.

So, after ten minutes of dead silence, she turned things over to instinct.

He was lying on his side facing away from her, on top of the covers. Carrie was beneath them, but she rolled over, edging herself up against his back. He wasn't asleep, or wasn't anymore. He froze as she pressed the fronts of her legs along the backs of his through the tangle of covers. With a guilty thrill, she rested her nose against his warm, hard shoulder and breathed him in.

"Are you awake?" he whispered.

She wrapped her arm around his middle, hand at his ribs and her forearm against his hard belly. "Yeah."

"What are you doing?"

"I'm spooning you. Forwardly."

"Because you're drunk?"

"I don't feel drunk." She felt a lot of things just now, but impaired was *not* among them.

"Is this a pity spooning?"

"It was you," she murmured, and pressed her lips to the collar of his tee. The soft hair at the nape of his neck tickled her nose.

"What was me?"

"You were the boy I wanted so bad that I knew I'd have to break up with…him." She couldn't say the name anymore. He had no place in whatever might come next.

Daniel's body was as rigid as wood. "You're just saying that."

"No, I'm not."

"I know you. You're just saying that so I won't feel like an asshole for telling you what I did."

"I'm nice, Daniel. That's not the same as patronizing. Plus, you're already kind of an asshole."

The tiniest laugh sparked in the dark room, and his muscles softened in her embrace.

"I never let myself really have a crush on you, because I assumed you hated me," she said. "But I wanted you, like I'd never wanted a guy before. More than I probably have since." And for a long time she'd assumed that attraction had been inflated in her memory, some trick of teenage hormones, or blown out of proportion in its one-sidedness, its impropriety, amid all that longing. But lying against him now, smelling his skin, feeling his voice vibrate through both their bodies… "I still feel it. As much as I did then."

A long, reedy exhalation escaped him.

He doesn't believe me. "You used to wear a gray sweat-shirt," she said. "Every day, practically."

"Yeah."

"It was a size medium from Old Navy. I know, because once, when you guys were practicing, I smelled it."

He made a funny little noise, a flustered huff warmed by amusement.

"I felt stupid doing it," she went on. "And scared, like someone would come up from the basement and catch me, and *know*. But nobody did. I sort of held it to my nose for a minute. I studied the tag, and how the cuffs were frayed. One of the grommets for the drawstring was missing."

After a long pause, he said, "Your hair used to smell like strawberries. And you wore the same scarf every winter from maybe eighth grade until we graduated. Red and black stripes."

She smiled. "I still have it. It's in my suitcase. Shawn saved up his money and bought it for me. He must have been about eleven. It's from Hot Topic."

His ribs hitched in a little laugh.

"I dragged him in there while our parents were waiting in the RMV for something. I'd forgotten I'd even mentioned wanting that scarf until Christmas morning. He'd never done anything that thoughtful for me before that, not since he'd been really little, anyhow."

"If it makes you feel like any less of a creeper, if I'd been alone in a room with that scarf, I probably would've smelled it," Daniel said.

She splayed her fingers over his heart. It was beating fast beneath taut muscle and the skin she'd never imagined she would ever touch. Boldly, she slipped her palm under the hem of his shirt and up his hard belly and chest. His only response was a silent gasp that swelled his ribs. The heat of him took away her breath. She felt the chest hair he hadn't had back when she'd first lusted for him, and the firm bulk that a physical job had put on his frame.

"Daniel."

He swallowed audibly. "Yeah?"

She slid her palm back down, taking in the planes of his bare body before slipping her hand from under his shirt. "Turn over."

He did. Carrie's vision had adjusted to the ambient light, and she could see emotions in his eyes that she never had before. Vulnerable ones. Uncertainty and wonder. And fire. She did the thing she'd fantasized about so many times, so many years ago, and touched his face. His jaw was stubbly, and it felt good against her palm. As their noses brushed, his eyes closed, but not Carrie's. She watched a furrow gather between his brows, watched his lashes quiver. With a final breath, she pressed her lips to his.

Warm, soft, smooth skin contrasted with his rough chin. She shivered.

His fingers slid through her hair to cup her head, and all at once, his hesitance was gone. His hold was needy and loaded. With a tiny moan, he angled his face and kissed her deeply. It could have been his fingertips between her legs for the way her body reacted. Her desire drew tight in her belly and her arousal demanded more, begged her to wrap her legs around him and feel the evidence of his excitement pressed against her. The blankets were as maddening as a straitjacket.

His tongue stroked hers with a boldness she wouldn't have expected, and through the covers she sensed his hips moving. She let his face go to touch him, memorizing his shapes— the firm swell of his backside, the dip at the side, the hard bone of his hip. The touch only spurred him. His kisses and thrusts intensified, and the fingers in her hair slid down her back under the covers. Carrie eased her hand beneath his pajamas. No shorts. Just her palm on his bare ass. The kiss fell apart. Daniel's lips fled hers to settle against her throat with a groan.

She touched his belly next, thrilled by the taut planes of him, and the sprinkling of hair from his navel to his waistband. His breaths steamed against her skin and he palmed her butt.

As her own hand slid lower, she realized this moment was nothing like the one she'd lived a thousand times over in her teenage fantasies. She'd always imagined her fingertips brushing the cool metal of the buckle and the studs of that old belt Daniel had always worn back then, and the thick denim of his jeans. Not all this soft flannel closed only by a drawstring.

He was stiff already, kicking her pulse into overdrive as she kneaded him through the fabric. He grew harder. Longer. Thicker and heavier until his desire beat against her palm.

"Carrie."

You don't talk during sex, huh? Oh, she'd see about that. She rubbed him until he was panting and she was aching, and the hand on her butt was squeezing in a thoughtless, distracted rhythm.

She plucked the bow of his drawstring free and slipped her fingers under his bottoms, their tips met by soft hair, then hot skin. She was poised to take her time and draw out the teasing for the both of them, when Daniel's hand covered hers, wrapping it around his erection with a curt moan.

She gasped, but Daniel mistook her excitement for alarm. He let go of her. "Sorry."

"Don't be." She gave him a squeeze to prove her hand was right where she wanted it.

"I can get kind of pushy," he murmured. "When I'm…"

"I don't mind. As long as you're not *too* rough." The thought of this cagey man losing control and turning gruff, proving that he had needs and desires… No, she didn't mind at all. "I'd like to see you like that. Passionate."

"That's a nice way to put it."

That was Carrie, always taking a highlighter to the positive. And Daniel was just the opposite, she imagined, underlining whatever disappointments affirmed his surly worldview. Well, she wouldn't be leaving him disappointed tonight. She'd get him so hot all those storm clouds would burn away to nothing.

"There are condoms in the bathroom," Daniel said between harsh breaths. "Should I get them?"

She nodded, releasing him. She kissed his forehead. "Yeah. Get them."

He left the bed, hand cupped to his erection. The shyness of the gesture charmed her. The bathroom lit up, blinding after all that darkness. As Daniel was about to return, she called, "Leave the light on—but close the door partway."

He eased it half-shut behind him, looking at her.

"A little more."

He shut it another inch.

"Perfect." The closest they'd get to mood lighting in this, the world's least romantic honeymoon suite. "Now come to bed."

7

DANIEL'S BLOOD WAS pumping so quickly it was as if he'd never taken a drink. The wine's haze had burned away the second Carrie had rolled over and touched his shoulder. He'd waited too long for any kind of sensual contact with this woman. His body wouldn't stand to dampen it.

As for whether Carrie was still feeling the wine…

What she'd said about his jacket, that couldn't be made up. Only someone who'd suffered from the same infatuation Daniel had could've thought of such a thing. But no one had ever expressed those kinds of feelings to him before. He believed her, but he couldn't begin to absorb it or own it or even trust it.

What his body wanted from hers, though, that was a fact he felt in every cell. He had no choice but to surrender to it.

He set the condom on the nightstand, barely believing what he was looking at. Carrie Baxter, in bed. She was sitting up, hugging her knees and the covers, waiting for him. He took a moment to simply study her.

She smiled. "Yes?"

"Just looking at you. Trying to figure out how this is happening."

"Fate?" she offered. "Christmas miracle?"

"Like a really dirty made-for-TV movie?"

She nodded. "Let's hope so." She moved to her knees, reached for him. He still had one hand cupped over his crotch, and she took his wrist and gently moved it away. Hooking her fingers under his waistband, she drew him closer, and he stepped forward until his knees were touching the mattress. His breath fled as her hand closed around his hidden cock, the pleasure a bolt. The world spun and he put his hand on her shoulder, steadying himself.

With a tug, she exposed him, and that eager hand closed around his pounding erection.

"Carrie."

She touched him as though he mesmerized her. As he'd never been touched before—with patience and wonder. The contact warmed him through. She made him feel soft things, sensations Daniel didn't tend to attract. And maybe for the first time ever, he didn't want to rush past the polite pregame stuff to the sex itself. This felt so good. Not like usual.

Though he knew it made him a jerk, Daniel hated foreplay. It asked of him things he wasn't good at giving—patience and finesse and attentiveness. He knew what he was good at, what he had to offer. It was rough and fast and intense, and usually blessedly impersonal. It wasn't that he disliked the women he hooked up with. It wasn't laziness, not even selfishness...not quite. It was fear of all that soft stuff. Fear of being bad at it. Or incapable of it. Fear of proving himself broken.

But this, he thought, eyes shutting as Carrie's hand stroked and measured. This could go on forever. She made him helpless in a way that liberated him, as if his anxieties simply didn't apply tonight.

The room was hot. The world was hot, the ice storm swallowed in the heat wave. Daniel let go of Carrie's shoulder to peel off his shirt. Her gaze took him in. That, he was used to. There was something that certain women liked about how he looked that apparently trumped his sour personality enough for him to get laid. His job kept him fit, and the way Carrie's eyes moved over him.... Yeah, the risk was worth it on a whole different level, just now.

The pressure was building in him, hot and maddening. He took her hand and moved it away, cool air enclosing his feverish flesh. He flung the covers wide and got to his knees between her legs. She welcomed his body as he lowered himself, her slim thighs wrapping around his hips. He braced himself on his arms, stroked his cock along her sex. His bottoms and her yoga pants were cruel, but the tease felt good. He didn't want to rush tonight. Didn't want to miss a second of this.

"You feel good," she said, stroking him from the shoulders to the wrists.

"You, too. What do you like for...you know, foreplay."

"I like this," she said, thighs squeezing his hips. "And kissing. Touching. Anything. I just want to mess around with you."

Mess around—yes, exactly. The clumsy, excited experimentation that typified teenage sex. He moved, drawing her against him, facing, on their sides. She brought her leg up, hugging it to his hip.

"Wait." He eased her leg away and reached between them to push her stretchy bottoms down. His thumbs found no underwear, and his excitement surged.

She helped him get them all the way off, and Daniel studied her as she stripped away her tee. Between her legs, she was just as he'd always imagined. The girl who'd shunned makeup had grown into a woman who kept things natural. And her bra was simple, just tan cotton. Her sexuality was all in her body—a physical expression, not a trick of packaging. Her body *fascinated* him. It was lean and vital, probably boyish by popular standards, but she'd been shaped by her talents and her passion. Her hands weren't soft. She had calluses, from climbing, he guessed. He loved things like this about her. All that imperfection and humanity and evidence of living. Her personality, perfectly translated to her physical being. He wished he felt so united himself. His body was the doing of his job, his disposition a thing to be endured.

"Here," she whispered. Slender fingers slipped under his waistband, and together they pushed his pants down. Daniel eased her onto her back, ran his hands beneath her to undo her bra clasp. She stripped it away and rolled back onto her side, their naked bodies pressing flush.

"Oh." He had to shut his eyes and just *feel* this. Every

square inch of her naked skin against his. Her small, smooth breasts against his chest, the soft hair between her legs tickling the underside of his cock. Her mouth sought his, and Daniel let his kiss tell her everything he felt for her. He was aching, needy, a little unsure, utterly eager. Things he never expressed through sex—never expressed, period. She brought up her leg and he shifted his hips, his erection pressing along her lips. That changed things, transformed his excitement, making it dark and chaotic and as hot as a jungle. Fiercely biological. It got his hips moving, every instinct demanding he angle his cock and drive it deep. She was wet, their contact a mix of friction and slickness, the latter soon dominating. He moved faster with every breath and every tease of her tongue against his. His hands roamed hungrily over her body.

All at once she wasn't kissing him anymore. Her breaths were heavy and harsh on his jaw, her fingers clutching at his hair, hips frantically mirroring his with every gliding stroke. *Holy shit.*

"You going to come?" he whispered, his palm riding the restless muscles of her lower back.

"Yeah. I am."

"From this?" He made it quicker, their bodies practically quarreling.

"Don't stop."

Not for a billion dollars. Not if the motel was burning to the ground around them.

His heart was pounding, pulse thumping everywhere in his body. Cock throbbing and begging to be quenched.

Then she touched him in a way that transcended sex—stroked him in some pleasurable place suspended between his dick and his brain and his heart. She said, "Daniel."

Her body went stiff, her fingers grasping his hair nearly hard enough to hurt.

He kissed her forehead as she rode her orgasm, urging her hips with his palm. "Good." When she stilled, he slipped his hand between them, fingertips seeking her clit. She jerked at the contact, then eased. He held still, wanting to feel the pulsations and record the rhythm of her excitement. Wanting so much more. To make it happen again against his fingers or his tongue.

He was good at giving women head, but not for reasons he was proud of. Jerk or not, he believed the woman came first, and oral kept the intimacy contained. As deeply personal as the act was, it felt safe to him. It demanded no eye contact, precluded the dirty talking he found so deeply awkward. And it was a giving act, feeling like it earned him the fast, urgent sex he favored.

But with Carrie, he wanted the contact only. Not the safety. He wanted to know what she tasted like and smelled like, wanted her hands on his head, and her moans and sighs filling the room.

When her breathing slowed, he began to move his fingertips against her softening clit. Her palm had grown hot and damp on his neck, and she squeezed him there.

"You want to…?"

"Not yet," he murmured and kissed her temple. "Lie back."

CARRIE FELT DRUNK on the orgasm. Wine had nothing on infatuation. She did as Daniel urged, her head finding the pillow, her back the rumpled covers. As he moved, she admired all that lean muscle. His body matched the intensity of his face and his personality perfectly. She was excited to watch those muscles really work, braced above her, but no—he moved down on the bed.

Oh.

He got positioned on his elbows and she stroked his hair. "You're full of surprises."

He met her eyes, his face in shadow. "You like this, right?"

She nodded. "I'll miss your voice, though."

"I promise you won't be thinking about that in a minute."

Her smile fled the second his tongue glanced her clit. Her short nails raked his scalp and the breath left her in a gasp. She was still sensitized there, though the too-much shock of it was good. Everything with Daniel felt saturated, hyperreal.

He was amazing with his mouth. Every slick, firm stroke wound her tighter. But it wasn't right. Not quite. He felt too far away with Carrie on her back and his face obscured.

"Wait," she whispered, tracing his ear.

He pulled back, looking expectant.

"Would you mind kneeling on the floor? Or is that too—"

It wasn't. He was on the carpet in a breath.

"This side," she said, swinging her legs over the edge. "I want to see you."

He came around to kneel before her. So much better with that handsome face lit dramatically on one side. She didn't lie back, but instead curled in a bit, cupping his head as he brought his talented mouth back to her sex. Her heels rubbed at his shoulder blades as his tongue slid deep, and his hands gripped her hips, rough and possessive. He felt close now that she could hold him this way. He felt like *hers*.

"That's amazing," she murmured.

His lids were shut and she traced his brows, willing his eyes to open. But he seemed lost in concentration. She hoped this felt as wonderful to him as it did to her. Was he tasting the evidence of how badly she wanted him, of how good he'd made her feel?

As the pleasure grew, her hands moved to his neck and shoulders, rubbing, grasping, kneading.

"I want you," she said, eyes shutting. "So much." He could stand right now, sink deep with a single push and let her feel his excitement pulsing, hugged by her own. She tugged at his shoulders. "Daniel."

He paused for only a beat—just long enough to say, "Yeah?"

"I want you." She tugged again. "Now."

"I want to make you come again."

"You will—and you would if you kept going. But I want all of you. Please."

He sat back on his heels, breathing heavily, and met her gaze.

"What?" she asked. His hands were still on her hips, and she stroked the backs of them with her fingertips. The touch seemed to knock his thoughts free.

"I like it kind of…rough."

"Okay. How rough?"

"Nothing crazy…and it's not that I only like it that way. I need that to…you know."

"Sure." Good, yes. Amazing. She'd give anything to see this closed-up man turned frantic and desperate with excitement.

He cleared his throat. "I want to make sure I get you there again first. In case what I need doesn't…work for you."

She smiled. "I'm pretty sure it will. Unless you're leaving something out?"

He shook his head, clearly uncertain.

He didn't trust himself. In exactly what way, she couldn't guess. "You're not going to hurt me or anything," she prompted.

"No, of course not. I mean, not on purpose. I just need it fast. And kind of selfish."

God, please. "If it means you'll be excited, then I guarantee you it'll work for me."

He might have nodded. It was hard to tell, the gesture was so subtle. He took in her sex from where he knelt, his gaze so loaded she swore she could feel it against her swollen lips and clit. Then, out of nowhere, he smiled up at her.

Surprised, she laughed, and squeezed his hands. "What?"

"It's nice down here."

"Oh?"

A sheepish sort of smile. "Being on my knees, for you."

Except then he was standing, urging her back on the mattress and climbing on above her, his legs knocking hers wide. "It's nice with you in general." His eyes surveyed her body beneath his, and she returned the admiration. He was still stiff, hovering thick and ready above her belly. She reached between them to clasp him, giving a long, slow pull. He dropped his head with a groan, shoulder blades jutting.

"Better than nice," she said softly and reveled in his reactions for a few more strokes.

His face came up, his look so intense that her hand froze. For a long breath they merely held each other's gazes, Daniel's hazel eyes nearly black in the dim room.

"This is the best thing that's ever happened to me," he said.

Carrie blushed. "It's high up there on my list, too."

He moved her hand from his erection. Dropping down on his forearms, he linked his fingers with hers, holding her hands against the mattress, framing her face. "No," he said. "This is the actual best thing that's ever happened to me. No moment of my life is ever going to be as perfect as this one. Here. With you."

Nothing she could think to say deserved to follow that, so she only regarded him. Memorized those words and his face and this suspended second shared by only the two of them. He swallowed and let go of her hands, sitting up to kneel between her thighs. Grazing her legs, he seemed calm but for the quick breaths flexing his belly. She drew her calves along his sides.

"You know what?" she asked.

"No, what?"

"This really is an awesome honeymoon."

His smile was broad and open, but then his expression darkened as his gaze went to the nightstand and the condom. She remembered what he'd said about needing it rough, and a hot wave of nervous excitement got her blood pumping.

"I'm ready if you are," she said.

"I imagined this for years, but I don't think I could ever be ready for it."

"Too bad for you," she said. "Because it's happening."

Daniel nodded. "Yes. Yes, it is."

8

CARRIE MOVED, GRABBING the condom and then settling against the pillows. Her fingers were clumsy as she opened the wrapper, but she saw that same anticipation mirrored in Daniel. She'd imagined being with him a million times when she'd been younger, but never felt able to guess how he'd be. He'd been so prickly, roughness had usually factored into her hypotheses—even rudeness—but she'd never imagined what sweeter intimacies he might offer. She *never* would have imagined him saying the heartbreaking things he just had.

"Here," she said, tugging him close. His knees were braced wide beneath her legs. She rolled the latex down his length, savoring the moment. Savoring the view—Daniel's strong masculine body looming, backlit and seeming dangerous. He dropped down, planting his palms beside her waist. She held his erection, angling as his hips guided him close. She swept his head along her lips, rocked by a surge of pleasure as it stroked her clit.

"Look at me," he murmured.

She did. Her hand went still, and she let his gaze hold her in thrall as the pressure came. Pressure but no resistance. She was lush and ready, welcoming his slow, measured intrusion. She let go to hold his sides, feeling his muscles flex as he gave her more. Just a tiny pang, a small adjustment of her angle, and when he next slid home he was gliding.

How a man could feel so familiar and so new, she didn't understand. And that was Daniel, essentially. A boy she'd grown up with, yet had never really known, who'd shared her exact secret—an off-limits and confounding infatuation, one neither of them had ever expected would lead to this moment.

"You feel so good," she whispered. To speak any louder might scare reality away.

"So do you." He eased back, slid deep. "Even better than I'd ever guessed."

She reached between them to touch herself, but he stopped her, pinning her hand against the bed. She shivered, the coolness chased by heat to feel that bossy grip on her wrist, that little taste of restraint.

I like it kind of rough.

"Let me," he said. He released her and slipped his hand low, thumb seeking her clit. All his weight was on one arm, the tendons and muscles locked and thrilling.

"I want to see what you like," she said, nudging his hand out of the way. If this was the only night they ever got together, she wanted to know exactly who this man was.

Again, he grabbed her wrist and held her hand down. "What I want," he said slowly, "is to be doing everything."

"Oh." Controlling. "Sure."

He shoved his legs even deeper beneath hers, sharpening the angle. His weight was off his arms now, and he took both of her wrists, pinning them above her head. Not so tight that it alarmed her. Not at all. She was physical. She craved the edgy sensation of her body being challenged, especially like this. His hold was everything dark that she'd tried to project onto him in her bygone fantasies. Rough and pushy but sensual, too. His hips moved with an unexpected grace, strokes smooth and lengthening by the second. He worked his strong body with a sureness she hadn't anticipated.

"You want me to do anything special?" she asked.

"No." He swallowed, eyes closing, hips speeding. "No, I just want to feel like you're mine."

Those words spread fever through her body, and she told him, "I *am* yours."

His eyes opened. For a glorious minute the world was his hands wrapped around her wrists, his muscles pumping, his hard length owning her. Then he let her go. A rough palm cupped her breast as the other slid low. One thumb strummed her clit, the other her nipple. The pleasure met and melded in her belly, urgency sparking.

She reached for him, but he said, "No," the word dark and hard. Exciting. "Keep them above your head."

His cock was surging, the slick motions caressing her lips as that rough thumb circled and rubbed. His racing breaths had become labored moans now, rhythmic and guttural, utterly male. The dynamic he'd set didn't welcome instruction, but if it had, she'd have told him, "Talk to me." She settled instead for these dark sounds, let them stoke her excitement as surely as his hands, or the sight of his laboring muscles.

"I'm close," she panted. She moved the only part of her body she dared, flexing her hips to heighten the penetration. *Talk to me.* "Don't stop. Please."

He controlled her pleasure, and although this wasn't what she'd have given herself—rougher, slower—the fact that he was giving it to her made the mechanics moot. And then he did the thing that trumped any touch. He spoke.

"You gonna come for me?" His eyes were hard and hot, same as that circling thumb.

"Yes."

His hips sped, and Carrie felt the promise of release becoming an inevitability. The pressure he spurred was blazing, tight, almost painful, and she groaned.

"Good. Come on."

And she was there, this orgasm so much more intense than the first, multiplied by his rough voice, his firm touch and his dark eyes burning down at hers. It roared through her, forcing her back off the sheets and making her nails bite into the pillow above her head. As the onslaught eased, Daniel's hips relented. His erection slid slow and luxurious and then stopped all together.

She broke his rule, reaching up to touch his face and neck.

His pulse thumped below his ear, echoed by the stiff heat of him inside of her. He looked disbelieving. And electrified. And beautiful.

"Thank you," she said, her voice thick. She cleared her throat and held his hard arms. She let her hips tell him that his turn had come.

He began to move, building gradually until he was speeding again, pounding hard. His eyes were wild, skin surely flushed.

He groaned. "Turn over. Please."

She made it to her hands and knees—more by his urging than by her own volition. She felt the weight of his hard body pushing into her, his length sliding deep once more. The show was over, Daniel chasing his release with an animal ferocity. His hips hammered and his grip was rough at her waist. One palm slid between her shoulder blades, fingers splaying. She felt held in place, exploited even—and, goddamn, it felt amazing.

She'd been with dominating guys before, and those experiences had run the gamut from exciting to a touch degrading. But with Daniel she felt nothing she had before. She felt a man turned wild from desire. She felt wanted in the most primitive, intoxicating way. She felt high and powerful to have done this to him.

"Oh." His moan was deep and ragged, full of wonder. His hands grew slick against her skin, and those masterful hips were frenetic. She could picture them—picture the entire length of his body in profile, gorgeous and rough.

She reached one arm back, found his fingers with her own. He seemed to rattle apart at the contact, his breathing coming in a string of tight gasps and his motions jerky. The pressure built until she had to steal her hand back, bracing against the impact. Then all at once he went perfectly still.

In that quiet space she listened to his panting breaths and memorized the pulse of his length, held tight inside her. His damp palm slid down her back, and he eased himself out with a breathy groan. Carrie turned onto her back as he collapsed across the covers. He drew his legs in, rubbing his knees.

"All right?" she asked.

"I think I got rug burn. Or sheet burn."

"Poor baby." She flopped her arm against his chest.

"I'll sue the motel for my injuries."

She gasped dramatically and thumped his ribs with her knuckles. "Never. I love this horrible motel. And this horrible room."

His fingertips teased the sensitive skin of her inner forearm. "I'm forgiving them for the spider in light of the free condoms."

"Oh, my God, yes. That alone must be worth a five-star Yelp review."

Once her body had cooled some, Carrie rolled onto her side and tucked her knees against Daniel's hip. "That was awesome."

He nodded, gaze on the ceiling. "Yeah, it was."

"I can't figure out if you're exactly how I'd expected or totally different. Either way, you were exactly how you should be. All gruff and fast and...Daniel Barber-y."

"Not too much, I hope."

"No way."

"That stuff's a preference, really. I don't *always* have to be like that—pushy, I guess. I got smacked around some, when I was a kid." He said it without angst, like it was a flat and faded scar to him now rather than a wound. "I think it's made me kind of...weird. About feeling like I'm having physical stuff directed at me. Stuff I can't predict."

"Oh." Made sense. "You liked when I stroked you, though."

He smiled. "Yeah, I did. Though I wanted like hell to grab your hand and control what you were doing, too."

"I wouldn't have minded that." She kissed his shoulder.

"I like what you had me do, though. I liked kneeling on the

floor for you, and feeling how you held my head. I wouldn't, usually. Usually I'd get annoyed, feeling like somebody was trying to direct me."

"I just wanted to feel connected to you."

He seemed to consider that. "It was nice. Made it feel like…like it excited you, touching me. That you weren't just excited by what I was doing to you."

She stroked his hair and held his gaze. "There's never been anyone I was more thrilled to be with. It could have been the worst sex of my life, and it still would have been amazing, because I was getting to know you that way."

"But it wasn't the worst sex of your life, right?" He'd made his expression so grave she had to laugh.

"I don't think I need to tell you that."

"Good. Because it was the best sex of mine. I mean, I know I don't really know you anymore. And I know I never *really* knew you that well when we were kids, despite us being in school together for twelve years."

"Plus kindergarten—thirteen years. Like cicadas," she whispered in a spooky voice, drumming her fingers along his forearm.

"I didn't let you know *me* well enough for that to happen. But if there's some version of love where you don't have to actually know the other person all that deeply…I feel that for you."

She blinked. "Wow."

"And it feels amazing."

She squeezed his hand. "So the next time you play Never Have I Ever and somebody says 'I've never had sex with someone I love'…?"

"Totally not drinking."

She smiled and stroked his knuckles, hummed a happy noise. "Daniel Barber…*making love.*"

"Must be a Christmas miracle."

"Very Dickensian. I think that makes me the Ghost of In- fatuation Past or something to your Ebenezer."

"We really ought to get some sleep," Daniel murmured, lips teasing her cheek. "Much as I never want this night to end."

"Yeah." She craned her neck, the clock on the nightstand telling her it was pushing four. "Oh, Jesus. We might want to rethink that six a.m. wake-up call."

"I'll get up when it's light out," he said through a yawn. "See what the road's looking like. We'll take it slow, and we'll probably make it home by dinnertime, if not in time for you to meet your brother at the station. Sorry."

"It's not your fault. And as bummed as that makes me, the stupid weather got us together. I can't be mad at that."

His laugh was a warm little hum. "No, me neither."

She turned over, spooning her back to his chest, smiling as his strong arm wrapped her up tight. "I'd say, 'See you in the morning,' but it's already morning."

"Say Merry Christmas instead."

"Indeed." She cleared her throat. "Thank you for my gift."

"Both of them."

She laughed, but he had that wrong. "Not the orgasms. Just you. Just us, getting to be this way. Thanks for being brave enough to come out and say what you did."

"Drunk enough, you mean."

"Semantics." Carrie yawned.

"Thank you," he whispered, sounding uncharacteristically earnest. "For…for all of this."

"My literal pleasure."

"Now I get to wake up next to you."

She smiled. "If we ever fall asleep."

"Night," he said, and kissed her hair.

"Morning," she returned, and settled her buzzing body against the calming heat of his strong one. "And Merry Christmas."

9

THEY GOT ON the road around eight in the morning, finding the asphalt blessedly—if inadequately—dusted with sand. It was still slick and the going slow. Daniel's knuckles were white, reflexes alert for the faintest tug of the wheel, the briefest slip of the tiny Fiat's tires. By the time they climbed back in after a quick lunch stop outside Eugene, he at least felt confident they'd survive to see their respective families.

The morning had been nice. He'd fought every self-defeating script programmed into his personality and forced himself not to shut down in the wake of all that soul bearing. It felt awkward and hurt a little in his chest, but he wouldn't trade it for the cold comfort of his usual armor.

He took a deep drink of the coffee they were sharing. Normally, he drank it black, but he had deferred to Carrie, and the creamy, sugary result was pretty disgusting. Yet he had to wonder if the memory of this trip just might change his preferences. There was something to be said for this sweetness.

"What do you think?" she asked. "Another five hours, with these roads?"

He set the cup back in the holder. "Maybe four if the ice eases up the farther north we get."

"Fingers crossed." After a pause, she amended that. "Not that this road trip isn't pretty nice in itself."

Nice? *Try the best gift I could have asked for.*

Though they made terrible time, the nearer they got to Grafton the better the roads became. The world seemed to thaw, just as Daniel had en route to finding himself so at home in easy small talk. He felt calm, for the first time in ages—and right at the moment he'd been anticipating dread and anxiety, as their hometown drew closer under a darkening sky.

AFTER A HALF hour of companionable silence, Carrie said, "You know, I bet we were supposed to be on the same flight to Portland. Leaving at seven-ten?"

Daniel nodded.

"Maybe we'd have wound up seated next to each other. Maybe fate had it in for us all along."

"How long are you in Grafton for?" he asked.

"I fly out the day after tomorrow. All the time I could get off, sadly. You?"

"Same." Three days had sounded like ages when he'd made the promise to his grandma, but seeing how he'd lost nearly an entire day, he was grateful for it now. "Early flight."

"Mine's not until dinnertime."

"You mind if I return the car at PDX?" Daniel asked. "It'll save me having to ask one of my parents for a lift. And spare me their company. And spare you the headache of telling the rental people we're returning it short a headlight and side-mirror and a load of paint."

"No problem. Shawn was planning on taking me."

"Cool."

"Actually, no doubt he'll want to go to the bar while we're both home. So tomorrow night I'll probably be playing des-ignated driver, in case you wanted to hang out at Paulie's, not drinking. Check out how old our fellow GHS alums have gotten."

"Maybe… Late, maybe. I, um, I'm going home mainly to spend time with my grandma. She doesn't think she's going to see another Christmas, so I may just hang out with her playing cards and watching movies."

"Oh, sure. Of course." As they passed by the big wooden sign, she read, "'Welcome to Grafton.'"

"But if my grandma goes to bed early, maybe I could swing by," Daniel added. Could be really weird, though, if Matt happened to be at the bar, or any of their old classmates, he thought as they drove past the high school. If people saw him and Carrie there together, the news would surely spread like a rash.

Whatever. It's time to start making some nice memories in this town for a change.

"We'll swap numbers," Carrie said. "I'll let you know what I end up doing."

"Sounds good."

She laughed softly. "And every thirteen years on Christmas, we'll return to the Evergreen Motor Inn, cicada-like, and resume this…whatever it is."

That got his pulse pounding, left his throat dry. He met her eyes for a moment, then looked back to the road, nervous.

"What?"

"We don't…I mean, we don't live *that* far apart, really, in the grand scheme of things. Maybe three hours' drive."

Carrie kept her voice light and level. "Hour and a half apiece if we met in the middle."

His chest filled. "Good old I-5. Maybe we could meet up in Modesto or wherever, sometime."

Did she have any clue how fast his heart was beating waiting those two seconds for her reply? It felt like a hummingbird between his ribs.

"What are you doing on New Year's Eve?" she asked.

And here he'd been hoping she'd want to see him in the next couple *months.* Next week? Shit, yes. "Nothing."

"I RSVP'd for a friend's party already. She has an amazing apartment with a view of the bay. Would you have any interest in coming up for that?"

He answered honestly. "You could invite me to come and pump your septic tank and I'd say yes."

She laughed, the best sound in the world. "I'll bear that in mind. And if parties aren't really your thing, I can just cancel. We could do whatever we wanted."

"No, I'd love to come."

He wanted to see where she lived and what her life was

like. He still wanted all the things he'd had when they'd both been living in this little town—a glimpse of her bedroom, a snoop through her bookshelves. He wanted to sit at her kitchen table or on her couch and drink coffee with her in the morning. Go out to eat with her. Shower with her. Run errands with her. Walk around her neighborhood or along the cold beach. Make a meal with her. Watch a movie. Take her to bed. Get taken there himself. He wanted to spend such a perfect January first with Carrie that the rest of the year could be complete misery and it wouldn't even matter.

"I ought to warn you," she said. "It's a one-bedroom."

He snorted. "Scandal. Also, this is all barring a fire, obviously."

"Sure."

"Though this time of year, luck's probably on my side."

"Let's hope California doesn't take a page out of western Oregon's book and order an ice storm."

"No kidding."

When he glanced her way, she was smiling, attention aimed forward as they drove through the town's center where the trees twinkled with white lights. He doubted he would've even noticed those lights without this woman beside him.

"You're still the prettiest girl I've ever seen," he told her, feeling naked in the nicest way.

She met his eyes with her dark ones and Daniel looked back to the road, feeling shy.

"Thanks."

He swallowed. "Sure."

"You probably need both hands on the wheel, huh?"

"Definitely."

She leaned over and rested her palm on his thigh. Daniel felt his neck and face flush with pleasure, and he hazarded a quick rub of her knuckles.

"Thanks for driving," Carrie said.

Daniel remembered the miles and miles of grit-messy

dangerous asphalt, the endless trees drooping and depressed under coats of ice. The speed limit-signs that had made a joke of their progress. The flat gray winter sky, now dark.

"Thanks for the best Christmas of my life," he replied. He punched the stereo button and filled their ridiculous little car with the bright chaos of pop music.

* * * * *

BABY IN THE MAKING

ELIZABETH BEVARLY

For Eli,

My greatest creation ever.

Love you, Peanut.

One

Really, it wasn't the gaping hole in the shirt and pants that troubled Hannah Robinson most. It wasn't the bloodstain, either. She'd seen worse. No, what troubled her most was how little Yeager Novak seemed to be bothered by the six tidy stitches binding his flesh just north of the waistband of his silk boxers. Then again, as far as Yeager's garments were concerned, this was par for the course. Such was life sewing for a tailor whose most profitable client made his living at cheating death—and planning similar travel adventures for others—then brought in what was left of his clothing after the most recent near miss to have them mended. Or, in the case of the shirt, completely recreated from scratch.

Yeager towered over her from her current position kneeling before him, tape measure in hand. But then, he towered over her when she was standing, too. Shoving a handful of coal-black hair off his forehead, he gazed down at her with eyes the color of sapphires and said, "I'll never let a bull get that close to me again." He darted his gaze from the stitches on his torso to the ruined clothing on the floor. "That was just a little too close for comfort."

Hannah blew a dark blond curl out of her eyes and pushed her reading glasses higher on her nose. "That's what you said last year when you ran with the bulls."

He looked puzzled. "I did?"

"Yes. It was the first time you came to see us here at Cathcart and Quinn, because your previous tailor told you to take a hike when you brought in one too many of his masterpieces to be mended." She arched a brow in meaningful reminder. "Except when you were in Pamplona last July, you escaped into a cantina before the bull was able to do more than tear the leg of your trousers."

"Right," he said, remembering. "That was where I met Jimena. Who came back to my hotel with me while I changed my clothes. And didn't get back into them for hours." His expression turned sublime. "I probably should have sent that bull a thank-you note."

Even after knowing him for a year, Hannah was still sometimes surprised by the frankness with which Yeager talked about his sex life. Then again, his personal life sounded like it was almost as adventurous as his professional life, so maybe he had trouble distinguishing between the two on occasion.

"Or at least sent Jimena a text that said adios," Hannah said, striving for the same matter-of-factness and not sure if she quite managed it.

He grinned. "Hey, don't worry about Jimena. She got what she wanted, too."

I'll bet, Hannah thought, her gaze traveling to the elegant bumps of muscle and sinew on his torso. Yeager Novak might well have been sculpted by the hands of the gods. But the scar left behind by his latest stitches would be in good company, what with the jagged pink line marring the flesh above his navel and the puckered arc to their left. He had scars all over his body, thanks to his extreme adventurer ways. And thanks to his total lack of inhibition when it came to being fitted for clothes, Hannah had seen all of them.

"So you think you can fix the shirt and pants?" he asked.

"The pants will be fine," she told him. "They just need a good washing. But the shirt is a goner." Before he could open his mouth to protest, she added, "Don't worry, Mr. Novak. I can make a new one that will look just like it."

He threw her an exasperated look. "How many times have I told you to call me Yeager?"

"Lots," she replied. "And, just like I told you all those other times, it's Mr. Cathcart's and Mr. Quinn's policy to use 'Mr.' or 'Ms.' with all of our clients."

Just like it was Cathcart and Quinn policy that Hannah wear the ugly little smock she had to wear while working and always keep her hair confined, as if the shop's sole female employee was a throwback to the Industrial Revolution.

"Anyway," she continued, "I learned pretty quickly to keep all of your patterns and cut enough fabric for two garments whenever I make one."

He smiled in a way that was nothing short of devastating. "And I love you for it," he told her.

She smiled back. "I know."

Yeager told Hannah he loved her all the time. He loved her for making him clothes that fit like a glove. He loved her for mending them when he thought he'd ruined them. He loved her for being able to remove bloodstains, oil stains, pampas stains, baba ghanoush stains, walrus stains...stains from more sources than any normal human being saw in a lifetime. And, hey, she loved Yeager, too. The same way she loved cannoli and luna moths and sunsets—with a certain sense of awe that such things even existed in the world.

She went back to measuring his inseam, pretending the action commanded every scrap of her attention when, by now, she had Yeager's measurements memorized. There was no reason he had to know that, was there? Sometimes a girl had to do what a girl had to do. Especially when said girl was between boyfriends. Like eight months between boyfriends. None of whom had torsos roped with muscle or smelled like a rugged, windswept canyon.

"Have you ever been to Spain, Hannah?" Yeager asked.

"I lived for a while in what used to be Spanish Harlem," she told him as she penned his inseam measurement onto the back of her hand. She lifted the tape measure to his waist. "Does that count?"

He chuckled. "No. You should go to Spain. It's an incredible country. Definitely in my top five favorite places to visit."

Hannah would have told him her top five were Queens, Manhattan, Brooklyn, the Bronx and Staten

Island, since she'd never ventured outside the five boroughs of New York. For fifteen of her first eighteen years, it was because she'd been a ward of the state, and even though she'd been shuffled around *a lot* during that time, she'd never landed outside the city's jurisdiction. For the last nine years, she hadn't had the funds to pay for something as frivolous as travel. What didn't go to keeping herself housed and fed went toward funding the business she'd started out of her Sunnyside apartment. Things like travel could wait until *after* she was the toast of the New York fashion industry.

"What are your other top four favorite places?" she asked.

She was going to go out on a limb and say that, to a man who'd built a billion-dollar company out of creating extreme adventure vacations for other alpha types, Sunnyside and what used to be Spanish Harlem probably weren't going to make the cut.

He didn't even have to think about his response. "New Zealand, Slovenia, Chile and Iceland. But ask me tomorrow and it could be a whole different list."

Hannah jotted the last of his measurements onto the back of her hand with the others, returned the pen to its perennial place in the bun she always wore for work and stood. Yep, Yeager still towered over her. Then again, since she stood five-two, most people did.

"All done," she told him. Reluctantly she added, "You can get dressed now."

He nodded toward the clothes on the floor. "Thanks for taking care of this."

"No problem. But you know, you could save a lot

of money on tailoring if you stayed in New York for more than a few weeks at a time."

"There's no way I can stay anywhere for more than a few weeks at a time," he said. "And I won't apologize for being an adventurer."

Hannah would never ask him to. She couldn't imagine Yeager sitting behind a desk punching a keyboard or standing on an assembly line screwing in machine parts. It would be like asking Superman to work as a parking attendant.

"All I'm saying is be careful."

He flinched. "Those are the last two words somebody like me wants to hear."

And they were the two words Hannah lived by. Not that she was a fearful person by any stretch of the imagination. You didn't survive a childhood and adolescence as a ward of the state by being timid. But after nearly a decade on her own, she'd carved out a life for herself that was quiet, steady and secure, and she was careful not to jeopardize that. Oh, blissful predictability. Oh, exalted stability. Oh, revered security. She'd never had any of those things growing up. No way would she risk losing them now.

"Your pants and new shirt will be ready a week from today," she told Yeager.

He thrust his arms through the sleeves of a gray linen shirt Hannah had made for him and began to button it. "Great. That'll be just in time for my trip to Gansbaai. South Africa," he clarified before she could ask. "I'm taking a group to go cage diving with great white sharks."

"Of course you are. Because after nearly being gored to death by a gigantic bull, why wouldn't you risk being bitten in two by a gigantic shark? It makes perfect sense."

He grinned again. "After that, it's off to Nunavut with a couple of buddies to climb Mount Thor."

"I would love to see your passport, Mr. Novak. It must be as thick as a novel."

"Yeah, it is. Like *Harry Potter and the Order of the Phoenix* size."

And the stories it could tell were probably every bit as fantastic.

"Well, have a good time," she told him. "I'll be at home, inventorying my swatches and organizing my bobbins."

He threw her one last smile as he reached for his charcoal trousers—also fashioned by Hannah. "And you say I live dangerously."

The bell above the shop entrance jingled, making her turn in that direction. "Excuse me," she said as she backed toward the fitting room entrance. "Your claim check will be at the register when you're ready."

The minute Hannah disappeared through the fitting room door, Yeager Novak's mind turned to other, more pressing, topics. When your life's work was creating extreme adventures for wealthy clients, you had to make plans, sometimes years in advance. In putting together vacation packages, he had a million things to consider—a country's culture and politics, its potential safety, its seasonal climate, how many people needed to be bribed for all the requisite permissions… The list was endless. And he always tried out the travel packages he designed for his clients first, to be sure they were doable without risk to life or limb.

Well, without *too* much risk to life or limb. *No* risk kind of defeated the purpose.

He knotted his tie, grabbed his suit jacket and headed for the register. Hannah's blond head was bent over her receipt pad as she wrote in her slow, precise hand, a few errant curls springing free of the prim little bun she always wore. Nice to know there was at least some part of her that wanted to break free of her buttoned-up, battened-down self. He'd never met anyone more straitlaced than Hannah…whatever her last name was.

As if she'd heard him say that out loud, she suddenly glanced up, her silver-gray eyes peering over the tops of her black half-glasses. She did have some beautiful eyes, though, he'd give her that. He'd never seen the color on another human being. But the rest of her… The shapeless jacket-thing she wore completely hid her gender, and if she was wearing any makeup, he sure couldn't see it. He guessed she was kind of cute in a wholesome, girl-next-door type of way, if you went for the wholesome, girl-next-door type—which he didn't. He liked talking to her, though. She was smart and funny. And, man, did her clothes make him look good. He knew nothing about sewing or fashion, but he knew excellent work when he saw it. And Hannah Whatshername definitely did excellent work.

"A week from today," she reiterated as she tore the receipt from the pad and extended it toward him.

"Thanks," he replied as he took it from her. "Any chance you could make a second shirt like it by then? Just in case?" Before she could object—because he could tell she was going to—he added, "There could be an extra hundred bucks in it for you."

She bit her lip thoughtfully, a gesture that was slightly—surprisingly—erotic. "I'm not allowed to take tips."

"Oh, c'mon. I don't see Leo or Monty around."

"Mr. Cathcart is on a buying trip to London," she said. "And Mr. Quinn is at lunch."

"Then they'll never know."

She expelled the kind of sigh someone makes when they know they're breaking the rules but they badly need cash for something. Yeager was intrigued. What could Ms. Goody Two-shoes Hannah need money for that would make her break the rules?

With clear reluctance she said, "I can't. I'm sorry. I just don't have time to do it here—we're so back-logged." Before he could protest, she hurried on. "However, I happen to know a seamstress who does freelance work at home. She's very good."

Yeager shook his head. "No way. I don't trust anyone with my clothes but you."

"No, you don't understand, Mr. Novak. I guarantee you'll like this woman's work. I know her *intimately*."

"But—"

"You could even say that she and I are *one of a kind*. If you know what I mean."

She eyed him pointedly. And after a moment, Yeager understood. Hannah was the one who did freelance work at home. "Gotcha."

"If you happened to do a search on Craigslist for, say, 'Sunnyside seamstress,' she'd be the first listing that pops up. Ask if she can make you a shirt by next week for the same price you'd pay here, and I guarantee she'll be able to do it."

Yeager grabbed his phone from his pocket and

pulled up Craigslist. He should have known Hannah would live in Sunnyside. It was the closest thing New York had to Small Town America.

"Found you," he said.

She frowned at him.

"I mean…found *her*."

"Send her an email from that listing. I'm sure she'll reply when she gets home from work tonight."

He was already typing when he said, "Great. Thanks."

"But you'll have to pick it up at my—I mean, her place," she told him. "She can't bring it here, and she doesn't deliver."

"No problem."

He sent the email then returned his phone to one pocket as he tugged his wallet from another. He withdrew five twenties from the ten he always had on him and placed them on the counter. Hannah's eyes widened at the gesture, but she discreetly palmed the bills and tucked them into her pocket.

Even so, she asked, "Don't you want to wait until you have the extra shirt?"

He shook his head. "I trust you."

"Thanks."

"No, thank *you*. That was my favorite shirt. It will be nice to have a spare. Not that I'll be letting any sharks near my clothes, but you never know when you'll meet another Jimena."

She nodded, but he was pretty sure it wasn't in understanding. Someone like her probably wouldn't let a lover that spontaneous and temporary get anywhere near her. She was way too buttoned-up, battened-down and straitlaced for idle encounters, regardless of how beautiful her eyes were or how erotically she bit her lip. Hannah, he was certain, only dated the same kind of upright, forthright, do-right person she was. To Yeager, that would be a fate worse than death.

"I'll see you in a week," he said, lifting a hand in farewell.

As he made his way to the door, he heard her call after him, "Have a great day, Mr. Novak! And remember to look both ways before you cross the street!"

A week later—the day Yeager was scheduled to pick up his new shirt at her apartment, in fact—Hannah was in the back room of Cathcart and Quinn, collecting fabric remnants to take home with her. Everyone else had gone for the day, and she was counting the minutes until she could begin closing up shop, when the store's entrance bell rang to announce a customer. Hoping it would just be someone picking up an alteration, she headed out front.

She didn't recognize the man at the register, but he had the potential to become a client, judging by his bespoke suit from... Aponte's, she decided. It looked like Paolo's work. The man's blond hair was cut with razor-precision, his eyes were cool and keen, and his smile was this just side of dispassionate.

"Hello," Hannah greeted him as she approached. "May I help you?"

"Hannah Robinson?" he asked. Her surprise that he knew her must have been obvious, because he quickly added, "My name is Gus Fiver. I'm an attorney with Tarrant, Fiver and Twigg. We're a probate law firm here in Manhattan."

His response only surprised her more. She didn't

have a will herself, and she knew no one who might have included her in one. Her lack of connections was what had landed her in the foster care system as a three-year-old, after her mother died with no surviving relatives or friends to care for her. And although Hannah hadn't had any especially horrible experiences in the system, she could safely say she'd never met anyone there who would remember her in their last wishes. There was no reason a probate attorney should know her name or where she worked.

"Yes," she said cautiously. "I'm Hannah Robinson."

Gus Fiver's smile grew more genuine at her response. In a matter of seconds he went from being a high-powered Manhattan attorney to an affable boy next door. The change made Hannah feel a little better.

"Excellent," he said. Even his voice was warmer now.

"I'm sorry, but how do you know me?" she asked.

"My firm has been looking for you since the beginning of the year. And one of our clients was looking for you long before then."

"I don't understand. Why would anyone be looking for me? Especially when I'm not that hard to find?"

Instead of answering her directly he said, "You did most of your growing up in the foster care system, yes?"

Hannah was so stunned he would know that about her—few of her friends even knew—that she could only nod.

"You entered the program when you were three, I believe, after your mother, Mary Robinson, died."

Her stomach knotted at the realization that he

would know about her past so precisely. But she automatically replied, "Yes."

"And do you remember what your life was like prior to that?"

"Mr. Fiver, what's this about?"

Instead of explaining he said, "Please, just bear with me for a moment, Ms. Robinson."

Hannah didn't normally share herself with other people until she'd known them for some time, and even then, there were barriers it took a while for most people to breach. But there was something about Gus Fiver that told her it was okay to trust him. To a point.

So she told him, "I only have a few vague memories. I know my mother was a bookkeeper for a welding company on Staten Island and that that's where she and I were living when she died. But I only know that because that's what I've been told. I don't have any mementos or anything. Everything she owned was sold after her death, and what was left in her estate after it was settled was put into trust for me until I turned eighteen and was booted out of the system."

Not that there had been much, but it had allowed Hannah to start life on her own without a lot of the stress she would have had otherwise, and she'd been enormously grateful for it.

"Is your mother the one you inherited your eyes from?" Mr. Fiver asked. "I don't mean to be forward, but they're such an unusual color."

Hannah had fielded enough remarks about her singularly colored eyes—even from total strangers—that she no longer considered them forward. "No," she said. "My mother had blue eyes."

"So you at least remember what she looked like?"

Hannah shook her head. "No. But I take back what I said about mementos. I do have one. A photograph of my mother that one of the social workers was kind enough to frame and give to me before I went into the system. Somehow, I always managed to keep it with me whenever they moved me to a new place."

This interested Mr. Fiver a lot. "Is there any chance you have this photograph with you?"

"I do, actually." Hannah had taken it out of the frame when she was old enough to have a wallet, because she'd always wanted to carry the photo with her. It was the only evidence of her mother she'd ever had.

"May I see it?" Mr. Fiver asked.

Hannah was about to tell him no, that this had gone on long enough. But her damnable curiosity now had the better of her, and she was kind of interested to see where this was going.

"It's in my wallet," she said.

He smiled again, notching another chink in her armor that weakened her mettle. "I don't mind waiting."

She retrieved her purse from beneath the counter and withdrew the photo, now creased and battered, from its plastic sheath to hand to Mr. Fiver. It had been cropped from what must have been a studio portrait, and showed her mother from the chest up, along with the shoulder of someone sitting next to her.

"And your father?" he asked as he studied the picture.

"I didn't know him," Hannah said. "He's listed as a Robert Williams on my birth certificate, but do you know how many Robert Williamses there are in New

York alone? No one ever found him. I never had any family but my mother."

Mr. Fiver returned the photo to her. "The reason we've been looking for you, Ms. Robinson, is because we have a client whose estate we've been managing since his death while we search for his next of kin. That's sort of our specialty at Tarrant, Fiver and Twigg. We locate heirs whose whereabouts or identities are unknown. We believe you may be this client's sole heir."

"I'm sorry to disappoint you, Mr. Fiver, but that's impossible. If my mother had had any family, the state would have found them twenty-five years ago."

He opened his portfolio and sifted through its contents, finally withdrawing an eight-by-ten photo he held up for Hannah to see. It was the same picture of her mother she had been carrying her entire life, but it included the person who'd been cropped from her copy—a man with blond hair and silver-gray eyes. Even more startling, a baby with the exact same coloring was sitting in her mother's lap.

Her gaze flew to Mr. Fiver's. But she had no idea what to say.

"This is a photograph of Stephen and Alicia Linden of Scarsdale, New York," he said. "The baby is their daughter, Amanda. Mrs. Linden and Amanda disappeared not long after this picture was taken."

A strange buzzing erupted in Hannah's head. How could Gus Fiver have a photo of her mother identical to hers? Was the baby in her mother's lap Hannah? Was the man her father? What the hell was going on?

All she could say, though, was "I don't understand."

"One day, while Stephen Linden was at work in the city," Mr. Fiver continued, "Alicia bundled up ten-month-old Amanda and, with nothing but the clothes on their backs, left him." He paused for a moment, as if he were trying to choose his next words carefully. "Stephen Linden was, from all accounts, a…difficult man to live with. He…mistreated his wife. Badly. Alicia feared for her and her daughter's safety, but her husband's family was a very powerful one and she worried they would hinder her in her efforts to leave him. So she turned to an underground group active in aiding battered women, providing them with new identities and forged documents and small amounts of cash. With the assistance of this group, Alicia and Amanda Linden of Scarsdale were able to start a new life as Mary and Hannah Robinson of Staten Island."

By now, Hannah was reeling. She heard what Mr. Fiver was saying, but none of it quite registered. "I… I'm sorry, Mr. Fiver, but this… You're telling me I'm not the person I've always thought I was? That my whole life should have been different from the one I've lived? That's just… It's…"

Then another thought struck her and the air rushed from her lungs in a quick whoosh. Very softly, she asked, "Is my father still alive?"

At this, Mr. Fiver sobered. "No, I'm sorry. He died almost twenty years ago. Our client, who initially launched the search for you, was your paternal grandfather." He paused a telling beat before concluding, "Chandler Linden."

Had there been any breath left in Hannah, she would have gasped. Everyone in New York knew the name Chandler Linden. His ancestors had practically built this city, and, at the time of his death, he'd still owned a huge chunk of it.

Although she had no idea how she managed it, Hannah said, "Chandler Linden was a billionaire."

Mr. Fiver nodded. "Yes, he was. Ms. Robinson, you might want to close up shop early today. You and I have *a lot* to talk about."

Two

Yeager Novak didn't find himself in Queens very often. Or, for that matter, ever. And he wasn't supposed to be here now. His assistant, Amira, was supposed to be picking up his shirt at Hannah's. But she'd needed to take the afternoon off for a family emergency, so he'd told her he would deal with whatever was left on his agenda today himself—not realizing at the time that that would include going to Queens. By train. Which was another place he didn't find himself very often. Or, for that matter, ever. This time of day, though, the train was fastest and easiest, and he needed to be back in Manhattan ASAP.

But as he walked down Greenpoint Avenue toward 44th Street, he couldn't quite make himself hurry. Queens was different from Manhattan—less frantic, more relaxed. Especially now, at the end of the workday. The sun was hanging low in the sky, bathing the stunted brick buildings in gold and amber. Employees in storefronts were turning over Closed signs as waiters at cafés unfolded sandwich boards with nightly specials scrawled in bright-colored chalk. People on the street actually smiled and said hello to him as he passed. With every step he took, Yeager felt like he was moving backward in time, and somehow, that made him want to go slower. Hannah's neighborhood was even more quaint than he'd imagined.

He hated quaint. At least, he usually did. Somehow the quaintness of Sunnyside was less off-putting than most.

Whatever. To each his own. Yeager would suffocate in a place like this. Quiet. Cozy. Family friendly. Why was a healthy, red-blooded young woman with beautiful silver-gray eyes and a surprisingly erotic lip nibble living somewhere like this? Not that anything Hannah did was Yeager's business. But he did kind of wonder.

Her apartment was on the third and uppermost floor of one of those tawny brick buildings, above a Guatemalan *mercado*. He rang her bell and identified himself, and she buzzed him in. At the top of the stairs were three apartments. Hannah had said hers was B, but before he even knocked on the door, she opened it.

At least, he thought it was Hannah who opened it. She didn't look much like the woman he knew from Cathcart and Quinn. The little black half-glasses were gone and the normally bunned-up hair danced around her shoulders in loose, dark gold curls. In place of her shapeless work jacket, she had on a pair of striped shorts and a sleeveless red shirt knotted at her waist. As small as she was, she had surprisingly long legs and they ended in feet whose toenails were an even brighter red than her shirt.

But what really made him think someone else had taken Hannah's place was her expression. He'd never seen her be anything but cool and collected. This version looked agitated and anxious.

"Hannah?" he asked, just to be sure.

"Yeah, hi," she said. She sounded even more on edge than she looked. "I'm sorry. I totally forgot about your pickup tonight."

"Didn't my assistant email you yesterday to confirm?"

"She did, actually. But today was…" She shook her head as if trying to physically clear it of something. But that didn't seem to work, because she still looked distracted. "I got some, um, very weird news today. But it's okay, your shirt is finished." She hurried on. "I just…" She inhaled a deep breath, released it in a ragged sigh…and still looked as if she were a million miles away. "I forgot about the pickup," she said again. Almost as an afterthought, she added, "Come on in."

She opened the door wider and stepped back to get out of his way. Good thing, too, since the room he walked into was actually an alcove that was barely big enough to hold both of them. As he moved forward, Hannah wedged herself behind him to close the door, brushing against him—with all that naked skin—as she did. It was then he noticed something about her he'd never noticed before. She smelled like raspberries. Really ripe, really succulent, raspberries.

Another step forward took him into her apartment proper, but it wasn't much bigger than the alcove and seemed to consist of only one room. Yeager looked for doors that would lead to others, but saw only one, which had to be for the bathroom. The "kitchen" was a couple of appliances tucked into another alcove adjacent to the single window in the place, one that offered a view of a building on the next street. The apartment was furnished with the bare essentials for living and the tools of a seamstress's trade—a sewing machine and ironing board, a trio of torso stands for works-in-progress, stacks of fabric and a rack of plastic-covered garments.

"I guess my place is a little smaller than yours, huh?" Hannah asked, obviously sensing his thoughts.

Smaller than his *place*? Her apartment was smaller than his bedroom. But all he said was, "A bit."

She squeezed out of the alcove, past him—leaving that tantalizing scent of raspberries in her wake—and strode to the rolling rack, from which she withdrew one of the plastic-covered garments. As he followed, he noted a half-empty bottle of wine on one of the end tables by the love seat. He thought maybe he'd interrupted a romantic evening she was spending with someone else—the bathroom door was closed—then noted that the near-empty glass sitting behind the bottle was alone.

"Do you want to try it on before you take it?" she asked. "Just to be sure it fits?"

Yeager figured it probably wasn't a bad idea, since he was leaving in two days for South Africa and there wouldn't be time for Amira to come back for it if it needed alterations. Truth be told, he also wasn't sure he should leave Hannah alone just yet, what with the wine, the distraction and the anxious look…and, okay, all that naked skin.

"Yeah, I guess I should, just in case," he replied.

As she removed the plastic from the shirt, he tossed his suit jacket onto the love seat, tugged free his tie and unbuttoned the shirt he was wearing. By the time he shed it, she was holding up his new one for him to slip on. She looked a little steadier now and seemed more like herself. His concern began to ease a bit. Until he drew near and saw that her eyes housed a healthy bit of panic.

It was obvious there was something bothering her. A lot. Yeager told himself that whatever it was, it was none of his business. But that didn't keep him from wondering. Boyfriend troubles? Family conflicts? Problems at work? He knew nothing about her outside her job. Because there was no reason for him to know anything about her outside her job. There was no reason for him to care, either. That wasn't to be cold or unfeeling. That was just how he was. He didn't care about much of anything outside his immediate sphere of existence. Somehow, though, he suddenly kind of cared about Hannah.

"I'm sorry," she said as he thrust his arm through the shirt's sleeve, "but the fabric isn't exactly the same as the original. Since I was moonlighting, I couldn't use what we have at work, and that came from Portugal. But I found a beautiful dobby in nearly the same color. I hope it's okay. It brought the price down a bit."

Yeager couldn't have cared less about the price. He cared about quality and style. Maybe it was superficial, but a man who was the face of a Fortune 500 company had to look good. And, thanks to Hannah, he always did.

"No, this is good," he said. "It's got a great texture. I actually like this one better than the one you made for me at Cathcart and Quinn. Why aren't you the one they're sending on buying trips to London and Portugal?"

"You'll have to ask Mr. Cathcart that question," she said in a way that made him think she'd already broached the topic with her employer and been shot down. Probably more than once.

"Maybe I will," he said, wondering about his sudden desire to act as her champion. "Or maybe you should just open your own business."

As she studied the fit of his shirt, she gestured to the rack of clothes against the wall. "I'm trying."

Out of curiosity, Yeager walked over to look at what she'd made for her other clients. He was surprised to see that the majority of items hanging there were children's clothes.

"You mostly make stuff for kids?" he asked.

Instead of replying, Hannah moved to her sewing machine to withdraw a business card from a stack and handed it to Yeager. It was pale lavender, imprinted with the words, Joey & Kit, and decorated with a logo of a kangaroo and fox touching noses. Below them was the slogan, "Glad rags for happy kids." At the bottom were addresses for a website, an email and a PO box.

"This is your business?" Yeager asked, holding up the card.

She nodded. "I'm an S-corporation. I trademarked the name and logo and everything."

"Why kids' clothes? Seems like other areas of fashion would be more profitable."

"They would be," she said. He waited for her to elaborate. She didn't. He was about to ask her to when she told him, "Turn around, so I can make sure the back darts are aligned."

He did as she instructed, something that left him looking out the apartment's solitary window. He didn't know why, but it really bothered him that Hannah only had one window from which to view the world. His West Chelsea penthouse had panoramic views of Manhattan and the Hudson from floor-to-ceiling windows in most rooms—including two of the three-and-a-half baths. Not that he spent much time at home, but his office in the Flatiron District had pretty breathtaking views of the city, too. No matter where Yeager went in the world, he always made sure he had a lot to look at. Mountain ranges that disappeared into clouds, savannas that dissolved into the horizon, oceans that met the stars in the distant night sky. Some of the best parts of adventure travel were just looking at things. But Hannah lived her life in a square little room with one window that opened onto a building across the way.

"You know, I don't usually have to put darts in a man's shirt," she said. "But the way you're built... broad shoulders, tapered waist..."

Yeager told himself he only imagined the sigh of approval he heard.

"Anyway," she went on, "I think this looks good."

She ran her hand down the length of his back on one side, then up again on the other, smoothing out the seams in question. The gesture was in no way protracted or flirtatious. Her touch was deft and professional. Yet, somehow, it made his pulse twitch.

She stepped in front of him, gave him a final once-over with eyes that still looked a little haunted, and told him, "You're good to go."

It was one of his favorite statements to hear. Yeager loved going. Anywhere. Everywhere. Whenever he could. Strangely, though, in that moment, he didn't want to go. He told himself it was because, in spite of the relative ease of the last few minutes, there was still something about Hannah that was...off. He'd never seen her be anything but upbeat. This evening, she was subdued. And that just didn't sit well with him.

Before he realized what he was doing, he asked, "Hannah, is everything okay?"

Her eyes widened in now unmistakable panic. She opened her mouth to reply but no words emerged. Which may have been his biggest tip-off yet that there was something seriously wrong. Hannah was never at a loss for words. On the contrary, she was generally one of those people who had a snappy reply for everything.

He tried again. "You just don't seem like yourself tonight."

For a moment she looked as if she was going to deny anything was wrong. Then she made a defeated sound and her whole body seemed to slump forward.

"Is this about the weird news you got today?" he asked.

She nodded, but instead of looking at him, she lowered her gaze to the floor. Hannah never did that. She was one of the most direct people he knew, always making eye contact. It was one of the things he loved about her. So few people did that.

"What kind of news was it?"

She hesitated again, still not looking at him. Finally she said, "The kind that could not only completely change my future, but also confirmed that my past could have—should have—been a lot better than it was."

"I'm not sure I understand."

At this, she emitted a strangled chuckle completely devoid of humor. "Yeah, I know the feeling."

Maybe the wine had affected her more than he thought. Probably, he ought to just drop it and pay her for his shirt. Definitely, he should be getting the hell out of there.

Instead he heard himself ask, "Do you want to talk about it?"

At that, she finally pulled her gaze from the floor and met his squarely...for all of a nanosecond. Then she lifted both hands to cover her beautiful silver-gray eyes. Then her lips began to tremble. Then she sniffled. Twice. And that was when Yeager knew he was in trouble. Because Hannah crying was way worse than Hannah panicking. Panic eventually subsided. But sadness... Sadness could go on forever. No one knew that better than he did.

She didn't start crying, though. Not really. After a moment she wiped both eyes with the backs of her hands and dropped them to hug herself tight. But that gesture just made her look even more lost. Especially since her eyes were still damp. Something in Yeager's chest twisted tight at seeing her this way. He had no idea why. He barely knew her. He just hated seeing anyone this distraught.

"Holy crap, do I want to talk about it," she said softly. "I just don't have anyone to talk about it with."

That should have been his cue to get out while he still had the chance. The last thing he had time for—

hell, the last thing he wanted—was to listen to someone whose last name he didn't even know talk about her life-altering problems. He should be heading for the front door stat. And he would. Any minute now. Any second now. In five, four, three, two...

"Give me one minute to change my shirt," he told her, wondering what the hell had possessed him. "Then you can tell me about it."

While Yeager changed his shirt, Hannah moved to the love seat, perching herself on the very edge of the cushion and wondering what just happened. One minute, she'd been double-checking the fit of his shirt and had been almost—*almost*—able to forget, if only for a moment, everything she'd learned today from Gus Fiver. The next minute, Yeager had been offering a sympathetic shoulder to cry on.

Not that she would cry on him. Well, probably not. She didn't want to ruin his shirt. But she appreciated his offer to hang around for a little while. She hadn't felt more alone in her life than she had over the last few hours.

She'd taken Gus Fiver's advice to close Cathcart and Quinn early, then had sat with him in the empty shop for nearly an hour as he'd given her all the specifics about her situation. A situation that included the most stunning good news/bad news scenario she'd ever heard. Since then she'd been here in her apartment, combing the internet for information about her newly discovered family and mulling everything she'd learned, in the hope that it would help her make sense of the choice she had to make. Maybe someone like Yeager, who didn't have any personal involvement, would have a clearer perspective and some decent advice.

She watched as he changed his shirt, doing her best not to stare at the cords of muscle and sinew roping his arms, shoulders and torso. But in an apartment the size of hers, there wasn't much else to stare at. Then again, even if she'd had the frescoes of the Sistine Chapel surrounding her, it would still be Yeager that drew her eye. So she busied herself with filling her wineglass a third time, since the two glasses she'd already consumed had done nothing to take the edge off.

"You want a glass of wine?" she asked Yeager, belatedly realizing how negligent a hostess she'd been.

Also belatedly, she remembered she'd picked up the wine at Duane Reade on her way home from work. She reread the label as she placed it back on the table. Chateau Yvette claimed to be a "wine product" that paired well with pizza and beef stew. It probably wasn't a brand Yeager normally bought for himself. But it was too late to retract the offer now.

"Yeah, that'd be great," he said as he finished buttoning his shirt.

She retrieved another glass from the kitchen and poured the wine. By then, Yeager had draped the plastic back over his new shirt and was sitting on the love seat—taking up most of it. So much so that his thigh aligned with hers when she sat and handed him his glass. She enjoyed another healthy swig from her own and grimaced. She honestly hadn't realized until then how, uh, not-particularly-good it was. Probably because her head had been too full of *Omigod, omigod, omigod, what am I going to do?*

"So what's up?" he asked.

She inhaled a deep breath and released it slowly. It still came out shaky and uneven. Not surprising, since shaky and uneven was how she'd been feeling since Gus Fiver had dropped his Chandler Linden bombshell. There was nothing like the prospect of inheriting billions of dollars to send a person's pulse and brain synapses into overdrive.

If Hannah actually inherited it.

She took another breath and this time when she released it, it was a little less ragged. "Have you heard of a law firm called Tarrant, Fiver and Twigg?" she asked.

Yeager nodded. "Yeah. They're pretty high-profile. A lot of old money—big money—clients."

"Well, I had a meeting with one of their partners this afternoon."

Yeager couldn't quite hide his surprise that someone like her would be in touch with such a financial powerhouse, though he was obviously trying to. Hannah appreciated his attempt to be polite, but it was unnecessary. She wasn't bothered by being working class, nor was she ashamed of her upbringing. Even if she didn't talk freely about her past, she'd never tried to hide it, and she wasn't apologetic about the way she lived now. She'd done pretty well for herself and lived the best life she could. She was proud of that.

Still, she replied, "I know. They're not exactly my social stratum. But I didn't contact them. They contacted me."

"About?" he asked.

"About the fact that I'm apparently New York's equivalent to the Grand Duchess Anastasia of Russia."

Now Yeager looked puzzled. So she did her best to

explain. Except she ended up not so much explaining as just pouring out her guts into his lap.

Without naming names, and glossing over many of the details, she told him about her discovery that she'd been born to a family she never knew she had in a town she would have sworn she'd never visited. She told him about her father's addiction and abuse and about her mother's custodial kidnapping of her. She told him about their false identities and their move from Scarsdale to Staten Island. She told him about her mother's death when she was three and her entry into the foster care system, where she'd spent the next fifteen years. And she told him about how, in a matter of minutes today, she went from living the ordinary life of a seamstress to becoming one of those long-lost heirs to a fortune who seemed only to exist in over-the-top fiction.

Through it all, Yeager said not a word. When she finally paused—not that she was finished talking by a long shot, because there was still *so much more* to tell him—he only studied her in silence. Then he lifted the glass of wine he had been holding through her entire story and, in one long quaff, drained it.

And then he grimaced, too. Hard. "That," he finally said, "was unbelievable."

"I know," Hannah told him. "But it's all true."

He shook his head. "No, I mean the wine. It was unbelievably bad."

"Oh."

"Your life is… Wow."

For a moment he only looked out at her little apartment without speaking. Then he looked at Hannah again.

And he said, "This isn't the kind of conversation to be having over unbelievably bad wine."

"It isn't?"

He shook his head. "No. This is the kind of conversation that needs to be had over extremely good Scotch."

"I don't have any Scotch." And even if she did, it wouldn't be extremely good.

He roused a smile. "Then we'll just have to go find some, won't we?"

Three

Instead of extremely good Scotch, they found a sufficiently good Irish whiskey at a pub up the street from Hannah's apartment. She'd ducked into the bathroom to change before they'd left, trading her shorts for a printed skirt that matched her shirt and dipping her feet into a pair of flat sandals. By the time the bartender brought their drinks to them at a two-seater cocktail table tucked into the corner of the dimly lit bar, she was beginning to feel a little more like herself.

Until she looked at Yeager and found him eyeing her with a scrutiny unlike any she'd ever had from him before. Normally he showed her no more interest than he would...well, a seamstress who was sewing some clothes for him. Sure, the two of them bantered back and forth whenever he was in the shop, but it was the kind of exchange everybody shared with people they saw in passing on any given day—baristas, cashiers, doormen, that kind of thing. In the shop, his attention passed with the moments. But now…

Now, Yeager Novak's undivided attention was an awesome thing. His sapphire eyes glinted like the gems they resembled, and if she'd fancied he could see straight into her soul before, now she was certain of it. Her heart began to hammer hard in her chest, her blood began to zip through her veins and her breathing became more shallow than it had been all day. This time, though, the reactions had little to do with the news of her massive potential inheritance and a lot to do with Yeager.

He must have sensed her reaction—hyperventilation was generally a dead giveaway—because he nudged her glass closer to her hand and said, "Take a couple sips of your drink. Then tell me again about how you ended up in Staten Island."

She wanted to start talking now, but she did as he instructed and enjoyed a few slow sips of her whiskey. She wasn't much of a drinker, usually sticking to wine or some sissy, fruit-sprouting drink. The liquor was smooth going down, warming her mouth and throat and chest. She closed her eyes to let it do its thing, then opened them again to find Yeager still studying her. She was grateful for the dim lighting of the bar. Not just because it helped soothe her rattled nerves but because it might mask the effect he was having on her.

"According to Mr. Fiver," she said, "my mother got help from a group of women who aided other women in escaping their abusers. They paid counterfeiters to forge new identities for both of us—fake social security numbers, fake birth certificates, the works. I don't know how my mother found them, but she needed them because my father's family was super powerful and probably could have kept her from leaving him or, at least, made sure she couldn't take me with her."

"And just who was your father's family?"

Hannah hesitated. During her internet search of her birth name, she had come across a number of items about her and her mother's disappearance from Scarsdale a quarter century ago. Some of them had been articles that appeared in newspapers and magazines shortly after the fact, but many of them were fairly current on "unsolved mystery" type blogs and websites. It had been singularly creepy to read posts about herself from strangers speculating on her fate. Some people were convinced Stephen Linden had beaten his wife and daughter to death and disposed of their bodies, getting away with murder, thanks to his social standing. Some thought baby Amanda had been kidnapped by strangers for ransom and that her mother had interrupted the crime and been killed by the perpetrators, her body dumped in Long Island Sound. Other guesses were closer to the truth: that Alicia escaped her abusive marriage with Amanda in tow and both were living now in the safety of a foreign country.

What would Yeager make of all this?

Since Hannah had already told him so much—and still had a lot more to reveal—she said, "My father's name was Stephen Linden. He died about twenty years ago. It was my recently deceased grandfather, Chandler Linden, who was looking for me and wanted to leave me the family fortune."

Yeager studied her in silence for a moment. Then he said, "You're Amanda Linden."

She had thought he would remark on her grandfather's identity, not hers. But she guessed she shouldn't be surprised by his knowing about Amanda's disappearance, too, since so many others did.

"You know about that," she said.

He chuckled. "Hannah, everyone knows about that. Any kid who was ever curious about unsolved crimes has read about the disappearance of Amanda Linden and her mother." He lifted a shoulder and let it drop. "When I was in middle school, I wanted to be a private investigator. I was totally into that stuff."

"Yeah, well, I wasn't," she said. "I had no idea any of this happened. Let alone that it happened to me."

She took another sip of her drink and was surprised by how much she liked the taste. Since Yeager had ordered it, it was doubtless the best this place had. Maybe her Linden genes just had a natural affinity for the finer things in life. She sipped her drink again.

"So you were destined for a life of wealth and privilege," Yeager said, "and instead, you grew up in the New York foster care system."

"Yep."

"And how was that experience?"

Hannah dropped her gaze to her drink, dragging her finger up and down the side of the glass. "It wasn't as terrible as what some kids go through," she said. "But it wasn't terrific, either. I mean a couple of times I landed in a really good place, with really good people. But just when I started to think maybe I'd found a spot where I fit in and could be reasonably happy for a while, I always got yanked out and put somewhere else where I didn't fit in and wasn't particularly happy."

She glanced up to find that he was looking at her

as if she were some interesting specimen under a microscope. A specimen he couldn't quite figure out. So she returned her attention to her glass.

"That was the worst part, you know?" she continued. "Never feeling like I belonged anywhere. Never feeling like I had a real home or a real family. Now I know that I could have and should have—that I actually *did* have—both. The irony is that if I'd grown up as Amanda Linden, with all her wealth and privilege, I would have had a terrifying father who beat up my mother and very well could have come after me. Foster care was no picnic, but I was never physically abused. Dismissed and belittled, yeah. Neglected, sure. But never harmed. As Amanda, though…"

She didn't finish the statement. She didn't dare. She didn't even want to think about what kind of life she might have lived if her mother hadn't rescued her from it. What kind of life her mother had endured for years before her daughter's safety had compelled her to run.

"Some people would argue that neglect and belittlement *are* harm," Yeager said softly.

"Maybe," she conceded. "But I'd rather be neglected and belittled and shuffled around and have nothing to my name than live in the lap of luxury and go through what my mother must have gone through to make her escape the way she did. I just wish she'd had more time to enjoy her life once she got it back."

And Hannah wished she'd had more time herself to get to know her mother. Mary Robinson, formerly Alicia Linden, might very well have saved her daughter's life—both figuratively and literally. Yet Hannah had no way to thank her.

"Your grandfather, Chandler Linden, was a billionaire," Ycager said in the same matter-of-fact tone he'd been using all night.

Hannah's stomach pitched to have the knowledge she'd been carrying around in her head all evening spoken aloud. Somehow, having it out in the open like that made it so much more real. Her heart began to thunder again and her vision began to swim. Hyperventilation would come next, so she enjoyed another, larger, taste of her drink in an effort to stave it off.

"Yeah," she said quietly when she set her glass on the table. "He was."

"Which means that now you're a billionaire," Yeager said in the same casual tone.

Oh, by . There went her stomach again. "Well, I *could* be a billionaire," she told him.

"*Could* be?" he echoed. "You said your grandfather bequeathed his entire estate to you. What are they waiting on? A DNA test?"

"Mr. Fiver took a sample of my saliva while we were talking," she said. "But that's just a formality for the courts. There's no question I'm Amanda. I didn't just inherit my father's unique eye color. I also have a crescent-shaped birthmark on my right shoulder blade that shows up with some regularity in the Linden line. And, yes, my grandfather wants his entire estate to go to me. But there are certain…terms…of his will that need to be met before I can inherit."

"What kind of terms?"

Hannah threw back the rest of her drink in one long gulp. Before her glass even hit the table, Yeager was lifting a hand to alert the bartender that they wanted another round. He even pointed at Hannah and added, "Make hers a double."

Hannah started to tell him that wouldn't be necessary. Then she remembered her grandfather's demands again and grabbed Yeager's drink, downing what was left of it, too. She would need all the false courage she could get if she was going to actually talk about this. Especially with someone like Yeager.

Once the whiskey settled in her stomach—woo, that warmth was starting to feel really good—she did her best to gather her thoughts, even though they all suddenly wanted to go wandering off in different directions. And she did her best to explain.

"Okay, so, as rich as the Lindens have always been," she said, "they weren't particularly, um, fruitful. I'm the last of the line. My father was an only child, and he didn't remarry before his death. My grandfather's sister never married or had children. Their father had twin brothers, but they both died from influenza before they were even teenagers. The Linden family tree prior to that had been growing sparser and sparser with each ensuing generation, so I'm all that's left of them."

Her thoughts were starting to get a little fuzzy, so Hannah drew in another long breath and let it go. There. That was better. Kind of. Where was she? Besides about to have a panic attack? Oh, right. The dried-up Linden family tree.

"*Any*way…" She started again. "I guess my grandfather was sort of horrified by the idea that the world would no longer be graced with the Linden family presence—we were, I have learned, some of the best fat cats and exploiters of the proletariat out there—so he tied some strings to my inheritance."

"What kind of strings?" Yeager asked.

"Well, actually it's only one string," she told him.

"A string that's more like a rope. A rope that's tied into a noose."

He was starting to look confused. She felt his pain.

"Hannah, I think I can safely say that I have no idea what you're talking about."

She tried again. "My grandfather included a condition I'll have to meet before I can inherit the family fortune. He wanted to make sure that I, um, further the Linden line."

"Further the line?"

She nodded. Then nodded some more. And then some more. Why couldn't she stop nodding? And why did her head feel like it was beginning to disconnect from her body? With great effort, she stilled and tried to think of the most tactful way to tell Yeager how her grandfather had stipulated that, before she could inherit the piles and piles and *piles* of Linden moolah, she'd have to become a Linden baby factory.

Finally she decided on, "My grandfather has stipulated that, before I can inherit the piles and piles and *piles* of Linden moolah, I have to become a Linden baby factory."

Yeager's eyebrows shot up to nearly his hairline. "He wants you to procreate in order to inherit?"

Yeah, that would have been a much more tactful way to say it. Oh, well. "That's exactly what he wants," she said. "It's what he demands. In order to inherit the family fortune, I have to either already be a mother or on my way to becoming one."

"Can he do that?"

"Apparently so. The wording of his will was something along the lines of, if, when I was located after his death, I had a child or children, then no problem, here's more money than you could have ever imagined having, don't spend it all in one place."

"But you don't have a child or children," Yeager pointed out.

"Nope."

"So what happens in that case?"

"In that case, I have six months to get pregnant."

Yeager's eyebrows shot back up. "And what happens if you don't get pregnant in six months?"

"Then *aaaallllll* the Linden money will go to charity and I'll get a small severance package of fifty grand for my troubles, thanks so much for playing. Which, don't get me wrong, would be great, and I'd be most appreciative, but…"

"It's not billions."

"Right."

He opened his mouth to say something then closed it again. For another moment he studied her in silence. Then he said, "Well, that sucks."

"Yeah."

The bartender arrived with their drinks and Hannah immediately enjoyed a healthy swallow of hers.

"See, though," she said afterward, "the problem isn't with me having children. I've always planned on having kids someday. I want to have kids. I love kids. I wouldn't even mind being a single mother, as long as I had the time and money to make sure I could do it right. Which, of course, I would, with billions of dollars. But to only have six months to make the decision and put it into action?"

"Actually, you don't even have six months, if that's the deadline," Yeager said oh, so helpfully. "I mean, I'm no expert in baby-making—and thank God for that—but even I know it doesn't always happen the first time. Or the second. Or the third. You're going to need all the time you can get."

Hannah closed her eyes at the reminder of what she already knew. "Thanks a lot, Grandpa. There's nothing like the pressure of a ticking clock to bring a girl's egg delivery to a crawl."

She snapped her eyes open again. Oh, God, did she actually just say that out loud? When she heard Yeager chuckle, she realized she had. Then again, this whole situation was kind of comical. In an over-the-top, stranger-than-fiction, absolutely surreal kind of way.

She leaned forward and banged her head lightly against the table. In some part of her brain, she'd already realized that, if she wanted to inherit this money—and she very much wanted to inherit this money, since it would enable her to realize every dream she'd ever dreamed—she was going to have to make a decision fast and get herself in the family way as soon as possible.

But now that the rest of her brain was getting in on the action, she knew the prospects weren't looking great. She had nothing remotely resembling a boyfriend. She didn't even have a boy who was her friend. And only one attempt at in vitro was way beyond her financial means. She'd already checked that out, too.

Which left visits to a sperm bank, something she'd also been researching online tonight. If necessary, she could afford a few of those—barely—but if none of the efforts took, and she didn't conceive by the six-month deadline, she would have drained what little savings she had. And fifty grand, although an impressive sum, wasn't going to go far in New York City.

These things came with no guarantees, especially if her anxiety about everything really did turn her eggs into the same kind of shrinking violets she was.

What Hannah needed was something that could counter her potentially diminished fertility. A super-tricked-out, ultra-souped-up, hypermasculine testosterone machine that could fairly guarantee to knock her up. And where the hell was she supposed to find a guy like—

She sat back up and looked at Yeager—and the super-tricked-out, ultra-souped-up, hypermasculine body that housed him. Talk about testosterone overload. The guy flew MiG 29s over the Russian tundra for kicks. He'd climbed Mt. Everest. Twice. He served himself up as shark bait *on purpose*, for God's sake. The man probably produced enough testosterone for ten men. If he couldn't put a woman in the family way, nobody could.

Maybe it was the wine. Maybe it was the whiskey. Maybe it was the wine followed by the whiskey. Or maybe it was just the unmitigated terror of having finally discovered who she was and where she belonged and everything she could attain. It wasn't just the reclaiming of a life that had been denied her, but the promise of a happiness she never thought she would have—and realizing she could lose it all in the blink of an eye or the shrink of an egg.

And she heard herself saying, "So, Mr. Novak. Have you ever thought about donating your sperm to a good cause?"

Before he could stop himself, Yeager spat back into his glass a mouthful of whiskey, something that had never happened to him before. Then again, no one had ever asked him about his intentions for his sperm before, either, so he guessed he was entitled to this one social lapse.

As he wiped his chin with his napkin, he tried to tell himself he'd misheard Hannah's question. "Excuse me?" he asked.

"Your sperm," she said, enunciating the word more clearly this time. "Have you ever thought about donating it?"

So much for having misheard her. "Uh…no," he said decisively.

She eyed him intently, her gaze never wavering from his. For a minute he thought she was going to drop it. Then she asked, "Well, would you think about it now?"

"No," he said even more decisively.

Still, she wouldn't let it go. "I mean, if you would consider it—donating it to me, I mean—I'd sign any kind of documents you want me to, to relieve you of all legal and financial obligations for any offspring that might, um, you know, spring off me. And I'd really, really, really, really, really…"

Her voice trailed off and her brows knitted, as if she'd lost track of what she was going to say. Then her expression cleared. A little.

"I'd really appreciate it," she finally finished. "A lot."

He was about to tell her she was delusional. But another look at her expression, especially her piercing silver-gray eyes—which were a lot less piercing at the moment than they usually were—told him what she really was was drunk. Hell, of course she was drunk.

No woman in her right mind would ask a man she barely knew to father her child.

He never should have encouraged her to drink whiskey on top of bad wine. Hannah wasn't the kind of woman who could drink a man under the table, the way women he dated generally were. The only reason she was asking him such a ridiculous question was because her judgment was clouded. He should just let her down gently, explain why what she was asking him to do was a terrible idea, then make sure she got home safely.

He should also, as inconspicuously as possible, scoot both of their drinks out of her reach. Which he did. She didn't even notice, because she was hanging so heavily on his reply.

"Hannah, I… I'm flattered," he finally said. "But it's not a good idea for me to do something like that."

She looked crestfallen. "Why not?"

"Because I'm not good father material."

At this, she looked aghast. "Are you kidding? You're incredible father material. You're smart and interesting and brave and funny and, holy cow, you're *gorgeous*."

He bit back a smile. "Thanks. But those aren't things that necessarily make a good father."

"Maybe not, but they make an *ex*cellent breeder."

He wasn't sure how to respond to that. Part of him was inordinately proud of the suggestion. Another part felt kind of tawdry. Strange—no woman had ever made him feel cheap before.

He pushed the thought away. "Well, I appreciate you considering me that way—" *I think* "—but it's still not a good idea."

"Why not?" she insisted.

There were so many reasons he could give her. There was just no way Yeager was going to be a father at all. Ever. Not in any universe, known or unknown. Not in her dreams or in his. Children were a constant reminder of a person's mortality—nothing marked the passage of time and the steady march to old age better than a child growing by leaps and bounds. The last thing he wanted to be reminded of was that, someday, he would be too old—or too dead—to enjoy life to its fullest. Not to mention that if he knew there was a kid in the world he was responsible for, it might make him more cautious, something that would put a major crimp in his extreme-adventure, thumbing-his-nose-at-death lifestyle. And there was nothing Yeager loved more than his lifestyle.

There was just no way he was going to become a father. Period. No—exclamation point. No—double exclamation point. Triple. Quadruple. Quintuple. Whatever the "uple" was that came after infinity. But, how to make that clear to Hannah?

"It's not a good idea," he said again, more gently this time.

For some reason his softer tone had a greater impact in conveying his opposition than his decisive one. She slumped back in her seat and covered her face with her hands the way she had earlier in her apartment.

He felt that weird tightening in his chest again. But what was he supposed to do? Hannah definitely had a major problem on her hands. But it was *her* problem, not his. She was a resourceful person. She'd figure out what she needed to do. Tomorrow, after the shock had worn off some, she could assess with a clearer head. If she didn't have a boyfriend—and since she'd just asked Yeager to be her sperm donor, it was clear she didn't have a boyfriend—then maybe some other friend with a, um, Y-chromosome would, ah, rise to the occasion. To put it crassly. Or there had to be dozens of sperm banks in New York she could use. Women did that all the time. It was no big deal.

Even if, somehow, Hannah doing that felt like kind of a big deal.

"Come on," he said, "let's get you home."

He withdrew his wallet and threw a handful of bills down on the table. Then, as gently as he could, he pulled her hands away from her face. There were tears in her eyes again, but he did his best to make himself immune to them. He almost succeeded. Then he led her through the bar and out onto the street. It was fully dark now, but there were still plenty of pedestrians. Muted music filtered through the open doors of the bars they passed, and the air was heavy with the aroma of summer in the city.

Hannah said not a word as they made their way back to her apartment. Absently, she withdrew her keys from her purse and promptly dropped them, so Yeager scooped them up and did the honors. It wasn't that hard. She only had three keys on her ring and he lucked into the correct one right off the bat. One of the others opened her front door at the top of the stairs. The third was probably for Cathcart and Quinn.

His own key ring held a dozen keys that he needed to get through a typical week. Hannah only needed three for the whole of her life. But then Hannah lived in one room with one window, too. He pushed her front door open and stood back for her to enter. A family fortune would certainly make her life better. *If* she was able to inherit.

She would be, he assured himself as he followed her into her apartment. She was a smart, capable person. She'd figure out how to make it happen. Eventually.

"Are you going to be okay?" he asked.

She headed to the love seat and folded herself onto it. "Yeah," she assured him in a way that wasn't at all reassuring.

"You sure?"

She nodded. "Don't forget your shirt."

Damn. Good thing she'd reminded him. He actually had forgotten about it. And it was the whole reason he'd come there tonight. He crossed to the rack to retrieve it.

He'd already paid her the extra hundred he'd promised, but he hadn't paid for the shirt itself. So he asked, "How much do I owe you?"

She cited a price significantly lower than he would have paid had she made the shirt under the auspices of her employer, presumably because of the different fabric. So he pulled out all the bills that remained in his wallet, which was actually more than what the shirt would have cost him at Cathcart and Quinn, and handed them to her.

"That's too much," she said, handing a few bills back.

He started to insist she take them anyway, but something in her voice made him stop. She sounded almost offended that he was giving her more than she asked for. So he returned the bills to his wallet. She stretched out on the love seat, tucked a throw pillow under her head and closed her eyes. He wondered where she slept at night and then noted that the wall behind the love seat looked like it housed a Murphy bed. Lying there the way she was now, she looked even smaller than she usually did, swallowed by the tiny room in which she lived.

Business concluded, it was time for Yeager to go. His flight to the other side of the world left in thirty-six hours. He had a million things to do between now and then. So why was he hesitant to leave Hannah's cramped little apartment that looked at the back of a building across the way?

"I'm not leaving for South Africa until the day after tomorrow," he said. "If you need to talk between now and then, just…"

Just what? he asked himself. If she needed to talk, she should just call him and he'd come right over? Hell, on days as busy as tomorrow was promising to be, he didn't even answer his phone, let alone take on any activities that weren't absolutely essential.

"If you need to talk, you can call me," he told her.

"That's okay," she replied softly, not opening her eyes. "I'll be fine. Thanks."

"You're sure?"

She nodded.

"Okay," he said. And still didn't leave.

She opened her eyes and he felt better when he saw that some of the life had returned to their silvery depths. "Bon voyage," she told him. "Try not to bleed on anything this time, okay?"

He grinned. "I'll see you when I get back."

Because he always saw her when he got back. He invariably had something that needed mending or clcaning. Funny, though, how that was the last thing he was thinking about at the moment. She really did have beautiful eyes.

"Be careful," she told him.

"I told you those are the last words—"

"Break a leg," she amended.

"Actually, that's probably not the best thing to say to an extreme adventurer, either."

"Have fun."

"That's more like it."

Even though he didn't want to, Yeager made himself cross to the front door and open it. Hannah lifted a hand in farewell then he stepped across the threshold and closed the door behind him. Leaving him to focus on all the other things he needed to do before he left town. Instead, as he made his way down Greenpoint Avenue toward the train, Yeager found himself wondering what two eye colors had to mix in a set of parents to make such an interesting combination of gray and silver in their child.

And he wondered if, when Hannah had her baby—and he was sure that somehow, some way, that would definitely happen—her child would have silver-gray eyes, too.

Four

Three weeks after Hannah asked Yeager if he would consider donating his sperm for a worthy cause, she still couldn't believe she'd done it. Every time she remembered that conversation, she was mortified all over again. And she promised herself she would never mix acceptably good Irish whiskey and bad wine products again.

Not that she would be doing that anyway, since she'd taken the plunge and contacted a Manhattan sperm bank to begin the process of artificial insemination. With any luck, she'd be pregnant soon, something that would put an end to imbibing for a while. It would put an end to a lot of things, actually. If—no, when—Hannah became pregnant, she would enter an entirely new phase of her life, one from which she would never be able to backpedal.

She'd spent the entire week following her first conversation with Gus Fiver sorting out her thoughts, weighing the pros and cons and ins and outs of her prospects. And in the end she hadn't been all that surprised to realize that, even more than inheriting a fortune, she wanted to get pregnant because she was ready to start a family—and probably had been for some time.

She'd wanted to be a part of a family her entire life, after all. She'd just always assumed she would need to have a life partner to achieve that. Not only because of the biological requirements, but because of the financial ones, as well. As much as Hannah wanted to have kids, there was no way she could afford to do that on her own with the life she led now. But if she'd had the financial means to raise a child, she would have started a family years ago.

If things worked out the way she now hoped—and they would work out…she hoped—she would not only have the funds to establish Joey & Kit as a driving force in the children's fashion business, she'd also be surrounded by family as she did it. Because if she inherited the funds to raise a child right, then no way was she stopping at one. Hannah wanted a houseful of children. Children who would never, ever, be told they had to leave.

Thank goodness for twenty-first-century medical progress and social mores, enabling women who wanted a family to start one, with or without a life partner.

Which was how Hannah came to be sitting on her love seat three weeks after her first meeting with Gus Fiver, laptop open, chamomile steeping, as she perused all the online forms and documents provided by the sperm bank she would be using. And, wow, there were a lot of them. In addition to the registration form, there was the Agreement to Purchase Donor Sperm form, the Authorization to Release Frozen Sperm form, and the Authorization to Transport Frozen Specimen form. Also, the Sperm Cryopreservation form, the Sperm Storage form, and the Egg/Embryo/Ovarian Tissue Storage form.

And then there was all the stuff she had to read and sign off on. Articles about andrology and semen analysis and sperm-washing techniques. More articles about infectious disease screening and genetic testing and karyotyping. It was all so scientific. So clinical. So...

She sighed. So sterile.

She'd had no idea how much time, work and expense went into baby-making when a person wasn't doing it the old-fashioned way. Still, if this was what it took, she would persevere. What was a little carpal tunnel if it meant there was a family at the end of it? Family was what she'd wanted all her life. Family and security. Now both were within her reach. Of course she would do whatever she had to do to win both.

Even if it did feel kind of cold, impersonal and dispassionate, which was the last way a child should be conceived.

It didn't matter, she told herself again. All that mattered was that she would be able to start a family and a business and support them both. All that mattered was that she would never be separated from a family—her family—again. All that mattered was that her children would be loved to distraction and grow up in a secure, stable, permanent environment.

Okay. Pep talk over. Hannah had things to do. She had forms to fill out, a donor to choose, an egg to release… Her evening was full. Cracking her knuckles, she went to the Donor Search tab to fill in her specifications. Unfortunately, when she input her preferred traits of Caucasian, blue eyes, black hair, six-feet-plus and postgraduate degree—she knew Yeager had a master's in Geopolitics, not that she was trying to recreate Yeager or anything like that—the search resulted in *No donors available at this time.*

She tried again, leaving out the part about six-feet-plus. Still nothing. Okay, fine. The donor didn't *have* to have a master's degree. Again, no results. Ultimately the closest she could get to her original preferences was a five-foot-eleven, green-eyed brunet with a BA in philosophy.

She had nearly finished filling out the initial application form when her intercom buzzer rang. Since she wasn't expecting anyone for a pickup from Joey & Kit, she figured it was someone looking for her across-the-hall neighbor Jeannette, who seemed to know everyone in New York, though no one in New York could seem to remember that Jeannette was in unit A, not B.

Hannah went to press the buzzer, ready to tell whoever it was that they had the wrong apartment. Before she had the chance, she heard a familiar voice coming over the intercom. "Hannah? It's Yeager. Are you home?"

After a moment of stunned surprise she replied, "Yeah, come on up," and buzzed him in.

She knew a moment's chagrin when she remembered she was already in her pajamas. Or, at least, what passed for pajamas on her—cotton pants decorated with fat cartoon sheep and a purple T-shirt whose sleeves she'd cut off to use for trim on one of her Joey & Kit creations. But she didn't have time to change, so she opened her front door and stepped into the hallway at the top of the stairs to wait for Yeager.

He climbed them sluggishly, his left hand dragging along the rail beside him. She immediately knew something was wrong. That was hammered home when he finally reached the landing and looked at her. His blue eyes, usually so animated and laughing, were flat and empty. His hair was unkempt. He was unshaved. He looked as if he'd slept in his khaki trousers and white shirt, which he hadn't even tucked in.

"Hey," she said gently by way of a greeting when he topped the last step.

"Hi," he said softly.

She was about to ask him what he was doing there, but something about his demeanor prevented her. Whatever his reason for coming to her place tonight, he would get to it eventually. Right now, he didn't seem inclined to talk.

"Come on in."

She entered first, waiting for him to pass her before closing the door behind him. He strode slowly to the love seat and heavily sat, staring straight ahead but not seeming to see anything.

Hannah sat beside him, closing her laptop and moving it to the floor to make room. "I'm sorry. I'm all out of bad wine," she said, hoping to lighten his mood. "Would you like something else? Coffee? Tea?"

He shook his head, not even smiling at her attempt at levity. "No, that's okay. Thanks."

Finally he turned to look at her. She waited for him to start talking, but he remained silent. So she asked the same question he'd asked three weeks ago, the one that had led to her spilling her troubles out to him.

"Is everything okay?"

He was silent for another moment. Then he said, "Not really." His dark brows arrowed downward and he met her gaze levelly. "I need to ask you a question."

Heat pooled in her belly at the seriousness of his tone. Even so, she told him, "Sure."

There was another bout of silence as he studied her face with great interest. And then, out of nowhere, he asked, "Is that offer to father your child still on the table?"

Yeager really hadn't meant to just blurt out the question the way he had. He'd intended to preface it with all the other things he had to tell Hannah first, so it wouldn't come as such a shock to her when he finally asked it. Then again, after what had happened in Nunavut—and how he'd felt since—the realization that he wanted to ask the question still came as a shock to him. Even more of a shock was how much he hoped she wouldn't tell him he was too late.

It had just been a hell of a few weeks, that was all. The trip to South Africa had been everything he'd hoped for and then some, one rush of adrenaline after another, an intoxicating brew of exuberance and euphoria. But the trip to Nunavut, the one that was supposed to have been no business and all pleasure...

"Yeah, the offer is still good," Hannah said, interrupting his thoughts, something for which he was grateful. "I mean, if you're the onc who's interested, it is."

"I am," he replied immediately.

Although he could see surprise reflected in her silvery eyes, her voice was level and matter-of-fact when she replied.

"O-o-okay."

Well, except for the nervous stammer.

She wanted to know why he'd changed his mind—the look in her eyes made that clear, too. He waited for her to ask, but the question that came out instead was, "Are you, um, sober at the moment?"

For the first time in weeks he smiled. Not a big smile, but it was good to know he could still manage one. "Stone cold," he assured her.

"Okay," she said again, more steadily this time. "Just wanted to make sure."

"You want to know what's brought about this one-eighty, don't you?"

She nodded. He sighed. In spite of having gone over it in his head a million times, he still didn't know how to explain it. Ultimately he decided to begin with what had reawakened the idea of fathering a child with Hannah in his head.

"I lost a good friend a couple of weeks ago," he said.

"And by 'lost,' you mean..."

"He died."

"Oh, Mr. Novak. I am so sorry."

"Yeager," he corrected her, since this wasn't going to be the kind of conversation a person had with some-one who only knew him on a last-name basis. "Call me Yeager, Hannah. What's your last name?" he added, since this wasn't the kind of conversation a person had with someone he only knew on a first-name basis, either.

Surprise flashed in her eyes again but she recovered quickly and told him. "Robinson."

Hannah Robinson. The name suited her. Sturdy, no-nonsense.

She tried again. "I'm so sorry for your loss… Yeager."

"Thanks," he replied, marveling at the curl of pleasure that wound through him when she spoke his name. Where had that come from?

He waited for her to ask what had happened, but she didn't. Hannah Robinson was evidently the sort of person who didn't pry. Normally it would have been something else he loved about her. But it would help to have her guide him through what he had to say.

"You remember how I told you I was going to Nunavut to climb Mount Thor with friends?" he began.

She nodded.

"While we were there, one of those friends… One of them had a… There was an accident," he finally said. "We're still not sure how it happened. I mean, I guess it doesn't matter how it happened. But he…he fell to his death."

"Oh, no…"

"One minute he was there and the next…"

"Oh, Yeager."

Something in his chest grew tight and cold, a sensation that was becoming too familiar. So he did what he always did when that feeling threatened to overwhelm him. He pushed it away.

And he made himself continue. "He and I met in

college. We started Ends of the Earth together. I had the head for business and he was the tech whiz. After we incorporated, I became President and CEO, and he was VP and Chief Technology Officer." He grinned. "He was the only VP Chief Officer of anything for the first three years. He was a great guy. A good friend. Full of life. I still can't believe he's—"

Yeager felt himself starting to blather, so he shut himself up. Hannah seemed to understand, because she scooted closer to him on the love seat. She extended a hand toward him, hesitated, then settled it gently on his forearm. It was a careful, innocent touch, but he felt it to the depths of his soul. Maybe because it was the first comforting gesture someone had made to him since he'd returned to the States.

Hell, even before then. No one ever tried to comfort Yeager. For one thing, he had the kind of life that didn't invite comforting, since it included everything a human being could ever want. For another thing, he had barriers in place that kept people far enough away from him to prevent them from doing things like offer comfort. At least, he'd always thought he had barriers like that in place. Hannah, however, evidently couldn't see them.

"Did he have a family?" she asked.

Yeager shook his head. But her question was the perfect segue for where he needed to steer the conversation. Maybe she'd be able to guide him through this, after all.

"His dad died when he was still a baby and he lost his mom a couple of years ago. He didn't have any brothers or sisters. It was another thing that bonded us when we first met, since I was an only child, too."

"Sounds like you two were a couple of lone wolves who made your own pack," Hannah said.

She lightly squeezed his arm and smiled a gentle smile. That was nice of her. Not many people tried that with Yeager, either.

"Yeah," he said. "Back in the day, being lone wolves suited us. Hell, last month, being lone wolves suited us. He was no more the marrying kind than I am. But suddenly..." Yeager hesitated again. "Suddenly, being a lone wolf has its drawbacks. I mean, there's nothing left of him in the world now, you know? Nothing left behind after his death that might bring comfort to the people who knew him and cared about him in life."

"But you must have some wonderful memories," Hannah said.

"I do. But that's just it. All any of us who knew him has is memories. Memories that will gradually fade then die when we do. After that, there won't be anything left of him at all. No indication that he ever even existed. He was such a larger-than-life person. He lived with such passion and exhilaration. For there to be nothing left now that was a part of him... That just seems wrong, you know?"

Hannah loosened her hold on Yeager's arm but didn't let go. There was something in her eyes now that told him she wasn't following him. Then again, she wasn't the kind of person who wanted to make her mark on the world. She'd said as much herself that time she'd told him what a prudent life she led.

But Yeager did want to make his mark on the world. He wanted to be remembered—and remembered well—long after he was gone. He wanted to leave behind a legacy of some kind. He'd never been sure exactly what kind of legacy, but it had to be something that people could point to and say, "Yeager Novak was here." Something that would keep his name and his spirit alive for years. For generations. Hell, forever. He'd always assumed he had plenty of time to figure out the particulars. But now he understood, too well, that life was fleeting, and he'd damned well better make the best of it because it could be snatched away anytime, without any kind of warning.

"I guess I just always thought he was immortal." Yeager tried again to explain. "That he'd go on forever. I thought both of us would. But now I know the clock is ticking on the immortality thing, and I realize that, if I died tomorrow, the same thing would happen to me that's happened to him. There'd be nothing of me in the world anymore."

"You want to leave behind a legacy after you're gone," she said.

He nodded, stunned that she'd used the same word he'd been thinking. "Yeah."

"And you think a child would be a good legacy."

"Yes."

She hesitated a moment, her gaze never leaving his. "There are other kinds of legacies that would—"

"No, there aren't," he interrupted, fearful she might be reconsidering her offer. "Other legacies can deteriorate or fall apart or be stored somewhere and forgotten about. But a child to carry on after I'm gone will be a literal part of me. And then his—or her—children will be a literal part of me. And their children will be, too. And then their children, and their children, and their children…" He forced a smile then was surprised to realize it wasn't forced at all. "When you get right down to it, Hannah, having a kid to carry on after you're gone damned near makes you immortal."

She smiled back. And something in that smile made Yeager feel better than he'd felt in a very long time. "I guess you're right."

"So I started thinking about that," he continued. "And I started warming to the idea of fathering a child." He might as well admit the rest, since that part had been as surprising as anything else. "I started warming to the idea of fathering *your* child."

Because he'd thought about all the other women he knew who might be amenable to that—there were actually more than a few—and realized Hannah was the only one he could honestly imagine doing the job right.

"If," he concluded, "like I said, the offer is still open."

"It's still open," she assured him again, even more quickly than she had the first time.

"Then I'd like to humbly offer my chromosomes to your cause," he told her.

He hesitated again, not sure how she was going to feel about the next part since it included conditions. He was sure she'd already had enough of those placed on her by her grandfather.

So, being careful for the first time he could remember, he said tentatively, "I have three conditions for my offer, though."

She released his arm. She didn't drop it like a hot potato or anything, but she did withdraw her hand. She also scooted a little bit away from him on the love seat and straightened her spine—a couple more telling gestures.

"What conditions?" she asked a little warily.

He didn't blame her for her caution. But he wasn't going to go into this thing lightly any more than she was.

"Number one," he began, "I'd like you to name the child after the friend I lost."

Her posture eased some. "Okay."

"Don't you want to make sure he didn't have a weird name, or one that's gender-specific?"

She smiled again; a softer smile that changed her whole demeanor. For the first time Yeager was seeing that she wasn't all diligence and pragmatism. There was a lot of gentleness and warmth there, too.

"It doesn't matter," she said. "It's a sweet, loving gesture you want to make, Yeager, and I would never say no to a sweet, loving gesture. There are too few of them in the world."

"His name was Thomas Brennan," Yeager said. "Tommy Brennan. I figure Brennan would suit a boy or girl."

She let it settle in then nodded. "Brennan Novak. That's a good name."

"You don't have to give your baby my last name," Yeager said. Even though, for some reason, he suddenly kind of liked the idea.

"Yeah. I kinda think I do," she said with a smile that was cryptic this time. "He or she will be Brennan Robinson Novak. That's a very good name."

"That is a very good name, now that you mention it," he agreed, feeling strangely gentle and warm himself.

"Okay, so that's settled," she said. "What else?"

His second condition wasn't going to be quite as easy to put on the table as the first. Even so, there was no reason to gloss over it. He might be seeing a softer side of Hannah this evening, but she was still the most practical woman he knew—something he suddenly kind of loved about her—and he knew she would appreciate his forthrightness.

"The second condition is that you and I have to make your baby the old-fashioned way, not with vials and test tubes and syringes. Having an adventurer's legacy come about by syringe just isn't very... I don't know. Adventurous."

"I guess I can see that."

"I'd just prefer to ensure my legacy—and honor Tommy's name—by having this baby come about through natural means and during an epic adventure. That just feels right for some reason. So you and I are going to have to have sex, Hannah. And we're going to have do it in epic proportions on some kind of epic adventure. I hope your passport is up to date."

He was relieved when she didn't look like she wanted to negotiate on the matter. In fact, from her expression, it kind of looked as though she wanted to get started right away.

She blinked a few times then said, pretty amenably, "Okay. If we *have* to."

"We do."

She was silent for another moment. "What's the third condition?"

The third condition was the only one he feared Hannah wouldn't agree to, and it was the most important one. At least, to Yeager. But where her refusal of the first condition would have been disappointing, but not a deal-breaker, and her refusal of the second was never really in doubt—all modesty aside, since he didn't have any, and he'd seen the way she looked at him in the shop when he was half-dressed—his third condition was sacrosanct. If she didn't go along with this one, then he would pull out of the deal.

"I want to be…" he began then changed his mind. "No, I *have* to be a part of the child's life." He hurried to clarify before she could object. "I won't be an intrusion in your life, Hannah. Hell, I don't want to alter my life very much, either. I'll definitely keep adventuring. You'll call the shots when it comes to child rearing. But I want my son or daughter to know me, and I want to know my son or daughter. Yes, you will be the child's primary parent. But I want regular visitation, and when the child is old enough, I want to include him or her in my travels whenever and wherever possible."

He thought she would tell him she'd need time to think about that. Ask if she could she sleep on it and get back to him tomorrow. Instead she told him without hesitation, "No problem."

His surprise that she conceded so easily must have been obvious, because she quickly explained.

"Yeager, I'm the last person to deny a child the right to know his or her parents, since I never knew my own and would have loved nothing more than to have had them in my life. I mean, yeah, it sounds like my father left a lot to be desired as a human being, but I would have still liked the opportunity to know him. Or at least know who he was when I was growing up. Good or bad, a lot of our identity is linked to our parents and where they come from. I never had a chance to know that part of my identity. And I never will. Of course I won't deny you the chance to be a part of your child's life. And I won't deny your child a chance to be a part of your life."

Yeager didn't know what to say. So he only said, "Thanks."

For a long time they sat on the love seat, staring at each other, as if neither knew what to do next. Then again, speaking for himself, Yeager had no idea what to do next. Naturally, he knew the mechanics that went into making a baby. But he also knew there were other things to consider beyond the act itself. Things like timing and opportunity, for instance. He had a pretty hectic schedule mapped out for the next six months. Not that he thought they'd need the full six months to conceive, since they were both young and healthy, but he did need to make some arrangements for the foreseeable future where the workings of Hannah's biological clock were concerned. He'd be there for her whenever she needed him, but, as was the case with living life, he needed some kind of timetable to work with for generating life, too.

"So," he finally said, "what do we do next?"

She lifted her shoulders a little self-consciously then let them drop. When she did, her shirt shifted enough to drop over one shoulder, exposing the delectable skin of her collarbone and the faint upper curve of one breast. In addition to having beautiful eyes, Hannah had some beautiful skin. Even if some of it was, at the moment, clothed in cartoon sheep.

"Well, you said we have to have sex," she replied softly, "so I guess we have sex."

Yeager was still pondering the creaminess of her breast when her words finally registered and, bizarrely, he knew a moment's panic. "Wait, what? You mean right now?"

Why was he panicking? He should have been—and normally would have been—standing up to go to work on his fly by now. But he could tell he wasn't the only one responding uncharacteristically. Hannah was blushing furiously. And seeing that made something inside him that hadn't been warm in a very long time go absolutely incandescent. He'd never seen a woman blush before. Certainly not with the adeptness with which Hannah managed it. And where before a woman blushing would have been off-putting, with her, it was...not. On the contrary...

"No, not right now," she said. "I'm not... I won't be..." She expelled a restless sigh. "My body has a schedule for this kind of thing," she finally said.

"Yeah, I know that much," he assured her. "But I need to know if I should book an extra ticket for my trip to Argentina next week or if we'll be...you know... before then."

You know? he echoed incredulously to himself. Had he just referred to sex as *you know*? What, was he twelve years old? Hell, he hadn't even referred to sex as *you know* when he was twelve.

Hannah blushed again. And that hot place inside him grew hotter still. What was going on with his body tonight? She was the one who was supposed to be experiencing physiological changes, not him.

"It won't be before next week," she told him. "I've mapped out my cycle for the next three months as best I can, and although there's going to be some give-and-take there, because I'm not exactly regular, I can say that the middle of next week will be prime time. But

I can't go to Argentina with you," she added. "I don't have a passport."

She didn't have a passport? Yeager marveled. What kind of person didn't have a passport? Oh, right. A seamstress in Sunnyside, New York, who had to work two jobs to make ends meet.

"Okay, we can get around that," he said. "I can send one of my senior agents on the Argentina trip in my place and stay here in the States. But you need to get a passport ASAP in case this first time doesn't work. Like I said, I really think, to honor Tommy's spirit and make this a legacy in the truest sense, the child should be conceived on an epic adventure."

"And I think that's a gallant and honorable gesture," Hannah told him. "But you need to find something epic to do here in New York. Because I can't take time off from Cathcart and Quinn."

"We have to go someplace other than New York. There's no epic adventure to be had here."

She gaped at him. "Are you out of your mind? New York is nothing but epic adventures. Have you taken the subway lately? Walked through the Garment District after dark? Eaten one of those chimi-churro-changa-chiladas from Taco Taberna? Nobody gets out alive after ingesting one of those things."

"Look, I'll figure out something. But you're going to have to take some time off from work next week, because we're going on an adventure, and that means getting out of New York. Do you have a specific day for us to…?" He would *not* say *you know* again. "A specific day for us to, um…"

"Wednesday," she hurriedly replied.

"Great," he said. "That gives me a few days to figure out where we'll be going."

"But I can't afford to take any days off from work," she insisted. "I barely save anything from my paycheck as it is. Speaking of, I don't have enough money to travel anywhere, anyway. I'm not a billionaire's granddaughter yet. Not financially, at least. I need that paycheck, and I can't lose my job in case you and I aren't successful at—"

"Oh, we'll be successful," he stated in no uncertain terms.

"You'll excuse me if I'm not as full of bravado as you are," she said.

"It's not bravado I'm full of," he assured her.

She sighed. "Fine. You're a raging tower of testosterone."

"Damn straight."

For the first time that evening she looked a little defeated. "Maybe I'm not quite as confident about my own contribution to the venture as you are of yours."

He wanted to tell her she had nothing to worry about there. Hannah Robinson was more woman than most women he knew. Funny that he was only now noticing that. "If it will help, I could talk to your bosses for you. Tell them I need you to do some work for me out of town for a couple of days or something and that I'll make it worth their while."

She was shaking her head before he even finished. "I appreciate it, but I'll talk to Mr. Cathcart and Mr. Quinn myself. Maybe they'll let me work over next weekend to make up for being out a couple of days during the week."

"But you shouldn't have to—"

"It's okay, Yeager. I've made my own way in the world this long. I can take care of myself."

He remembered how she'd told him she'd grown up in New York's foster care system. She hadn't gone into detail about it. But anyone who'd gone through something like that and come out on the other side as happy and well-adjusted as Hannah seemed to be could definitely take care of herself. There was a part of Yeager, though, that really wanted to help her out. He was surprised at the depth of his disappointment that she wouldn't let him.

He pushed those thoughts away. For now. Something told him he'd be coming back to them in the not too distant future. "So I should make plans for us to be away for...how long?" he asked.

Her gaze deflected from his, moving to something over his right shoulder, and she bit her lip in the thoughtful way that had intrigued him so much at the shop that day. It had the same heated effect on him now, except stronger, making a part of him twitch that had never twitched in Hannah's presence before. Interesting.

"Well, according to my reading," she said, "There's a three-day window for me to be at peak, and it's best for you to wait twenty-four hours between attempts to, um, replenish your, uh, stock."

Yeah, right. Like that was going to be necessary for him. "Okay, so we'll need three nights." For some reason he suddenly kind of liked the idea of spending that much time with Hannah. "We can leave early Tuesday morning and come back Friday. Let me see what I can arrange."

"But—"

"Kauai is the obvious choice for domestic adventure," he decided immediately. "The twelve-hour flight to Hawaii makes that kind of difficult, under the circumstances, though."

"But, Yeager—"

"Maybe the Grand Canyon or Yosemite. Or there are a few places in Maine that would be closer. Hell, even the parts of the Adirondacks might work."

"But, Yeager, I—"

"Don't worry about it, Hannah. I'll take care of all the arrangements. It's what I do for a living."

"It's not the arrangements I'm worried about," she told him. "It's the expenses."

"Don't worry about that part, either. I'll cover those, too. I'll take care of everything."

At this, she looked angry. "The hell you will. This is my baby, too."

Why was she getting so mad? It was ridiculous to argue about this. Yeager had more money than he knew what to do with. He could afford this better than Hannah could, and he was the one who was insisting that the conception be an adventure in its own right.

Even so, he relented. "Fine. You can pay me back after you inherit."

"But what if I don't—"

"You will," he assured her. Because there was no question about that.

She thought about it for a moment and then finally nodded. "Keep an itemized list of what you spend for this," she said. "Every mile, every meal, every minute. And bill me for my half of everything after I conceive. I intend to pay my fair share."

Of course she did. Because even with the flashing

eyes, the erotic lip nibble and the luscious skin, she was still, at heart, practical, pragmatic Hannah.

"Agreed," he said. And then, before she could offer any more objections, he told her, "I'll pick you up here Tuesday morning and return you here Friday afternoon. Pack for being outdoors, for warm and cool weather both. Bring clothes and shoes for walking and climbing. And sunscreen. I'll take care of everything else."

Well, except for the second set of chromosomes that would be necessary for conceiving a child. He'd need Hannah for that. Weird. Yeager hadn't needed anyone for a long time. Since his parents' deaths, he'd come to rely only on himself and had figured it would be that way for the rest of his life. He'd gotten to a point where he almost resented relying on other people for something. But needing Hannah…and needing her for this… He wasn't resentful at all. Needing her felt oddly appropriate. Even natural.

Probably, it was some primal instinct making him react that way. Man's inherent need to carry on the species that dated back to the beginning of time. Yeah, that had to be it. Because, seriously, what else could it be?

Five

When Yeager had told Hannah to pack for walking and hiking, she figured that meant they would be walking and hiking. So what was she doing sitting in a four-seater inflatable raft, wrapped in a life jacket and staring down a river in North Carolina that would eventually become miles and miles of whitewater?

She looked at Yeager, who was still on the dock, double-checking whatever he needed to double-check before they hurtled headlong into self-destruction. Not that he seemed concerned about that. Then again, had it not been for the raging aquatic disaster ahead, she might have been just as Zen-like as he was, because North Carolina was the greenest, the bluest, the most gorgeous and peaceful place she'd ever seen.

The closest Hannah ever came to the Great Outdoors was Central Park, a place she didn't even have an opportunity to visit as often as she liked. And as beautiful as it was, it was often crowded with people and was still surrounded by towering skyscrapers and bumper-to-bumper buses and cabs, its sky crisscrossed with air traffic. This was her first taste of actual, honest-to-god nature. And it was incredible.

Evergreens sprouted along both sides of the river, a hundred feet high, stretching into a cloudless blue sky that was as clear and bright as a gemstone. And the air. Holy cow, it was amazing. Warm and languid, touched with just a hint of humidity and filled with the scent of pine and earth and something vaguely, but not unpleasantly, fishy. Although the water wasn't yet rough enough to be called whitewater, it whirled and gurgled past in a hurry, tugging at the raft and vying with the wind for whose rush of sound was most eloquent.

It was hard to believe fewer than six hours had passed since Yeager had picked her up in Queens in a shiny black car, complete with driver. They'd driven to a small airport in New Jersey where they'd boarded a private jet—because, of course, Ends of the Earth had its own private jet—then made the two-hour flight to Asheville, North Carolina. It was Hannah's first time on a plane and her first time outside New York.

They'd ventured into Asheville long enough to eat breakfast, and although the town was small by New York standards, it was still kind of urban and cosmopolitan, so it hadn't felt *too* different from Queens. Well, except for the great green bumps of mountain surrounding it. But as they'd driven away from the city in the Land Rover that had been waiting for them on arrival, everything—*everything*—had changed.

So much green. So much sky. So little traffic. So few people. The farther they'd traveled, the more isolated they'd become, even on the highway. And once they'd exited the interstate, they might as well have been the only two people on the planet. Instinctively, Hannah had rolled down her window and turned her face to the breeze, closing her eyes to feel the warmth of the sun on her face and inhaling great gulps of air that was unlike anything she'd ever drawn into her body.

Yeager had driven up, up, up into the mountains, until they arrived at a secluded dock on the Chattanooga River, where they'd found the very raft in which she now sat. It had been conjured, presumably, by magic, along with its contents of life jackets, cooler and oars, because there wasn't another soul in sight. Just Hannah and Yeager and the primordial earth spirits she was sure still lived here.

She eyed the river again, battling a gnarl of fear curling up in her belly. He'd told her he would go easy on her this trip and make the outing low-risk, since she was still new to the adventure thing. He'd promised the danger to her would be nonexistent. She wasn't sure she believed him. There was a bend in the river not far ahead, and she was worried about what lay around it. Where her idea of staying safe was not climbing into a tiny inflatable raft on a raging river—or, you know, *any* river—Yeager's idea of safety probably meant there was enough oxygen to last ten minutes or fewer scorpions than usual.

Potato, potahto.

"Are you sure this is safe?" she asked him.

He was shrugging his dun-colored life jacket over a skintight black T-shirt and khaki cargo shorts. Well-worn hiking boots, a gimme cap emblazoned with the Ends of the Earth logo and aviator sunglasses completed the ensemble. He looked every inch the wealthy epic adventurer. She could almost smell the testosterone oozing from every pore. She gazed down at her attire—cut-offs and a T-shirt she'd received for making a donation to public radio. Coupled with her sneakers and retro cat-eye sunglasses, and with her unruly hair stuffed into an even more unruly ponytail, she was going to go out on a limb and say she did *not* look like a wealthy epic adventurer. Especially in a life jacket that was two sizes too big for her.

"Of course it's safe," he assured her. "The rapids here are only Class Two. They have camps for middle-schoolers along this stretch."

Hannah eyed the river again. Yeah, right, she thought. Feral middle schoolers, maybe. Who'd been raised by wolves. She couldn't imagine any halfway responsible parent allowing their child anywhere near a river like this. Maybe she'd been too hasty in agreeing to Yeager's condition that they leave New York. She'd rather their adventure involve eating sushi from a food truck or crossing Queens Boulevard against the light. Now *that* was living dangerously.

She tried to object again. "But—"

"It's fine, Hannah," Yeager interrupted before she had the chance, cinching the belt of his life jacket. Then he threw her one of those smiles that always kindled something inside her. "You'll have fun. I promise.

C'mon. Do you really think I'd endanger the mother of my child?"

The warmth inside her sparked hotter at that. The mother of Yeager Novak's child. That was what she would be for the rest of her life if everything went the way it was supposed to. What a weird concept. What they were planning would bond the two of them together forever. She'd realized that when she'd accepted his last condition, of course, but she was only now beginning to understand exactly what that meant. The man standing above her looking like some omnipotent earth god would be moving in and out of her life *forever*. Was she really, truly, sure she wanted that?

He hopped down into the raft with her, making it rock back and forth enough for her to seize the ropes on its sides nearest her. Her stomach pitched. If she had ever doubted that she wasn't the risk-taking type— and, actually, she had never doubted that at all—she was now certain. They hadn't even left the dock yet and she was already bracing for a spectacular death.

Yeager leaned across the raft, reaching past her to grab a strap she hadn't even noticed was there. He tugged it across her lap and latched it to another one on her other side, effectively securing her in place. She should have been grateful there were seat belts in the raft. Instead, all she could do was panic that now she would drown if the damned thing tipped over.

"What do I do if—"

"The raft won't invert," he interrupted, reading her mind. Again. "The way it's designed, that's impossible. Not to mention—in case I haven't already—this part of the river is in no way dangerous."

Ever the optimist—kind of—Hannah countered, "Nothing is impossible."

Yeager grinned again. "You getting hurt on this trip is."

"Then why do I have to wear a seat belt?" she asked. "If this is as safe as you say it is, then how come even you put on a life jacket?"

"I'm an adventurer, Hannah. I'm not stupid."

Before she could say anything more, he threw off the last line and the raft was moving away from the dock. Hannah opened her mouth to scream—it might be her last chance to draw breath, after all—then realized they were only going about five miles an hour. If that. The raft floated along the water serenely, hitting the occasional gentle bump before turning a bit and gliding forward again.

Yeager held one oar deftly in both hands, maneuvering it first on one side of the raft then the other, steering it simultaneously forward and toward the center of the river. As they gradually picked up speed, so did the wind, until it was buffeting her hair around her face in a way that was actually kind of pleasant. She shoved it aside and gripped the ropes on the sides of the raft, but more out of reflex than because she was actually frightened. They really weren't going very fast and their surroundings really were beautiful.

For long moments they simply glided along the river, the raft rising and falling gently with the swells, turning left, then right, as Yeager guided it forward. Eventually, though, the water did grow rough and the raft's movements became more irregular and jarring. But he handled it expertly, switching the oar from right to left to keep the raft on track. Water splashed up over the sides, wetting Hannah's feet and face, but instead of being alarmed, she thrilled at the sensation. Every new jolt of the raft or pull of the current sent a wave of adrenaline shooting through her, making her pulse dance and her heart race. By the time the water began to cascade over the side of the raft, soaking her legs and arms, her entire body was buzzing with sensations unlike any she had ever experienced before. She held on tighter, but instead of panic it was elation that bubbled up inside her.

And then the water grew very rough and the raft was pitching over rocks and shoals, spinning and leaping and crashing down again. Water splashed fully over both sides of the craft, dowsing both of them. But instead of fearful, Hannah felt joyful. Especially when she saw how Yeager reacted to what must have been a minor feat of derring-do for him. He was grinning in a way she'd never seen him grin before, with a mix of ecstasy and exhilaration and exuberance, as if being right here, in this moment, was the absolute pinnacle of experience—and she was a part of it. Such pure, unadulterated happiness was contagious, and she was swept up into it as fiercely as he was, until she was whooping with laughter.

The journey continued for miles; the river, by turns, as turbulent as a whirlpool and as smooth as glass. During the smooth times, Hannah marveled at the scenery and the wildlife—She saw her first deer! Three of them! Right there on the riverbank!—and asked Yeager what kind of bird that was flying above them and how big pine trees could grow, and did it snow here in the winter. During the turbulent times, he schooled her in how to use her oar and laughed with her whenever she turned the raft backward—which was often.

By the time they reached the end of the course two hours after starting it, Hannah felt more alive than she'd ever felt in her life. As Yeager steered them toward a dock much like the one from which they'd departed, she was keenly disappointed that the ride was coming to an end. So when he slung a rope over a wooden post to secure the raft and turned to look at her to gauge her reaction, she responded in the only way she knew how.

"Can we do it again?" she asked eagerly.

Yeager could hardly believe that the Hannah at the end of their ride was the same one who'd climbed so carefully into the raft upriver. He'd never seen her smile like she was now, with such spirit and wonderment and…something else, something he wasn't sure he could identify, something there probably wasn't even a word for because it was so uniquely Hannah. She just looked more animated than he'd ever seen her, more carefree, more full of life.

Happy. She just looked happy. And he thought it odd that, as many times as he'd seen her and had conversations with her, and she'd seemed contented enough, she'd never really looked happy until now.

Then her question finally registered and he shook the other thoughts out of his brain. Or, at least, tried to. There was something about Hannah's newly found happiness that wouldn't quite leave him.

"We can't go again," he told her. "At least, not from here. We have to hike back upriver first."

She looked a little dejectcd at that.

"But we can go again tomorrow, if you want to."

"I want to," she immediately replied. Her smile brightened again and something inside Yeager grew brighter, too.

He stood, extending a hand to her. "Come on," he said. "We can do a little exploring before lunch."

She unhooked her safety belt and settled her hand in his, and he pulled her to standing, too. When he did, the raft rolled toward the dock a bit, pitching Hannah forward, into him. Instinctively he settled his hands on her hips as hers splayed open over his chest. Her touch was gentle, but he felt it to the depths of his soul. His hands tightened on her hips and, not sure why he did it, he dipped his head to kiss her. She gasped when he did, and he took advantage of her reaction to deepen the kiss, tasting her leisurely, taking his time to enjoy it. And he did enjoy it. A lot.

Hannah seemed to enjoy it, too, because, without missing a beat, she kissed him back, curling her fingers into the fabric of his shirt to pull him closer. He felt her heart beating hard against his torso, heard the catch of her breath, inhaled the earthy scent of her, becoming more intoxicated by her with each passing second.

He would have taken her right there, right then, shedding their clothes in the raft and settling her naked in his lap astride him. He was already envisioning just how erotic the union would be, but she ended the kiss—with clear reluctance—and pushed herself away from him as far as she could in the small raft. Her face was flushed and her breathing came in rough, irregular gasps. What was weird was that Yeager's breathing was ragged and uneven, too. It was just a kiss, he reminded himself. No big deal. He'd kissed dozens of women. Kisses were nothing but a prelude. There was no reason for him to feel so breathless. So weightless. So senseless.

"We, um, we should probably wait until tonight," she said softly. "Just to keep things as close to Wednesday as possible."

Right. They were on a schedule here. Yeager understood schedules. His entire life was scheduled. Of course they should wait until tonight to ensure optimum results. Even if he suddenly didn't want to wait. His *body* didn't want to wait, he hastily corrected himself. What had just happened between him and Hannah was just a chemical reaction to a physical stimulus. He himself could wait just fine. It was only sex. No problem waiting until tonight.

Even if tonight seemed way too far away.

"You, uh, said something about exploring?" she asked tentatively, her breathing still a little frayed.

Yeager nodded. "Right. Then we can hike farther downstream to where we'll be camping."

"Which is how far?"

"About three miles."

Her mouth dropped open at that. "We're going to hike three miles?"

"Piece a cake," he told her. "It'll be a walk in the park."

She shook her head. "I've walked in the park lots of times. *That's* a walk in the park. Three miles over rugged terrain is—"

"A great way to build up an appetite," he finished

for her. He'd let her decide for herself what kind of appetite he was talking about.

Evidently she knew exactly what kind he meant, because color suffused her face again. He'd never seen a woman with such a propensity for blushing. It should have been a turnoff. Yeager liked women who were as audacious and intrepid as he was. But something about Hannah's seeming innocence tugged at a part of him where he wasn't used to feeling things.

Before she could object again, he cinched her waist tighter and lifted her easily up onto the dock, setting her down on her ass as she sputtered in surprise. Then he unfastened the cooler from its mooring in the raft and raised it to the dock, too, placing it beside her. After hoisting himself up effortlessly, he stood and extended a hand to her as he had before. This time, though, he was more careful when he pulled her up alongside him.

Careful, he echoed to himself. He was actually being careful with Hannah. He was never careful with anyone. Anything. Careful was the last thing he ever wanted to be. But then, Hannah was a careful person, and what the two of them were trying to do—create a life together—took care. That was all there was to his reaction. It wasn't like he'd actually begun to, well, *care* for her. No more than he had before, anyway.

The dock was attached to a clearing on the riverbank that disappeared into the forest a few hundred feet away. Yeager was familiar with the area and knew it was rife with common fossils and less common arrowheads, so they shed their shoes to dry in a patch of sunshine and spent some time looking around. When he pointed out a handful of brachiopods and trilobites to Hanna, he might as well have been pouring diamonds into her lap, so delighted was her reaction. He reminded himself again that, in spite of her rocky upbringing, she'd led a fairly sheltered life. It was hard to fathom the contradiction. Hannah just seemed like such an anomaly sometimes.

By the time they finished lunch, their clothes and shoes were dry. Yeager packed the remnants of their meal in the cooler and secured it back in the moored raft, then rejoined Hannah on the dock.

"Don't we need to take those with us?" she asked.

He shook his head. "Someone will be coming for them later."

"The same someone who dropped them off at the first dock?"

Now he nodded. "Ends of the Earth contracts with other travel professionals all over the world. I found one in Raleigh that got everything set up for us here, from where we started in the raft to where we'll be camping. They'll pick up the Land Rover, too, and deliver it to the campsite so we'll have it if we need it."

She eyed him thoughtfully. "You know, when you said we'd be having an epic adventure, I had a picture of us machete-ing our way through the Everglades while dodging alligators or hang gliding across the Grand Canyon. I wasn't planning on coolers full of lobster and San Pellegrino and Land Rovers at our disposal."

Yeager smiled. "Yeah, well, normally machete-ing among alligators *is* the kind of trip Ends of the Earth puts together. The hang gliding is more likely to happen over an active volcano."

She started to laugh, then realized he was serious.

"Anyway, I'm having to break you in gently," he pointed out. Not to mention he'd been trying to do something a little romantic, which rarely included machetes and often included lobster.

"I didn't say you had to break me in gently," she told him. "I just said I couldn't travel outside the US this first time."

"Fine. Next time, we can go someplace where there's a political coup happening during a tsunami."

"If there is a next time," she said.

Right. Because if her calculations were correct, and everything went according to plan, this would be the only time the two of them did this. For some reason the realization didn't sit well with Yeager. In spite of what he'd just said about political coups and tsunamis—as fun as that would have been—he already had their next time planned, and it would be a shame to have spent an entire week working on it for nothing. Hannah was going to love canyoneering in Morocco. Which reminded him…

"Just in case, did you apply for your passport?"

"Yes."

"And did you—"

"Yes, I paid the extra fee for expediting it," she answered before he could even put voice to the question. "I should have it in a couple of weeks."

"Good."

"If I need it."

Why was she harping on *if*? Was it such a hardship for her, sexing it up with him? Hell, she'd enjoyed that kiss as much as he had.

He decided to change the subject. "Ready to hike? We're burning daylight here."

He told himself he did not sound impatient. There were still a lot of hours to fill before bedtime and the hike to their campsite would only use up a few. But that was okay. Just because Hannah wanted to wait until nightfall for the main event didn't mean they couldn't enjoy themselves before they enjoyed each other.

Six

It was dusk by the time Hannah and Yeager arrived at their campsite, made even duskier by the trees that towered overhead, obscuring what little was left of the sunlight. She was more than ready to call it a day. A walk in the park. Ha! Maybe if it was Yellowstone Park and the walk involved all eight billion acres of it. She'd figured hiking and walking were two different things, but she'd assumed those differences lay mostly in hiking being more vertical and walking being more horizontal. She now knew that hiking was actually different from walking in that it was like dousing your legs and feet in gasoline and then setting them on fire.

When they finally reached their destination, however, her mood improved considerably. Because, as the hiking path emptied into a clearing surrounded by evergreens that disappeared into a purpling sky, she saw a campsite setup that was more reminiscent of a vintage Hollywood epic than a modern epic adventure.

A round, canvas tent stood in the center, its flaps thrown back to reveal a platform bed with a pile of pillows. There was a copper chandelier with a dozen candles flickering in its sconces—the kind that worked on batteries, not the kind that could, left unattended, leave the Smoky Mountains in ashes—and a few others twinkled on a bedside table. To the right of the tent was a copper fire pit ready for lighting and a love seat laden with more pillows. On the other side was a table and chairs—set with fine china and crystal—and an oversize copper ice chest brimming with bottles and other containers. Across it all zigzagged strings of tiny white lights that glimmered like stars. Hannah had never seen a sight more dazzling.

"You didn't tell me we'd be glamping," she said with much delight.

"Glamping?" Yeager echoed dubiously.

When she turned to look at him, she could see he wasn't as charmed by the tableau as she was. In fact, the expression on his face probably would have been the same if he were staring at the stuff in the back of the butcher shop that never made it into the case.

"Yeah, glamping," she repeated. "Part glamour, part camping. I saw it on *Project Runway*."

"There is no glamour in camping," he stated decisively. "I mean, I didn't expect us to kill and clean our own dinner or sleep out in the open, but this…" He shook his head. "Adventure travel should never include throw pillows and wineglasses. I knew it was a bad idea to hire a company called Vampin' 'n' Campin'. There are way too many apostrophes in that name for it to be taken seriously. Unfortunately they were the only ones available on short notice."

"Well, I'm glad you did," she told him. "This is wonderful."

He made his way toward the site. Still sounding disgusted, he muttered, "The privy is probably copper-plated, too."

"There, see? We will, too, be roughing it," she said. "I've never spent a day of my life without plumbing or electricity." Although a couple of her foster homes had come close. She kept that to herself. No need to spoil the beauty of the moment. "And there's no tech out here. Talk about primitive conditions."

He made his way to the ice chest, withdrew a bottle to inspect its label, then grinned. "I guess this glamping thing has its upside. We won't have to drink our *Clos du Mesnil* warm. Now *that* would be roughing it."

Hannah joined him. "That ice isn't going to last three days," she said.

"No, but the solar-powered fridge and freezer they set up behind the tent will."

"Ah. Is the privy solar-powered, too?" she asked hopefully.

"It is. And compostable."

"And I think that's all I want to know about the plumbing. Unless," she added even more hopefully, "you also arranged for a solar-powered shower."

He chuckled. "It's not solar-powered, but there is a shower."

Considering the amount of sweating she'd done in the last few hours, Hannah definitely wanted to hear about that. "Okay, you can tell me about the shower."

"Actually, I can do better than that. I can show it to you."

She sighed. "That would be wonderful. I'd love to get clean before dinner."

"There should be some towels in the tent," he said. "Our bags should be in there, too. Grab whatever else you need."

When she entered the tent, she did, indeed, find their overnight bags, so she opened hers to collect some clean underwear, a red tank top and striped pajama bottoms, all of which would doubtless be a far cry from what Yeager's usual girlfriends wore for a night with him. But it was the best she could do on short notice and short funds. Not that she was Yeager's girlfriend, so she couldn't be held to that standard, anyway. Even so, she was now wishing she'd had the foresight to cough up a few bucks for something that at least hinted at seduction. She tried to remind herself that she and Yeager weren't here for romance. But that didn't quite feel right, either.

She found the towels on a folding wooden chair, underneath a bar of soap and bottle of shampoo, both environmentally friendly. Hannah didn't care what Yeager thought about Vampin' 'n' Campin'. As far as she—a lover of the Great Indoors—was concerned, they did camping just fine.

She emerged from the tent to find him waiting for her near a break in the trees, looking almost otherworldly in the growing darkness. His black hair was silvered by the moonlight, his biceps strained against his T-shirt, and a shadow fell across his face, imbuing him with just enough of the sinister to send a ribbon of apprehension shimmying through her.

Was she really going to go through with this tonight? Could she? Even considering everything that
was at stake, she was beginning to have her doubts.
Yeager was just so...so... She battled a wave of apprehension. So intimidating. He was almost literally
twice the man of any guy she'd ever dated. She normally went for guys who were born to be mild. The
ones who carried a novel by some obscure author in
their messenger bags and whose clothes were always
adorably rumpled. Guys who spent the weekend working on their bicycles and whose dinner orders never
included substitutions. Safe guys. Predictable guys.
Uncomplicated guys. How was she going to react to
guys like that after a few nights with Yeager? Especially if he would be popping in and out of her life
forever once those nights were concluded?

Maybe she should go the sperm bank route. If she
changed her mind right now and asked Yeager to take
her back to New York tonight, she might still have
time to get pregnant this month. Her baby's father
would be anonymous and in no way a part of their
lives. Then, someday, she'd meet a safe, predictable,
uncomplicated guy she could have more children with.
She and Safe Guy could spend the rest of their days
raising their family among *Consumer Reports*–en-
dorsed products in their picket-fenced, asbestos-and
lead-free home that was landscaped with noninva-
sive, allergen-free plants, while they protected their
children from perils like sugary breakfast cereal, dog
breeds weighing more than seven pounds and team
sports.

Yeah. That sounded like a *great* life. She couldn't

wait to get started on that. Then she'd never have to suffer the heart-racing dangers of Yeager again.

"Did you forget something?" he asked when she made no move to join him.

Yeah. Her sense of self-preservation. But that was way too big to pack in an overnight bag.

"No, I think I'm ready."

Overstatement of the century.

He tilted his head toward the opening in the trees, so she forced her feet to move forward until she came to a halt beside him. Up close, he looked a little less sinister and a lot more seductive, so she decided— *oh, all right*—she could go through with having sex with him if she *had* to. She didn't want to waste a perfectly good ovulation, after all. At least, she hoped it was perfect.

Yeager eyed her thoughtfully for a few seconds and Hannah was torn between wishing she knew what he was thinking and hoping she never found out.

All he said, though, was, "It's this way." Then he preceded her down the path.

Oh, joy. More hiking.

The trees swallowed them up again, but Hannah didn't mind so much this time. With the sun down, the night was growing cooler and a gentle breeze rocked the leaves in the trees. Soft bursts of light erupted here and there, and it took her a moment to realize they were fireflies. She'd never seen even one, let alone the dozens that suddenly surrounded them, and she couldn't help the laughter that rippled from inside her.

"What's so funny?" Yeager asked, glancing over his shoulder.

"Fireflies," she said. "I've never seen them in person."

He stopped abruptly, turning to look at her. "You're joking."

She halted, too, since his big body blocked the path. "No, I'm not. I told you—I've never been out of New York."

"There are fireflies in New York," he said.

"Not in the neighborhoods where I've lived."

"You've never been outside the *City* of New York?" he asked incredulously. "I thought you meant the state."

She shook her head. "No, I meant the five boroughs."

He studied her in silence for a moment, but his face was in shadow again, so she couldn't tell what he was thinking. Finally he said, "What, one of the families you lived with couldn't even take you to Jones Beach for the day?"

In response Hannah only shrugged. Of course none of the families she'd lived with took her to Jones Beach. For most of them, she'd just been a way to add some money to their bank accounts. And for the few who had genuinely cared for the children they took in, all the money they received went to feed and clothe those children. There had never been anything left for luxuries like day trips.

"But you've seen the ocean, right?" Yeager asked. "Surely you hit Coney Island or Rockaway Beach at some point when you were a teenager."

"I didn't, actually," she confessed. "My friends and I preferred prowling Manhattan whenever we had a little free time. And, truth be told, on those rare occasions I found myself with a little extra money to do stuff, I spent it on fabric instead."

He said nothing for another moment. "You've never seen the ocean?"

"No. I haven't. Or, if I did before I lost my mom, I don't remember it."

"How is that possible?"

Again she shrugged. Even as an adult freed from the confines of the foster care system, Hannah had never felt the need or desire to explore beyond the city. She just wasn't one to stray outside her comfort zone, even for small adventures. She liked knowing where she was and how to navigate her surroundings. The thought of taking a day trip someplace had just never appealed to her.

Yet here she was, hundreds of miles away from home—and for more than just a day—and she didn't feel unsettled at all. She hadn't even been nervous about boarding a plane or leaving New York. On the contrary, she'd been excited before they'd left, and she'd had a lot of fun today. Enough to make her think she should have tried something like this a long time ago.

But it was only because Yeager was with her, she told herself. He was familiar enough to her to offset the strangeness of this trip. She couldn't do this all the time, especially not alone. And, hey, she didn't *want* to do this all the time. Once she was settled back in New York, she'd return to being her usual complacent self again. She was sure of it.

Another sound suddenly joined the rustle of leaves overhead, drawing her attention away from her thoughts and back to the night surrounding them.

Because even though this was her first time in the Great Outdoors, she recognized the sound. A waterfall. The shower Yeager had promised her was a waterfall. She'd assumed they were finished with adventures for the day—well, except for the greatest adventure of all that was still looming—yet here he was, presenting her with another. His life really was one exploit after another.

They exited the trees onto the banks of the river they'd navigated earlier, though here, it wasn't wide and rough with rapids. Here, it was narrow and flowed like silk. The waterfall was only about eight feet high, spilling into the river with a gentle percussion that sent ripples gliding outward. The sun had well and truly set by now, and the moon hung overhead like a bright silver dollar, surrounded by hundreds of glittering stars. Hannah had never seen the moon so bright and had never seen more than a few stars in the sky above her. She made her way carefully toward where Yeager had stopped on the edge of a rock, but she was so busy staring at the sky, she nearly walked right past him and into the river. He stopped her with a gentle hand to her shoulder, turning her until she faced him.

"Easy there, Sacagawea," he said. "The trail you're about to blaze could be your last."

She laughed, still looking at the sky. "I can't help it. It's so beautiful here."

"It's just your run-of-the-mill woods, Hannah."

Now she looked at Yeager. "It's not run-of-the-mill for me."

As she toed off her sneakers, she thought about how she must seem like an absolute freak to him. Her world was so tiny in comparison to his, her life experience virtually nonexistent. He lived for risk and danger, two things she wanted no part of. They couldn't be more different or less suited to each other. But that was good, right? It meant there was no chance of any messy emotional stuff getting in the way of their, ah, enterprise.

For a moment they only gazed at each other in silence. Well, except for the chirping of the crickets and the whisper of the wind and the shuffle of the waterfall. And, okay, the beating of Hannah's heart, which seemed to be loudest of all.

Yeager, however, seemed not to notice any of it, because he reached behind him and grabbed a handful of his T-shirt, pulling it over his head. "Come on," he said. "Last one in's a rotten egg."

Hannah scarcely heard what he said, because she was too busy staring at a half-naked Yeager. And even though she'd seen him half-naked a dozen times before, she'd never seen him as he was now—gilded by starlight and moonbeams and fireflies, looking like a creature of the night, if not the night itself. And then he was going to work on his fly, and she remembered he hadn't brought any clothes to change into after their swim—or even *for* their swim. And then she realized his half-naked state was about to become a full-naked state. And then... And then...

And then she was jumping into the river fully clothed, turning her back on him to feign much interest in the waterfall that was suddenly way more interesting than it should be, even for someone who'd never seen a waterfall in person before. The river was shallow enough here that she could stand with her head out of the water—just barely—but that didn't keep her knees from shaking. Though she was pretty sure that had nothing to do with the chill of the water. Especially since the water was surprisingly warm.

When she heard a splash behind her, she knew Yeager had joined her. And when she turned to see hiking boots and a pile of garments on the rock where he had been, she knew he was naked. She also knew that by the way he was grinning at her when he broke the surface of the water, jerking his head to sling back his wet hair.

And by his tone of voice when he said, "Most people undress before they bathe."

She bit back a strangled sound. "I just didn't want to be a rotten egg."

"Right."

"And I figured it might be a good idea to rinse out my clothes."

"Uh-huh."

"I mean, they did get pretty dirty today."

He swam toward her, quickly enough that Hannah, growing more panicky by the moment, didn't have a chance to swim away before he reached her.

"Well, then, let me help you," he said.

She felt his hands at the hem of her T-shirt and, before she could stop him, he was pushing it up over her torso. He took his time, though, opening his palms over her naked skin under the wet fabric, sliding his hands up over her waist and rib cage, halting just below her bra, the L of his index finger and thumb brushing the lower curves of her breasts. Her heart hammered even harder in her chest and heat pooled deep in her belly. His expression remained teasing, though, so she knew he was feeling none of the tumult she did.

"Lift your arms," he said softly.

Automatically she did and he tugged her shirt over her head, tossing it behind him toward the rock, where it landed perfectly alongside his own.

"Now the shorts," he said, moving his hand to the button at her waist.

Deftly, he undid it and the zipper, then tucked his hands inside the garment, settling one on each of her hips. For a moment he only held her in place, the warmth of his palms permeating the cotton of her panties, a sensation that made the heat in her belly spiral outward, kindling fires in every part of her. Then he gripped her shorts and tugged them down, lifting first one leg then the other, until that piece of clothing, too, had been stripped from her and tossed to the riverbank.

Although she was still in her bra and panties, the equivalent of a bathing suit, the sensations coursing through her made Hannah feel like she was as naked as Yeager was. It didn't help that his teasing expression had gradually grown into something much more heated. And when he began to dip his head toward hers...

She quickly turned around and began swimming toward the waterfall with all her might. But she was no match for Yeager, who caught up to her immediately.

"There," he said as he drew up alongside her. "After that swim, everything you have on should be totally clean. Time to take it off."

Well, golly gee whiz. Nothing like getting right to it. Talk about a wham-bam-thank-you-ma'am.

"Are you always this pragmatic when it comes to sex?" she asked.

"I'm never pragmatic when it comes to sex," he assured her. "But I've never had sex on a timetable. It's always a lot more spontaneous than this. And the reason for it is never baby-making. It's always merry-making."

"You don't think sex for making a baby can be fun?" she asked. "You just want to get this thing over with as quickly and cleanly as possible? Am I that un-appealing to you?"

His response was to pull her close and cover her mouth with his, kissing her in a way that assured her he found her very appealing indeed, that he didn't in-tend for this thing to be in any way quick—never mind clean—and that he planned to have quite a lot of fun making a baby with her. By the time he pulled away from her, they were both breathing raggedly.

"Well, okay, then," Hannah managed to say.

But she still didn't take off her underwear. She just wasn't ready yet. It was a nice night. She was in a beautiful place with a beautiful man. She didn't feel the need to rush. So she turned onto her back to float on the water and look at the night sky. She heard Yea-ger emit a sound of reluctant resignation and then turn onto his back, too.

"Hey, that's the Big Dipper," she said, pointing to-ward a group of stars to the left of the moon. It kept her from looking at a naked Yeager floating on his back, gilded in moonlight.

"It is," he told her. "And you can follow the arc—"

"Follow the arc to Arcturus," she chorused with then finished for him. "I remember that from ninth-grade science. Isn't that weird? I don't think I remember anything else from that class. I'm not sure I even remember much from the rest of ninth grade. I moved around a lot in high school. Even more than when I was in elementary school."

He paddled closer to Hannah, so she paddled away. She really wasn't ready yet for a naked Yeager.

He growled restlessly, clearly frustrated that she was going to draw this out as long as she could. Despite that, he asked, "Where did you live when you were in ninth grade?"

"For the first three months, I was in Mott Haven," she told him. "Then they moved me to Vinegar Hill. After school broke for summer vacation, I went to Bed-Stuy for a while."

He was silent for a moment. Then softly he said, "You lived in some pretty rough neighborhoods."

"Yeah, well, you don't find too many people taking in foster kids on the Upper East Side. Go figure."

He was silent again.

"It wasn't all bad, Yeager," she told him. "I lived with a handful of families who were truly good people, and I still have friends I made while I was in the system. You only hear the horror stories about foster care in the news. But a lot of kids ended up way better off there than they were with their birth families."

"Did you ever wonder about your real family?"

"Sure. There were times when I would fantasize that someone must have made a mistake somewhere, and I really did have a mom and dad out there somewhere. Like I was mistakenly switched with another baby at the hospital. Or the woman who died that they thought was my mom was actually misidentified and my mom was still out there in the world somewhere, looking for me." She sighed. "But I knew it wasn't true. I knew I was right where I was supposed to be. It's just a weird irony that I actually wasn't."

"Sounds like little-kid Hannah was as down-to-earth as grown-up Hannah," Yeager said.

She didn't know whether to take that as a compliment or not. From his tone of voice, he seemed to respect down-to-earth people. On the other hand, he didn't spend much time in one place on the earth himself.

"How about you?" she asked, still gazing up at the sky. "Where were you in ninth grade?"

He hesitated for a telling moment. Then he said, so quietly that Hannah almost didn't hear him, "Peoria, Illinois."

His response surprised her enough that she forgot about his nakedness and glanced over at him. Fortunately—or not—it was dark enough now that the water had turned inky, hiding most of him. Of all the places she could have imagined Yeager being from, Peoria, Illinois, would never have made the cut.

"You actually grew up in the city that's an icon of Midwestern conservatism?"

"I actually did."

It occurred to her then how little she really knew of Yeager. Sure, he'd revealed snippets of his life from time to time during their conversations at Cathcart and Quinn, but she knew nothing about what had made him Yeager Novak, global adventurer. And suddenly, for some reason, she wanted to know that very badly.

"Did you live your whole life there?" she asked.

"I did until I was eighteen."

"What brought you to New York?"

"A full-ride hockey scholarship to Clarkson University in Potsdam."

"You play hockey?"

"I used to."

"What do your mom and dad do for a living?"

He sighed in a way that made her think he really, really, *really* didn't want to talk about this. Despite that, he replied, "My mom managed a bookstore and my dad was an accountant."

The son of a bookstore manager and an accountant had grown up to be one of the world's greatest risk-takers? How the hell had that happened?

"So how did you wind up—"

Before she could finish her question, he righted himself in the water and strode toward her. Hannah straightened, too. She thought he just wanted to get closer to continue their conversation. Instead, the moment he was within reaching distance, he wrapped an arm around her waist, pulled her toward him until she was flush against him and kissed her.

As he did, he reached behind her to unfasten her bra, slipping it over her arms and releasing it into the flow of the river. Hannah started to object at the loss of the garment, but Yeager moved his hands to her breasts, covering both with sure fingers, and anything she might have said got caught in her throat. He brushed the pad of one thumb over her sensitive nipple. When she gasped, he took advantage of her reaction to taste her more deeply. She opened her mouth wider to accommodate him, splaying one hand wide over the ropes of muscle on his torso, threading the fingers of the other through his silky, wet hair.

He growled something unintelligible against her mouth, then dragged soft, butterfly kisses along her jaw, her neck and her shoulder. The hand at her waist moved to her back, skimming until he gripped the wet cotton of her panties and pulled them down. Then he was caressing her naked bottom, curving his fingers over the swells of her soft flesh, guiding his fingers into its elegant cleft, penetrating her with the tip of one.

When Hannah cried out loud at the sensation, he moved again, pulling down her panties in the front to push his hand between her legs. She felt his fingers against her, moving through the folds of flesh made damp by her reaction to him, furrowing slowly at first, teasing her with gentle pressure. Hastily, she shed her panties completely, then opened her legs wider, silently inviting more. But instead of escalating his attentions, Yeager only continued with his slow and steady cadence, gliding his fingers over her until she felt as though she would burst into flame.

"Please, Yeager," she whispered. But those two words were the only ones she could manage.

He seemed to understand, though, because he slipped a finger closer to the feminine core of her, drawing languid circles before venturing inside. He entered her with one long finger, once, twice, three times, four, each with a single, long stroke to her clitoris that sent tremors of need shuddering through her. Before she could climax, though, he moved his hand away. She was about to beg him to touch her again, but he circled her wrist and guided her hand toward him instead, wrapping her fingers around his long length.

She opened her eyes to find him watching her intently, his blue eyes dark with wanting. So she enclosed his shaft at its base and stroked upward, curving her palm over its head before moving back down again. This time Yeager was the one to close his eyes, and this time it was his breath that hitched in his chest. When Hannah pulled her hand up and down him again, he reached for her, aligning her body against his, covering her mouth with his, tucking his hand between her legs once more.

For a long time they only kissed and caressed, their gestures growing bolder and more invasive, until both were close to climax. Then Yeager lifted Hannah by her waist and wrapped her legs around his middle to enter her. Up and down he moved her body, going deeper inside her with every thrust. Gently he curved his hands under her bottom to lift her higher, bringing her down harder, entering her as deeply as he could.

The hot coil inside Hannah cinched tighter with every thrust, until she knew she was close to crashing. Then she felt his finger behind her again, pushing softly inside her, and she came apart at the seams.

Yeager held on for a few more moments then climaxed hard, spilling himself hot and deep inside her. He held her in place for a long time afterward, as if he wanted to ensure every drop of his essence found its way to her center.

Hannah lay her head against his shoulder and clung to him, shivering, though not from the soft circles of water eddying around them.

"Are you cold?" he whispered against her ear.

Somehow she managed to murmur, "No. I'm good."

She stopped herself before saying she was better than good, better than she'd ever been in her life, because she knew she must be imagining that. She'd just never had a lover like Yeager, that was all. He really was larger than life. A part of her was thrilled by that, but a part of her was sobered by it, too. She might never have another experience—another adventure— like Yeager Novak again. And she just wasn't sure if that was a good thing or not.

Seven

Yeager was working in his office in the Flatiron Building, his tie loosened, the top two buttons of his dress shirt unfastened, when his assistant, Amira, texted him from her desk in End of the Earth's reception area. She only did that when she was trying to be discreet about something. In this case, it was that there was a Hannah Robinson, who didn't have an appointment, here to see him. Should she just show her the door the way she usually did with the women who came to see Yeager at the office without an appointment, or should she tell her to wait until he had a free moment, which would probably be in a couple of hours—maybe—and hope Hannah left on her own after sitting in the waiting room for a while?

Instead of texting back that she should do neither, Yeager headed out to the reception area himself and ignored Amira's astonished expression when he got there.

Hannah was standing with her back to him, studying an enlarged photo of the Sinabung volcano on Sumatra that he'd taken five years ago. The first thing he noticed was that her clothes matched the photo, her shirt the same rich blue as the sky, her skirt printed in the same variegated yellows as the sulfur. The second thing he noticed was that she didn't look pregnant.

He mentally slapped himself. Of course she didn't look pregnant. She could only be a couple of weeks along, at most, since it had only been eleven days since he'd last seen her and twelve since he'd made love to her. But she must be pregnant. Otherwise, why would she have come to his office? If their first effort had failed, she could have just texted him to say, *Sorry, see you next month.*

"Hey," he said by way of a greeting, his heart racing at the prospect of good news, way more than he expected it would in these circumstances.

She spun around, her gaze connecting immediately with his. That was when something cool and unpleasant settled in Yeager's midsection. Because he could tell by the look on her face that she *wasn't* pregnant.

"Come on back to my office," he said. Then, to Amira, he added, "I'm unavailable for the rest of the morning. Maybe the afternoon, too."

"Sure thing, Yeager," Amira said, sounding even more shocked than she looked.

Hannah threw a soft but obviously manufactured smile at his assistant and murmured a quiet, "Thanks." Then she crossed her arms over her midsection and followed him silently to his office.

He closed the door behind them and directed her to one of two leather chairs in front of his massive

Victorian desk. His office, like the rest of Ends of the Earth, was cluttered with antique furniture and vintage maps and artifacts. A deliberate effort to replicate a time when world travel was full of intrigue and danger, attempted by only the most intrepid explorers. He pulled the second chair closer to Hannah's and sat.

"It didn't work, did it?" he asked. "You're not pregnant, are you?"

She shook her head.

Even though he'd already known that was what she was going to say, he was surprised by the depth of his disappointment. He really had thought they'd be successful the first time they tried. They were healthy adults with even healthier libidos, and when they'd made love in North Carolina, it had been with exuberance and passion and a *very* long finish. In the days in between, they'd bungee jumped from an abandoned train trestle and zip-lined through the mountains. He still smiled when he remembered Hannah's expression and half-baked objections both times as he cinched her safety harness to his, followed by her unmitigated elation at the end of each adventure.

But his disappointment wasn't just for a failed effort after his confidence that they would succeed. He felt genuine sadness that there wasn't a tiny Yeager or Hannah growing inside her at this very moment. And it wasn't until now that he understood how very much he wanted to have this child with her.

"It's okay," he said. Even if it didn't really feel okay at the moment. "We'll try again."

Hannah nodded but she didn't look convinced. Not sure why he did it, Yeager lifted a hand and cupped her cheek in his palm. Then he leaned forward and pressed his lips lightly to hers. It was a quick, chaste kiss. One intended to reassure. But the moment his mouth touched hers, desire erupted inside him. It was all he could do not to swoop in for a second, more demanding kiss. Instead he dropped his hand to hers and wove their fingers together.

"Are you all right?" he asked.

Very softly she replied, "I think so."

He could tell she wanted to say more, but no other words came out. "Do you want to talk about it?" he asked.

"No," she said. Then she quickly amended, "Yes." She expelled a frustrated sound. "I don't know. I feel so weird right now."

That made two of them.

"It's just…" She inhaled a deep breath and released it slowly, then met his gaze. Her beautiful silver-gray eyes seemed enormous and limitless, filled with something he had never seen in them before. Not just disappointment, but uncertainty. He'd never known Hannah to be a victim of either of those things. She was always so sunny and contented whenever he saw her. Even in her tiny apartment that offered so little to be sunny or contented with, she'd seemed to be both.

Hannah was one of those rare people who was satisfied with what life had brought her, even after life had brought her so little. Not that she didn't have aspirations or goals, but she wasn't blindsided by a single-minded, driven ambition that overshadowed everything else, the way most people were when they were going after what they wanted. She took life day by day and enjoyed what each of those days brought. At least, she had until now.

"It's not about the money, you know?" she said. "I mean, at first, it was. I did always plan on having kids someday, but my timetable was fluid where that was concerned, and I didn't really give it that much thought. Then, when I found out about my grandfather and all that money..." At this, she managed an almost earnest chuckle. "Well, hell, yeah, it was about the money. I could do everything I ever wanted if I inherited the Linden billions. But this morning, when I discovered I wasn't pregnant, it wasn't the money I thought about first. It was the baby. And how there wasn't going to be one. And I just felt so..."

She blinked and a single, fat tear spilled from one eye. Yeager brushed it away with the pad of his thumb before it even reached her cheek. Then he kissed her again. A little longer this time. Maybe because he needed reassuring as much as she did, which was the most surprising thing of all this morning.

"It's okay," he repeated. "I bet no one gets pregnant the first time they try." He smiled gently. "Really, when you think about all the logistics that go into procreating, it's amazing anyone ever gets pregnant at all."

He had meant for the comment to lighten the mood. Instead, Hannah looked horrified.

"I'm kidding," he said quickly. "It'll happen, Hannah. Don't worry. This just gives us the chance to go to Malta next time. I know this very isolated, extremely wild beach where there are some incredible caves for diving. You'll love it. I promise. A few days in the Mediterranean, lying on a sunny beach, eating all that great food..." He stopped himself from adding the part about the virile young stud she'd be spending her nights with, since that part went without saying. "Who wouldn't get pregnant with all that as a backdrop?"

She smiled again and, this time, it was a little more convincing. "You're taking me to the beach," she said.

"I am."

"I'll finally get to see the ocean."

"You will."

"How long have you been planning this trip?"

Yeager had started planning it in North Carolina, the minute she'd told him she'd never seen the ocean. For some reason, though, he didn't want to admit that. So he hedged. "I've had a few ideas for destinations in my head all along. Malta was just one of them."

Which was true. He just didn't mention that Malta had been at the bottom of the list, since beaches, even the Mediterranean ones, were usually pretty lacking in adventure, and besides, when you've seen one beach and ocean, you've pretty much seen them all. Except, of course, for Hannah. So Malta it was.

"That's sweet of you, Yeager."

It wasn't sweet of him. He just didn't think it was fair that a perfectly nice person like Hannah had never seen the ocean, that was all. And, hey, that Mediterranean diet was supposed to be all kinds of healthy.

"Will it be a problem for you to take the time off from work?" he asked.

"I'm sure Mr. Cathcart and Mr. Quinn won't be too crazy about me asking off again. But when I remind them how, in the ten years I've worked for them, I hadn't had a single vacation before last month, they'll probably grudgingly concede. I'm not sure how many more times I'll be able to play that card, though. And it really will eat into my paycheck."

Yeager started to offer to intercede on her behalf with her employers for her again and cover any of her lost wages. Then he remembered how adamant Hannah had been that she could make her own way. Besides, he really was sure the trip to Malta would be, ah, fruitful. There was a good chance Hannah wouldn't need to ask for any more time off, because she'd be able to quit that job and follow her dreams.

"It'll be okay, Hannah," he told her a third time. Because three was a charm, right?

Except in baby-making, he quickly amended. In baby-making, two was. They *would* be successful next time. Yeager was sure of it.

Hannah stood on the balcony of the breathtaking suite in the luxury hotel Yeager had booked for them in Valletta, gazing out at the Grand Harbour at night, waiting for him to finish his shower.

She was beginning to understand why he lived the way he did. This place was amazing. The city was awash with light against the black sky, practically glowing with a golden grandeur reflected in the water of the bay. The moon and stars, too, were gilded with an otherworldly radiance that made her feel as if she'd completely left the planet and arrived on some ethereal plane. She couldn't be farther removed from her life in New York than she would be if she were standing at the outer reaches of the universe.

The mere view from a European balcony wasn't enough to satisfy Yeager's idea of adventure, though. For him, the adventure for this trip had lain in the ocean caves where they'd spent yesterday diving. And that had certainly been fun. But to Hannah, the true adventure was simply being in a place that was so different from her own. There really was a lot more to the world than the neighborhoods she'd called home. And she'd only visited two places at this point. Maybe, if everything worked out the way it was supposed to, once her life settled down, she'd think about doing a little more globe-trotting with her child or children in the future.

A wave of apprehension spilled over her. Right now, that *child or children* was still a big *if.* Though she and Yeager were spending this trip at a more leisurely pace than their days in North Carolina. The cave diving yesterday had been peaceful—even the heart-racing moments of interacting with a real, live, albeit small, octopus—and today, they'd lain in the sun and strolled along the streets of Valletta and stuffed themselves with local cuisine. With any luck, Hannah would drop an egg at some point tomorrow—or the next day—that was ripe for fertilization. And tonight…

The thought stopped there. Yeah. Tonight. Tonight was… Tonight would be… She sighed. This time last month she'd been looking at the night ahead as a task necessary for her to complete to claim her legacy. Not that she hadn't liked the idea of having sex with Yeager—a lot—but, originally, that was all it was supposed to be: sex with Yeager. Something that would conveniently lead to her achieving her goal of starting a family. After actually having sex with Yeager, however, everything seemed to…shift. She still couldn't put her finger on what was different about this attempt to become pregnant from the last one, but there was definitely something. Something different about Yeager. Something different about her.

When she heard a door open in the suite behind her, she spun around to see him emerging from the bathroom wearing nothing but a pair of midnight blue boxers, scrubbing his black hair dry with a towel.

She watched as he crossed to the walk-in closet and stepped inside it. He then withdrew, wearing buff-colored trousers and buttoning up a chocolate-brown shirt. She recognized both as pieces she had made for him, and a ribbon of unexpected pleasure wound through her. She didn't know why. She'd probably made, or at least altered, half his wardrobe, the same way she had for many of Cathcart and Quinn's clients. His wearing of her clothes had never affected her any more than some other man's wearing of them. For some reason, though, she suddenly liked the idea of Yeager being wrapped in garments she had sewed for him.

She continued to watch him as he strode to a table where a bottle of champagne had been chilling since they'd returned from their day in town. Deftly, he popped the cork and poured two flutes, then nestled the bottle back into the ice. Hannah didn't think she could ever get tired of just looking at him. He moved with such ease and elegance, utterly assured in himself but completely unconscious of that confidence. She remembered how, in North Carolina, he'd revealed his seemingly quiet upbringing in the heart of the Midwest. Try as she might, he hadn't let her bring up the subject again. And she was dying to know how that little boy from Peoria had become such a raging scion of world adventure.

He made his way toward the French doors leading to the balcony, where Hannah awaited him in the darkness. His eyes must not have adjusted from the light of the room because he didn't seem to see her at first. Then he smiled and headed toward her. He halted just before reaching her, though, and gave her a thorough once-over.

"Wow," he said. "You look incredible."

She warmed at the compliment. They had reservations for a late dinner at some upscale seafood place he'd told her was one of his favorite places in the world. She'd had to scramble to find something to bring with her that would be suitable, since *upscale* didn't exist in her normal wardrobe—or her normal life, for that matter. Fortunately she'd had a couple of large enough fabric remnants to stitch together a flowy, pale yellow halter dress and had found some reasonably decent dressy sandals at her favorite thrift shop.

She was also wearing the strapless bra and brief panties Yeager had given her their first day in Valletta to compensate for the ones he'd sent down the river in North Carolina. Or so he'd said. Somehow, though, the sheer ivory silk-and-lace confections bore no resemblance to the cotton Hanes Her Way that they'd replaced. And she was reasonably certain they didn't come in two-and five-packs.

"Thanks," she said, the word coming out more quietly and less confidently than she'd intended. "You look pretty amazing yourself."

He smiled. "Thanks to you."

Another frisson of delight shuddered through her. Why was his opinion suddenly more important to her than it had been before? She knew she was good at her job—she didn't need the approval of others to reinforce that. But Yeager's approval suddenly meant a lot to her.

He handed her a glass of champagne then turned to look at the city lights she'd been marveling at. "I think this may be one of the most beautiful cities I've ever visited," he said.

There was a wistfulness in his voice she'd never heard before. She wouldn't have thought Yeager Novak could be wistful. She smiled. "You talk like there are actually cities you haven't visited."

He chuckled. "One or two."

She shook her head. "I can't imagine living the life you do. Are you ever in one place for any length of time?"

"I try to spend at least one week a month in New York," he said.

"One week is not a length of time," she told him.

"Maybe not to you. But even a week in one place can make me restless. Besides, I can pretty much run Ends of the Earth from anywhere. And there are times when I have to be out of the country for months."

"Have to be?" she echoed. "Or just want to be?"

He lifted one shoulder and let it drop. "Could be they're one and the same."

Interesting way to put it.

"So, what?" she asked. "You just live in hotels?"

"Sometimes. Or in tents. Or out in the open. Depends on where I am. I do own homes in the places I visit most often."

"Which are?"

He turned to look at her full-on. "I don't want to talk about me. Let's talk about you."

She shook her head adamantly. "Oh, no. No way. We talked about me the whole time in North Carolina. You know everything there is to know about me. This time, we're going to talk *aaalll* about you."

He bristled palpably at the comment. Hannah didn't care. The last time they were together, he'd avoided every effort she'd made to learn more about him, always turning the conversation back to her.

Yeager really did know everything there was to know about her. About how she'd nearly failed phys ed at her Harlem middle school because she was so bad at gymnastics. About the four stitches and tetanus shot she'd had to get when she was seven, after slicing open her knee in a vacant lot on Lexington Avenue. About how, to this day, she still missed the grumpy, one-eyed tabby named Bing Clawsby that had lived in one of her homes.

He knew her favorite color was purple, her favorite food was fettuccine Alfredo, her favorite movie was *Wall-E* and her favorite band was the Shins. He knew she was a Sagittarius, that she'd never learned how to drive, that she believed in ghosts and, how, if she could be any animal in the world, she'd be a fennec fox. All she knew about him was that he was the only child of a quiet-sounding couple from Peoria and that he'd played hockey for a college so far upstate he might as well have been in Canada. He wasn't going to avoid her this time.

"Oh, come on," she said. "How bad can your secrets be? You barely have two thousand hits on Google."

He arched his eyebrows at that. "You looked me up online?"

"Of course I looked you up online." Hell, she'd done it after the first time he'd come into Cathcart and Quinn. There was no reason he had to know that part, though. "You're going to be the father of my child." She hoped. "But all that turned up was your social media accounts, stuff about Ends of the Earth, and mentions in some extreme adventure blogs. Even that article about you in *Outside* magazine didn't reveal anything about the real Yeager Novak."

He enjoyed a healthy taste of his champagne and avoided her gaze. Hannah remained silent as she waited him out. She was surprised when she won the battle after a few seconds and he turned to gaze out at the bay again.

Quietly he said, "That article in *Outside* revealed everything you need to know about me."

"It didn't tell me you're from Peoria."

"That's because Peoria isn't a part of my life."

"But it's where you grew up," she objected. "Where and how a person grows up is a huge part of who they are."

"It's a huge part of who they *were*," he argued. "You can't go home again."

"Everyone goes home again at some point, Yeager, in some way. It's inescapable." When he said nothing she asked, "Do your folks still live in Peoria?"

He sighed that sigh of resignation she was beginning to recognize fairly well. "No," he told her. "They died within a year of each other when I was in college."

"Oh," she said soberly. "I'm sorry."

She was sorry for his loss, not sorry that she'd asked. This was exactly the sort of thing two people should be sharing when their lives were going to be linked—she hoped—by a child. The things that had impacted them, the things that had shaped and moved them.

"I was one of those late-life surprises," he said. "My mother was fifty-two when I was born. My father was nearly sixty. He had a fatal heart attack my junior year of college. My mom had a stroke ten months later."

Which could explain one of the reasons Yeager kept himself so physically fit. It didn't, however, explain why he kept traversing the globe over and over.

"I'm sorry," Hannah said again.

He gazed down into his glass. "It was a long time ago."

Maybe. But two losses like that, so close together, had to have taken a toll on a college kid hundreds of miles away from home.

Hannah changed the subject from his parents to his school. "So…hockey scholarship. You must have been pretty good."

He nodded. "I was, actually. I had interest from a couple of pro teams before I graduated."

"Why didn't you stay with it?"

He shrugged again, even more half-heartedly. "Hockey was something I shared with my dad. He was my coach when I started in a youth league at five. He took me to Blackhawk games once a month before I even started school, even though Chicago was a three-or four-hour drive one-way. We'd make a weekend of it—my mom would come, too—and we'd do touristy stuff while we were there. Hit Navy Pier or the Shedd Aquarium or the Field Museum or something. And my dad never missed one of my games, all the way through high school. He even hung around the rink to watch me practice when he could. After he died, it wasn't the same. Hockey didn't mean as much to me as it did before. I just didn't have the heart for it anymore, you know?"

Hannah didn't know, actually. She could no more imagine what that had been like for Yeager than she could swim from here to New York. She'd never had a relationship like that—had never shared anything like that—with anyone. So she didn't respond.

He didn't seem to expect an answer, anyway, because he continued. "That was when Tommy and I started talking about going into business together. He'd spent his childhood living all over the world, thanks to his mom's job, and after my parents' deaths, going someplace else in the world—anywhere else in the world—sounded pretty damned good to me. So that was where we put our efforts."

Hannah had thought it would take the entirety of their trip this time—and then some—to uncover what it was that made Yeager tick. But in less time than it took to drink a glass of champagne, she was beginning to understand exactly why he'd become the traveler and risk-taker he was. It was clear he'd been very close to his parents, and that they'd been a loving family. A family he'd lost while he was still a kid and whom he missed terribly. A part of him might even still be looking for that family, in his own way.

Maybe, deep down, she and Yeager weren't quite so different as she'd first thought. But where her way to deal with that loss was to stay put in one place to try to a build a life there, his was to escape any reminder of what he'd once had.

He lifted his glass, drained its contents, then gazed at the bay again. Hannah sipped her champagne carefully—the way she did everything—and studied him in silence. After a moment he almost physically shook off his sober mood and looked at her again. He even smiled. Kind of.

Evidently heartened by having overcome the most difficult hurdle she could throw in front of him, he asked, "So what else do you want to know about me?"

She smiled back. "Favorite color?" Even though she already knew it was blue.

"Blue."

"Favorite food?"

"Anything from the ocean that's been blackened and grilled."

And on it went until she knew his favorite movie was *High Noon* and his favorite band was whatever happened to be streaming that didn't suck. That he was, ironically, a Virgo. That he even knew how to drive—and actually preferred—a stick shift. That he thought ghosts were a lot of hooey and that, of all the animals in the world, he'd choose to be not a lone wolf but a Komodo dragon because, hey, dragon.

By the time Hannah finished her interrogation, Yeager was pouring the last of the champagne into their glasses, and she was feeling mellower than she'd ever felt in her life. In North Carolina, they'd scarcely had a single minute when they weren't doing something adventurous. Including the sex, which, even though they'd had a perfectly good bed in their glamping tent, had happened that last time on a blanket in a clearing in the woods, under the stars, surrounded by fireflies. They'd been stargazing at the time, then one thing had led to another and, suddenly, Hannah had been naked, and then Yeager had been naked, and then she'd been on all fours with him behind her, thrusting into her again and again and again, and, well... It had just been, you know, super, super adventurous the whole time.

Anyway.

This time felt a lot less demanding. A lot less needful. A lot less urgent.

Until she looked at Yeager again and realized that, somehow, he was thinking about the exact same things she'd just been thinking about. Right down to the nakedness, the all fours and the thrusting again and again and again.

"You know," he said softly, "we can always cancel our dinner reservation."

Heat erupted in Hannah's belly at the suggestion. "But I thought you said it was one of your favorite places to eat in the whole, wide world."

His gaze turned incandescent. "I can think of other places I like better."

"How do you always know what I'm thinking?" she asked, her voice scarcely a whisper.

"I don't," he told her. "Except when you're thinking about sex. It's your eyes. They get darker. And there's something there that's just...wild. You have the most expressive eyes I've ever seen in a human being. At least, they are when it comes to wanting something."

"Or someone," she said before she could stop herself.

He took her glass from her hand and set it with his

on the balcony railing. "We should definitely cancel our dinner reservation," he said decisively.

"Okay," Hannah agreed readily. Although she was certainly hungry, dinner was the last thing on her mind. "If we *have* to."

Yeager took her hand in his and tugged her to him. Then he dipped his head and kissed her. It was a gentle kiss, with none of the heat and urgency she knew was surging through both of them. He brushed his lips over hers, once, twice, three times, four, then covered her mouth completely with his, tasting her long and hard and deep.

Oh. Okay. There was the heat. There was the urgency. There was the…

He skimmed one hand over her bare shoulder and down her arm, settling it on her waist to pull her closer.

Hannah went willingly, looping her arms around his neck, tangling the fingers of one hand in his still-damp hair. His heat surrounded her, pulling her into him, until she wasn't sure where her body ended and his began. Slowly he began moving them backward, into their suite. He paused long enough to switch off the single lamp that had been illuminated, and then they were bathed in the pale light of the moon and the golden city outside.

Yeager continued to kiss her as he guided them toward the bed, his tongue tangling with hers, his mouth hot against her skin. He reached for the tie of her halter at the same moment she reached for the button of his trousers. As she unzipped his pants, he unzipped her dress, until the garment fell into a pool around her feet. She felt his member surge against her fingers, hard and heavy against the soft silk of his boxers. So she tucked her hand inside to cover him, bare skin to bare skin. He was so... *Oh*. And she could scarcely wait to have him inside her again.

As she stroked him, he bent his head and tasted her breast over the fabric of her bra, laving her with the flat of his tongue until her nipple strained against the damp fabric. His hand at her waist crept lower, his fingers dipping into the waistband of her panties, then lower still, between her legs. Somehow, Hannah managed to take a small step to the side to open herself wider to him, and he threaded his fingers into the damp folds of her flesh. She gasped at the contact, gripping his shoulder tight when her legs threatened to buckle beneath her, her caressing of his erection growing slower and more irregular.

Yeager didn't seem to mind. As he fingered her with one hand, he moved the other to her back, expertly unfastening her bra until it fell to the floor, too. Then he pulled as much of her breast as he could into his mouth, the pressure of his tongue against her nipple coupled with his hand between her legs bringing her near orgasm. When he realized how close she was, he moved his hand away, dragging his wet fingers up over her torso to cradle her breast in his palm.

He lifted his head again and covered her mouth with his, kissing her deeply. His member twitched beneath her hand, and she knew a keen desire to have him inside her *now*. With trembling fingers, she freed him long enough to unbutton his shirt and shove it from his shoulders. Then she tugged his trousers and his boxers down over his hips, kneeling before him to skim them off his legs completely. When he stood in front of her, towering over her, his member straight and stiff, Hannah couldn't help herself. She wrapped her fingers around him and guided him toward her mouth.

He groaned his approval at her gesture, tangling his fingers in her hair. She ran her tongue down the length of him, back up again, then covered the head of his shaft completely, pulling him deep inside. Eagerly, she consumed him, taking her time to pleasure them both until she knew he was close to his breaking point. Only then did she rise again, dragging her fingers up along his thighs and taut buttocks, over the ropes of sinew and muscle on his torso, pushing herself up on tiptoe to kiss him as hungrily as he had her.

He reached for her panties and pushed them down over her hips, and she pulled them the rest of the way off. Then he lifted her up off the floor and, after one more fierce kiss, threw her playfully to the center of the bed. She landed on her fanny with a laugh, until he joined her, spreading her legs wide to bury his head between them.

Now Hannah was the one to gasp—and moan and purr—as he devoured her, drawing circles with the tip of his tongue, nibbling the sensitive nub of her clitoris until she thought she would come apart at the seams. Then he was turning their bodies so that he was sitting on the edge of the mattress again, with her astride him, facing him. Gripping her hips, he lowered her over his shaft, bucking his hips upward as he entered her, long and hard and deep. Hannah did cry out then, so filled was she by him. He moved her up, then down, then up again, until she picked up his rhythm fluently. Over and over their bodies joined, until they seemed to become one. And then they were climaxing together, Yeager surging hotly inside her.

Immediately he turned them again, so that Hannah was on her back and he was atop her, bracing himself on his strong forearms. He murmured something about staying inside her until he was sure she was pregnant this time—because he was sure she would be pregnant this time—then kissed her again for a very long time.

All Hannah could do was open her hands over the hot, slick skin of his back and return the kiss, and hope like hell he was right.

Eight

It was raining in New York the second time Hannah came to see Yeager at his office. Since undertaking this…this…this whatever it was with her—since *deal* didn't seem like the right word anymore—he'd been trying to stay close to his home base as much as he could. That way, when Hannah had good news to tell him, she could do so in person.

But he knew the moment she stepped into his office—he'd told Amira weeks ago to send Hannah back anytime she showed up—that she didn't have good news. Her dark expression was completely at odds with the bright pink-and-orange dress she was wearing, and she didn't look as if she'd slept for days.

Something cold and unpleasant settled in Yeager's midsection. He'd been disappointed last month when she'd told him she wasn't pregnant, but this… What he was feeling now went beyond disappointment. It went beyond sadness. He wasn't even sure there was a word to cover the emotions swirling inside him at the moment.

Hannah, though, looked even worse than he felt. So he rose and rounded his desk, ushering her to the same chair she'd sat in before, drawing his up alongside hers. As he had before, he took her hand in his and wove their fingers together.

And he did his best to inject a lightness he didn't feel into his voice when he said, "Another miss, huh?"

She nodded silently.

"It's okay, Hannah," he told her, just as he had the first time. And, just like the first time, it didn't feel okay at all. "There's still plenty of time before the deadline." Even though he sincerely doubted it was the deadline she was worrying about right now.

Her reply was a heavy sigh, followed by a soft, "I know."

Still forcing his cheerfulness, trying not to choke on it, he added, "And, hey, bonus, we'll get to spend more time together."

It wasn't until he said it that he realized that actually would be a bonus. He'd enjoyed his two trips with Hannah more than he'd thought he would. He liked being around her. She brought an aspect to his travels he'd never had before—the newness of the experience. He'd forgotten how much fun going someplace for the first time could be. Hell, he couldn't even remember the last time he'd gone someplace for the first time. Watching Hannah's exuberance rafting down the Chattanooga River and seeing her euphoria in the underwater caves of Gozo, he'd felt like he was seeing it all for the first time, too.

He supposed, in a way, he had been. Because he didn't think he'd ever approached adventuring the way she did. For Yeager, going someplace else in the world felt like an escape. Hell, it was an escape. For Hannah, it was a discovery. Which, maybe, was what an adventure was supposed to be about in the first place.

He pushed the thought away. He pushed all his thoughts away and focused on Hannah. He hadn't been lying when he'd said she had the most expressive eyes he'd ever seen on a human being. He had been lying when he'd told her they were only expressive when it came to sex. He'd said that in Malta because he'd wanted sex at the moment, and so had she, and it had been the perfect segue to it—not that either of them had really needed one. Her eyes really were the proverbial window onto her soul. He always knew what Hannah was thinking lately, no matter what she was thinking about. Just by looking into her eyes.

And what she was thinking now was that she was never going to get pregnant. Yeager begged to differ. They'd tried twice. Big damn deal. He knew people who had tried for years to get pregnant, then had two or three rug rats in a row. Not that he and Hannah had years—although, he had to admit, the idea of that wasn't as off-putting to him as it might have been a couple of months ago—but they did still have time. The clock on her inheritance had started ticking in July. That meant she had until January to get pregnant. It was only October. Including this month, they had three more shots. So to speak. Was it crazy that Yeager was suddenly kind of hoping they'd have to use up them all?

Hannah still hadn't replied to his last comment about how getting to spend more time together would be a bonus. Maybe she didn't think of it that way. Maybe what no longer felt like a deal to him was still very much a deal to her. Maybe she wasn't enjoying this as much as he was. Maybe she was just going through the motions and—

Yeah, right. As though the way the two of them had come together in Valletta, and before that, in North Carolina, was going through the motions. Hannah Robinson might be circumspect and careful when it came to living her life, but when it came to sex, she'd been surprisingly, gratifyingly adventurous.

An idea suddenly struck him. "Hey," he said, "if you could go anywhere in the world you wanted, where would you go?"

She gazed at him questioningly. "What do you mean?"

"I mean the two trips we've taken so far have been ones I've put together. I'd still like to honor Tommy's spirit and leave my legacy through an adventure, but maybe the secret to this baby-making is to go some-place *you* want to go. Do something *you* want to do. What do you think?"

Although the question seemed to stump her, it also seemed to pull her out of her funk. "I don't know," she said. "I've never really thought about it." Then she braved a soft smile. "Jones Beach?"

He smiled back. But there was no way he was going to let her get away with a day trip she could take anytime she wantcd to when he could take her anywhere in the world.

"Come on," he coaxed. "When you were a kid, there had to be someplace you dreamed about going. Something you dreamed about doing."

"Yeager, I've spent my whole life imagining being able to *stay* in one place and *not* move around."

He didn't buy it. "There's not a kid in the world who hasn't wanted to go someplace far away at some point and do something they've never done before. Think about it for a minute."

For a minute, she did. Then she smiled again. A better smile this time. One that did something to Yeager's insides he'd never felt before. Weird.

"Okay, so when I was about six or seven," she said, "I read this book. *Stellaluna*. Are you familiar with it?"

He shook his head. He'd never been a huge reader growing up and what little reading he had done was always about sports or superheroes.

She continued. "It's about a baby fruit bat named Stellaluna who gets separated from her mother and is taken in by a family of birds. She has to live by the birds' rules, which are totally counter to her own bat instincts, but they become a family. All the while, though, Stellaluna's mother is looking for her. In the end, she finds her and they live happily ever after. So you can see why I read the book a million times when I was a kid and why I identified so much with a fruit bat."

"I can absolutely see that," Yeager agreed. And he absolutely could.

"For a while," she went on, "I got onto this fruit

bat kick. I read a lot about them, and I decided that, even though the book never mentions where Stellaluna lives, she lived in a rainforest in Madagascar. And I thought Madagascar sounded like a really cool place."

"So you want to go to Madagascar," he said.

Hannah nodded. "Either that or Hogwarts."

He laughed. He was still disappointed that Hannah wasn't pregnant. But there was something about the prospect of trying again that made him feel better. He told himself it was because he hadn't been to Madagascar for a long time. But it was probably more because, this time, he'd be seeing it with Hannah.

"I can't help you with Hogwarts," he said. "But we can definitely go to Madagascar. Did you know there are treehouses there that you can rent?"

At this, Hannah lit up in a way he hadn't seen from her in months. Not since that night in North Carolina when she'd seen her first fireflies.

"We could really live like Stellaluna?" she asked.

"Yeah."

And if living out her childhood dream didn't put Hannah in the family way, Yeager didn't know what would.

Then another thought struck him. "Will it be a problem to take time off from work again?"

She sighed. "Yeah. But I'll handle it. I may have to finally explain to Mr. Cathcart and Mr. Quinn about my grandfather's will, which was something I really didn't want to share with anyone until I got pregnant, since I may nev—"

"Yes, you will," Yeager cut her off. And before she could say anything else, he added, "I'll have Amira clear my morning. You and I can make the plans together."

The light in Hannah dimmed some at that. "I can't," she said. "I have to be at work in a half hour."

"Right," he said. "But you have an hour for lunch, don't you?"

She nodded.

"So I'll meet you at one at Cathcart and Quinn. I'll bring lunch and my tablet with me. We'll make the arrangements then."

"Are you sure you have the time for all that?"

Was she nuts? Yeager Novak not have time for the mother of his offspring?

"Of course I have time. I'll see you at one."

"Okay."

"A Madagascar treehouse, Hannah. That will do the trick," he promised her. "This time next month, you'll be pregnant. I'm sure of it."

But the Madagascar treehouse didn't do the trick. And neither did the isolated castle in Scotland—the closest thing Yeager and Hannah could find to Hogwarts—in November. By the middle of December, she was so convinced there was something wrong that made it impossible for them to conceive that they both had their doctors do a second workup to see if that was the case.

But the results were the same then as they'd been in the summer, before they'd even started trying to conceive—they were both healthy, fertile adults for whom conception should pose no problem. Hannah's doctor tried to reassure her that it was perfectly normal for some couples to take several months to conceive and that, sometimes, the harder two people tried, the more elusive conception became. "Relax," her doctor told her. "Don't worry about it. It will happen."

Which was all well and good, Hannah thought a few evenings later in her apartment, if there weren't other factors at play. Billions of factors, in fact. If she wasn't able to inherit the Linden family fortune—her family fortune—she could be working for the rest of her life at a job that barely enabled her to take care of herself, never mind a child. Her fifty thousand dollar consolation prize would make the start of a nice nest egg, but it wasn't enough to start a business and keep it going here in New York. And without the funds to get Joey & Kit off the ground, there was no way she would ever be able to support a family. Yes, she might someday meet Mr. Right and get married and settle down. With two incomes coming in, she might be able to launch Joey & Kit and eventually turn it into a viable business.

Then again, she might not do any of those things. Nothing in life was guaranteed. Unless maybe you had billions of dollars.

And with or without the Linden fortune, Hannah knew now without question that she wanted to start a family. That had become clearer every time a pregnancy test came back negative and she was overcome by a sadness unlike any she'd ever known. Finding her Mr. Right would be beneficial in more than just a financial sense. But finding him was going to become more and more difficult the more time she spent with Yeager. The last five months with him had been the most enjoyable she'd ever spent. And not just because of the travels and adventures, either.

With every moment she spent with him, he crept further under her skin. She wasn't sure she'd ever be able to forget him once their time together came to an end—with or without a child. Before going into this venture with him, she'd considered him a frivolous, one-dimensional player. A guy who was fun to talk to and easy on the eyes, but who could never take anything in life seriously—especially a woman or a family. But she knew now that wasn't true. Yeager Novak was... He was...

She gazed out the only window in her apartment, at the back of the building on the next block. During the warm months, the backyards and fire escapes of both that building and hers were alive with activity, from Mr. Aizawa's tending of his bonsai trees to Mrs. Medina's courtyard flamenco lessons to the luscious smells wafting over from the Singhs' rooftop tandoor. In December, though, everything was still and quiet. Christmas lights twinkled from the Blomqvists' balcony, the Gorskis had lit the first candle in their window menorah and Lilah Windermere was revving up for Saturnalia, her share of the fire escape bedecked with suns and crescent moons.

Yeager Novak, Hannah continued with her thoughts, was the sort of man a woman could easily—oh, so easily—fall in love with. There was just something inside him that connected with something inside her—she didn't know any other way to put it. He was kind and smart and funny. And, for the last couple of months, he'd put her needs before his own.

She had always thought his incessant travels were due to some misplaced desire to prove he could live forever. He'd said as much himself, both that first night when he'd turned down her offer to father her child, and again the evening he'd agreed to. Now she understood, even if Yeager didn't, that he moved around so much to escape the loneliness of having lost his family when he was young. There were times when she even wondered if his agreement to donate a second set of chromosomes for her child might be the result not of his wish for a legacy, but of an unconscious desire to recreate the family he no longer had.

He was a good man. A complicated man. A multi-layered man. A man with more substance and appeal than anyone she knew. Not the kind of guy Hannah normally went for at all. Which, maybe, was why she was falling for him so much harder.

The buzz of her doorbell interrupted her thoughts and she was grateful. She somehow knew before she even crossed to the intercom and heard his voice that it would be Yeager. But she didn't know why he'd be dropping by on a wintry Wednesday evening. They weren't supposed to meet again until Saturday morning, New York time, when they would arrive separately in Fiji for their final adventure together—this one to camp near a volcano on Koro Island. Yeager had read it was the site of an ancient fertility ritual and he intended to recreate it, right down to the running naked across hot coals after ingesting copious amounts of kava from a coconut shell. He had to leave tomorrow for a trip to Vancouver, but would take a red-eye to Suva and meet her within an hour of her own arrival.

A few months ago Hannah would have been excited by the idea of an adventure in Fiji, especially with Yeager. Tonight the thought of another quick trip—the most exotic one of all—only to return to her normal life a week later held no appeal. Her normal life, period, didn't hold much appeal these days. Which was, perhaps, the most troubling realization of all. Even if it hadn't been remarkable, her life five months ago had been perfectly acceptable to her. Then Gus Fiver of Tarrant, Fiver & Twigg walked in and everything— *everything*—changed. She wondered now if she would ever be content again.

She buzzed Yeager in and opened her front door, meeting him at the top of the stairs. He was still dressed for work, in a tailored, black wool coat flapping open over a charcoal suit—though he'd unbuttoned his shirt collar and loosened his tie. Hannah, too, was still in her work clothes, a black pencil skirt paired with a red sweater and red-and-black polka-dot tights.

As he topped the last stair, she started to take a step back toward her apartment to give him room. Before she could, though, he swept her up against him and dropped a swift kiss on her lips. The gesture surprised her. Especially when, after he completed it, he made no move to release her.

Instead he gazed into her eyes and murmured, "Hi. How you doing?"

"I… I'm good," she stammered. And then, because she couldn't think of anything else to say, thanks to the way the blood zipping through her veins made her a little—okay, a lot—muddleheaded, she added, "How are you?"

He grinned. "I'm good, too. I thought maybe we could do something tonight."

Her eyebrows shot up at that. "Why?"

He chuckled. "Why not?"

"Because I'm not… I mean, it's not time for me to… I still have a couple of days before I…"

He laughed again. Something inside Hannah caught fire.

"I wasn't planning on getting you pregnant tonight," he told her. "I was in the neighborhood, meeting with a potential contractor, and I thought I'd drop by and see if we could grab some dinner together. Maybe go over our itinerary for Fiji one more time. I have a car waiting downstairs. We can go anywhere you want."

It wasn't that unusual of a request. Well, okay, the car waiting downstairs was a little outside her usual experiences, since Hannah normally bused or trained it everywhere. Even so, it took her a moment to reply.

"Anywhere?" she finally repeated. Because, if he was offering, she did have something kind of specific in mind.

"Anywhere," he promised.

"Okay," she said. "Dinner would be good. Just let me get my coat."

In retrospect, Yeager decided a couple of hours later, maybe he shouldn't have told Hannah they could go anywhere she wanted. Because she'd chosen the Russian Tea Room. Not that he had anything against it, but…it was the Russian Tea Room, which wasn't exactly his cup of tea. But Hannah had never been before and had always wanted to go, so here they were. And, truth be told, his cheese and cherry blintze had been pretty freaking amazing.

It wasn't even nine o'clock when they exited the restaurant, and Yeager didn't want the evening to end just yet. He didn't have to be at the airport for his flight to Vancouver until eleven tomorrow morning, so it wasn't like he had to be in bed early. He started to ask Hannah what else she wanted to do, but hesitated. She might tell him she wanted to go to the roof of the Empire State Building. Or, worse, on one of those cruises to see the Statue of Liberty. Or, worst of all, go ice-skating under the Christmas tree at Rockefeller Center.

He risked it anyway. "What do you want to do next?"

And heard an answer that was far, far worse.

"Can we take a carriage ride around Central Park?"

Yeager flinched as if she'd just hit him with a brick. Seriously? What was this, Prom Night?

Then he remembered how she'd once told him she hadn't gone to her prom because no one had asked her and she'd been too scared to ask anyone herself. She'd just transferred to a new school a few months before all the senior events started happening. All the kids had steered clear of her once they learned she was in the system because they'd figured she was, at best, a weirdo and, at worst, a psycho.

"Please, Yeager?" she asked, sounding very much like a high school senior who'd just moved to a new school and had no friends. "It'll be so much fun. The Christmas lights will be up in Central Park, and it's supposed to snow."

Oh, good. The only thing that would make a carriage ride through Central Park more fun would be doing it in a snow globe they could buy later from some guy in a trench coat in Times Square. But Hannah's heart was in her eyes again. Standing there in her red coat with its multicolored buttons, her striped scarf wound around her neck what looked like a dozen times, her mittened hands before her in a way that made her look like she was praying he would say yes...

He sighed with resignation. "Yeah, okay. Why not?"

Her eyes went incandescent at that and, somehow, he minded a lot less that he was doing the crass tourist thing in New York with Hannah when he could have, quite literally, been anywhere in the world doing anything he wanted. He liked being here with Hannah. He liked being anywhere with her. It didn't matter what they were doing.

They found a free carriage at 7th Avenue and 59th Street. The driver introduced himself as Yuri and his horse as Arthur, the latter delighting Hannah since, as she told Yeager, she'd never been this close to a horse before. When Yuri heard that, he handed her a carrot to feed the animal and, by her reaction as she fed Arthur, she might as well have been donning the Crown Jewels. Then they climbed into the white carriage with red velvet seats and settled in for the ride, nestled under a red-and-black-plaid blanket to chase away the chill.

Central Park opened up before them like a Christmas card, surrounding them with a winter wonderland of lamplight and moonlight and twinkling white tree lights. All was calm, all was bright, with silver lanes aglow and kids jingle-belling and chestnut vendors roasting their fare on an open fire and passersby dressed up like Eskimos. Barely ten minutes in, snow began to swirl around them, giving everything an otherworldly glow and buffering the sounds of this frosty symphony. Hannah looped her arm through his as if it were the most natural thing in the world to do, leaning her head on his shoulder. And Yeager had to admit there were worse ways to spend an evening than inside a Christmas snow globe with Hannah Robinson.

They rode in silence for a little while then Hannah sighed with much feeling. "I knew it would be like this," she said.

"Like what?" Yeager asked.

She hesitated, sighed again and whispered, "Magical."

On any other night, with any other person, Yeager would have said that was ridiculous. There was no such thing as magic. This was just Central Park, a place they both must have visited dozens of times. Lights ran on electricity. Snow was just frozen pieces of water. There was an explanation for every single thing around them.

Except, maybe, for why he wanted so badly to kiss her when there was no reason to do it.

"When you were a kid," she said quietly, "did you believe in Santa Claus?"

"Of course I believed in Santa Claus," he told her. Hell, he'd held out on the Santa-being-real thing way longer than his classmates, something that had brought him no end of ribbing. He hadn't cared. He'd been absolutely certain a white-bearded man dressed in red came down their chimney every year to scatter toys across every inch of the living room, leaving cookie crumbs and a half-empty glass of milk behind. What other explanation could there be? Such had been the innocence of his childhood. An innocence that was shattered one night in upstate New York, when his mother called him from almost a thousand miles away to tell him he would never see his father alive again.

"How about you?" he asked Hannah, pushing the memory as far to the back of his brain as he could. He thought she would reply the same way. So he wasn't quite prepared for the answer she gave him.

"I don't think I ever had the chance to believe in him. I mean, maybe when I lived with my mom before she died, I did. I don't know. But I don't remember ever looking out the window, up at the sky, waiting for his arrival. Someone must have told me at one of my first homes that there was no such thing as Santa."

When he and Hannah had their baby, Yeager thought, no one was ever going to do that. Every child should have the opportunity to believe in magic for as long as they wanted to believe. Even if Yeager didn't believe in it anymore.

"Did you at least have presents to open on Christmas morning?" he asked.

"Usually."

Usually, he echoed to himself. Meaning there had been some Christmas mornings when Hannah had gone without the breathtaking exhilaration that came with ripping brightly colored paper off boxes to see what treasure was inside. That wasn't going to happen to their child, either.

"What kind of Christmas traditions did your family have?" she asked. Probably because she'd never been in one place long enough to establish traditions of her own.

There was a time when Yeager would have refused

to answer, since he generally hated talking about his parents and the life he'd had with them. That life just didn't feel like it was his anymore. In a way, it felt like it had happened to someone else. With Hannah, though, he didn't mind talking about it so much. With Hannah, that life didn't seem so alien. It didn't feel so far away.

"Every Christmas Eve," he said, "my mom made Cornish hens, with sweet potatoes and Brussels sprouts as a side."

None of which he'd eaten since her death.

"We had this Christmas china she got somewhere," he continued, "and she'd break it out for that meal and Christmas Day, then it would be boxed up again and stowed for another year."

Yeager still had that china. Somewhere. For some reason, he hadn't been able to part with it when it came to disposing of his parents' possessions after graduating from college. Maybe he'd look around for it this year. Break it out before Christmas. Maybe he and Hannah could—

But he wouldn't be in New York for Christmas, he reminded himself. He had long-standing plans to be skiing with friends in Vail.

"I got to open one gift on Christmas Eve," he continued for Hannah, "and I always took about an hour to pick out which one. Christmas morning, I wasn't allowed to get out of bed before eight, even though I was always awake by six. But at one second after eight, I'd run downstairs and behold the glory that was Christmas morning."

For the first time in a long, long time, he was able to smile at the recollections. Hell, it was surprising that he was even able to tolerate the memories in the first place. How the tree lights would be on when he awoke, even though his father was adamant they be turned off before he went to bed. How, somehow, there were already cinnamon rolls baking in the oven and hot chocolate heating on the stove and Christmas carols playing on the CD player. Back then, he'd put it all down to Santa. Santa and the magic of Christmas.

He told Hannah about all that and more, until the snow was falling furiously around them and he was dipping his head toward hers and she was lifting hers in return to meet him halfway. Their lips connected gently at first, the subtle brush of their mouths against each other a warm counterpoint to the night around them.

They chatted and canoodled for the rest of the ride around the park. When Yuri pulled Arthur to a halt where they had begun, Yeager was surprised by the depth of his disappointment. Part of him wanted to go around again. But another part of him—a bigger part—just wanted to be alone with Hannah.

As they drew up in front of her building in the car he'd hired for the day, he grew more disconcerted. Why did he feel so annoyed at having to say goodnight to her? He'd be seeing her again in Fiji in a few days. For some reason, though, the days between now and then felt like an interminable—intolerable—period of time. But how to finagle an invitation to…oh, he didn't know…spend the night with her, without sounding like a jerk.

"So, Hannah, what would you think if maybe I—"

"So, Yeager, is there any chance you might want to—" she said at the same time.

They stopped talking as one, their gazes connecting. Then, as one, they both smiled.

"I think it's a great idea," she told him.

"I'd love to," he said at the same time.

He sent the driver on his way after that, emptying his wallet for the tip, not wanting to waste any more time doing something as mundane as keeping track of his cash flow.

Hand in hand, he and Hannah climbed the stairs to her apartment and entered. The moment they were inside with the door closed behind them, he kissed her. Strangely, it wasn't like the kisses that had preceded their couplings in other places. It wasn't hot and urgent, filled with need. It was slow and sweet, almost innocent, as if this were the first time for both of them, and neither was sure exactly what to do.

Later, Yeager wouldn't even remember moving the love seat to pull down the Murphy bed. Later, he wouldn't remember the two of them undressing each other and climbing into it. Later, he would only remember making love to Hannah in a way they hadn't made love before. With care and attention, and something else that hadn't been there earlier, either. Something he wasn't sure how to describe or what to call. But it felt as natural and necessary as breathing.

After they spent themselves, when he wrapped his arms around her and pulled her close, she nestled into him and tucked her head beneath his chin. As Hannah slept beside him, Yeager looked out the window—the only window she had onto the world—and watched the snow fall.

And he wondered what he was going to do if he and Hannah weren't successful with their final attempt at conception in Fiji. Worse, he wondered what he was going to do after their baby was born, when he would be moving in and out of their lives, and Hannah would never have a need for a night like this again.

Nine

Hannah was throwing the last of her toiletries into the suitcase she'd be carting to Fiji in an hour when her phone rang. She wasn't surprised to see Yeager on the Caller ID, since he always called just before she was due to leave to remind her to bring sunscreen—even to Scotland—which she'd always already packed.

She thumbed the answer button and lifted the phone to her ear. "Yes, I packed sunscreen, and yes, it's SPF thirty," she greeted him.

Silence met her from the other end for a moment. Then, in a quiet, too steady voice, Yeager replied, "Hannah, I have some bad news."

Something seized up in her chest at the absolute absence of emotion in his voice. She'd never heard him sound this way before. "Are you okay?"

"Yes," he told her quickly. "But I'm not in Vancouver."

He was supposed to have been in Vancouver yesterday afternoon, West Coast time. He'd planned to check out a site for some new mountain adventure today, then take a late-night flight that would put him in Suva before breakfast on Sunday morning, Fiji time, which would be Saturday afternoon New York time. That gave them plenty of time to get settled, since that would be the day before Hannah was set to ovulate. They'd planned everything down to the minute. At least, they had before Yeager turned up someplace he wasn't supposed to be.

"Where are you?" she asked.

He muttered an exasperated sound. "I'm in Alberta. Long story short, what was supposed to be an uneventful flight, both time-and weather-wise, got delayed a couple of hours, then a storm blew in out of nowhere just as we were approaching the Rockies. The jet I chartered had to make an emergency landing on a little airstrip at a research station in the middle of nowhere."

Hannah's tension increased with every word he spoke. "That happened yesterday?"

"Yeah."

"Why didn't you call me?"

"I didn't think it would be that big a deal. I figured the storm would blow over and we'd still make it to Vancouver today. Worst case scenario, I'd have to cancel my day trip to look at the property I'm interested in and just head right on to Fiji as planned."

"So you think you'll still be able to do that?"

His answer was way too quick for her liking. "No."

Okay, so they wouldn't be going to Fiji. That was all right. Hannah hadn't been all that keen on flying fifteen hours one way, anyway, with or without a fer-

tility volcano—and Yeager—at the end of the journey.
She was totally okay with their next attempt at conception being right here in New York. They could check
into a nice hotel, have dinner—maybe even take another carriage ride around Central Park, which, of all
the experiences she'd shared with Yeager, had been,
hands down, the most enjoyable. Well, except for all
their, um, attempts at conception.

"So I guess we're not going to Fiji then," she said.

"No," he told her. "I'm definitely not going to get
out of here in time for that."

He still sounded way too somber for her liking.
Way too serious. Way too worried.

"Well, when will you be able to leave?" she asked.

This time, there was a long pause followed by a
quiet, "I honestly don't know."

Now Hannah felt somber, serious and worried, too.
"Why not?"

"Because we're completely snowed in here. And
another storm is coming right at us."

She told herself not to panic. There was still plenty
of time for him to get back to New York, right? Sunday was still two days away. A flight from Alberta
couldn't take more than four or five hours, could it?
A third of the time it would have taken to fly to Fiji.

"But you'll be back in New York by Sunday, right?"
she asked.

There was another pause, longer this time. Then a
very weary-sounding Yeager told her, "I don't know,
Hannah."

"But—"

"The jet took a beating before we landed. My pilot
almost didn't get us to the ground in one piece."

Her nerves went barbed-wire sharp at that. "Yeager! You nearly died? And you didn't call me yesterday to tell me?"

What the hell was the matter with him? Okay, yeah, they weren't girlfriend and boyfriend, so he wasn't obligated to keep her apprised of everything that happened in his life, even when his life was threatened. But they were friends, weren't they? Kind of? Sort of? In a way? Okay, maybe they weren't friends, either—she wasn't sure what they were, actually. But they *were* trying to make a baby together, so the least he could do was keep her informed about things that put him in danger.

Then she remembered he made his living courting danger. He lived his life courting danger. Yeager wasn't happy unless he was thumbing his nose at death with some kind of crazy adventure. Nearly crashing into the side of a mountain in a private jet was probably nothing compared to some of the activities he undertook. How could she have thought it would be a good idea to have a baby with a guy like that? She was going to be worrying about the safety of her child's father for the rest of her life.

Or not. Because it was starting to sound like they might miss their last chance for her to conceive before the time ran out on the Linden fortune. If Yeager got stuck in Alberta much longer...

"The jet landed safely," he hurried to reassure her. "But not before it developed some mechanical problems that are going to keep it grounded until it can be repaired. And this place is totally closed off by road this time of year. The only way in and out is by plane, and there aren't any others here right now. Even if this new storm subsides soon, I'm going to be stuck until someone else can get in and fly us out. And I just don't know how long that will take. There must be three feet of snow on the ground."

With every word he spoke, Hannah's fears grew worse. Not just for Yeager's safety, but that the last chance she had to conceive a child with him—to start a family with him—was gone. Sunday was supposed to be her fertile day. She knew that an egg, once dropped, could be viable for, at best, twenty-four hours. If her calculations were correct—though, honestly, she had no idea these days if they were, and the fertility monitors and ovulation tests she'd tried to use hadn't been all that helpful—she could still become pregnant if Yeager made it back to New York by Monday night.

Maybe. Possibly. Perhaps.

But if he didn't make it back by then, that was it. No baby for Hannah. No Linden fortune that would have ensured the rest of her life was a happy, safe, secure one. Instead she'd be dogged forever by the specter of what might have been.

She tried not to think about the irony. Had she never discovered she was the missing Linden heir, the rest of her life would have been happy. Happy enough, anyway. She would have lived it as she always had, day by day, satisfied with what she had, working toward a future she hoped and dreamed would eventually happen. She would have had a vague idea about starting a family someday, but wouldn't have been in any big hurry. And if it never happened, well, that probably would have been okay, because she never would have known what she was missing. But now...

Now she would have to live with the very real knowledge that she wanted a family badly and might never have one. Worse, now she knew she wanted that family with Yeager, and she would never have him, either. Without him as the father of her child, there would be no reason for him to stay in her life. Not as anything other than one of her regulars at Cathcart and Quinn—though one she would now know quite a bit better than most. The only reason he would have continued to be a part of her life otherwise would have been because he was her baby's father. He wasn't the kind of man to settle down in one place with one woman—any woman. Sure, he was determined to be a father to their child, but only between trips to all four corners of the world. His idea of parenting would be swooping in with *Matryoshka* dolls and *Mozartkugel* and didgeridoos to regale his progeny with stories of his travels, then fly off again for another adventure— most likely with someone named Luydmila or Fritzi or Sheila.

Yes, Yeager Novak wanted to be a father. But he didn't want to be a *father*. Not the kind who dealt with the skinned knees and carpools and picket fences. Or with the hand-holding strolls and the Sunday-morning snuggles and the firefly-spattered evenings on the patio after the kids went to bed, the way Hannah wanted to be a mother. And the way she wanted to be—she might as well admit it—a wife.

So if Yeager didn't make it back to New York soon…

"Well, when do you think someone will be able to fly you out?" she asked.

There was another one of those uncomfortable silences. "I just don't know, Hannah. I'm sorry."

"It's okay," she told him. Even if it wasn't. Even if it kind of felt like she was stranded alone in an icy, isolated wilderness herself. "I'm sure you'll get out of there soon. I'm not supposed to ovulate until Sunday. Maybe it'll even happen Monday. As long as we can get together by Tuesday, we should be fine. You'll be back by Tuesday, right?"

The silence that met her for that reply was the worst one yet. So was the hopeless, defeated tone in Yeager's voice when he said, "Yeah. Sure. Sure, I will. It'll be fine. Look, I'm sorry, but I have to go. The power here is iffy, too, right now, and I'm not sure how long I'll have my battery. I'll call you again when I can, okay? Let you know what's going on."

"Okay," Hannah said. "Keep me posted. And, Yeager?"

"Yeah?"

She knew he hated to hear the words, but she was going to say them, anyway. "Be careful."

"I will," he said.

And that, more than anything, told her all she needed to know. He was worried, too.

She said goodbye and thumbed off the phone, then looked at the suitcase she hadn't yet closed. On top was the lacy underwear Yeager had given to her in Malta. She'd worn it every trip since, thinking it would bring them luck. And also because of the look in Yeager's eyes whenever he saw her wearing it. Automatically, she began removing everything she'd packed, piece by piece, putting it all back where it belonged. Then she gazed at the empty suitcase, feeling every bit as empty.

She told herself there was probably still time to go the sperm bank route. She'd finished the application process last summer and been cleared while she was waiting for Yeager to see a doctor about his health to ensure he was up to the task of conceiving a child. It was possible they might be able to accommodate her, especially if she explained the situation to them. She might still be able to conceive a baby this month with some anonymous donor.

But she didn't want to have a baby with some anonymous donor. She wanted Yeager to be the father of any child she might have. Having a baby wasn't about winning the Linden billions anymore. It hadn't been about that for a long time. Hannah didn't want to just start a family, not even for a family fortune. She wanted to start a family with Yeager. Because, somewhere along the line, Yeager had begun to feel like family.

Surely he'd make it home by Tuesday. Surely her egg would wait until he was there before it made an appearance. Surely this time—this last, final time— would be the one that worked.

Surely it would. Surely.

It took Yeager a full week after becoming stranded in Alberta to get back to New York, much too late for him and Hannah to even attempt conception. For the last couple of months she'd been using one of those prediction kits that indicated a surge in some hormone that happened prior to ovulation. By Wednesday afternoon, when Yeager finally called her to tell her he would be flying out the next day, that surge was nonexistent. Hannah's egg had come and gone without him. They'd never stood a chance.

He'd told her on Sunday night to go to the sperm bank on Monday and get pregnant that way. But she'd said she would wait for him. He'd been surprised by her decision—she was almost certainly not going to get pregnant if she waited for him to get back to New York, and by the time they could try next month, it would be past the legal deadline for her to inherit. But a part of him had been delighted by her decision, too. He still liked the idea of having a child with Hannah. Now, though, there wouldn't be any financial benefit to her, so he couldn't see her wanting to continue the effort.

Even if he offered to pay for everything the child needed—and then some—he couldn't see her going along. Hannah wanted to make her own way in the world. She wanted to have a child on her terms, not his, which was perfectly understandable. But she wouldn't be able to do that until she was at a place in her life where having a child fit in. Now that she wouldn't be claiming her family fortune, who knew when she'd be able to swing it? And by the time she could, there would probably be some other guy in the picture who could provide the paternity. And maybe provide a life with her, too. She wouldn't need Yeager for any of it. Not that he wanted to spend a life with Hannah—or any woman. But the idea of her starting a family with someone else now was just...inconceivable. No pun intended.

He wished her grandfather was still alive. Not just so Yeager could tell the guy what an incredible granddaughter he had—so it was unfair to put some ridiculous condition on her inheritance like insisting she have a child—but also so he could strangle the guy with his bare hands. Seriously, what kind of jerk turned a woman into an incubator, just so he could ensure his family line remained intact?

Okay, so, in a way, maybe Yeager had kind of done that to Hannah, too. That was beside the point. The point was...

He sighed with much feeling as he gazed out the window of his office at the snow falling over New York. The point was that he and Hannah had both wanted a child for their own reasons, and now they wouldn't be having one. What could either of them say or do at this point that would make that better? It wasn't like either of them was at fault for what had happened, but that didn't make it any easier to bear.

So where did that leave them? What would they be to each other now? It wasn't like they could go back to just being seamstress and client. But they didn't feel like just friends, either. Sure, they were lovers—or maybe former lovers—but even that didn't feel like the right word to use. Yeager had had lots of lovers—and he had lots of former lovers—but he'd never felt for any of them the way he felt for Hannah.

He forced himself to turn away from the window and go back to his desk, where a mountain of work awaited him after his stay in Alberta. He told himself he was way overthinking this. He and Hannah *were* friends. Period. That was why he felt differently about her than he had other women he'd dated. Those women had been great, and he'd liked all of them, but they'd never been... Hannah. And he didn't kid himself that he'd ever meet another woman who was like her. Who would be a *friend* like her, he corrected himself. Women would come and go in his life the way they always had, but Hannah would be constant. The way friends were.

Yeah, that was it. They were friends. Friends who would stay friends, no matter what. Even if they didn't have a child to tie them together. Wouldn't they?

Surely they would. Surely.

Hannah awoke on New Year's Day with *the* weirdest feeling, after having some of *the* weirdest dreams she'd ever had. In one, she was underwater, but perfectly capable of breathing, and was suddenly surrounded by and swimming among dolphins. In another, she was tending to a garden full of lotuses and turtles kept coming up out of the soil. Yeager was in another, bringing her a basket of acorns that she up-ended and consumed in one gulp. Just…weird.

She also realized she'd slept way past the usual time she awoke on days when Cathcart and Quinn was closed. It was nearly eleven when she finally opened her eyes and looked at the clock.

Still feeling as if someone had wrapped her in cotton gauze, she rolled over and, for some reason, settled both hands over her lower abdomen, splaying her fingers wide. It shouldn't have been an unusual gesture. Except that she never did it. Usually, when she awoke and turned to lie on her back in bed, she tucked both hands behind her head. What the hell was up with those dreams, and why did she have her hands on her abdomen instead of—

Heat suddenly flared in her belly. She dared not hope…but did anyway. Was her body trying to tell her brain something it hadn't yet figured out? Like maybe…

She was supposed to have started her period yesterday or the day before, but she'd put down the lateness as a result of, number one, her cycle never being all that regular to begin with and, two, the stress of the last several months taking its toll. She shouldn't have been fertile the night she and Yeager made love in New York, and sperm normally weren't viable for more than three days after they launched. On the other hand, she'd read that it was possible for some of those little swimmers to hang around for five days after their release. And, hey, it *was* Yeager's little swimmers she was talking about.

It was also possible she'd dropped an egg before she thought she would. Those ovulation predictor kits were iffy. They only told you your hormones were in the right place for you to ovulate, but not exactly when you would. So maybe, *maybe*, that snowy night when they'd made love right here in her bed, the circumstances had been right.

She had a pregnancy kit in her bathroom she'd bought after their last attempt failed. Her hands were actually shaking as she withdrew it from the medicine cabinet. And she didn't think she took a single breath while she counted down the seconds it took for the indicator to produce the word *Yes* or *No*. Five times she had performed this ritual. Five times, it had ended with the word *No*. She waited a full minute longer than she needed to to check the results this morning. And she had one eye closed, and the other narrowed, when she finally picked up the indicator to look at it. So it was no wonder she was still doubtful when she saw that the answer this time was—

Yes.

Heat exploded inside her at those three little letters. She didn't believe it. Couldn't believe it. Wouldn't believe it until she took a second test. Which she didn't have. So she yanked on some pants and threw her coat on over her pajama shirt, tugged snow boots on over her bare feet, grabbed her wallet and ran downstairs to the *mercado* below her apartment…only to find it closed for the holiday.

She knew a moment of panic. Until she remembered the twenty-four-hour Duane Reade two blocks up. She knew it was closed on Thanksgiving and Christmas. Oh, *pleasepleaseplease*, Pregnancy Gods and Goddesses, don't let it be closed on New Year's, too.

The gods and goddesses were good to Hannah that day because a half hour later she was counting down to see the results of the second test. The sample wouldn't be nearly as strong as the first, because she'd been storing up that one all night, and this one was the result of two hastily consumed cups of coffee purchased along with the pregnancy test. But even with the weakened sample, when she picked up the wand, studying it with both eyes wide open this time, the word she saw was—

Yes.

No matter how many times Hannah looked at it, and no matter from what angle, the word she saw, again and again, was *Yes.*

Yes. *Yes.* YES. *Yessssss!*

Holy cow. She was going to have a baby. She and Yeager were going to have a baby. She was going to have a family. A real family. The way she'd always wanted. The way she'd never really thought she would.

She had to tell him. Immediately. In person. She could shower and change and be at his place by—

By never, because she realized in that moment that she didn't even know where he lived. There had never been a reason to visit him at his place, and other than one vague mention of his having a condo in West Chelsea, the topic of where he lived had never come up in their conversations. Why should it? There had never been a reason for her to visit him at home, and there never would be, unless—until—they had a child together. Which had seemed less and less likely with every passing month.

They weren't boyfriend and girlfriend, she reminded herself for perhaps the hundredth time since going into this venture with him. They weren't even lovers, at least not on Yeager's part. It didn't matter that Hannah was battling some weird emotions on that front herself. Maybe she had grown to love him over the last six months—maybe—but she would fall out of love again, once the two of them weren't so involved. Right? Of course.

They were partners. That was all. And they would always be partners, thanks to this baby. But it was more like a business arrangement than anything else. They'd even signed paperwork outlining their obligations to each other during the conception process and to the child once its conception was achieved. They had each gone into it with individual needs and goals, and this baby—they were going to have a baby!— would fulfill those needs and goals for each of them. Yes, that sounded kind of indifferent and calculating, but that was exactly what their agreement had been at first. Nothing personal. Everything planned. And now…

A wave of something that was in no way indifferent or calculating—or impersonal or unplanned—rolled through her midsection. Oh, God. Now it was so, *so* much more than any of those things. Now it was…it was…

She grabbed her phone to text Yeager, asking him only where he was. They hadn't spoken since his return to New York—probably because neither of them had known what to say. He might not even be in New York at the moment. How did billionaire adventurers celebrate New Year's Eve, anyway? For all she knew, he'd followed the holiday around the world, celebrating it a dozen times, starting in Samoa and ending in Pago Pago.

He texted back immediately, telling her he was at home. Why?

She didn't want to announce something like this with a text. Or even a phone call. So her text back to him was simple, if vague. Would it be okay if I came over for a little while?

He again replied immediately. Sure. Everything ok?

Fine, she returned. Just want to talk. Then she backspaced over the last part before hitting Send and amended it to Just need to talk.

Yeager texted back his address on West 21st and said he'd be working at home all day. Hannah told him she'd be there in an hour or so. The 7 train on holidays never ran very efficiently, after all. Fortunately for Hannah, though, her body finally was.

Ten

Damn the 7 train, anyway, Yeager thought as he waited for Hannah's arrival nearly two hours later. It never ran well on holidays.

He'd given up trying to work after she'd sent her last text, because he'd been too busy wondering what she needed to talk about. He'd at least showered and shaved and changed into a pair of jeans and an oatmeal-colored sweater, but that had only eaten up about thirty minutes. For the last—he glanced at the Bavarian clock on his mantel nestled between the Turkish *Iznik* bowl and a Puerto Rican *vejigante* mask—seventy-eight minutes, he'd done little more than pace from room to room trying to find something to occupy himself. He hadn't even eaten lunch because his stomach was too full of apprehension.

Two hours and sixteen minutes after Hannah's last

text, there was finally a knock at his front door—Yeager had already notified Baxter, the doorman, that he was expecting her and to send her right up. He couldn't believe how nervous he was when he went to answer the door. As he strode down the long gallery from the living room where he'd been pacing, it did that cinematic stretch thing where it seemed to quadruple in length.

It had just been too long since he'd seen her, that was all. Since July, they'd never gone more than a couple of weeks without contact. Then he realized it had only been a couple of weeks since he and Hannah had taken that carriage ride through Central Park. No different from most other months and hardly an eon. Even if it did feel like one.

He opened his front door to find her standing there in her red coat with the funny, different-colored buttons that she'd designed and made herself, her striped scarf tripled around her neck. Her hair was damp and glistening from the snow that had begun to fall not long after she'd texted. And her eyes...

Damn. Those eyes. Even after knowing her as long as he had, even after making love to her a dozen times, her eyes still seized something deep inside him and held fast. Yeager would always be startled by the clarity and depth of emotion in Hannah's eyes.

"Hi," she said.

Still feeling as nervous as a schoolboy at his first dance—even though he hadn't even been this nervous as a schoolboy at his first dance—he replied, "Hi."

He took a step backward and gestured her inside, and she strode past him slowly, almost cautiously, as if she weren't sure of her reception here. Why was this the first time she'd ever been in his home? He should have invited her over a long time ago.

He closed the door behind her and followed her down the gallery, Hannah unwinding her scarf as she went. By the time they reached his living room with its panoramic windows on both sides, she had shrugged it off, along with her coat. Beneath, she was wearing jeans and a fuzzy white sweater. She transferred her coat restlessly from one hand to the other.

"Let me take your coat," Yeager said, reaching toward it.

She looked a little confused by the gesture at first, as if her thoughts were a million miles away. Then she awkwardly extended her coat to him. He awkwardly took it from her. Then he shifted it from one hand to the other a couple of times before tossing it onto the chair nearest him.

"So," he began...then realized he had no idea what else to say. Finally he went with, "How've you been?"

And immediately regretted the question. How the hell did he think she'd been? She wasn't going to have the family or the fortune that had been dangled in front of her for six months then cruelly yanked away from her to leave her with neither. He was going to go out on a limb and say she hadn't been too great.

Instead of replying, she darted her gaze around his living room, from the travel trophies on his mantelpiece to the Russian mosaic on the wall above them to the Chilean pottery lining one windowsill to the Indonesian shadow puppets hanging above the door to his office. Her gaze seemed to light on every item he'd ever brought home with him from his adventures—and there were scores of them in this room alone.

Finally she looked at him again. "I didn't think you'd be home," she said softly.

"Why not?"

"I just figured you'd be somewhere else. I mean, look at this place, Yeager. It's incredible. How many people can live the way you do? I just thought you'd be celebrating New Year's somewhere besides New York, that's all."

He started to tell her he hadn't felt like celebrating. The New Year or anything else. Instead he told her, "I have a lot that needs attention here right now."

One of those things should have been Hannah. One of those things was Hannah. He just wasn't sure yet what kind of attention to direct her way. He wasn't sure he'd ever know.

"Hannah, is everything okay?" he asked.

She opened her mouth to reply then something over his shoulder caught her eye. She moved to the side of his living room that looked out onto the Hudson.

"You can see the Statue of Liberty from here," she said.

Yeager had forgotten about that. He'd lived here long enough that he guessed he took it for granted. And why the hell wasn't she answering his question?

She walked to the other side of the living room and looked out the windows there. "And you can see the Empire State Building from here," she said.

Yeah, he'd forgotten about that, too. He'd honestly stopped seeing the views as anything other than New York City in general and Manhattan in particular. Not that he didn't appreciate the view, he just hadn't really given it much thought in the last few years. To someone like Hannah, though, who'd spent who knew how long in her cramped Sunnyside studio with one window that looked at the apartment building on the next street, his view of the city was doubtless pretty incredible.

Why had he forgotten about that when it was what had impressed him about the place so much the first time he'd looked at it? The minute he'd seen the views Hannah had just seen, the little boy from Peoria had surged up inside him and hadn't been able to believe it was possible to see so much from one room. It was like looking at the whole, wide world in one swoop. And at night, when the city lights were on, it was like the world went on *forever*.

When Hannah turned to look at him again, she had tears in her eyes. The only other times Yeager had seen her cry were the night he'd initially turned down her request that he be the father of her child and that first time she'd come to his office to tell him she wasn't pregnant. Both times she'd been in a position where she thought she would miss out on inheriting her family's fortune—or, at least, that was why he'd thought she was crying at the time. He knew now that the money wasn't the primary reason Hannah had wanted to get pregnant—she genuinely wanted to start the family she'd never thought she might have. But, come on—who wouldn't cry at the prospect of losing billions of dollars? Yeager almost felt like crying himself.

Even so, it had been weeks since they'd realized they wouldn't make the deadline for the terms of her grandfather's will. Why was she crying now?

"Hannah?" He tried again. "Are you okay?"

She nodded, wiping at each eye. "Yeah, I am. It's

just that standing here, looking at your place… It's just… It's *huge*, Yeager. And it's gorgeous. It embodies everything good that money can make happen. All morning, I've only been thinking about what it will be like to finally have a family. I'm just now remembering I'll have enough money to live the way you do. I'd actually forgotten about that. Isn't that weird? When I realized this morning that I'm pregnant, I didn't even think about the Linden fortune. All I could think about was the baby and you."

Yeager had pretty much stopped hearing what she said after the words *I'm pregnant*. Probably because the roar of adrenaline that started rushing through him made it impossible to register anything else.

"You're pregnant?" he asked, his breath shallow.

She nodded.

"You're sure?"

She nodded again. "I took two tests. They were both positive. I mean, I need to see the doctor for a blood test, too, I guess, but those home tests are pretty freaking accurate."

Yeager still couldn't believe it. "But how? I was in Alberta."

Hannah laughed. "It didn't happen when you were in Alberta, obviously. It happened here in New York. That night we went to the Russian Tea Room and took the carriage ride through Central Park."

He shook his head. "So all those times we planned down to the minute, all those adventures, all those exotic places…"

She shrugged. "Turns out I just needed some spontaneity in familiar surroundings to be at my most, um, fertile."

Hey, whatever worked. That night at the Russian Tea Room and riding around Central Park with Hannah had still been an adventure, Yeager realized. He'd done things that night he'd never done before, and he'd felt as exhilarated by them as he had by any other risk he'd ever taken. Hell, any time he spent with Hannah was an adventure. They'd still be doing his legacy—and Tommy—proud.

"We're going to have a baby?" Yeager asked. Because he *still* couldn't believe he'd heard her correctly.

"Yeah, Yeager. We're going to have a baby."

They were going to have a baby. Even though they'd been working toward the goal for months, he had no idea what to say or how to act. He'd been so certain the first time they'd tried that it would happen immediately. He and Hannah could pat each other on the back and say, *Job well done.* Then they'd see each other again in a year or so—after she'd had a few months to get used to the whole motherhood thing—to arrange a visitation schedule. When he'd initially envisioned the arrangement, he hadn't seen much point in visiting the baby when he or she was still an infant, since babies couldn't communicate or interact or do much of anything but lie there and stare at you. They sure as hell couldn't travel or have adventures. But by the time the child was three or four, it would be a good time to get to know his progeny and gradually start introducing him or her to the world. Now, however…

He'd been such an idiot.

Because now, after months of disappointment and fear that he would never become a father, Yeager realized he wanted a lot more than to just put a miniature version of himself on the planet to be his legacy after he was gone. He couldn't just settle for visiting his child a couple of times a year and taking him or her on age-appropriate adventures. Sending an exotic gift and having a Skype conversation from the other side of the world on birthdays and holidays wouldn't be enough. Yeager wanted...

He wanted to be a father.

"So, pretty cool, huh?" Hannah said, her voice sounding like it was coming through an echo chamber on the other side of the planet.

Cool? Yeah, it was cool. Among other things. A million, billion other things that Yeager would be able to identify if his brain wasn't trying to light on every single one of them at the same time.

When he still didn't say anything—because he honestly couldn't figure out yet what to say—Hannah continued, less enthusiastically. "I mean, it's what we both wanted, right?"

Yeager nodded. But he still couldn't find his voice.

"I'll get my family and my family fortune," she said, "and you'll get your legacy to carry on after you're gone."

He still couldn't believe it was that easy. Then again, he knew it hadn't been easy. On either of them. But it had probably been tougher on Hannah than on him. With or without a child, his life—or, at least, his lifestyle—wasn't going to change all that much. But hers...

Now she could live her life any way she wanted to. She would have everything she'd ever hoped for, everything she'd ever wanted. A family. Financial freedom. A business empire she built all by herself. Yeager knew how gratifying all of those things could be. He was happy for Hannah. He was. It just felt kind of weird that she'd have all those things without him.

She was still looking at him expectantly, her eyes full of joy and wonder and relief, but also apprehension and fear and a host of other emotions that cut right to his soul. And then he felt the joy and wonder, too, and he realized it didn't matter that he couldn't find the words. He didn't need words. He crossed the room to where she was standing and swept her into his arms.

"We're going to have a baby," he said in the same astonished, ecstatic way she had.

And then they were laughing and staring at each other in disbelief and both of them were groping for words.

"Wow, we're really…"

"And we're…"

"I know, right? It's just so…"

"Exactly. How can…?"

"I don't know. It's just so…"

"Yeah. It really is the most…"

"And it's…"

"Totally unbelievably…"

"Awesome," they finally said as one.

And that word, more than any other Yeager knew, captured everything that needed to be said. At least for now. The rest…

Well, he'd worry about the rest of it later. Once he had it all figured out. In a million years or so.

It was dark by the time it occurred to Hannah that she should be going home. She and Yeager had spent hours trying to get accustomed to the new life growing inside her and how it was going to change *everything*.

They fixed lunch together in his kitchen and ate it in his dining room, and talked some more about how the baby was going to change *everything*. Not so much for Yeager, since he would still be living his life the way he always had, arranging his schedule here and there to visit his son or daughter, but for Hannah.

She had called Gus Fiver at his home—as he'd told her to do, should there be any developments like this outside regular office hours—to tell the attorney the good news and had arranged to meet with him in a few days, after she'd had a chance to see her doctor to confirm what she already knew. She wasn't sure what kind of legal hurdles still lay ahead or what kind of time frame she was looking at for coming into her inheritance, but she figured it was probably safe at this point to give her two weeks' notice to Cathcart and Quinn. And then...

She had no idea. She had to find a bigger place to live, obviously, someplace with a yard that was close to good schools and lots of child-friendly places and activities. But she didn't want to move too far from where she lived now, since Queens was familiar and she liked it a lot. Maybe she could find a house with a nice yard in Astoria or Jackson Heights. Someplace that had a lot of families and things for families to do and places for families to go. Because once she had this baby, she would be part of a family. A family who could go anywhere and do anything and live any way they wanted.

Before the realization of that started making her woozy again, she told Yeager, "I should probably head home."

They were sitting on his sofa, gazing out the windows that faced the Empire State Building, the city sparkling like fairy lights against the black sky. When night had first fallen, Hannah thought the view breathtaking. Now, though, she marveled at how Yeager could see so much of New York from his place, but knew nothing about the people who were living out there. Maybe her tiny apartment didn't boast a spectacular view like this one, but she knew most of the people who populated it. That, she hoped, would never change, no matter where the future took her.

"Go?" Yeager echoed from beside her. He had his arm comfortably draped across the sofa behind her, his feet propped on the antique steamer trunk he used for a coffee table. His posture suggested this was something the two them did all the time instead of this being Hannah's first visit to his home. "But you just got here."

"We've been talking for hours," she said. "And it's getting late."

"Stay here tonight," he told her.

His tone of voice was as comfortable as the rest of him, but Hannah was surprised by the invitation. And she had mixed feelings about accepting it. On one hand, she absolutely wanted to spend the night with Yeager. She wanted to spend every night with him. She wanted to spend her life with him. On the other hand, their "business" together really was concluded, at least until after the baby was born. There was no reason for her to prolong her time with him. Especially since she knew that the more time she spent with him, the more difficult that parting was going to be.

"I can't," she said reluctantly. "I have to work tomorrow and I don't have any of my stuff with me."

"You can use my stuff."

The intimacy inherent in that statement made her toes curl. He was speaking as if the two of them shared this space all the time. He was probably accustomed to having his girlfriends spend the night on a regular basis—even though, Hannah reminded herself again, she wasn't his girlfriend. They weren't intimate, even if they had made love several times and were now expecting a baby. Intimacy was more than the sharing of bodies. It was the sharing of souls. It was the sharing of everything. And *everything* was the last thing Yeager wanted to share with anyone.

"I can't use your stuff," she told him. "Your clothes won't fit me."

He grinned lasciviously. "Who said anything about wearing clothes?"

Her heart raced. He still wanted to have sex with her, even without the goal of getting her pregnant. Maybe...

Maybe nothing, she told herself firmly. He was Yeager Novak. He wanted to have sex with every woman in North America. And South America. And Europe, Asia, Africa, Australia and Antarctica.

"I have to work tomorrow," she told him, hoping she only imagined the husky, sex-starved quality her voice seemed to suddenly have. "And Cathcart and Quinn has a strict dress code."

"Then don't go to work," he said.

"I have to go to work."

"Why? You're rich."

She started to tell him—again—that she wasn't rich yet, then remembered that, at this point, that was no longer true. It was merely a formality. She would be rich—her stomach pitched at the reminder. But she wouldn't breathe easy about that until everything was official. And she couldn't just quit her job impulsively. Maybe Misters Cathcart and Quinn hadn't been the most accommodating employers all the time, but they'd done her a solid favor ten years ago, giving her a job while she was still in high school with little work experience. And once she'd explained her situation with her grandfather's will, they'd granted her all the time off she needed. It would be ungrateful and mean to just walk away without warning.

"I have to give my two weeks' notice," she said. "I can't leave Cathcart and Quinn hanging without a seamstress. That would be irresponsible. Not to mention just a crappy thing to do."

She hesitated a moment, then made herself say the rest of what she had to say. Especially since she and Yeager both seemed to need to hear it spelled out. "Besides, you and I aren't... We won't be... It's not necessary for us to..." She sighed in frustration and tried again. "We don't...need each other anymore, Yeager."

Which, she told herself, was the truth. Although she needed him—although she loved him—he didn't need or love her. So the *each other* part of that statement kept it from being a lie.

His gaze locked with hers but he said nothing. Unable to tolerate the intensity of his blue, blue eyes, Hannah looked out at the city and said the rest. "I appreciate everything you've done. Oh, God, that was a terrible platitude." She hurried on when she realized what she was saying. "I just mean..." She muttered a ripe oath under her breath. "I'm honestly not sure what I can say that *won't* sound like a platitude, but I'll give it a shot."

She made herself look at him again. And wished she hadn't. Because there was something in his eyes she'd never seen before, something she couldn't identify, except to say that it wasn't good. In spite of that, she pressed on.

"Thank you for everything you've done for me over the last six months, Yeager. Not just in providing the biological essentials I needed to make a baby, but in showing me the world, too. I'm a different person, a better person now than I was five months ago, thanks to you. And not just because of the new life growing inside me. But because of other things inside me now, too."

Probably best not to dwell on those *other things*, since they included being in love for the first time in her life and the knowledge that she would never love anyone like this again.

"I know this…this venture…was time-consuming for you and I know it kept you tethered in one place for a lot longer than you're used to being confined. I understand you need to get back to business as usual. I need to get back to business as usual, too. Even if things are going to be a lot different for me now. So you don't have to invite me to spend the night because it's getting late. I'll be okay on my own. I promise. I've been okay on my own for a long time."

She deliberately used singular pronouns when she spoke, because she knew she and Yeager weren't a collective anymore. This baby was her baby, and it was his baby, but it wasn't *their* baby. In the agreement they'd signed, Hannah alone would be responsible for her pregnancy, without any obligation on Yeager's part. She would contact him after her baby was born to see when he wanted to start visiting his son or daughter and work from there.

That was how they'd both wanted it five-and-a-half months ago. It was doubtless how Yeager still wanted it. Just because Hannah had begun to wish he would be there for her now...that he would be there for her forever... It was irrelevant. *Their* time was at an end. From here on out, Hannah would have her time, and Yeager would have his time, and they would only interact whenever he could fit a visit to his child into his schedule.

"So...thanks," she said again. "But I've got this."

Yeager studied her in silence for a long time. Then he said, "And what if I want it, too?"

Heat suffused her, but not for the same reason it usually did when Yeager looked at her the way he sometimes did. This look was certainly heated. But it was heated in a way she'd never seen before.

"What do you mean?" she asked.

He hesitated again then he said, "I mean, what if I want to be a part of your pregnancy? What if I want to be there when our baby is born?"

"I..." she began.

Then she halted. She really did want to get on with her life without Yeager as quickly and cleanly as possible. It was going to become more and more difficult to do that the longer he stayed a part of it. But her baby was his baby, too. If he wanted to be there for its birth, could she really deny him that?

"All right," she said reluctantly. "If you don't mind sticking close to New York when the due date approaches, then I'll call you when I leave for the hospital and you can be there when the baby is born."

"I can definitely stay close to New York," he said. And there was something in his voice when he said it that made it seem like he was talking about more than just for the baby's due date. "And what if I want to be… What do you call it? Like a pregnancy coach or something? What if I want to be there for your pregnancy, too?"

"I don't think there's such a thing as a pregnancy coach." Hannah hedged, avoiding an answer. "But the person who coaches you through labor is a doula."

"Okay, so what if I want to be a doula?" he asked.

His request surprised her. "I don't know if a man can be a doula."

"It's the twenty-first century, Hannah. Gender roles are fluid."

Still stalling, she replied, "Oh, sure. Tell that to all the women making seventy-nine cents for every man's dollar."

He smiled at that. She felt a little better. Though she still felt plenty weird. Just what was Yeager asking, really?

"Then maybe I can be a dude-la," he said. "Be there for you during your pregnancy, whenever you need me. What would you think about that?"

She narrowed her eyes at him. "I think it would be tough for you to do that from places like Kyrgyzstan and Djibouti."

He lifted a shoulder and let it drop. "Like I said, I can stay close to New York."

Well, this was certainly news to Hannah. She could count on all her fingers and toes and then some the times he'd told her he could never stay in one place for too long. "Since when?" she asked.

This time Yeager didn't hesitate at all when he replied. "Since the minute you told me you're pregnant."

"You've always said you'd suffocate if you had to stay in one place for any length of time," she reminded him.

"That's what I used to think," he agreed. "Back when I was an idiot. But now..."

"Now what?"

He sat forward, removing his feet from the steamer trunk to place them firmly on the floor. As if he were trying to anchor himself here.

"Look, I won't lie," he said. "There's still a lot I need to figure out about this whole fatherhood thing. But that's just the point, Hannah. I want to figure it out. I don't just want a legacy. I'm beginning to wonder if that was what I really wanted in the first place. I don't know. I don't know a lot of things. But there's one thing I *do* know. I want more than to be a long-distance parent."

He turned to face her fully, then lifted a hand to cup her cheek. "And I know one other thing, too," he said softly. "I want *us* to be more than long-distance parents. I want us to be more than parents, period. I don't want us to be you and me. I want us to be...us."

Hannah covered his hand with hers, worried he might take it back. Worried he might take it all back. But she had no idea what to say.

Yeager didn't seem to be finished, though, because he continued. "I've spent my adult life circling the globe, trying to find the thing that will make my pulse pound hardest, my heart hammer fastest and my soul sing loudest. I've done things no normal human being has ever done, and I've had one adrenaline buzz after another. But today, when you told me you're pregnant… Hannah, I've never felt anything like that in my life. And I'm still reeling from it. It's intoxicating, this feeling of…of…"

"Joy," she finished for him. Because she'd had more time than he to identify it for what it was.

"Yeah," he agreed. "Joy. And, yes, it's partly because of the baby, but even more, it's because of you. Even before this baby happened, I knew I wanted more with you. Since I started spending time with you, Hannah, *everything* in my life has been different. No matter where I've been, as long as I've been with you, I've been…happy. Since my parents died, I was beginning to think I'd never feel that way again. Maybe that's why I keep circling the globe—I'm looking for that. But I don't need to keep running all over the world. I only need to be where you are. Where you and our baby are. Because starting a family with the woman I love? That's the ultimate adventure. One I want to live over and over again."

Now Hannah was the one experiencing the heart-hammering, pulse-pounding, soul-singing adrenaline rush. And all because of three little words. Very softly, she asked, "You love me?"

Yeager nodded. "It may have taken me a while to figure that out, too, but I finally did. I do love you. I've probably loved you since that first trip we took together. And I will love you for the rest of my days, no matter where I spend them."

"Just for the sake of clarification," she said, not sure why she was belaboring this, "you love me for more than being able to stitch up your clothes and clean out the walrus stains, right?"

He smiled. "Yeah. For more than that. A lot more."

He waited for Hannah's response and, when it didn't come—mostly because she was too stunned to say anything—he sobered some. And he said, "Please tell me this isn't a one-sided thing. I mean, I know you were doing your best to keep us separated with all the 'I' and 'you' talk a minute ago, but I can't help feeling maybe you at least like me more than you did when we first went into this thing."

"No, I don't like you more," she told him. "I love you. Always."

His smile turned dazzling. "So what do you say then? You want to hitch our stars together? See where it takes us?"

She thought about that for a moment. And after another moment, she smiled back. "I'll agree on two conditions," she told him.

"Conditions?" he asked, smiling at the echo of their conversation six months ago.

She smiled back, obviously remembering. "Number one, we *have* to have a home base here in New York where we can put down roots. A place where we can take hand-holding strolls and have Sunday-morning snuggles and enjoy firefly-spattered evenings on the patio after the kids go to bed."

"Kids," he repeated. "As in plural?"

She nodded. "That's the second condition. We *have* to keep traveling and having adventures in exotic places to get pregnant again. I want to have lots of kids, Yeager, which means we have to have lots of epic sex."

He eyed her speculatively. "Well, okay. If we *have* to."

They smiled as one and wove their hands together. Then they leaned back on the sofa and gazed at the lights of Manhattan, marveling at what their lives ahead held. Maybe Hannah could spend the night here tonight. And maybe she could call out from work tomorrow. It would only be one day. And, hey, she and Yeager were celebrating.

"Happy New Year, Yeager," she said softly.

"Happy New Life, Hannah," he replied.

And she knew in that moment, it would be. Because no matter where life took them, no matter what adventures awaited, they were a family. And they always would be.

* * * * *

COMING SOON!

We really hope you enjoyed reading this book.
If you're looking for more romance
be sure to head to the shops when
new books are available on

Thursday 19th December

To see which titles are coming soon, please visit

millsandboon.co.uk/nextmonth

MILLS & BOON

LET'S TALK

Romance

For exclusive extracts, competitions and special offers, find us online:

f MillsandBoon

X @MillsandBoon

◎ @MillsandBoonUK

♪ @MillsandBoonUK

Get in touch on 01413 063 232